MR. BOOKER'S
SUMMER
VACATION

MARK LAGES

authorHOUSE®

AuthorHouse™
1663 Liberty Drive
Bloomington, IN 47403
www.authorhouse.com
Phone: 1 (800) 839-8640

Published by AuthorHouse 09/19/2017

ISBN: 978-1-5462-0984-3 (sc)
ISBN: 978-1-5462-0983-6 (e)

Library of Congress Control Number: 2017914717

Print information available on the last page.

Any people depicted in stock imagery provided by Thinkstock are models,
and such images are being used for illustrative purposes only.
Certain stock imagery © Thinkstock.

This book is printed on acid-free paper.

CHAPTER 1

A MORNING ABDUCTION

So who is Mr. Booker? He's a real person, but I'm not going to give you his actual name, since I'm keeping his identity secret. I'm calling him Mr. Booker, a name I pulled out of a hat, and I'm not going to tell you where he lives or works. For the purpose of this story, let's just say he lives in the low-crime, stucco, red-tile-roofed town of Mission Viejo, under the sunny skies of Southern California. Mr. Booker is a high school history teacher, and I'm going to say he teaches at Lincoln High School, also in Mission Viejo. I made up the name of this high school, so don't try to Google it. There's no Lincoln High School anywhere in Mission Viejo.

When Mr. Booker first came to me, he said that it was essential I not reveal him to anyone and that he would tell me his fantastic story only if I kept his identity secret. Usually when I write about this kind of encounter, I'm more forthcoming about the details of the storyteller, but I agreed to Mr. Booker's request because I felt the public needed to hear what he had to say.

Wow, what a story! I've been reporting on alien abductions for more than twenty years, and I've made a decent living at it. Maybe you've already heard of me. Many people read my books, and everyone comes to me with his or her wild stories. But no one has ever come to me with a story like Mr. Booker's. If you're not the sort of person who finds these kinds of tales interesting or believable, please don't be discouraged right off the bat. Don't dismiss this book as just another crazy fantasy concocted by an attention-seeking crackpot. If you're interested in the past, present, and future of humankind, I suggest you keep reading. I know many people find the subject of aliens to be absurd, but I can assure you Mr. Booker's account will be unlike anything you've ever read. Mr. Booker's story does not involve seeing a UFO, having an unexpected encounter with aliens on a quiet stretch of rural road, having implants inserted into his body, or meeting little green men. Mr. Booker's story is altogether different.

Before I begin telling you what happened to this man, I will give you some background information about him. If you are to have any faith in Mr. Booker's integrity, you must know him a little better. He is now forty-three years old. When he first came to me, he was forty-two; he celebrated a birthday in between the time we first made contact and the time I started writing this book. He came to me in the summer of 2016. I had no idea where he got my name. He knew I was something of an expert on the subject of abductions, and he hoped I would not dismiss him as just another goofball with a made-up story. I could tell from his demeanor that he wanted to be taken seriously.

Mr. Booker was born in 1973 as the only son of Edgar and Julia Booker. He grew up in a little stucco tract house in the city limits of Anaheim. Mr. Booker's father was a manager at an auto parts store, and his mother was a stay-at-home wife. They were not wealthy, but they lived a satisfactory and stable life. Mr. Booker told me he had no complaints about his childhood. Mr. Booker loved school, and his favorite subject was history. He not only did well in his classes but also did a lot of reading on his own. It would be accurate to call the young Mr. Booker a history buff.

I interviewed a few of Mr. Booker's childhood friends, and an important quality of his personality stood out. Everyone agreed Mr. Booker had a reputation for being honest, and they said he was not prone to telling lies or even exaggerating. I think you can tell a lot about a person from his or her behavior as a child. Many adult predispositions manifest themselves early on in childhood, so

Mr. Booker's behavior as a child was of importance to me. Further investigation into his behavior as an adult simply confirmed what I'd learned about him as a child. He was precisely the kind of person I wanted to write about, for in my opinion, Mr. Booker was an honest and rational man.

I'll tell you another thing that impressed me about Mr. Booker: he didn't want to be tied to the book in any way. He wanted no percentage of the profits and none of the possible media popularity that might go along with telling his story. He was seeking neither fame nor fortune. He simply had a story that he felt needed to be told to the public. I came to like Mr. Booker a lot. He didn't seem to be driven by ego or greed; rather, he was motivated by a desire to inform the world of an experience he thought was important. How many people do you meet in this day and age who are simply inspired to help others without asking for a reward? At the risk of sounding cynical, I would say not many. Mr. Booker was unique in this way.

Mr. Booker had nothing to gain by telling his story, and his life was fine before he reached out to me. He could've kept this abduction story to himself, and no one would've been the wiser. I've written about a lot of abductions over the years, and I have to be honest: the more of these books I write, the more skeptical I become. I'm fully aware that many who claim to have been abducted by aliens are people who, upon realizing how boring their lives are, convince themselves they deserve attention by concocting these fantastic abduction tales. I don't think Mr. Booker is one of these people. In fact, while telling me his story, he stopped midsentence several times and told me he'd changed his mind and didn't want to go on. "This all sounds so crazy," he'd say. I'd have to encourage him to continue.

"If Linda hadn't passed away, none of this would've happened," Mr. Booker told me. Linda was Mr. Booker's wife. They met in college, and they married shortly after graduating. They both went to UCLA, where Mr. Booker studied history, and his wife majored in chemistry. Mr. Booker has kept many old photographs of Linda in his house; they were hanging on walls and standing on tabletops and counters. I noticed the photos when I came to Mr. Booker's house for our interviews. From the photographs, I could see that Linda was a handsome woman. I wouldn't call her pretty or cute; I think *handsome* is the right adjective. Her eyes were kind yet serious, and her face looked as though it had been chiseled from a block of marble by a Roman sculptor. She had a prominent nose and a strong jaw—not masculine but not entirely feminine either. Her hair was golden blonde, and it was always tied back, often braided. I could tell from some of the photos that she was taller than Mr. Booker by a couple of inches.

I suppose now is as good a time as any to describe Mr. Booker's appearance. He was about five feet eight inches tall. He was trim but not particularly athletic or fit. Just from his appearance, I'd guess the man hadn't exercised a day in his life. His arms weren't thin, but they lacked muscle definition, and his shoulders were not broad; they fell downward from his neck as though the weight of his arms were pulling on them. If I had to choose a single word to describe Mr. Booker's face, I would choose *nondescript*. He reminded me of Walter Mitty, a sort of everyman who could easily get lost in a crowd. I guess the most prominent feature of Mr. Booker's face was the scar on his left cheek, which ran from the bottom of his eye and nearly reached the corner of his mouth. The scar was the result of an accident Mr. Booker had when he was in high school. He and several friends were climbing over a chain-link fence to gain access to a construction site. There was no reason for them to be climbing the fence other than youthful curiosity. In other words, if you put up a fence, mischievous boys will be inclined to climb it. Mr. Booker's head was above the top of the fence, when his foot slipped, and he fell. His face snagged the sharp top of the chain-link fence, resulting in a nasty and bloody gash that required sixteen stitches. However, other than the scar, there isn't much I can tell you that sets Mr. Booker apart.

Come to think of it, I probably shouldn't have used the Walter Mitty comparison to describe Mr. Booker, for he didn't have an overactive imagination. He was anything but a Walter Mitty. Mr. Booker dealt with facts and the truth. He had no use for fiction, unless it told the truth. "The world is so bizarre just as it is. Why waste time making things up?" he said to me.

I'll tell you another thing that impressed me about Mr. Booker: his intelligence. He not only was well educated but also had a mind capable of sorting through experiences and information and making rational sense of things. When it came to political issues, for example, he did not get caught up in the emotions of taking sides. He was an independent thinker. I wouldn't call him a liberal or a conservative, and I wouldn't call him a Democrat or a Republican. He was one of those rare individuals who thought through every issue presented to him in a logical manner, not joining forces with fanatics but seeking the most intelligent opinion he was capable of coming up with, given what he knew. I think he was proud of his ability to do this and proud of his God-given ability to reason. He told me he had a high IQ and was a member of not only Mensa but also Intertel, an even more exclusive society for the top 1 percent of high IQs among the population. There was no disputing the man's ability to think clearly and understand the world.

I've already mentioned his wife, Linda. I told you she passed away, but I didn't tell you how she died. Linda died four years ago from breast cancer. It was a loss that took Mr. Booker a long time to accept; in fact, he probably still isn't quite over it. Her passing shook him to his core. He talked to me about her while he was telling me his story, and he said if she'd been alive, he'd never have been abducted. "She's probably turning over in her grave just thinking about everything I'm telling you. She wouldn't approve at all." Like Mr. Booker, Linda was a rational person. She was alert and intelligent, and she had a distaste for flights of fancy. That was one reason the two of them got along so well. They both liked to see the world for what it was, not twisted by overactive imaginations and emotional longings.

I found it interesting that both Mr. Booker and Linda believed in God. They weren't Bible thumpers, but they did believe there was someone or something in charge. Mr. Booker liked to quote Einstein and say, "God does not play dice with the universe." According to Mr. Booker, Einstein was indeed referring to God—perhaps not the guy with the white beard but the entity who had a hand in the creation of everything we see and experience. The idea that things just happened as a result of random events in nature was inconceivable to Mr. Booker. There was someone or something, and it had to be both powerful and good, an intelligent force that mortal men would probably never comprehend.

Mr. Booker and Linda never had children. They decided they were both too busy with work to invest the time necessary to properly raise a child. Mr. Booker took his job at Lincoln High School seriously, and he worked all day and into the evenings. When she was alive, Linda was a chemist at a large local pharmaceutical company, and she too worked long hours. They both brought home decent paychecks, and they lived comfortably, always within their means. They put their leftover money toward their passion of traveling. Both of them loved to fly all over the world, and every summer, the two of them would take vacations to places that interested them. After Linda died, Mr. Booker kept taking vacations, going by himself, and so begins our story.

During the summer of 2016, Mr. Booker planned to visit the United Kingdom for a week or so. He had been to England with Linda years earlier, and they'd had such a great time that he wanted to visit again. In his mind, his wife would be with him in spirit, taking everything in and sharing every wonderful moment.

Mr. Booker was ready to go. It was early on a June morning, and his suitcases were packed. The shuttle to the airport was due in a half hour. He had just finished breakfast and was working on his second cup of coffee, when the doorbell rang. He stepped to the front door to see who was there. He wasn't expecting anyone that early. He opened the door and found two policemen standing on his porch. They asked if they could come inside. "Is there some kind of problem?" Mr. Booker asked.

"We just need to talk to you," one officer said. He was thin and tall and had a mustache. He had a friendly face that put Mr. Booker at ease.

"We just need a minute of your time," said the second policeman.

He was shorter and heavier than the first. He too had a friendly face but had no mustache.

"Come on in," Mr. Booker said. "But you'll need to make this brief since I'm leaving for the airport in a half hour."

"Going somewhere?" the thin officer asked.

"Overseas."

"Ah, yes, of course," the thin officer said.

"Are those your suitcases?" the other man asked. He was looking at Mr. Booker's bags, which were standing in the hallway, ready to go.

"Yes," Mr. Booker said.

"Is that everything?" the thin cop asked.

"Yes, that's my luggage."

"Do you have a carry-on?"

"It's right there." Mr. Booker pointed to the leather bag sitting on his dining room table.

"And your boarding pass?"

"It's in the carry-on."

"And your wallet and passport?"

"They're in the carry-on too. Say, why all the questions about my things?"

"Just curious," the second officer said.

Mr. Booker told me he should've realized something odd was up. First, the appearance of the two men in his house was unusual. At a glance, they seemed entirely normal, but the longer Mr. Booker looked at them, the stranger they seemed. It was hard to put a finger on what was different about them, but they were not quite right. They looked like people who'd had too much plastic surgery. Second, they had an odor—a strong smell of spearmint. He figured one of them must have been chewing on a fresh stick of gum. However, the smell wasn't coming from a mouth; it was coming from one or both of their bodies.

"You're probably wondering why we're here," the tall cop said.

"I am," Mr. Booker said.

"There was an incident last night."

7

"An incident?"

"With a young woman down the street. Her name is Tami Appleton."

"Tami?"

"You know her?"

"I don't really know her. I know of her. I mean, I know who she is."

"There's no pleasant way to put this."

"To put what?"

"She was raped last night."

"Raped? Really?"

"By a man fitting your description."

"Certainly you don't think I did it."

"Well, did you?"

"Of course not."

"Then you won't mind taking off your shirt," the tall cop said. "She says she scratched the attacker's back with her fingernails. We'd like to see if you have any scratch marks."

"I have no scratch marks."

"Then your shirt, please? Can you take it off?"

"Okay," Mr. Booker said. "I suppose I can remove my shirt."

"Good, good. We can clear this matter up right now if you'll give us a look."

Mr. Booker unbuttoned his shirt. He then removed the shirt and stared at the two men.

"Could you please turn around so we can have a look?" the tall cop said. "Let's see what we have."

Mr. Booker turned around, and the heavier cop stepped forward and examined his back. Then the strangest thing happened. Mr. Booker felt something cold on the back of his neck, like a wet ice cube. "What the heck?" Mr. Booker said.

"You'll be good in a few seconds."

"Good for what?"

"You'll feel very good," the cop said.

"What's going on?" Mr. Booker asked, but the police officer was right. Mr. Booker felt wonderful. A powerful euphoria overwhelmed his consciousness, and he came to the giddy conclusion that he'd been drugged. His face felt warm, and his extremities tingled. It was a delightful feeling, and he was not afraid of anything. In fact, he was no longer the slightest bit suspicious of the two officers, and he was glad they were in his home. "Do you see any scratches?" he asked.

"None at all," the tall cop said, laughing.

"Of course, that's not why we're here," the other cop said.

"Of course," Mr. Booker said. He turned around to face the officers. "What do you want me to do?"

"You'll need to come with us."

"I'll do whatever you say," Mr. Booker said. He wanted to be compliant. "Where are we going?"

"You'll see soon enough."

"Okay," Mr. Booker said.

One of the officers went to the front door and opened it, and in came a third man. Mr. Booker laughed when he saw him. Dressed in a golden robe, the man was facing Mr. Booker. Could this be? The third man was the spitting image of Mr. Booker, right down to the scar on his cheek. He was like Mr. Booker's twin. Mr. Booker felt as if he were looking in a mirror. Except for the different clothing, no one would ever have been able to tell the two apart. "Mr. Booker, meet Mr. Booker," the tall cop said to the man who'd just entered. Then, to the real Mr. Booker, he said, "Please take off the rest of your clothes."

"You mean everything?" Mr. Booker asked.

"Yes, well, except for your shorts. You can leave those on."

"Very well," Mr. Booker said.

Still under the influence of the drug, Mr. Booker took off his clothes. It didn't take him long, and he was now standing in his underwear. This was interesting to Mr. Booker. He was ordinarily shy when it came to exposing his body to strangers. He wasn't proud of his physique, but that morning, he stood disrobed in front of the three men without feeling the slightest bit uncomfortable. His twin then removed the robe he was wearing, and he handed the robe to

Mr. Booker. "Put this on," he said. It was so strange! His twin's voice sounded exactly like his own. Mr. Booker laughed at this.

"Okay, okay," Mr. Booker said. He did as he was told and put on the robe. It smelled of spearmint, and it was still warm from his twin having just worn it.

The twin then proceeded to put on Mr. Booker's clothes, and when he was dressed, the tall cop pointed to the suitcases in the hallway and said, "There's your luggage. And the carry-on is over there on the table. Your driver's license, passport, and boarding pass are in the carry-on. The shuttle to the airport will be here any minute, so the three of us have got to get going. You know what to do?"

"I know exactly what to do," the twin said.

"Cheerio then," the cop said.

"What about me?" Mr. Booker asked.

"You're coming with us."

"Where are we going?"

"Follow us," the officer said. Mr. Booker followed the two officers through the front door and to their patrol car parked in the driveway, and they all climbed in. "Still feeling okay?" the officer asked.

"Feeling great," Mr. Booker said. And he meant it. He'd never felt so safe and pleasant in his life. He knew he'd been drugged, but he didn't care. In fact, he was glad they'd done it.

The thin officer was driving the patrol car, and the other rode in back with Mr. Booker. The cop beside Mr. Booker took a small metallic object out of his pocket and pressed several buttons on it. He then asked Mr. Booker to face the window so he could have access to the back of his neck. Mr. Booker did as he was asked, and as he watched the scenery pass, he again felt something cold on his skin. He felt a slight sting, and at first, he felt light-headed. A few seconds later, everything went black, and he shut down completely.

He had no idea how much time had passed. It seemed like only seconds, yet it also felt like hours. He was in his bedroom, lying on his back, still dressed in the golden robe. He didn't feel well. His head was spinning, and his stomach ached as if he'd eaten too much food. He had a queer taste in his mouth. He ran to his bathroom and held his head over the toilet bowl, where he proceeded to vomit. He did this over and over until he finally stopped. "Jeez, what the hell is wrong with me?" he said. He then wiped the bad-tasting bile from his lips with the back of his hand. Then the queer taste returned in his mouth, and he hung his head over the toilet bowl and vomited again.

CHAPTER 2

MR. BOOKER'S CABIN

The vomiting lasted for hours, or at least it seemed like hours. It reminded Mr. Booker of his college days. He hadn't been much of a drinker back then, but during his freshman year, some of the boys in his dormitory had convinced him to join them while they were shotgunning beers. That was before he met Linda. For those of you who don't know what it means to shotgun a beer, the process involves piercing a hole at the bottom of a beer can. You then hold the hole to your mouth while holding the can upright. When you open the top, the beer gushes through the hole and down your throat. The boys timed themselves, and some were able to finish entire cans in less than three seconds each. Imagine doing that over and over. That was exactly what they all did, and when they were done, they were surrounded by empty beer cans, and each boy was marvelously drunk. I say *marvelously* because all the boys seemed to like the way they were feeling—except for Mr. Booker. He had no idea how many beers he'd consumed, but it turned out to be far more than he could handle. The room started spinning, and he felt horribly sick. He wound up on his knees in the dormitory bathroom, puking his guts out. He thought he'd never stop.

That was exactly how he felt now, but why was he so sick? Obviously, he hadn't been drinking. He tried to recall what had happened over the past few hours, and the last thing he remembered was riding in the patrol car with the mysterious cops. He recalled the heavy scent of spearmint. The thin cop had been driving, and the other cop had put something cold on his neck. It was the same little metallic device they'd used to drug him. Then he remembered blacking out, but what had happened after that? How had he gotten back to his bedroom? Had they carried him? And why was he dressed in nothing but a pair of shorts?

"How are you feeling?" someone asked. Mr. Booker was surprised to hear the voice, and he turned to look toward the bathroom doorway. Standing in the doorway was an elderly man wearing a golden robe. He was about Mr. Booker's height, but he was much older. He had snow-white hair and a kindly old face, and he held a wooden staff in his right hand. His eyes were the most remarkable color of blue, a brilliant shade of turquoise. He smiled, revealing a mouthful of perfect teeth that were unusually white for a man his age. "You'll feel better soon," he said.

"Who are you?" Mr. Booker asked.

"You can call me Sid."

"Sid who?"

"Just Sid will do."

"And what are you doing in my house?"

Sid laughed and said, "We're not in your house, and I'm here to check up on you."

"Check up on me?"

"To make sure you're okay. Until your body gets used to it, relocation can have some very uncomfortable side effects."

"Relocation?"

"Yes, relocation. In your case, from your planet to our ship."

"Your ship?"

"You're aboard our spaceship."

"I have no idea what you're talking about."

"You've been relocated."

"To your ship?" Mr. Booker said. He was beginning to feel dizzy again. "What kind of a gag is this?"

"It's no gag. We're in your cabin."

"We're in my home."

The old man laughed even louder. "Come with me, and have a look out your front room's window. Then I think you'll understand."

Mr. Booker spit into the toilet, and thinking he might now be okay, he flushed it. Wiping his mouth with one hand, he grabbed the countertop edge with his other hand and stood up. He followed Sid out of the bathroom and to the window in the front room. He opened the shutters and looked, but he couldn't believe his eyes. "What the heck?" Mr. Booker said. "What the hell is going on here? Where are we? I must be dreaming."

"No, no, you're not dreaming," Sid said. Looking out the window, Mr. Booker saw nothing but the light of the sun and planet Earth floating in space. He had to be dreaming. This was unbelievable. "We're orbiting your planet," Sid said. "You are aboard our *Peacekeeper 102*. You're now our guest. We've re-created the interior of your home aboard our ship to make you feel more comfortable. Everything in your house has been duplicated right down to the smallest detail."

"Okay," Mr. Booker said, still skeptical but willing to talk further. "I'll play along. So why are we here, and why are we orbiting Earth?" He was still sure he was dreaming, but he wanted to hear what the old man had to say.

"Have a seat," Sid said. He motioned toward the sofa, and Mr. Booker took a seat. Sid sat in the chair facing the sofa and, still holding his wooden staff in his hand, proceeded to explain. Mr. Booker listened patiently. What else could he do but listen? Sid said, "All of us aboard this ship are Ogonites, a species of living beings from the planet Og, which is light-years from your planet, Earth. I guess you could correctly refer to us as explorers. This ship was developed to seek out life-sustaining planets, such as yours. We are not here to conquer you or extend an empire. We are peacekeepers. That's all you need to know for now—that we are charged with keeping the peace."

"And I'm supposed to believe this?"

"Oh, you will believe it."

"I've been abducted by aliens?"

"That's one way of putting it. Of course, we see it a little differently. To our way of thinking, you are the alien. It depends on how you look at it. For the week, you, Mr. Booker, will be our guest. And you've been brought aboard for a very good reason."

"A good reason?"

"Everything will be explained. First, I need you to get over this idea that you're dreaming."

"And how will I do that?"

"Let some time pass. Dreams, being what they are, only last for finite periods of time. Once enough time goes by, you'll come to the realization that you're not dreaming at all, and you'll understand." Sid grinned at Mr. Booker, but Mr. Booker did not grin back. He wasn't sure what to make of all this. He wasn't sure what to make of Sid. He was not at ease with his predicament. Then Sid said, "There's a red button by the light switch on the wall, next to the front door. When you've decided you're not dreaming and feel you're ready to continue with me, simply press the button, and I'll return. In the meantime, I'm going to leave you here. You'll probably want to get dressed. There's a robe in your bedroom."

Sid stood up and walked to the front door. He turned his head and smiled at Mr. Booker, and then he opened the door to leave. "You're leaving me here?" Mr. Booker asked.

"Yes, until you summon me back."

"Until I decide I'm not dreaming?"

"Precisely," Sid said, and he stepped out and shut the front door behind him.

Mr. Booker was still sitting on the sofa in a confused state of shock. The entire situation was bizarre. Was it possible this wasn't a dream? He looked around at his front room. If it was a replica, it was a darn good one. Everything inside the room was exactly correct. His oak bookshelves lined the far wall, stuffed with all the history books Mr. Booker had collected over the years. His framed pictures hung on the walls, reproductions of famous paintings Linda had picked out, including Manet's *Music in the Tuileries Gardens*, one of Linda's favorites; a Rembrandt self-portrait; and one of Van Gogh's paintings of irises. He saw all the photographs of Linda, located exactly where they were in his house. Positioned near the bookshelves was the upright piano Linda used to play when she had free time. Atop the piano was a plaster bust of Beethoven, with a chip in its lower left shoulder. The bust had been chipped when the piano tuner accidently dropped it while removing it to tune the piano. Every little detail was right, just as Sid had said.

This had to be his house. A cabin in a spaceship? How could that be possible? Heck, it even smelled like his house; he detected the scents of dusty old books and aged oak shelves. There was no mistaking the old library scent of his house. It occurred to Mr. Booker there was one way to find out for sure whether he was in his house or aboard a spaceship: he would open the front door and view the outside—the front lawn, the plum trees, and all the houses across the street. Yes, he needed to see the outside. Mr. Booker stood up from the sofa and stepped to the front door, but when he grasped the doorknob, it would not turn. The front door was locked, and he was unable to open it. He was locked in his own house. He went again to the front window and stared at the surreal view of Earth. Only a dream could explain these strange circumstances—but it didn't feel like a dream. It felt real, and except for the view out the front window, nothing strange was happening. In a dream, strange things tended to happen. Dreams were always surreal and weird, weren't they?

Mr. Booker suddenly realized he felt much better than he had earlier; the dizziness and awful urge to vomit were gone. His stomach felt hollow and empty, as if he hadn't eaten for days, and he went to the kitchen and opened the refrigerator. It was filled with all sorts of food and drink, and he removed some bread, meat, and mayonnaise to make a roast beef sandwich. He made the sandwich on the kitchen counter.

As he ate, he surveyed the kitchen. The old pendulum clock on the wall seemed to be working, and it was nearly eleven. But was it eleven in the morning or eleven at night? If they were out in space, did it even matter? He tried to look out the kitchen window, but it was blocked off with wallboard instead of glass, and it was inoperable. He tried to open it, but like the front door, it wouldn't budge. He looked around. In fact, the only view available was that from the front room, and that view was no help at all.

The phone! It suddenly occurred to Mr. Booker that he could call someone and find out what was going on. He picked up the phone receiver from the kitchen wall phone and punched in the number for his next-door neighbors, Andrew and Vivian Cassel. They'd be able to come over and unlock his front door for him. They could certainly confirm he wasn't aboard some ridiculous spaceship. However, when Mr. Booker held the receiver to his ear, he heard nothing. The line was dead.

Mr. Booker continued to eat his sandwich. The food made him thirsty, so he poured a glass of milk. There had to be some way for him to contact the outside world, but short of knocking down the front door, he couldn't think of a good way. Could he knock the front door down? With a running start, maybe he could smash through the thing. He needed to at least give it a try. Standing around eating a roast beef sandwich wasn't getting him anywhere, so when Mr. Booker was done with his meal, he stepped into the front room. He gave the front doorknob another twist just in case, but it was still locked. Clearly, his only option was to break through the door. Ten steps away from the door, he lowered his shoulder and took a deep breath to prepare himself. Then, with all his might, he ran at the door like a charging bull. *Thud!* He tripped over his own feet and hit the door face first. The door didn't budge an inch, and Mr. Booker bounced off it and fell to the floor. Sitting upright, he held his nose. "Dammit!" he said. The door remained shut. He'd succeeded only in hurting himself, and blood was now running from both of his nostrils and into his mouth. "This is crazy," he said, and he stood back up, holding his nose and trying to stop the bleeding. He noticed a sharp pain as he pinched his nose. Had he broken it? *Of all the stupid things to have done!* Then he saw something that got his attention: the red button by the door, alongside the light switch—the

17

button Sid had told him to press. *Who breaks their nose in a dream? Who bleeds like this?*

Was he sure he wasn't dreaming? Not really. But he was getting nowhere without Sid, and he needed medical attention. He needed someone to attend to his nose. Mr. Booker pressed the red button and then went to the bathroom to grab a wad of toilet paper to soak up the blood running freely from his nostrils. He then went to the bedroom for some clothes, but the only garment available was the golden robe he had been wearing earlier. He put it on, went to the front room, and took a seat on the sofa, holding the toilet paper to his face and waiting for Sid to show up. The front door opened, and Sid stepped in with his wooden staff. He closed the door behind him and then looked at Mr. Booker and his bloody toilet paper. "Oh my," he said. "What did we do to ourselves?"

"I think I broke my nose."

"How did you do that?"

"I was trying to break down the door."

"With your nose?"

"No, of course not. It was an accident."

"Sit tight, and I'll get you a medic."

Sid stepped out again, but he was not gone long. He returned with a woman he called Anna. She was wearing a golden robe too. Her blonde hair was cut short like a boy's, and she appeared to be in her thirties. She had a nice face with big blue eyes and rose-petal lips. She seemed to be wearing a lot of rouge. Her teeth were perfectly white like the old man's. She was carrying a black bag, which presumably contained her medical supplies, and she took a seat on the sofa beside Mr. Booker. "Let's have a look," she said, and Mr. Booker removed the toilet tissue from his nose.

"Is it broken?" Mr. Booker asked.

"It could be," Anna said.

"Can you fix it?"

"Of course. Just hold still."

"It hurts."

Anna unlatched her bag, reached into it, and removed a silver device similar to the one the cop had used earlier. She placed the device alongside Mr. Booker's nose and pressed a couple buttons. There was no pain involved, only an icy chill. "That should do it," Anna said. While she packed the silver device back in her satchel, he reached up to his nose. It was no longer sore, and the bleeding had stopped. "You might want to go wash your face," Anna said. She smiled and then stood up and walked back to the front door. Sid opened the door for her, and she was gone. Sid shut the door, and Mr. Booker went to the bathroom to wash his face. Sid followed him to the bathroom.

"I feel so stupid," Mr. Booker said as he dried his face with a towel.

"It's no problem," Sid said.

"I guess I'm ready to listen."

"Listen to what?"

"Listen to what you have to say."

"Are you convinced you're not dreaming?"

"I'm not sure I'll ever be completely convinced. But for now, I'll accept that this is my reality. I might as well treat it as such. I might as well listen to you. I don't see an alternative."

"Good enough."

"So you'll explain?"

"Yes, I'll explain," Sid said. Mr. Booker followed Sid into the front room, where he took a seat on the sofa again, and Sid sat in the same chair he'd previously sat in. This time, rather than continuing to hold on to his staff, Sid leaned it against the chair. He then looked directly at Mr. Booker and took a deep breath. "Where to begin?" he said. "Where should I begin?"

"Wherever you want," Mr. Booker said.

"Yes, yes, wherever I want. I guess I should tell you who we are and what we're doing here. You have a right to know why we're concerned with your civilization and why we're interested in you specifically. I've already told you we're from the planet Og. It's true we're a very long way from home, yet here we are. Your astronomers know nothing about us, since Og is too far away for them to see. But our planet is about the size of your Earth, and we orbit a star similar to your sun, along with twelve other planets of various sizes. We are obviously way ahead of you with our technology, but we are not here to conquer you or make you our subjects. We are here simply on a mission to keep the peace. Believe me when I say that we are a peace-loving culture. We have learned some harsh and unforgettable lessons about peace, and we would not be here were it not for an experience we had with another planet also far away from here. It is home to a people who did not have our same values. I am referring, of course, to the Aktoon and the Great War."

"Where is Aktoon?"

"It's not a where. It's a who."

"Then who are they?"

"The Aktoon were a civilization we discovered in our galaxy. We found them during our early years of space exploration, and they took us completely by surprise. We were not accustomed to life-forms being so devious and aggressive, and we'll be the first to admit that we were very naive. They were not as advanced as us, so as an act of goodwill, we shared our technology with them. Little did we know that while we were sharing this information, they had designs for turning against us and using our technology to take over our planet. To make a long story short, they built up an enormous fleet of warships and attacked us. Their purpose was to make Og their own.

"You have to remember that Og is and has always been a peace-loving planet, and we had no experience fending off aggressors. The Aktoon attack took us completely by surprise, and we were unprepared to defend ourselves. We went into an immediate defensive mode, building our own warships and developing implements of battle. This was completely new to us, not to mention repugnant, but we had to act fast. The war itself was a living nightmare. We lost millions of lives—entire cities—and our planet was ravaged and badly damaged. The war went on for years and years, until finally, we devised a way to beat the Aktoon aggressors. It was either them or us, and with this in mind, our scientists developed a biological weapon that, when released into their atmosphere, would wipe out their entire species. We called it the Doomsday Plague, and we delivered it to their planet via a barrage of transport ships. The Aktoon destroyed most of these transport ships before they reached their destinations, but enough of them successfully made it to perform their horrid mission of releasing the Doomsday Plague into the Aktoon atmosphere and bringing death to their entire population. After a few months, everyone on their planet was dead, and realizing what we'd done, their fleets surrendered.

"I've simplified this war for you, but you get the general idea. Be advised, Mr. Booker, that there are some extremely dangerous life-forms in the universe, and ever since this war, we've made it a goal to seek them out and neutralize them before they become a threat. We do not want to find ourselves in another catastrophic war with a species like the Aktoon. Like I've told you, we're a peace-loving people. But there isn't much we won't do to keep our planet safe from future aggressors. We view our peacekeeping missions as very serious business."

"So you're here to investigate Earth?"

"We've been here for over twenty years."

"You have?"

"We've been monitoring and researching human beings on your planet exhaustively."

"What have you discovered?"

"That we're close to making a decision."

"A decision?"

"As to how we should deal with you."

"Do you consider us a threat?"

"Possibly. But before they decide, our Council for Peace would like to talk to you."

"Your Council for Peace?"

"Five highly respected Ogonites charged by our home planet with deciding exactly how to handle Earth and its human beings. The council has already processed a massive amount of information, and they've taken every fact and circumstance of this situation into consideration, but they'd like to have you visit their council chambers in person so they can talk to you. I think they have some questions for you."

"Why me?"

"Because our computer calculated that you're a human being they can trust to be both truthful and insightful. You were chosen by our computer."

"I was chosen by a computer?"

"It took only a few hours to come up with your name. It was a simple matter of logic and deduction."

"So you sorted through a world population of seven billion people in just a few hours?"

"Our computer is very efficient."

"How exactly did my name come up?"

Sid stared at Mr. Booker for a moment and then continued. "I see no harm in your knowing the parameters of the search." Sid reached for his staff, as though holding it would help him think. He tapped the staff several times on the floor and then said, "First, we had to pick a specific country. There are a lot of countries on your planet, but the United States stood out as having the most promising candidates. This isn't because it's well behaved or particularly full of bright and honest people, but it does have a remarkable tolerance for independent thought and expression. We wanted to find someone who would speak his or her mind without being intimidated. That was our first consideration. But obviously, there were many other factors we used."

"Such as?"

"Well, for example, we wanted someone who was alert and intelligent. The problem is that many of your species are rather dull and just not that bright. As I'm sure you know, your species uses a measure for gauging intelligence called an IQ. We found this useful. We used the IQ measurement to weed out ninety-nine percent of the US population, and this narrowed our search significantly. We then applied another parameter, searching for only those individuals who were high school teachers. You're probably scratching your head and wondering why we did this. You have to understand that our society is not like yours. On our planet, the task of teaching young people is the most admirable role a citizen can play. We wanted to interview someone we respected, and a high school teacher was the perfect choice. We weren't looking for one of your grade school teachers, who are really just glorified babysitters. And we weren't looking for a self-absorbed college professor. Rather, we sought a good old-fashioned, hardworking high school teacher, someone who truly gets down in the trenches to teach. So you see how easy this is getting, narrowing the field down?"

"There must have been more requirements."

"Of course there were. We looked for subjects who had a history of good behavior. Anyone with a criminal history of any kind was excluded. Further, we sought someone over the age of forty, so he or she would have some life experience. We also sought a subject who was widowed or unmarried and childless. This last requirement was very important because we planned on extracting the person from his or her environment, and it was essential that no one close to the subject notice anything peculiar. Your parents live clear across the country, your wife passed away, and you have no children. Your name was in a short list of candidates, but your trip to England clinched it. Your trip was at the exact time we needed someone to interview. Replacing you with a doppelganger was the ideal strategy. No one in England will notice the switch, and as far as everyone back home knows, you are off enjoying yourself on a weeklong vacation. At the end of the trip, your twin will bring home lots of photos on your cell phone, a stamped passport, suitcases of dirty clothes, and some leftover English cash. Then, when we return you to Earth, everyone will assume you went on your trip. Only you will know what happened, and you won't tell a soul, because anyone you told would think you were off your rocker. There isn't a sane person who'd buy your crazy story."

Mr. Booker thought for a moment and realized Sid was probably right. His twin had gone to England, and it might as well have been Mr. Booker. Who in his right mind would believe a twin had taken his place while he was taken aboard a spaceship? He then asked, "So when do I get to meet this Council for Peace?"

"Soon, Mr. Booker. Very soon."

"I have another question."

"Feel free to ask me anything."

"What's the deal with these golden robes?"

CHAPTER 3

THE GOLDEN ROBES

S id laughed. "Of course you're curious about the robes. I should've expected that, as you're so used to dressing like an earthling. We all wear these robes here on the ship as well as at home on Og. It's how we dress. We don't have the need to wear a variety of fashions, as you humans do. In fact, we find your desire to decorate your bodies egotistical and barbaric. In our society, everyone has a strong social conscience, and showing off our individuality through clothing isn't something we do. We're Ogonites, and we dress like Ogonites. How did your famous French author put it? 'One for all, and all for one'? It's a wonderful line, and it could've been written by an Ogonite. Yes, one for all, and all for one!"

"You've read *The Three Musketeers*?"

"I've read most of your classic literature, and so have our council members. In fact, so have most of the ship's crew. You'll find we're all quite well-read when it comes to earthly culture. This is not to say we don't have many questions. It's just to say we've done our due diligence."

"You said you have questions," Mr. Booker said. "What sort of questions do you have? I might be able to answer them for you now."

"I won't be asking the questions. It'll be up to the council to query you. That isn't my role. I'm not here as an interrogator. My role is simply to serve you as a gracious host and helpful counselor. I'm here to help you make sense of this process. You'll find we're not a secretive society, and we like transparency. So do you have any questions for me?"

"Oh, wow." Mr. Booker laughed. "I guess I have a lot of them."

"Well, feel free to ask. I mean, you can ask me anything at all."

"Well, back on the subject of these golden robes. Fashions have never been that important to me, but isn't it a little extreme to require all your people to wear the same thing? Don't you find it stifling? Don't you ever feel like expressing yourselves?"

"We're free to express ourselves. We express ourselves all the time."

"But the robes?"

"What about the robes?"

"Why require everyone to wear the same thing? That seems oppressive to me."

"Oh, you don't understand. No one is required to wear the golden robes. It's entirely voluntary. The truth is that none of us wants to dress differently; we all want to belong. We're proud to be Ogonites, and we're eager to display our comradery."

"I have another question."

"Go ahead."

"Why do you people look so much like human beings? You'd think being so far away and from another planet, you'd look different."

"Oh." Sid chuckled. "We do look much different."

"You look the same to me."

"It's an illusion."

"An illusion?"

"A magic trick. Do you believe everything you see when a professional magician performs his tricks? Don't you know you're being fooled? Don't you know there's a rational explanation for all the impossibilities you're observing?"

"I suppose so."

"Without getting into the details, that's the best way I can explain our appearance to you. It's a magic trick done for your benefit. I won't tell you how we do it. We've shared our technology with others before, and it's never worked out well for us. Just know that you're being fooled, and what you're seeing is an illusion. If you saw what we actually looked like, you'd probably be frightened or repulsed, and our goal is to make you feel comfortable with us, not to cause you unnecessary alarm. Thus, we make ourselves look like you. You may have already noticed our technology isn't perfect. If you look closely, you'll notice our skin isn't exactly like yours, and some features, such as our teeth, are a little too perfect."

"I've noticed that."

"And we smell like spearmint."

"Yes, I've noticed that too."

"We've been working on the spearmint issue for years, but no one has been able to solve it. Still, it's a rather impressive illusion, don't you think? I think it's good enough to fool most humans."

"Yes, it's very effective."

"Certainly good enough."

"So tell me—what exactly do you Ogonites look like?"

Sid looked up toward the ceiling for a moment, seemingly thinking over my question. He then said, "I'm not sure I should tell you."

"I'd really like to know."

"Well, we're kind of hard to describe. I can tell you we're between four and five feet tall. We have two eyes, a nose, a mouth, and a pair of ears, but they are unlike anything you're used to. We look something like a cross between a very large plucked chicken and a rattlesnake."

"I see," Mr. Booker said.

"You asked."

"Yes, I did. And I'm trying to visualize it."

"I've probably said more than I should have."

"I have another question."

"Feel free to ask."

"You said teachers on your planet were respected and admired."

"Yes, I did say that. And it's true. Teaching our children is held high above all other walks of life. Our children mean everything to us, and teachers are revered and treated specially."

"I like that idea."

"Yes, of course you like that. You should also know that on our planet, only the best and brightest are allowed to become teachers. Our educational system is nothing like yours. The truth is that we find your educational system flawed and primitive."

"Do teachers make a lot of money on your planet?"

"No one makes a lot of money."

"I don't understand."

"Everyone makes the same."

"Everyone?"

"Yes, everyone. We don't strive for the acquisition of material things and money. We live each day for the sake of living. Unlike humans, we do not set our sights on personal profits. We are rewarded with the knowledge that we've done our best to maintain and improve our culture."

"Like communism?"

"Something like communism."

"And this works for you?"

"You have to understand something about Ogonites. We are devoutly social creatures. We strive to contribute to the greater good. That is where we find fulfillment, not by struggling to hoard things for ourselves. It is one of the great differences between your species and our own. You'll find the council will be very curious to learn how your society functions with all its individual egotism. To our way of thinking, feeding egos is a bizarre way of doing things, and it seems to cause your people unnecessary and sometimes catastrophic problems."

"And Og is different?"

"Yes, much different. Any more questions?"

"Yes, you say you've been studying our planet for twenty years. Did I hear you correctly?"

"You did."

"How is it that no one on Earth has noticed your ship orbiting our planet?"

"To Earth, we're invisible."

"Invisible?"

"It's another magic trick. We're here just as big as life, and we've been here for the last twenty years, but no one on Earth can see us or detect us. We achieve our invisibility through a technology similar to what we use in order to appear like human beings. It's not exactly the same technology, but it's based on some of the same principles. Once you understand the physics behind it, it's really quite simple. But if you don't know how it's done, it's very effective and nearly foolproof."

"How about all the UFO sightings and alien abduction stories people have been recounting over the years? Are they true? Are these people talking about you and your ship?"

"No, those stories are fiction."

"No one has seen you at all?"

"Not a soul. The UFO sightings and abduction stories you're referring to are the result of overactive human imaginations. They're entertaining and thought provoking, but I can assure you that no one other than you knows we're even up here. And as far as we know, we're the first explorers from outer space to visit your solar system. You have a very young civilization, and it's unlikely anyone else has even noticed. Listen, it's a great big universe, and Earth is a tiny blip on the screen. And even if other civilizations knew of your existence, it's unlikely they'd take much interest."

"But Og has taken an interest."

"We're peacekeepers."

"You told me that."

"We believe in nipping problems in the bud—catching them before they catch us."

"I'm not sure what that means."

"By the last day of your visit here, our mission will become clear."

"Can we go outside?"

"Outside?"

"Out through the front door. I'd like to see what's outside my door."

29

"I see no reason why not. You're going to be out of here soon anyway, when it comes time for you to meet with the council. I'd be happy to show you around before then. Let's go right now."

Sid stood up, and so did Mr. Booker. Sid opened the front door, and the two of them stepped out of the cabin. Mr. Booker followed Sid into a long hallway. The hall was about eight feet wide and ten feet high. It was like nothing Mr. Booker had ever experienced. It wound through the spaceship like a snake, and the walls were paneled with ornately carved wood. The wood carvings were organized into strange geometric patterns Mr. Booker had never seen applied to any earthly architecture. The intricacy and attention to detail were astonishing, and the wood itself was intriguing—startlingly colorful, grainy, and neatly stained and finished. The ceilings were just as ornate as the walls, crisscrossed with beams, corbels, and more amazing designs. Every ten feet, there was a glass light fixture suspended from the ceiling. The fixtures reminded Mr. Booker of Dale Chihuly's artwork, except these lights were even more intricate. This was not the sort of environment Mr. Booker had expected to see in a spaceship. For some reason, he'd expected something more starkly functional. *All this wood and glass! Who would've guessed?*

Mr. Booker touched one of the wall carvings with the tips of his fingers. As he admired the unreal carpentry, Sid said, "We're proud of our woodworkers. Wood carving and craftsmanship are highly regarded on Og. The wood you are looking at is all from the efram tree. The tree is native to our planet, and it is plentiful and fast-growing. One thing we'll never run short of is efram. You'll find it everywhere on our planet. If you cut it down, it grows right back within a few years. We have more than we know what to do with."

"Where does this hall lead?"

"To everything. Our entire ship is built around this central hallway. It is the spine of our ship. Of course, you won't have access to all of it. You'll be restricted to a small segment. You'll notice it's been blocked off at two ends." As the two men continued to walk, they came upon a large door. There were some inscriptions carved in the door in a foreign language, presumably the language of the Ogonites. Sid opened the door by twisting its large doorknob, and the two men walked into a room. Sid then turned on the overhead lights, and a brilliant light flooded the room. Mr. Booker looked around in awe, astonished by what he saw. The room was an auditorium. More Ogonite woodwork covered the walls and ceiling. The patterns were even more impressive than those in the hallway. He'd never seen anything like it. "These are our council chambers," Sid said. "You'll be sitting right there in that chair, in the middle of the room, and the council members will be up on the stage, sitting behind that long desk. There are five council members, and one is the chairman. His name is Rock, and he'll be running things."

"Rock?"

"We've given all the council members ordinary English names to make you feel more at home."

Mr. Booker was a little overwhelmed by the room. He was still looking around with his mouth open. "Jeez," he said.

"Don't let the room intimidate you."

"This is much more than I expected."

"I'll be here with you during all the sessions, seated in that chair behind yours. You'll be able to consult with me during the questioning anytime you wish."

"So you're like an attorney?"

"No, you won't be on trial."

"Then what would you call it?"

"The council simply wants to ask questions. They want to make sure they understand your planet and its people as fully as possible."

"What if I don't have answers?"

"Then just tell them. There's no harm in saying you don't have an answer to a question. They won't expect you to know everything, and you won't be chastised for saying you don't know. I'm sure they know you won't be able to answer everything. They'll be expecting it."

Mr. Booker thought about that and then asked, "Can I be honest with you?"

"Of course," Sid said.

"I think they've picked the wrong guy to do this."

"Our computer is seldom wrong."

"But I'm not an important man. I'm just a high school history teacher. I'm sure there are others on Earth who are much more qualified to answer the council's questions."

"On our planet, being a history teacher would make you a very important man. Certainly, your thoughts and opinions will be helpful to them."

"That's not how I feel. I have very little real-life experience other than teaching my history classes for kids who'd rather be elsewhere."

"You sell yourself short."

"You really think so?"

"There is much to learn from you. Our computer says so. Listen, our computer picked you out of a pool of seven billion living souls, which says a lot. And like I said, the computer is seldom wrong. The fact that you feel inadequate is probably one of the strongest arguments for your adequacy. We're not looking for someone who thinks he has the answers; we're looking for someone who actually has them. And you have them. Our computer says so. And regarding your experiences on Earth, we don't want someone who has a vested interest in things. We want an impartial observer. If you have skin in the game, your answers are likely to be corrupted by your interests rather than being the result of your impartial honesty. You know, I could go on and on telling you why you're right for this, but you'll just have to trust me, Mr. Booker; we've been doing this for a long time, and we know precisely what we're doing. Take it from me: you are the right person. You will help us make the right decision."

"There you go again."

"Go again with what?"

"Telling me about making a decision. It sounds kind of threatening. It sounds ominous. What kind of decision are you talking about?"

"I'm simply telling you a decision has to be made. It is our purpose. We're peacekeepers."

Mr. Booker rolled his eyes. "And you want me to tell the truth to your council?"

"Yes, the truth."

The two men stared at each other for a moment. Then Mr. Booker said, "I'll tell you a story about the truth. It's a lesson I learned years ago."

"Okay," Sid said.

"When I was twelve years old, we had a neighbor named Mrs. Bartlett. She was in her late sixties, and what a sight this woman was. Her hair was thin and gray, a mass of emaciated snakelike ringlets; her head looked something like the head of Medusa. She wore too much makeup for a woman her age, as though by wearing it she could fool us into thinking she was younger. She always wore glasses that didn't fit her face. They were too large, and the lenses were thick and made her eyes appear small and beady. And she was always blinking, as if something was in her eyes. But I suppose looking back, I'd say the worst thing about her was her smile. Whenever she smiled, she'd make you feel like she was getting one over on you, like she had you in a jam and was enjoying it. It wasn't a kind or gracious smile. It made me feel uncomfortable, and I always wanted to look the other way when I saw her.

"I have to wonder how a person turns out to be like old Mrs. Bartlett. It was hard to imagine she was once a young girl or even a young woman. She was a mean and spiteful old lady. She seemed to hate us kids the most. She was always chasing us from her front yard, even if we weren't touching any of it. Our neighborhood was full of children back then, and I think we drove Mrs. Bartlett crazy. Maybe she would've been nicer if she'd had a husband or even a child or two of her own. But she had no one, and she was a childless widow. Yes, she was married once, but I'd never seen her husband. I heard he died years ago. I had to wonder what in the world her husband saw in her and why he married her. Maybe he died just to get away from her, the poor guy. Maybe he committed suicide. Who knew?

"Anyway, I remember my first encounter with Mrs. Bartlett, when I was eight years old. My mom was talking to her, and it turned out she was looking for a kid my age to help her with her yardwork. She was getting feeble in her old age and needed a young, energetic boy to work for her. The deal my mom struck with the woman was that I would help out on Saturday mornings, and in turn, she would pay me by the hour. It gave me the chance to earn some money, and it gave Mrs. Bartlett someone to boss around and help with her chores. She paid me a little over a dollar an hour. Truth is that I didn't want to work for the woman, but my mom insisted. She said it would be good for me to work and earn my own money."

"So you worked for her?"

"For three Saturdays in a row."

"And?"

"The woman was crazy. She treated me like a slave, and she had me doing the most ridiculous things. And every time I did what she asked, she'd say I did it wrong and have me do it over. Then, on the third Saturday, she accused me of stealing. She told my mom that she'd left her purse on the patio table while I was working. She said she definitely had over sixty dollars in her wallet, but when she went to the grocery store that afternoon, the cash was gone. Other than her, I was the only person who had access to the purse. Despite my protests, my mom paid her the missing money and had me apologize. I think she felt sorry for her. I don't think my mom thought I had taken the cash. She said, 'People get funny when they're old,' and then she said it'd probably be a good idea if I stopped working for the woman. And that ended my employment. You know, I didn't steal that money, and I didn't feel sorry for Mrs. Bartlett. The woman was lying and deliberately trying to get me in trouble. I swore to myself that I'd get even with the old bat, and when I was twelve, I did exactly that. Oh boy, did I ever get even."

"What'd you do?"

"In Mrs. Bartlett's front yard was a twenty-year-old century plant near the sidewalk. It turned out that her husband had planted it when he was still alive, and it was Mrs. Bartlett's pride and joy. Do you know what a century plant is?"

"No, I don't."

"It's a large, odd–looking succulent. It isn't much to look at, just a mundane bundle of thick, pointy leaves. But after twenty years, it shoots up a stalk twenty or thirty feet high with a step ladder of marvelous yellow blossoms. It really is something spectacular to behold, like a plant from another planet. Anyway, when I was twelve, Mrs. Bartlett's century plant finally grew its blooming stalk. I remember seeing her in her front yard, taking pictures of the incredible plant. I heard my parents talking about it and how much it meant to Mrs. Bartlett, and it occurred to me how I could finally get even. One night while everyone was sleeping, I went to our garage and got my dad's handsaw from his workbench. I snuck out to Mrs. Bartlett's front yard and cut down the stalk, and the thing fell across her driveway. The next day, Mrs. Bartlett was at our front door, demanding to know if I was responsible for the vandalism. I guess I was the most obvious culprit. My parents waited until I got home from school, and then my dad interrogated me. I never have been a very good liar, so I told my dad the truth: I had cut down Mrs. Bartlett's precious plant."

"What'd he do?"

"He was furious. At first, he just stood there, mad as a hornet. Then he took me next door and made me fess up to Mrs. Bartlett, and he made me apologize. It was horrible, having to face this woman and tell her what I'd done. She grinned at me with that awful smile of hers, obviously pleased to see that I was in trouble with my parents. When Dad and I got home, he grounded me for an entire month. He told me that what I'd done was inexcusable and that he was ashamed of me. It made me feel awful. To this day, I still tell the truth when I'm questioned. I don't seem to be able to help myself, but I don't expect to tell the truth without it having consequences. I know better. So when you ask me to tell the truth, I can say yes, I'll do that for you, but I think it's only fair that I be told the consequences. You said Ogonites liked transparency, so again I ask, what is the decision your council needs to make? You keep saying they have to make a decision. I think you should be honest with me."

"Point taken," Sid said.

"Well?"

Sid said, "Okay, I'll be honest with you. The future of your people is in your hands. It's all going to depend on you."

"The future of my people?"

"You asked, and I answered honestly."

"Do you mean the future of Americans?"

"I mean the future of everyone on your planet, all seven billion of you."

CHAPTER 4

TO TELL THE TRUTH

The tour continued. The next place Sid showed Mr. Booker was the cafeteria, which Sid said Mr. Booker was welcome to visit any time of the day or night. The usual ornate woodwork covered the walls and ceiling, and there were rows of carved wooden tables and chairs. Various members of the ship's crew occupied the tables, eating and talking to each other. The place smelled wonderful, like a culinary stew of enticing aromas, intergalactic spices, and exotic main courses and sauces. Sid said, "Our cafeteria is open twenty-four hours, and you'll often find our crew eating here. You're welcome to sit and converse with any of them while you enjoy your meals. You'll discover our people are cordial, and of course, they will be curious about Earth and eager to become friends with you. We are all familiar with your planet and its culture, but most of us want to learn more. You'll learn that Ogonites are by nature very inquisitive, so don't be surprised if they ask you many questions."

"What kind of food does the cafeteria serve?" Mr. Booker asked.

"A little of everything."

"Earth-type food?"

"Yes, of course. You'll find a wide variety of your native foods. You'll also find many Ogonite dishes on the menu, each of which I highly recommend. Food preparation is a high art on Og, and every citizen fancies him-or herself a gourmet. Although I'll warn you about one thing: we don't kill animals for eating. All our preparations are made from scratch."

"From scratch?"

"From plant life and various chemicals. We grow the plants here on our ship."

"That doesn't sound very appetizing."

"I think you'll be surprised at how good the food is. Each of our cooks has gone through many years of intensive training at our culinary colleges, and Ogonite food is second to none. We've been to many planets, and we've yet to find a civilization whose cooking skills come even close to ours."

"In that case, I guess I'll look forward to trying my first meal."

"As you should."

"I noticed you provided me with plenty to eat and drink back at my cabin. The refrigerator and the pantry are full."

"You always have the option of cooking for yourself, if you're so inclined."

"I'm not much of a cook."

"Then I strongly recommend the cafeteria. You won't be disappointed."

"Do they serve hamburgers?"

"I believe our chefs have put an American hamburger on the menu."

"I could really go for a hamburger."

"Ah, of course, but in due time. Let's finish up with our tour. Please follow me so we can continue." The two men stepped out of the busy cafeteria and back into the hallway. Sid took Mr. Booker to the physical activities center, which was a short walk from the cafeteria. The center housed rows of exercise machines, stacks of towels, and a door that went to a locker room. It also had a large heated swimming pool and a basketball court. "We know you're not an athlete," Sid said, "but we thought during your stay, you might feel inclined to exert a little physical energy. It seems to be something you earthlings like to do. Anyway, you're welcome to use this room as you see fit. It was built specifically for you."

Mr. Booker wasn't much for exercising, so he wasn't sure what to say. He just smiled at Sid and said, "I appreciate this."

"Some of our crew members have been using the room and have taken a liking to your basketball game. Do you know much about this sport? Maybe you can play with them and give some pointers."

"I'm not much of a basketball player."

"Well, neither are they."

Mr. Booker laughed.

"Anyway, I'm sure they'd enjoy playing with you."

"Maybe," Mr. Booker said.

Mr. Booker laughed again. *Basketball? Really?* Of all the silly things to pick for him to do! The last time Mr. Booker had held a basketball in his hands had been during gym class in ninth grade, when he'd been required to play with the other boys. He'd been unable to make a shot if his young life depended on it. Besides, sports were for kids who didn't like to study. Who in his right mind would waste hours of his life trying to toss a ball through a stupid metal hoop, when there were so many important books to read and so many things to learn?

After the fitness center, Sid took Mr. Booker to the ship's library. It wasn't a conventional library; there wasn't a single shelf or book in the entire room. Instead, there were rows of computer monitors mounted on several long wooden desks. The monitors were all tied to the ship's main computer, and there were no keyboards. Sid explained that each station was voice activated. He said, "Our ship's computer holds a complete collection of books in its memory, and while you're here on our ship, you'll have access to everything that's been stored. Our librarian, Margaret, can help you navigate the system for your more advanced searches. You'll find her very useful. She isn't here right now, or I'd introduce you to her. I think I saw her in the cafeteria, grabbing a bite to eat, but when she's here, you'll discover she can help you. Our computer translates all the works we have on file, so you can read anything, written in any language. There are millions of works available, many from Earth but also many from Og. There are even a substantial number of works from other planets we've visited."

"This is incredible," Mr. Booker said.

"We thought you'd like it."

"So can I look up anything?"

"Yes, anything. We believe everyone aboard this ship should have access to everything. Of course, this includes our guests, which obviously includes you. You'll find that nothing in our library has been deliberately omitted or censored in any way."

Sid demonstrated the system for Mr. Booker by bringing up the texts of several of Earth's classic books using one of the desktop monitors. He then brought up *Uncle Tom's Cabin* for Mr. Booker. That was the book Mr. Booker had packed in his satchel to read on the plane on his way to England. He'd read the book back in college, but he wanted to read it again. Mr. Booker looked at the monitor, amazed. Sid said, "See how simple it is? You just say the name of the book, the author, and the planet it came from, and up it comes."

Mr. Booker told Sid he was impressed. When they were done playing with the system, they left the library, and Sid took Mr. Booker farther down the hall to show him some of the other facilities. They spent a lot of time going in and out of doors, checking out rooms, and talking to some of the crew members. Everyone on the ship was friendly, and Mr. Booker felt like a celebrity. Never had he been to a place where so many people were wanting to meet him. Everyone on the ship was pleased to see him. When they were finally done with the tour, Mr. Booker told Sid he was tired and asked if he could return to his cabin. Sid suggested he first grab dinner in the cafeteria and then go to his cabin.

"Okay," Mr. Booker said.

"I suggest you turn in early tonight and get plenty of sleep. You'll have a busy day tomorrow, and you'll need to be well rested. You'll be meeting with the council, and their interrogations can be taxing. You should set your alarm for six. That will give you time to have breakfast and to shave and shower. You're due in council chambers at eight. Ogonites are very punctual, so you shouldn't be late. It's not that anything bad will happen if you're not on time; it's just that we find tardiness to be impolite. And it's best you don't offend the council."

"Can I get my food from the cafeteria to go?" Mr. Booker asked.

"To go?"

"Can I take the food to my room to eat it?"

"You wish to eat alone?"

"I'm tired, and I'm not in the mood for talking to anyone."

"I suppose it can be arranged. We'll have someone bring your food to your cabin. Do you still want a hamburger?"

"Yes, but with no cheese. Just add a slice of tomato, pickles, and a leaf of lettuce."

"Okay."

"And some french fries."

"A hamburger and fries."

"And some catsup."

"Yes, of course. Can you find your way back to your room, or do I need to show you how to get there?"

"I remember where it is."

"Fine. Then I'll see you tomorrow morning."

Mr. Booker and Sid shook hands and parted ways, and Mr. Booker found his way back to his cabin. He opened the front door and stepped inside. Everything was just as he'd left it, a perfect reproduction of his home on Earth. No, he thought, this was not a dream. It was unbelievable, but it wasn't a dream. He'd been on this ship for hours, and Sid had been right when he'd said that dreams didn't last that long.

There was a knock at the front door, and Mr. Booker answered it. "You're here already?" he asked. He was surprised to see his visitor. Standing in the doorway was a young man holding a silver tray over his shoulder, and on the tray were Mr. Booker's hamburger, fries, and a red bottle of catsup.

"Where should I put it?" the kid asked.

"Put it on the kitchen table."

The young man carried the tray to the table and set it down. "Do you want anything else?" he asked.

"No, this looks perfect."

"Enjoy your meal, sir."

Just like that, the kid was gone, and Mr. Booker was alone in his cabin with his hamburger and fries. It certainly smelled like a real hamburger, but what would it taste like?

There was a framed photograph of Linda on a shelf in the kitchen, near the table. He looked at the photograph and laughed. He said to the picture, "Even if you were here with me, you wouldn't believe any of this. No, you wouldn't believe it at all." He then took a bite of his hamburger. It was one of the best hamburgers he'd ever tasted. *Who would've thought this possible? Such a great hamburger made from Ogonite plant life and chemicals!* Mr. Booker was starving, and he ate everything on his plate.

When Mr. Booker went to bed, it was only nine o'clock, well before his normal bedtime, but he could barely keep his eyes open. He had no difficulty falling asleep, and he dozed like a baby in a deep and dreamless slumber. Then, early in the morning, he had the strangest dream, which took him far back in time.

In the dream, he was seated at a campfire at night. He was in a cold and thick forest with a group of other men. At first, he was confused, but soon he realized where he was, and more importantly, he understood who he was. One of the men put another log on the fire, and the flames crackled and ignited. The heat from the fire helped take the chill out of the night air. "So where have you been, Robin?" one of the men asked.

"You wouldn't believe me if I told you."

"Try me," the man said.

"Surely you can trust us," another man said.

"Can I really?"

"Were you breaking bread with the sheriff?" a third man asked, laughing.

"No, of course not."

"In bed again with Marian?"

"I wish it were so."

"Well, where then?" the first man asked. "Why all the mystery?"

"Because I've been up in the stars."

"The stars?"

"High in the heavens."

The Merry Men laughed at this, and one of them slapped his knee and asked, "How much mead have you been drinking tonight?" There was more laughter.

"Haven't had a drop."

"Then do tell us more!"

"You'll just laugh at me."

"No," the friar finally said. "We won't laugh. Will we, men? We're not going to laugh at Robin. I, for one, promise not to laugh. So tell us more. Tell us all about the stars."

With a serious expression on his face, in a low and deliberate voice, Mr. Booker said, "I was aboard a spaceship."

"A spaceship?"

"It was from another galaxy."

"Another galaxy?"

"Ho, ho!" One of the men laughed, but the friar gave him a stern look, and the man kept quiet.

"What's a galaxy?"

"Never mind," Mr. Booker said. "I wasn't abducted by men. I was abducted by creatures with the ability to look like men. They relocated me to their ship, a ship such as none of you have ever seen. It was not the sort of ship that navigates the seas or oceans but a ship that sails high in the sky, beyond the clouds, in the vastness of outer space."

"Beyond the clouds?"

The men were listening skeptically but not laughing. Had their leader lost his mind? He wasn't slurring his words, and he didn't smell of alcohol, but there was something about him—a seriousness in his manner that caused them to worry. Mr. Booker continued. "They've mastered secrets of sorcery. I was shown around the ship by a man named Sid, but he wasn't really a man. He made himself look like a man by magic."

"He was from another planet?"

"What did he actually look like?"

"He said he looked like a cross between a plucked chicken and a snake."

"A what?"

"I know it's hard to fathom, but I think he was telling me the truth. He had no reason to lie to me."

"So what did he want?"

"I'm to appear before a council."

"A council? For what purpose?"

"I'm not really sure what they want from me. Sid told me they had questions. I'm to be there first thing in the morning. Sid told me not to be late."

"What happens if you're late?"

"I'm not sure."

"Tell us more," the friar said. "We want to hear everything."

"Yes, more," the other men said in unison.

Mr. Booker cleared his throat, and looking into the campfire, he said, "Something tells me there may be trouble."

"You think Sid's a spy? Do you think he'll tell King John where we're hiding out?"

"No, it isn't that."

"Well, what then?" the friar asked.

"Yes, what?" the other men repeated.

"I think they want to know more about us."

"Us?" the friar asked.

"I mean they want to know about all of us—about all of England and all of France and all about every other nation on Earth."

"What sense does that make?"

"Have any of you ever heard of basketball?" Mr. Booker asked.

"Basketball?"

"It's a game. It's called basketball. There's a rectangular court, and at each end is a backboard with a metal hoop. The point of the game is to toss the ball so it goes through the hoops."

"Never heard of it," one of the men said.

"Is it a French game?" another asked. "It sounds like some dumb sport Frenchmen would play."

"They say it's American."

"What's American?"

"Americans eat hamburgers."

"What's a hamburger?" the friar asked.

Mr. Booker looked at his men. They were staring at him as if he had gone crazy. "Dear God," he finally said. "I think I'm dreaming."

"Get a hold of yourself, Robin," the friar said. He put a hand on Mr. Booker's shoulder.

"Why do you men keep calling me Robin? My name is Mr. Booker. And why are we in these woods? Why are we sitting around this campfire?"

"Robin?" a voice said.

"Wake up, Robin!" another voice said.

"You're going to be late. It's nearly seven, and you slept through your alarm. The council doesn't like to be kept waiting." This voice sounded familiar, but it didn't belong to any of the men around the campfire.

"Oh hell," Mr. Booker grumbled. He opened his eyes, and the campfire was gone. The forest was gone, and the men were nowhere to be seen. He was under his bedcovers, in his bedroom. He was no longer dreaming, and Sid was shaking his shoulder.

"Wake up, Mr. Booker," Sid said.

"I'm awake."

"It's time to get ready. It's a good thing I came to check on you. You would've been late."

"Yes, of course," Mr. Booker said. "Give me some time in the bathroom. I'll be ready to go in fifteen minutes."

"Fine. I'll wait for you. We can walk to the council chambers together."

Mr. Booker got ready and then stepped into his front room. Sid was waiting, seated on the sofa. When Sid saw Mr. Booker entering the room, he stood up, and the two of them left the cabin. "I was hoping you'd be able to have some breakfast," Sid said. "But you won't have time for it."

"It's okay," Mr. Booker said. "I'm not hungry."

"You can get something for lunch. There's a two-hour break at lunchtime."

"That'll be fine," Mr. Booker said.

"How was your hamburger last night?"

"It was great."

"Our chefs know what they're doing?"

"Yes, they seem to."

"Were the fries to your liking?"

"They were fine."

They reached the door to the council chambers, and Sid opened it. They walked into the room, and Sid raised his hand to get the council's attention. "We're here," Sid said in a loud voice. The council members were seated on the stage, just as Sid had described. Mr. Booker took a seat in his chair, and Sid sat behind him.

"Welcome, Mr. Booker," the chairman said. "My name is Rock."

"Good morning, sir."

"We hope Sid has been treating you well."

"Yes, he's been an excellent host."

"That's good to hear. I'm going to introduce you to our other four council members, but first, I want to explain something to you. It's important that you understand what I have to say."

"Okay," Mr. Booker said.

"I'm sure Sid's already told you we've been observing your planet for the past twenty years, and I think we have a pretty good idea of what makes you humans tick. But we still have some questions we'd like answered before we make our final decision as to the disposition of your species. We need you to be honest with us. I wouldn't say this if it wasn't important. Why do I make it a point to bring this up? It's because humans are so deceitful. We've been analyzing life-forms on planets for a long, long time, and it isn't often that we come across a life-form that is so relentlessly inclined to lie. It's truly remarkable. None of us has seen anything quite like it. We think it may be genetic, and you can't help yourselves, but we're not a hundred percent sure. Anyway, we're giving you a chance. You are being given this opportunity to provide honest and sincere answers. Am I making myself clear to you? Do you understand what we want from you?"

"Yes," Mr. Booker said. "I think you want me to be honest."

"Yes, that's it precisely. You should know that we considered having you take an oath. We've studied your courts of law and how they deal with this challenging aspect of human nature. When a human testifies in one of your courts, he or she is required to take an oath, correct? This oath says something like, 'Ordinarily, I would lie to you, but since I've agreed to swear on a Bible, I now promise to be truthful.' We asked ourselves, is it really all as simple as that? Is this all that needs to happen? In fact, doesn't an oath really say, 'Now I can say whatever I want, and you have to believe me unless you can prove for a fact that I'm telling a lie'? What are your thoughts on this?"

"I'm not sure."

"You don't have an opinion?"

"I guess an oath doesn't mean much."

"Humans under oath lie all the time?"

"They do," Mr. Booker said.

"That sounds like an honest answer. I'm glad you said that. Honesty is what we require. But it brings us back to where we started, which is determining how we'll know you're being honest with us."

"I guess you'll have to take my word."

"Ah, the word of a human being."

"That's about it."

Rock stared at Mr. Booker for a moment and then said, "Fine, let's do it this say. We will move on, and there will be no oath. We're going to ask you our questions, and we'll promise to take you at your word. But here's the hitch. One lie, Mr. Booker, and we'll shut this process down and send you back to Earth. One little lie, and we'll ignore everything you've said. We'll ask you for the sum of one and one, and if you say two, we'll believe you, but if you tell us three, it's all over. You must not lie to us under any circumstances. Do you understand? Does this sound fair to you?"

"Yes, it sounds fair."

"And is that a truthful answer?"

"It is truthful."

Rock looked at the other council members and asked, "Is this plan okay with the rest of you?" All of them nodded. Then Rock turned toward Mr. Booker and said, "Now that we've come to this understanding, I think we can move forward. Are you ready to move forward? Are you ready for our questions?"

"Yes," Mr. Booker said.

Chapter 5

Only Human

Rock was a handsome fellow with an angular face and friendly eyes. He must've been going for the mature movie star look when he picked out his appearance. Mr. Booker told me he looked like a Hollywood actor approaching his fifties. His hair was black and neatly styled, and he had a clean-shaven face and perfect teeth. Judging by the man's appearance, Mr. Booker had a feeling Rock would treat him respectfully. There was something about his countenance that made Mr. Booker feel at ease. Above his friendly eyes were two bushy eyebrows that wriggled when he spoke, as though they were attached to the nerves of his mouth. His eyebrows were his most expressive feature, and as the council meeting began, they seemed to be expressing both compassion and goodwill. Even though Rock had started off the meeting on a rather stern note, Mr. Booker liked the man, and he was glad Rock was chairman.

Before they started the questioning, Rock introduced the other council members to Mr. Booker. He started with Lucy, who was seated to his far left. "Lucy is our youngest member," Rock said. "But I think you're going to like her. She's very fond of your planet and its people. Lucy is what you earthlings would refer to as an anthropologist. Of course, she observes all sorts of different life-forms, not just humans." Lucy smiled at Mr. Booker after Rock said this, and Mr. Booker smiled back at her. Rock then went on to recite her educational background and some of her accomplishments. She seemed like a warm young woman, and Mr. Booker looked forward to answering her questions. There was nothing intimidating about her appearance. She had short brown hair cropped in a manner similar to the hairstyle of the medic who had tended to his nose. She was quite good looking—not flashy or glamorous, but she had an intelligent face that put Mr. Booker at ease.

Seated between Rock and Lucy was a dour-looking man whom Rock introduced as William. Rock said William was the eldest member of the council, and he was a retired medical doctor. His head was shiny and bald, and he wore a pair of wire-rimmed spectacles that sat on the end of his pointed nose. His jaw was bristly, as if he hadn't bothered to shave that morning, and the bristles were as white as snow. Mr. Booker guessed the man was in his eighties, and he was concerned with him. William didn't smile once while Rock talked about his background. He was a little too serious and unfriendly for Mr. Booker's taste. As Rock continued to speak about him, William removed his wire-framed glasses and rubbed the lenses on the lapel of his golden robe. With his glasses off, while cleaning the lenses, he squinted at Mr. Booker, looking at him suspiciously as if sizing him up. This guy was nothing like Rock or Lucy, and Mr. Booker did not look forward to his questions.

Seated on the other far side of Rock was a black man named Ernie. He had pronounced African features and an almost comical Afro hairstyle. His skin was coal black, and it made the whites of his eyes and his teeth seem even whiter than they were. He was introduced by Rock as the ship's resident historian, and Mr. Booker guessed Ernie was in his sixties. According to Rock, they were lucky to have Ernie on the council. Back on Og, he was supposedly highly respected, a man who could've taken an educational position at any of the planet's top universities. However, many years ago, he'd been bitten by the space-exploration bug, and he was now one of the council's most senior members. "Ernie's knowledge of intergalactic history is indispensable," Rock said. "As a history teacher yourself, you can probably appreciate what he brings to the table. I think in the days ahead, you'll come to like Ernie a lot."

Lastly, to Rock's immediate left sat the artist and gadfly of the group. Rock introduced him as Ralph and said he was one of Og's most beloved creative minds. He appeared to be in his forties. Rock said, "I'm not exaggerating his talents. Ralph is what you on Earth would refer to as a Renaissance man. He excels in all forms of artistic expression, and while you're here, you'll be given a chance to see and appreciate some of his work. We're proud to have him aboard this ship and delighted to have him on our council." As Rock spoke, Ralph stroked his bushy beard with his hand and smiled with his own perfect teeth. It was difficult to tell whether he was actually looking at Mr. Booker, since he was wearing a pair of sunglasses. Not only was his beard bushy, but so was the gray hair on his head. It had been forced into a ponytail that dangled down the middle of his back. "Like Ernie, Ralph was much in demand back home, but he too wanted to travel into space. We consider ourselves lucky to have him here with us."

Each council member had a monitor sitting on the desktop in front of him or her. Presumably, the monitors gave them access to the ship's computer. Having completed the introductions, Rock looked at his own computer monitor, reading something from the screen. This went on for a minute or so while everyone watched and waited for him to get things rolling. Then he peered over the top of the monitor toward Mr. Booker. "Shall we get started?" he asked.

"By all means," Mr. Booker replied.

"Are you ready, Sid?"

"Yes," Sid said. "I think we're both ready."

"Very well. I'm going to begin with William. He has a few opening questions, and he asked me if he could start things off."

"Fire away," Mr. Booker said. He wanted to sound enthusiastic, but the truth was, he was getting nervous. He hoped his apprehension wasn't obvious to the others, and he tried to disguise it by keeping a relaxed face. In all honesty, William was the last council member he'd wanted to hear from first. He had hoped it would be someone else.

William cleared his throat and said, "I'm going to give you

a hypothetical, Mr. Booker. Do you mind me giving you a hypothetical?"

"Not at all."

"Okay, let's say you're in a restaurant back on Earth, and you're minding your own business, eating your meal and chatting with a companion. Suddenly, at the table next to you, a man begins to hack and cough. His face turns blue; his eyes are bulging. He's holding on to his throat with both hands. Clearly, he's choking on a piece of food. Let's say it's a piece of fat from a steak he was eating, and now his wife begins to panic and starts shouting for someone to help. You know precisely what needs to be done. You were taught the Heimlich maneuver in your health class in high school, and you committed the procedure to memory just in case a situation like this ever arose. 'I can help your husband,' you say, and you walk to the choking man. You tell him to rise, and then you put your arms around him from behind. You give him several hearty squeezes, and out shoots the piece of fat. The guy gasps for air, finally able to breathe. Do you know about the Heimlich maneuver? Do you know what I'm talking about?"

"Yes, I do."

"Fine, fine. So have I described a reasonable hypothetical?"

"Saving the man's life? Yes, it could happen that way. Certainly, if I saw a man choking, I would try to help."

"This is a hypothetical, of course."

"Yes, of course."

"Tell me, Mr. Booker—would you expect to be paid by the man?"

"You mean with money?"

"Yes, of course with money."

"Certainly not," Mr. Booker said.

"Why not?"

Mr. Booker thought for a moment. William was staring at him, and it made him uncomfortable. Was it a trick question? Mr. Booker didn't trust William's motives. He seemed to have something up his sleeve, but Mr. Booker finally said, "I wouldn't ask to be paid because it wasn't a big deal. I'd have done something anyone who knew the maneuver would've done."

"But you saved the man's life."

"Yes, I did."

"Certainly you're entitled to some sort of reward for your services. What if the man offered to pay you a thousand dollars? What if he offered you five thousand? Wouldn't you take the money?"

"Probably not."

"No, of course not," William said, now agreeing with Mr. Booker. Finally, William smiled, but it wasn't a friendly smile. It was a self-satisfied smile, as though William had made an important point. "You simply did the right thing by helping another who was in need."

"Yes, something like that."

"You didn't help him for money."

"No, I didn't."

"That's very good. So can you explain something to us? How do you justify Earth's health-care system? Tell me why doctors on your planet are constantly demanding so much money for their services."

"It's the way things are."

"The way things are?"

"It's how our system works. Doctors go through years of school and internship to learn how to save lives, so they charge for their time just like people in any other profession. No one on our planet is expected to work for free."

"So if you're facing a life-threatening illness, you have to pay your doctor to be treated?"

"Yes, that's how it works."

"It amounts to a lot of money, doesn't it?"

"Yes, medical care is very expensive."

William leaned back in his chair. He threw up his hands and said, "I'm at a loss!"

"Are things different in your society?" Mr. Booker asked.

"They're quite different," William said. "For each of us, medical care is free. We believe in helping one another because helping is the right thing to do. No one assumes he or she will get rich from another's misfortunes. We help each other because we should—the same way you felt you should help the choking man in the restaurant."

Lucy then spoke to William and said, "They seem to know the difference between right and wrong, yet they often pick the wrong. It's fascinating."

"*Fascinating* isn't exactly the word I'd use," William said.

"What would you call it?" Rock asked.

"I'd call it offensive," William said. Then, fixing his gaze on Mr. Booker again, William asked, "Do you believe humans are selfish?"

"Yes, at times, we can be."

"They have many charities," Lucy said.

"Yes, they do," Rock agreed.

"Ah, human charities," William said, still looking at Mr. Booker. "Do you give money to charities?"

"Sometimes," Mr. Booker said.

"How much?"

"Not a lot, I guess."

"Why not?"

"I don't have a lot of money to give away. I live on a very modest income."

"Compared to others, teachers on Earth are paid very little," Lucy explained.

"I keep forgetting that," Rock said.

"We're getting off track," William said. "I was questioning Mr. Booker about health care. I wasn't asking him how much money he made or whether he donated any of his earnings to charities. My concern has to do with how his people treat one another. As the Council for Peace, we've been charged with determining whether humans present a future danger to Ogonites, and I'd say you can tell a lot about a species by the way it treats itself. Life-forms that extort large amounts of money from each other under the guise of altruism certainly can't be trusted to treat another species ethically. In other words, if they can't be trusted to treat each other right, how will they treat us?"

"He has a good point," Ernie said.

"He does," Ralph agreed. He was still stroking his beard, but he had put his sunglasses on the top of his head so that Mr. Booker could now see his eyes.

"Let me ask him a question," Lucy said.

"Please do," William said.

Lucy leaned forward and looked directly at Mr. Booker. "I'm going to give you another hypothetical," she said. "Let's say you're out at sea on a ship with a friend, and your friend accidentally falls into the water. This friend of yours does not know how to swim, and he isn't wearing a life vest. He's thrashing about in the water, screaming for help. You know that without your immediate assistance, he's going to drown. What do you do? I think I know your answer, but I'm going to ask you anyway. Do you demand he pay you money before you take any action? Or do you just throw him a life preserver so he can stay afloat? What would you do, Mr. Booker? Would you demand money?"

"No, of course not."

"Because you know throwing him the life preserver is the right thing to do?"

"Anyone would know that."

"Okay," William said. "Let's say you're a doctor in a hospital. You work in the emergency room, and they wheel in a car-accident victim who's in critical condition. The poor guy is barely hanging on. Without your help, this victim has no chance of making it. His life is in your hands, just as the life of your friend on the boat was. Remember, you're now a doctor. So what do you do, Doctor? Do you help the guy and save his life because it's the right thing to do, or do you charge him a fortune for your services? You're no longer a private citizen. You've spent years learning how to save lives."

"It's different when you're a doctor."

"Is it really?" William asked. "Let's go back to the boat and the drowning man. If you were a doctor, would you be right to charge your friend a fee? As a medical doctor, wouldn't you have a perfect right to demand money for throwing the friend a life preserver?"

"That's not what I meant."

"Then what did you mean?" William asked.

"There's a big difference between a friend falling off a boat and a car-accident victim being wheeled into an emergency room."

"Is there?"

"I think there is."

"Perhaps you can explain this difference."

Mr. Booker stared at William for a moment, and then he looked at the faces of the other council members. They all seemed anxious to hear his response. But what exactly was the difference? Without having the chance to really think things through, Mr. Booker said, "I think you're comparing apples to oranges."

"Am I?"

"Yes, I think you are."

"You're being honest, but I don't think you're being either rational or ethical."

"But being a doctor is a very difficult job. They should get paid for what they do."

"On Og, being a doctor is a privilege," William said. "Few other professions are as rewarding."

"But it's hard work, isn't it?"

"That's all the more reason to love the job," William said. "All the more reason to do it for free."

"I don't follow you," Mr. Booker said.

"He doesn't get it," Ralph said.

Everyone was quiet for a moment. Then Lucy said, "It's as they say: he's only human."

"Yes, that's good," Rock said. "He's only human. He certainly is that." Everyone laughed at this—except for Mr. Booker.

Sid tapped Mr. Booker on the shoulder with the head of his wooden staff and whispered, "Don't let it bother you, kid. They're just having a little fun."

CHAPTER 6

SHOOTING HOOPS

Following the first session with the council, Sid and Mr. Booker went straight to the cafeteria. "I have no idea what to order," Mr. Booker said. He was looking up at the sprawling menu board, which listed more than a hundred items to choose from.

"Try an Ogonite dish," Sid suggested.

"Such as?"

"The cocopees are popular."

"What exactly is a cocopee?"

"It's like an earthly meat dish, except it isn't made of meat. Of course, neither was the hamburger you had last night, and you seemed to enjoy that. Like I told you, all our dishes are made from scratch, and none of them contain any animal products. Our chefs are exceptionally talented and well trained, and they can whip up just about anything you can think of. But the cocopees are terrific, and everyone likes them. It's a cold diced protein dish served with a warm kambert sauce. I'm not sure exactly how to describe the sauce to you except to say that it's thick like your gravy yet also a little sticky like your syrup. Cocopees are a favorite of the Ogonites, and many of our guests enjoy them as well. It comes with a traditional side of salted arponots. The arponots are like your green peas on Earth, except they're bigger, about the size of your large black olives."

"Sounds so bizarre."

"Why not give it a try? You're only going to be with us for a short while, and you'll never have another chance to try the stuff out. It's what I'm going to order. I'm in the mood for some cocopees."

"Well, if they're good enough for you, then I guess they'll be okay for me."

"You won't regret it."

Having decided, Sid and Mr. Booker approached the counter, and Sid asked for two orders of cocopees. They were given two empty cups, which they took to the beverage dispenser. It only took a couple minutes for the lunch orders to come up, and they went to the pickup station to get them. The plates of food were on silver trays, and they carried the trays to an empty table.

"Wow, this sauce is so red," Mr. Booker said.

"Like human blood," Sid said.

"And what are these little brown cubes?"

"Those are the cocopees."

"I see," Mr. Booker said. His lunch didn't look the slightest bit appetizing, and he was beginning to wish he'd just ordered another hamburger.

"Don't be a wuss," Sid said.

"A wuss?" Mr. Booker laughed.

"Dig in. Go ahead and eat."

Mr. Booker stared at his plate full of odd-looking food while Sid stabbed one of his cocopees with his fork and poked the bite-sized cube into his mouth. He closed his eyes and chewed, savoring the flavors. Then Mr. Booker carefully did the same, stuffing one of the saucy cubes past his lips. He chewed carefully and was surprised at how good it was. The cocopee was something like a chunk of cold and tender lamb but was crispy on the outside. The warm kambert sauce was delicious too, despite the fact that it looked as if someone had cut an artery and bled all over his plate. He couldn't think of anything on Earth he could compare this crazy sauce to; it was slightly sweet but also thick and meaty. "This isn't too bad," he said, and Sid just nodded and ate another cocopee.

"Isn't it great?" Sid asked. "The cocopees here are as good as you'll find anywhere on Og. Yes, this really hits the spot!" Sid was talking with his mouth full, his teeth reddened savagely by the bright red sauce.

"I've never had anything quite like it."

"Ogonites know how to prepare food. You just can't beat our cooking."

"I have a question," Mr. Booker said, chewing on his second cocopee and now changing the subject.

"Yes?" Sid asked.

"Am I going to have a problem with your council?"

"A problem?"

"I feel like they're ridiculing me."

"Oh, I wouldn't put it that way."

"Then how would you put it?"

"The council is simply trying to ascertain the facts and get your opinions."

"To see if humans are a threat?"

"Something like that."

"Do you think we're a threat?"

"It doesn't matter what I think. It isn't my call to make. I'm here solely to serve you as a host and adviser, and that's all. What the council does with the information you give is their business and of no concern to me. I have no say in the matter, and neither does anyone else. My suggestion is not to worry. There's really nothing you can do to influence their final decision other than be sincere and truthful when you answer their questions. It won't prevent all negative consequences, but honesty and sincerity will count for a lot."

"Negative consequences?"

"I probably shouldn't have phrased it that way."

"Do you think they'll decide to interfere with our lives on Earth?"

"It's possible," Sid said. "The council will do whatever it takes to protect our planet and its citizens. They are peacekeepers, plain and simple. Sometimes actions are required, and sometimes not. But they're not here to take over your planet and enslave your species, if that's what you're worried about. Now, we should probably talk about something else. I don't blame you for being curious, but you're attempting to get information from me that I'm neither qualified nor prepared to give."

"Fine," Mr. Booker said. He stuffed another cocopee into his mouth and said, "I have another question."

"That's why I'm here."

"How old are you?"

"How old am I? Ha, such a question!"

"Why do you say that?"

"Because my answer is going to surprise you. Ogonites live a lot longer than human beings."

"How much longer?"

"I'm almost five hundred years old."

"You're what?"

"The life expectancy of the average Ogonite is over six hundred years. The oldest Ogonite on record lived to be six hundred seventy-eight."

"That's hard to believe."

"What reason would I have to lie?"

"None, I guess."

"This age disparity between our species makes for some interesting differences between our cultures."

"Such as?"

"Well, education for one. The average Ogonite is schooled for sixty or more years before he or she is let loose on society. Our young people are far better educated than your own."

"Sixty years of school?"

"Sixty, and often more. You'll find we're very proud of our schools. We view your school system as grossly inadequate. We would never consider letting our kids loose on our society with such minimal knowledge. Of course, you don't have much of a choice in the matter, seeing as how human life expectancy is so short. We recognize this as a problem for humans. The way we see it, even the most mature adult humans on your planet are really just adolescents.

It's no wonder your civilization has so many problems. It's being run by juveniles."

"We do have a lot of problems," Mr. Booker agreed.

A woman suddenly approached the table and asked if she could sit with Sid and Mr. Booker. It was Anna, the medic who'd treated Mr. Booker when he hurt his nose, and Sid invited her to take a seat. "I'm so hungry I could eat a horse," Anna said. Then, looking at Mr. Booker, she said, "Isn't that what you say on Earth?"

"Yes, that's what we say."

"But you don't eat horses, do you?"

"No, we don't. It's just an expression."

"Of course it is."

Mr. Booker looked at Anna's attractive face. She was still wearing too much rouge, but for some reason, she appeared even prettier than Mr. Booker remembered. He said to her, "I don't think I ever thanked you."

"For what?" Anna asked.

"For fixing my nose."

"It was nothing."

"I felt pretty stupid running into the door like I did. I should've known better."

"We've seen worse," Sid said.

"Much worse," Anna agreed.

Sid looked at Anna's plate. "I see you ordered the cocopees too."

"Best cocopees in the universe," Anna said.

Mr. Booker had liked the cocopees at first, but he was now growing weary of them. "Have you tried a hamburger?" Mr. Booker asked Anna.

"No, is it any good?"

"It's an American staple. It's very good. I had one last night, and it tasted just like the real thing." He was now wishing he'd ordered one rather than his screwball cocopees.

Anna then asked, "Did you meet with the council this morning?"

"I did," Mr. Booker said. "Sid and I have to be back at two."

"So you have some free time until then?"

"I guess I do."

"Do you like basketball?"

"I can take it or leave it."

"Would you like to watch me play?"

That was an interesting proposition, watching Anna play basketball. If Mr. Booker hadn't known better, he would have thought she was fluttering her eyelashes while she awaited his answer. Was she flirting with him? She certainly seemed to be, and Mr. Booker felt simultaneously uneasy and flattered. "We're playing in fifteen minutes, so I have just enough time to finish lunch. It'll be the Reds and the Blues. We play once a week, and I'm on the Reds. We think we're getting pretty good at the game, but it'd be fun to play for a real human audience. Maybe you could tell us how to improve."

"I don't know much about it."

"Doesn't every American like basketball?"

"No, not all of us. But I would like to watch you play. I think it'd be interesting."

"Oh yes, do come!"

"I will," Mr. Booker said.

"I'm going to leave you two alone," Sid said.

"You're leaving?"

"I have a couple personal matters to attend to. I'll catch up with you at the game."

"Okay," Mr. Booker said.

Sid stood up and walked away, leaving Mr. Booker alone at the table with Anna. "Sid is very nice," Mr. Booker said, not knowing what else to say. He suddenly felt a little bashful at being left alone at the table with this pretty girl.

"Do you know much about Sid?" Anna asked.

"Only that he's my host."

"I know a few stories."

"Such as?"

"Has he told you anything about his wife?"

"No, he hasn't," Mr. Booker said.

"Did he tell you why he's on this ship?"

"No," Mr. Booker said.

"Everyone here knows the story. It's no secret, so there's no harm in me telling you. I can tell you what happened if you're interested."

"I am," Mr. Booker said.

"Years ago, before I was born and before this ship departed from Og, Sid was the senior manager of a large hotel. There are many hotels on Og, since our people love to travel and are always in need of places to stay. Back then, Sid got married and had three children—two boys and a daughter. His wife's name was Areena, and she came from a respectable Ogonite family whose primary responsibility was running a large furniture-manufacturing company. They liked Sid, and they were pleased that he'd married their daughter. Well, for a while anyway."

"What happened?"

"You should know that there are three basic reasons you will find yourself aboard an exploration ship such as the *Peacekeeper 102*. The first is that you're actually passionate about discovering and studying other planets and civilizations. This would describe most of the people on this ship. They love what they do here and wouldn't trade their lives for anything. The second reason you might find yourself here is because you were born here. I'm one of those people, one of the ship's children. I was born here a little under a hundred years ago, and I don't know any other kind of life. My parents are wonderful people, and I share their enthusiasm about space exploration. But one day I hope to visit Og. There's so much I'd like to see on our home planet, and who knows? Maybe someday I'll live on Og rather than on a spaceship. But this brings me to the third reason why you might find yourself aboard this ship. Some people simply need to get away. Something may have happened, making this life a necessity. Our friend Sid falls into this third category. I think Sid likes what he does here, but he would've been just as happy back on Og. He joined us because he had difficulties on Og that he couldn't reconcile. He's not a bad person, mind you, but he did bring shame upon himself and his family, so he had to leave."

"What'd he do?"

"He took up with another woman."

"Another woman?"

"A woman named Lendoola."

"So he got a divorce from his first wife?"

"No, we don't divorce on Og. Divorce is never an option."

"What'd he do?"

"He left his wife and moved in with Lendoola. Then they had a child. Ogonites seriously frown on this kind of behavior, and Sid immediately became a pariah. There was only one solution to his difficulties, and that was to leave Og. This space mission provided him with the perfect opportunity. So he signed up, and he was accepted as a crew member. There's something about being so far away from home that allows you to escape past transgressions. Maybe it's because we are so far from home. I mean, we're still all Ogonites, but for some reason, we're less concerned about a man's past and more concerned about what's going on today. As long as you're a well-behaved member of the crew, that's all that really matters. Everyone here respects Sid and appreciates his skills. Having spent so much of his life working in the hospitality business back on Og, he's proven himself to be a very adept host, and he represents us honorably and graciously to our guests. I don't think there's another Ogonite who could do a better job with the creatures we've brought aboard."

"What happened to his other woman?"

"Lendoola?"

"Yes, and their child."

"They now live aboard the ship with Sid."

"So they all left Og together?"

"They did."

"And what happened to his original wife and three children back home?"

"His wife paired up with a man named Alfer. You could say Alfer is now a surrogate father and husband, something that is allowed if the first husband dies or leaves the family. But there will never be a divorce, not like the divorces humans get on your planet. Divorces simply don't happen on Og. Once a couple takes their wedding vows, the vows are vows for life."

"But Sid and his wife have nothing to do with each other. They're separated."

"That's true."

"And they both have new partners."

"Yes, that's also true."

"Then how are the vows still vows?"

"They just are. Anyway, that's Sid's story. That's why he's aboard this ship."

"Do you suppose I'll get to meet his new wife?"

"She isn't his wife. I just told you: he has only one wife, and she lives back on Og."

"Okay," Mr. Booker said.

"You might meet her. I've gotten to know her, and she seems like a kind person. She has a way of making you feel good about yourself, the same as Sid, and I can see why he fell for her."

"I'd like to meet her."

"Are you done with your lunch?"

"Yes, I'm full. I didn't eat it all, but it was very good."

"I liked mine too."

"Are we still going to the fitness center?"

"Does that mean you're coming?"

"Yes, I'd like to."

"Well, let's go then."

A young man appeared at the table to take away the trays and dirty dishes. Mr. Booker and Anna stood up to leave, and as they made their way out, Anna grabbed Mr. Booker's hand. They held hands as they walked, which made Mr. Booker feel strange. He said to Anna, "Do you know you're holding my hand?"

"Of course I do."

"But why?"

"Isn't this what male and female humans do when they like each other?"

"It is," Mr. Booker said.

"Well, don't you like me?" she asked. Anna batted her eyelashes again. It suddenly occurred to Mr. Booker just how attractive this young girl was. She was certainly good looking, but was she young? Of course, she wasn't young at all. In fact, she was nearly a hundred years old.

"I guess I do like you," Mr. Booker said.

"Well, I like you too. Don't let go. It's a nice custom, holding hands."

When they arrived at the fitness center, Anna guided Mr. Booker to the locker room. There was only one dressing area for both sexes, something Mr. Booker hadn't noticed during his tour with Sid. Once in the room, Anna let go of Mr. Booker's hand and proceeded to remove her golden robe. "I need to get my basketball clothes on," she explained. She was now standing before Mr. Booker in nothing but her bra and panties, and he could feel himself blushing. He tried to avert his gaze, but when he looked around, he noticed they were not alone. There were other young men and women, all wearing nothing but their underwear and putting on their basketball outfits. No one seemed the slightest bit bashful. "You're blushing," Anna said. She stood there for a moment, smiling.

"You took off your robe."

"You've never seen a woman's body before?"

"It isn't that."

"Well, what is it?"

"I don't know. Do you people always undress in front of each other? I mean, men and women together?"

"You humans are so modest." Anna laughed and then stepped into a pair of baggy basketball shorts. She then pulled a sleeveless jersey over her head. "How do I look now?" she asked.

"You look like a basketball player."

"Wait until you see me dribble."

"I'll be watching," Mr. Booker said. Anna grabbed his hand again and pulled him out of the locker room to the court. Mr. Booker took a seat in the bleachers while Anna walked out onto the floor. There was no one else in the stands, so he was sitting alone. There were no referees, game clock, or scoreboard. The other players showed up, half of them dressed in red and the other half dressed in blue. Soon everyone was ready, and they began playing basketball, running up and down the court, trying to get the ball into the hoops. It was the silliest thing Mr. Booker had ever seen. He actually laughed out loud. These players had no idea what they were doing. They were dressed in their jerseys and shorts, as though they were real basketball players, but they didn't have a clue. When one of them made a basket, they all jumped up and down and cheered for the person. They were all rooting for each other to win!

During this strange game, Sid appeared from behind the bleachers and took a seat next to Mr. Booker. "We need to get back to council chambers in about twenty minutes," he said.

"Okay," Mr. Booker said.

"What do you think of our basketball players?"

"I've never seen anything quite like this game."

"They're not too bad?"

"They all seem to be playing for the same team. They don't seem to be playing against each other or trying to win a game."

"Against each other?"

"They're divided into teams, red and blue, but each team seems to be helping the other out. No one is trying to block anyone's shots, steal the ball, or score more points."

"Well, of course not."

Mr. Booker looked at Sid. "Listen," he said. "I don't know much about basketball, but I know enough to understand the teams are supposed to play against each other and not for each other. What they're doing makes no sense. No one will win, and no one will lose."

"But they'll all win," Sid said.

Mr. Booker laughed. "I don't think you guys get it."

Sid put his hand on Mr. Booker's shoulder. "No, I don't think you get it."

"Get what?"

"Ogonites don't compete with each other in games or in real life.

It's not our nature. I told you before that we're a very social species. We always work in unison to achieve a common end. We constantly look out for each other and strive to make each other better. It's what makes us so successful."

"But this is so pointless. They're not even keeping score!"

"Precisely. And they're getting better at the game every day. You should've seen them when they first started playing. They were terrible."

"I'm no sports expert, but it's hard to imagine they were much worse than they are now."

Sid just smiled, and then he laughed. He removed his hand from Mr. Booker's shoulder and looked toward the clock on the far wall. "We should probably get going. When it comes to meeting with the council, it's always better to be early than late."

CHAPTER 7

MY DOUBTS

When Mr. Booker reached this point in his story, he asked if he could take a couple days off so he could attend to some personal business. Of course I said yes, and during the time off, I began organizing my notes. During that time, I also received a call from Julius Chesterfield. I realize Julius has nothing to do with Mr. Booker's story, but I'm now going to tell you a little about him because he was so typical of the people I wrote about prior to meeting Mr. Booker. If I describe him and his stories, maybe you'll see why I found Mr. Booker so compelling.

Julius was included in one of my more recent books, which described a dozen or so alien abductions I'd learned about over the past several years. Like Mr. Booker, Julius claimed to have been taken aboard an alien spacecraft. You may at first be inclined to say Mr. Booker's story was no different, just another far-fetched men-from-outer-space fantasy. But you'd be wrong. There was much more to Mr. Booker's story.

So what was the deal with Julius? When he called, he was out of breath, and he insisted we meet right away. I wanted to work more on Mr. Booker's notes, but the guy just wouldn't take no for an answer, so I scheduled a meeting with Julius at his home in Laguna Beach. He lived in a run-down cottage just a half mile from the ocean, a place he'd inherited when his parents passed away. We sat down at his kitchen table, and he recounted his most recent experience.

According to Julius, he was on his way home from work at dusk, when he stopped at a market to purchase some groceries. The parking lot at the grocery store was crowded, but he found a place to park.

Julius went into the store, bought what he needed, and then stepped outside with his bag of groceries. He opened his car door, placed the goods on the backseat, and climbed into the front to drive home. When he sat in the driver's seat, the radio began to blare despite the fact that he hadn't even put the key in the ignition. The radio was drifting from station to station. Then the windshield wipers started whipping back and forth, and the headlights began to flash. He told me that from his own past experiences, he knew exactly what was going on. Yes, it was happening again: he was being abducted. He looked at his wristwatch to check the time, and it was precisely 6:32. He remembered that for sure. He said there was then a sudden bright light from overhead, followed by a gust of hot air, and after that, everything was dark and silent. He blinked and felt a sharp pain in his groin. He was still sitting in the car, but when he looked at his watch again, it was after nine. It was no longer dusk, and the radio and car lights were off. It was dark outside, and except for his car, the parking lot was empty. "It happened again!" he told me. Two and a half hours had passed right under his nose, and he couldn't account for the lost time.

As with the first time he'd been abducted, his memories of what had happened came to him in a dream. While sleeping, he recalled bits and pieces of the two-and-a-half-hour gap in time. Now it all made sense, and he wanted to share it with me. He said he'd been strapped to a metal examination table in a spaceship that was orbiting Earth, and he was surrounded by almond-eyed aliens. None of them was over four feet tall, and not one of them wore a stitch of clothing. He too was stark naked, and one of the aliens held on to his penis while another inserted a plastic tube into his urethra. It was very painful, he said, and he asked them to please stop. But they wouldn't listen to him. They just chirped and mumbled to each other in a strange foreign language. That was the extent of what Julius could recall, but he told me he was sure the dream was accurate. He looked at me seriously and said, "They're now obsessed with our reproductive organs. I spent two and a half hours with them. God knows what other experiments they performed. My penis ached that night like I'd had sex with a lawnmower."

This talk I had with Julius brought back memories of the afternoon I first met him. When I first interviewed Julius, he told me he'd been abducted by aliens while working in his backyard. He was listening to the radio and trimming a hedge, when the same thing happened. The radio stations started jumping from one to the other for no apparent reason. Then he felt a gust of warm wind and saw a blinding light overhead. The next thing he knew, several hours had passed, and it was evening. At first, he had no idea what had happened, but then memories of the abduction came in his dreams. During this first abduction, the aliens were probing his nose. He said the process was very painful, but the aliens ignored his pleas to stop. This procedure went on for hours, until they were finally done with him. Not knowing any better, I included Julius's stories in my recent book, along with several stories of a similar nature told to me by others.

Not too long ago, I thought these tales were important for the world to read, and I wrote about them. I learned that many people enjoyed reading my books; I was not alone in my interest in alien abductions. However, after meeting with Mr. Booker, I started to have doubts about Julius and the others. Many of their tales were similar in nature. I used to think that was because there was truth to them. It made sense that the stories would be alike, since I figured the same group of aliens were probably pestering these poor people. But more recently, it occurred to me that the stories were similar for a different reason: these people were egging each other on. In other words, people were reading the stories and getting ideas for their own stories. Each story was being influenced by that which preceded it.

That wasn't the only reason for my skepticism. When you think about all these alleged alien experiments on our human bodies, they make little sense. For example, if aliens were truly interested in human anatomy, why wouldn't they just sneak down to Earth and get some copies of a few good medical textbooks? Surely if they're smart enough to travel light-years through space to visit us, they ought to have the means to come down to Earth and acquire a few books. Do you see what I mean? I hate to cast doubt on all the books and magazine articles I've written over the years, but I'm trying to be honest with you. I do now have my suspicions, and while I listened to Julius during our recent meeting, my mind was on Mr. Booker.

I liked Mr. Booker's tale. It was different. Sure, it was outrageous and a little hard to believe, but it didn't involve any metal examination tables, little green men, or probes being poked pointlessly into naked human abductees. His Ogonites had already done their research, just as one would expect intelligent alien visitors to do. They already had extensive knowledge of human beings. They simply wanted to talk to one of us to see what kind of information he or she could offer regarding our behavior. They were giving us a chance to explain ourselves, and that makes sense, doesn't it? I think it makes perfect sense, and I think it's what makes Mr. Booker's story so intriguing. It's about the kinds of questions intelligent alien life-forms would have for earthlings. Does this mean I believed everything Mr. Booker was telling me? I can't answer that, because the truth is that I don't know for sure. But one thing is for certain: Mr. Booker told this tale with conviction and an astonishing degree of detail. If he made it all up, he must have spent an awful lot of time and effort doing so.

Chapter 8

Kim Kardashian

After watching Anna and her friends play their crazy version of a basketball game, Sid and Mr. Booker went to the council chambers. They took their seats in the middle of the room. Rock called the session to order, and all eyes were upon him as he cleared his throat and spoke to Mr. Booker. "Did you enjoy your lunch?" he asked.

"Yes, it was fine," Mr. Booker said.

"What'd you have?"

"I tried the cocopees."

"Ah, an excellent choice. Did you like them?"

"They were good."

"At the risk of boasting, I can say our cafeteria serves some of the best food in the universe."

"I had a hamburger last night, and it was as good as any burger on Earth."

"A hamburger?"

"It's an American food," Mr. Booker said.

"Of course it is. Well, I'm glad you liked it." Rock paused for a moment and then got on with things. "We talked during the lunch break and agreed on a topic for our next line of questioning."

"Okay," Mr. Booker said.

"Several years ago, we conducted a poll on earthlings. We often do this for the civilizations we're studying. It was a popularity contest in a way, but it was a critical one. We asked a sample of a hundred thousand human beings if they were aware of certain people on your planet whom we considered to be important. In all civilizations, there are people worthy of being remembered and revered, and a lot can be learned about a culture by understanding just how popular these people are. I'm not talking about movie stars, popular musicians, or others who, by the very nature of their business, have to be popular. I'm talking about people who've made real and important contributions to your lives. Are you with me? Is this making sense to you?"

"Yes, I think so."

"We believe the more a society loves and respects its outstanding citizens, the more love and respect it has for itself, and the more love and respect it has for itself, the more it can have for others. Are you still following me?"

"Yes," Mr. Booker said.

"I asked each of our council members to come up with the name of an individual on your planet, past or present, who fits this criteria of worthiness in his or her field of expertise, and they came up with four. Then we polled your planet, asking your fellow men what they knew about them. I'll start with Lucy. She gave the matter a lot of thought and came up with the name of Louis Leakey. Mr. Booker, do you know who Louis Leakey was?"

"I know something about him."

"What do you know?"

"Wasn't he an American archaeologist?"

"He was an archaeologist," Lucy said. "But he wasn't an American."

"What was he?"

"He was Kenyan."

"I remember him being Caucasian."

"Not all Africans are black," Lucy said.

"And not all blacks are Africans," Ernie added. "I'm black, and I'm not even human." Everyone laughed at this, including Ernie. His laugh was especially loud. It was a booming chortle that rumbled out of his throat like the low-blasting notes of a tuba.

"Do you know anything else about Mr. Leakey?" Lucy asked.

Mr. Booker tried to recall what he knew about the man, but he couldn't come up with much, which was a little embarrassing. As a history buff, Mr. Booker prided himself on knowing a lot about Earth's influential and important people.

"I know his work had to do with mapping the origins of man," Mr. Booker said. "I think he made some important discoveries in Africa. He was an evolutionist, no?"

"Indeed he was," Rock said.

"Did you know his parents were missionaries?" Lucy asked.

"I didn't know that."

"Isn't it ironic that such an outspoken proponent of evolution was brought into the world and raised by a pair of missionaries?"

"Yes, it's ironic."

"Do you suppose his parents ever felt swayed by their son's ideas, or did they hold steadfastly to their Christian beliefs and insist mankind got its start in the Garden of Eden?"

"They probably opted for the garden."

"And the serpent and the apple?"

"Yes," Mr. Booker said. "Many people used to believe that story. Many still do."

"Don't you suppose it took a great deal of courage for Mr. Leakey to pursue a career that went against his parents' beliefs?"

"It probably did."

"What are you, Mr. Booker?" Lucy asked. "Are you a creationist or an evolutionist?"

"I'm not sure that I'm either."

"Mr. Leakey knew where he stood, and he fought for what he believed," Lucy said. "Do you stand up for what you believe?"

"Sometimes I do."

"Even at the risk of being publicly condemned or humiliated?"

"I don't know. I guess I try to avoid controversy. I don't actually enjoy disagreeing with others."

"Ah, of course not," Lucy said. "It's easier to go along with the crowd. Most life-forms do this. This is why I consider Leakey to be one of the great men of your civilization. It has little to do with whether he was right or wrong and more to do with the fact that he was a man of courage and intelligence. Ogonites revere courage and intelligence. In our civilization, everyone would know of Louis Leakey. There's no way we'd allow ourselves to forget the contributions he made."

"We asked your fellow human beings about Louis Leakey in our poll," Rock said. "We wanted to know how many knew anything about him."

"And what did you learn?" Mr. Booker asked.

"Two percent knew of him," Rock said. He stared at Mr. Booker for a moment, letting the number sink in. "That's the total percentage of your population who knew anything at all about Louis Leakey. Just two percent."

"A few thought he was a jazz musician," Lucy said, rolling her eyes.

"And a couple people thought he was a movie actor," Rock added. "They were even able to name some of his old movies."

"Ho, ho!" Ernie laughed.

Lucy said, "Seriously, Mr. Booker, can you imagine so few people knowing who Mr. Leakey was? And of that paltry two percent, only a handful knew any details about his life or the actual contributions he made to archeology."

"I guess it doesn't surprise me."

"You're okay with it?"

"I'm not saying I'm okay with it. I'm only saying it doesn't surprise me."

Rock whispered something to William, and they nodded in agreement. It was apparently William's turn. "Do you know anything about a physician named Ignaz Semmelweis?" William asked.

"Never heard of him," Mr. Booker said. At first, no one said anything, for it was clear that wasn't the answer the council had been expecting.

"That's most interesting," Rock said.

"Yes, very curious," Ernie added.

"Should I know who he was?"

"All of us on the council know who he was, and we're not even humans," William said. "He was a Hungarian doctor who practiced medicine in the nineteenth century. You claim to know a lot about history, Mr. Booker. Did you know that back when Semmelweis was alive, doctors didn't bother to wash their hands before touching their patients? They wondered why so many people were getting sick and dying in their hospitals. Then along came Dr. Semmelweis, predating the work of Louis Pasteur, telling physicians to wash their germ-laden hands. He demanded doctors clean themselves before working on patients, and what an uproar this caused! Right away, he was dismissed as a lunatic. His fellow doctors considered his ideas ridiculous. Highly respected physicians were offended at the implication that their gentlemanly hands could in any way be the cause of disease and death. They fought against Semmelweis and his assertions tooth and nail."

"So washing was frowned upon?"

"It was unheard of! Not until after he'd passed away did the practice of sanitizing one's hands and medical instruments become an accepted routine in hospitals. He was vindicated posthumously. But do you know how this great man's life ended?"

"No, I obviously don't."

"He was locked up in an asylum and beaten senseless by the guards, and he died in his cell. That was his reward for trying to help his fellow man. He died when he was in his forties."

"Why have I never heard this story?"

"Actually, that's our question for you. Why weren't you taught about him in school?"

"Maybe they teach about him in medical schools."

"Maybe," Rock said. "But the fact remains that barely one percent of the humans we polled had ever even heard of him. He was even less popular than Lucy's Mr. Leakey. He was a great human being but, sadly, forgotten."

"If you're interested, you should research Semmelweis in our library," William said. "Plenty has been written about him."

Mr. Booker stared at the two men, expecting them to say more. But now they were waiting for Mr. Booker to speak, so he asked, "Is our civilization failing in your eyes?"

"Failing?"

"Failing to respect its great men."

"And women," Lucy said.

"Yes, men and women."

Rock heard the question, but he wasn't going to answer it. Instead, he was determined to move on. He said, "Let's hear from Ernie. Since you're both intrigued by history, the two of you should be on the same page." Rock looked at Ernie and said, "Tell Mr. Booker who you picked."

Ernie looked at Mr. Booker. "There are a lot of fine historians on Earth, but I chose Will Durant."

"And Ariel," Lucy said.

"Yes, and Ariel. But I'm primarily talking about Will. Do you know about him, Mr. Booker?"

"Yes, of course," Mr. Booker said.

"Have you read *The Story of Civilization*?"

"It's on one of my bookshelves at home."

"But have you read it?"

"I honestly intended to read it, but I only got around to reading a few volumes. I think I stopped at the Renaissance."

"You should've kept reading."

"I probably should have."

"During my own research of your planet, I learned a great deal from Durant's books."

"To tell you the truth, I found it difficult to digest so much writing done by the same author," Mr. Booker said. "It was an awful lot of reading."

Ernie ignored Mr. Booker's excuse and continued. "When we polled your fellow human beings and asked about Will Durant, only six percent had heard of the man. The rest had no idea who we were talking about. Granted, Will performed a little better in the poll than Leakey or Semmelweis, but at six percent, he can hardly be called popular. He's just another great man in your civilization who no one seems to know about. There's a line Durant wrote in one of his books you ought to be aware of. He wrote, 'A great civilization is not conquered from without until it has destroyed itself within.' Are you familiar with this line, Mr. Booker?"

"No, I'm not."

"The people of Earth would be well advised to take these words to heart."

Rock cleared his throat. "This brings us to Ralph," he said. "I also asked him to come up with the name of an important human, and since Ralph is an artist, he picked a fellow artist."

"Yes, I did," Ralph said.

"And who is he?" Mr. Booker asked.

"Unless you have an interest in art, you probably haven't heard of him."

"Try me."

"Do you know of an artist named Klee?"

"Wasn't he the guy who painted the kids with the big eyes?" Mr. Booker asked.

"No, that was Keane. I'm talking about Klee. I'm talking about Paul Klee. He was active during the first half of your twentieth century, and while he was popular then, no one now seems to know who he was. In my opinion, his work was incredible, yet he barely registered one percent in our poll."

"Is there a particular work he's known for?"

"A particular work?"

"Yes, a trademark work—the way Michelangelo is known for the ceiling of the Sistine Chapel or Da Vinci is known for the *Mona Lisa*."

"No, I can't think of a trademark work. Klee is just known for being Klee. He reminds me a lot of one of my favorite Ogonite artists, a painter named Kapoochee. I've always been a big fan of Kapoochee. The work of the two men is very similar, and this is probably why I have such a high regard for Klee. His artwork is intelligent, playful, and precise. Whenever I look at a Kapoochee or a Klee, I feel lucid and liberated. I experience a calmness, while at the same time being challenged. All of you on Earth should be educated about the works of Klee. He deserves your admiration and recognition. But barely one percent? It's a travesty, this lack of respect humans have for such a great artist."

"I'll have to take your word for it."

"Do you see what we're up against?" Rock asked the other council members, and they nodded.

"Up against?" Mr. Booker asked.

Looking at Mr. Booker, Rock said, "We're faced with a society that has no great love or respect for its best and brightest. What should we make of this? What would you do if you were in our shoes?"

"I don't know."

"It's a recipe for disaster. Of all the living people on your planet, do you want to know who's the most popular? I mean, if this was a contest, do you know who would win?"

"Who?" Mr. Booker asked.

"This person isn't a scientist, a doctor, a historian, or an artist. The most popular living person on your planet is a woman, and we haven't been able to figure out what she does. We're hoping you can tell us why she's so popular."

"What's her name?"

"Her name is Kim Kardashian."

"Oh, her, of course."

"You know who she is?"

"Yes, I know."

"What does she do?" Lucy asked.

"And why is she so famous?" Ernie asked.

"I wish I had an answer," Mr. Booker said.

"You mean you don't know?"

"I honestly haven't a clue."

CHAPTER 9

PROMISES, PROMISES

"So what are you having?" Sid asked.

"I think I'll have another hamburger."

"No cocopees?"

"Not tonight."

It was time for dinner, and the two men were standing at the cafeteria counter, looking at the menu board. They finally placed their orders with the server, and when the food was ready, they grabbed their dinner trays and carried them to a table.

Mr. Booker was exhausted. The council inquiry had taken a lot out of him. Of course, it was never energizing to be interrogated, and he didn't feel he'd said much to impress the council members. In fact, he felt a little foolish. He could only imagine what the council thought of him and how they now viewed his fellow humans. "How do you think I've been doing?" he asked Sid.

"Doing how?"

"Answering the council's questions."

"You've been doing fine."

"I don't have the feeling they're impressed. In fact, they seem a little disappointed."

"It isn't that."

"Then what is it?"

"They're just curious. I told you that Ogonites were very inquisitive creatures. It's our nature to probe, pry, and ask lots of questions, and this can make even the most self-confident feel challenged and a little uncomfortable. They know this, and they know you're nervous. No one likes to be scrutinized, but you're doing fine. You're being honest and sincere, and that's exactly what the council asked for."

"Do you miss Og?" Mr. Booker asked, changing the subject, and he could tell the question took Sid by surprise.

"I do miss Og," Sid said.

"Anna said you had to leave."

"It was in my best interest."

"She said you abandoned your wife and children."

"I did," Sid said.

"Would it be considered impolite for me to ask you what happened?"

"No, it wouldn't be impolite."

"So why did you leave your family behind?"

"I suppose Anna already told you a good deal of the story, but I can fill in the blanks. You should know that unions between men and women are a very big deal on Og. We take our marriages very seriously, perhaps more than anything else."

"Marriages are also important on Earth."

Sid laughed. "A marriage on Earth is nothing like a marriage on Og."

"How is it so different?"

"The chief purpose of getting married on Og is to have and raise children. Our children mean everything to us. For earthlings, it's different. In most cases, a boy meets a girl, and the two of them fall in love. In a silly stupor, they decide they must never be separated, and they take vows promising to live together for the rest of their lives. They promise to be faithful and support each other in sickness and in health. They promise to be joined at the hip for the rest of their lives. Very little about children is even mentioned during the early years of a human marriage. But it's different for an Ogonite. Men and women on our planet do fall in love, but this isn't why they get married. Like I said, they get married in order to raise their kids. Just because a couple love each other, it's no reason for them to get married. It's only when they decide to have children that marriage becomes necessary. Most Ogonites marry around the age of two hundred, and having children is their first order of business. Marriages can last for hundreds of years, and there are only two ways a couple can call it quits. One is by the death of a spouse, and the other is by the death of all the children. But as long as everyone remains alive, the marriage is a lifetime commitment."

"What if the couple discovers they can no longer live happily together, or what if they just fall out of love and no longer wish to be married?"

"Not an option," Sid said.

"But you left your wife for another woman."

"I did."

"And you had a child with your new love."

"True enough. And this does happen now and again, but it doesn't happen often, and it certainly doesn't take place without serious consequences. My longing to have a child with Lendoola was overwhelming, and we acted on it. But I was immediately shunned by everyone. I was suddenly a social outcast, and those people in my life who were once my beloved family and friends no longer would have anything to do with me."

"So you found yourself aboard this ship?"

"It was my only option. I had nowhere else to go. On a spaceship so far away from home, I've found a new home. When you're out in deep space, you belong to a little subsociety, and if you have a questionable past, it tends to be ignored or forgotten."

"That's what Anna said."

"So here we are on this ship. Lendoola and I are able to raise our son and live our lives free from judgment and scorn. On this ship, we're treated with love and respect, as though we're a normal married couple with a healthy, normal child."

"On Earth, couples simply get divorced and start new lives. It's a common practice."

"Yes, of course. I'm aware of the divorce rate on Earth. About fifty percent, I think."

"That sounds right."

"Such barbarians!" Sid laughed.

"But happy barbarians. Are you a barbarian?" Mr. Booker asked.

"I don't think of myself that way. I like to think I'm what your people call the exception that proves the rule."

Mr. Booker thought about this. Sid was certainly an interesting fellow. He felt a little sorry for Sid for having to leave his planet. Since when should it be the end of the world just because a man or woman had a change of heart?

Mr. Booker looked at Sid's dinner plate and saw he was eating a strange dish made of thickly sliced sausage-like discs the diameter of silver dollars, all smothered with a runny bright blue sauce. Also served with the meal was a side of salted green arponots piled on a small dish beside the main plate. "What are you eating?" Mr. Booker asked. "I recognize the arponots, but what are those things in the blue sauce?"

"Goofoos," Sid said. "You should give them a try."

"Maybe tomorrow."

"You're missing out," Sid said.

"Maybe I am," Mr. Booker said.

Sid and Mr. Booker continued to talk and eat for nearly an hour, mostly discussing what had taken place with the council that day. When they were done, Mr. Booker retired to his cabin. He went to bed early that night, hoping to get some sleep. He wanted to be alert and well rested for tomorrow's session with the council. He did sleep well, but in the early morning, he had a curious dream. In the dream, he was sitting at a campfire again, but he was not in Sherwood Forest, and he was not Robin Hood. He was someone else.

The campsite was adjacent to a small creek in a copse of trees about a half mile from the highway. The year was 1933, and his stolen Ford was parked thirty or so feet away, covered with a thin film of dust. "Are we going to get caught?" Bonnie asked. "I think they want to fry all of us."

"We'll never be caught," Mr. Booker replied. "But we will be killed."

"So why are we doing this?"

"We're heroes," Mr. Booker said.

"Heroes?"

"The public is counting on us."

"Counting on us to do what?" Buck asked.

"They're counting on us to fight until the bitter end. They want us to go out in a blaze of glory, guns popping and blood gushing."

"I don't want to die," Blanche said.

"We're a sensation," Bonnie said to Blanche. "Haven't you read the papers? There's an article about us nearly every day."

"They claim to hate us, yet they secretly long to be us," Mr. Booker said. "Throughout the history of mankind, citizens have claimed to despise people like us, while at the same time idolizing us, wishing they had the nerve to fill our shoes—to shoot our Brownings and drive our stolen Fords. They pray we'll be shot to bits but not because they're opposed to evil and not because they're so good-natured and righteous. It's because they want to be able to say to themselves, 'See? A life of crime doesn't pay!' They want to justify their complacent lives and prove the dubious value of their cowardice."

"Where do you come up with this crap?" Buck asked, laughing. "You sound like a college professor."

"But it's true, isn't it?"

"I think it's true," Bonnie said.

"Bonnie understands me," Mr. Booker said. "Bonnie has always understood."

"So she says," Blanche said.

"The day is coming," Mr. Booker said. "When they finally zero in and kill us, every cowardly man and woman in this country will rejoice at the news."

"I really don't want to die," Blanche said.

"Well, I don't want to face the council this morning," Mr. Booker said. "But you don't hear me whining or complaining."

"What council is that?" Buck asked. Before Mr. Booker could answer Buck's question, they heard a high-pitched sound coming from the highway.

"Are those sirens?" Blanche asked.

"Everyone keep quiet," Buck said. He cupped his hand to his ear.

"I can hear them loud and clear," Mr. Booker said. "They're getting closer."

"We need to get the heck out of here," Buck said. "Let's go."

"No, those aren't sirens," Bonnie said. "It's the alarm clock on the nightstand."

"The alarm clock?"

"It's time to get out of bed."

Mr. Booker blinked and then opened his eyes. Sure enough, the sound was coming from his alarm clock, and he rolled over to turn it off. It was six in the morning, and he sat up straight. He climbed out of bed, yawning and stretching his arms. The details of his strange dream fell from his thoughts as he stepped into the bathroom. He showered and shaved and then put on his golden robe.

Sid arrived at the cabin at seven, and the two of them went to breakfast at the cafeteria. Mr. Booker ordered the pancakes, and he stuffed a forkful of them into his mouth and asked Sid, "Do Ogonites dream?"

"We have our dreams," Sid said.

"I mean at night or early in the morning while you're sleeping. Do you actually dream?"

"No, not the way you do."

"I had the strangest dream this morning."

"Do you want to tell me about it?"

"Not really."

"Then why bring it up?"

"I don't know."

"How are your pancakes?"

"They're great."

When they were done eating breakfast, they stood up and left the cafeteria.

They arrived at the council chambers right on time, and Rock called the session to order. He asked Mr. Booker if he'd slept well. Mr. Booker told him yes, he'd slept like a baby. Rock then said, "We understand you spoke with Sid at some length about the differences between Ogonite and human marriages."

Mr. Booker was a little surprised that Rock knew what he and Sid had been talking about, and he turned to look at Sid, who was seated behind him. Sid smiled and nodded, as if to say, "Go ahead; there's nothing we talked about last night that you can't discuss with the council."

"Mr. Booker, is there a problem?" Rock asked, noticing Mr. Booker looking at Sid.

"No, I suppose not," Mr. Booker said. "I guess I was just surprised that you knew about our conversation."

"Did you take lifelong wedding vows when you married your wife?" Rock asked.

"I did," Mr. Booker said.

"And you lived up to them?"

"Yes, I did."

"And your wife lived up to her vows?"

"She did, right up until the day she died. She was a good person."

"It pleases us to hear this."

"Okay," Mr. Booker said.

"You're aware, of course, that you're not a typical earthling. People on Earth seem to have a very difficult time living up to their vows. In fact, half of them wind up getting divorced."

"Yes, I'm aware of that."

"And you discussed this with Sid?"

"I did," Mr. Booker said.

"Can you see why this statistic alarms us?"

"I suppose I can."

"Wedding vows are meant to last a lifetime, are they not?"

"Yes, they are."

"What could be more critically important than the heartfelt promises made between a man and a woman? Last year in your country alone, there were over eight hundred thousand divorces. Think of it, Mr. Booker. Nearly a million people threw in the towel and reneged on their marital commitments."

"It does seem like a lot."

"Can you tell us why humans have such an affinity for going back on their word? We find it disturbing. Humans seem so eager to make promises, yet they're equally eager to break them. When we began this inquiry, I began by speaking to you about honesty, and I told you we wouldn't require you to take an oath. But the reason we decided against an oath wasn't because we were convinced of your honesty. It was because oaths and promises mean so little to humans. It would've been pointless to have you make any kind of promise, either written or verbal. We've observed that humans are willing to promise anything, signing their names on dotted lines, placing their hands on Bibles, and even swearing on their mothers' graves. Yet in the blink of an eye, they'll go back on their word without giving it a second thought. Are you with me, Mr. Booker?"

"Yes, I hear what you're saying."

"It's a real problem."

"I don't know what to say," Mr. Booker said.

"Are you familiar with the Hippocratic oath?" William asked, and Mr. Booker looked at him.

"Of course," Mr. Booker said.

"Your doctors on Earth like to take this oath, do they not?"

"Yes, I believe they do."

"Do you know what it says?"

"I've never actually read it."

William looked at the screen of his computer monitor. "I'm going to read some of it to you. It states, as follows, that a doctor will 'remember that I do not treat a fever chart, a cancerous growth, but a sick human being, whose illness may affect the person's family and economic stability. My responsibility includes these related problems, if I am to care adequately for the sick.'" After reading the passage, William peered over the top of his monitor at Mr. Booker and asked, "Don't you find this strange?"

"Strange?"

"How does a doctor who's taken an oath like this turn around and charge his patients and arm and a leg for his services, enriching himself at the expense of the sick and less fortunate? How does he rationalize his vacations to Europe, golf club memberships, imported luxury cars, and Rolex watches? Sure, the doctor takes an oath, but what's the point of the oath when he so readily ignores what it says and extorts money from the people he's sworn to help and save?"

"I think most doctors mean well."

"Do they?"

Did they? Mr. Booker didn't know how to answer the question and wasn't sure what he should say. The room was dreadfully quiet as everyone waited for him to speak. The council members were staring, hoping for some sort of illuminating explanation, but he had nothing illuminating to say. Mr. Booker knew that William had made an excellent point. He'd read the critical sentences straight from the oath itself, right off the screen of his monitor, and the words couldn't have been clearer.

"Mr. Booker, I have another question for you," Ernie said.

"Yes?" Mr. Booker said. He looked at Ernie, who drummed his fingers on the desktop.

"Are you proud to be an American?"

"I suppose I am."

"And you're a man of your word?"

"Yes, I'd say so."

"Do you know American history?"

"Yes, I do."

"Your country is a fascinating place—not so much because it is a free and democratic society but more because of how it was established. I'm talking about treaties, Mr. Booker. It was all about the treaties."

"Treaties?"

"I'm talking about the agreements signed with Native Americans. Do you know how many treaties were signed and broken by the white men?"

"I'm not sure of the exact number."

"There were hundreds of them."

"Okay," Mr. Booker said. "You're probably right about that. I know there were a lot."

"Hundreds of broken promises—a dripping, bloody paper trail of invaders and frontiersmen with no intention of keeping their word."

"I guess you could say it like that."

"Some say, 'Treaties are meant to be broken.' Have you heard that line before? Do you agree with it? Are all treaties made to be broken?"

"I've heard that line before, but no, I don't agree with it. They also used to say, 'The only good Indian is a dead Indian,' and I certainly don't agree with that, and I know a lot of people feel as I do."

"Yet do you live, work, and play on your stolen real estate with a clear conscience?"

"I feel bad for what happened."

"You feel bad?"

"I honestly do."

"So what have you done about it?"

"Nothing, really."

"You're like everyone else in your country—going on with your life and proudly imagining you're a citizen of the greatest country on Earth. But all these broken treaties, Mr. Booker. How do you sweep these under the rug? Over and over, your ancestors broke their promises. The truth is, none of these treaties were worth the cheap paper they were written on. They were promises made and signed by humans, and human promises have no value. Would you agree?"

"I don't know."

"All this marvelous real estate from sea to shining sea was overrun by immigrants with their lies held in one hand and loaded Winchesters clutched in the other. Am I misstating the facts?"

"I suppose not."

"You have to put yourself in our shoes, Mr. Booker. How can we trust a species with such a history of welching on its promises?"

Mr. Booker thought about this question but didn't offer an answer. Instead, he looked back at Sid for support. "What do I say?" he whispered.

"Just tell the truth," Sid said.

Then Rock chimed in. "We could go on with this line of questioning until we're blue in the face, but we aren't getting anywhere. I don't think Mr. Booker has an answer. Or am I missing something? Do you have anything you'd like to say?"

"Not really," Mr. Booker said. He was no longer looking at Sid and was facing the council.

"Read my lips!" Ralph suddenly exclaimed.

"Yes, read my lips," William repeated, laughing.

"No new taxes," Ralph said, and he hit his fist on the desktop to make his point. All the council members laughed uproariously. Even Sid was chuckling, and Mr. Booker wasn't sure what to do.

"Ho, ho!" Ernie roared with his trademark Santa Claus laugh. Then he said, "If an Ogonite ever tells you to read his lips, you'll be wise to pay attention. We take our promises seriously, Mr. Booker, and we expect the same from others."

CHAPTER 10

THE KISS

With two days of interrogations under his belt, Mr. Booker found himself alone in his cabin, looking out the window in the front room at the view of Earth. It was a little after nine at night, when someone knocked on his front door. He went to answer and was surprised to discover Anna standing in the hallway, just as pretty as ever. There was a leather-bound book in her hand, and she held it out to him. "Sid told me to give this to you."

"What is it?" Mr. Booker asked. He took the book and looked at its cover. "Ah, *Uncle Tom's Cabin*. I wanted to read this."

"Sid said you were trying to take it with you on your vacation before we abducted you."

"That's true."

"Can I come in?"

"Sure," Mr. Booker said. He stepped back so Anna could enter. She came in, and he shut the door behind her, looking again at the cover of the book.

"What's it about?" Anna asked.

"Slavery in America."

"You like reading about slavery?"

"It was an important book."

Anna stepped over to the window and looked at the view. "Earth is such a lovely planet," she said. "You'd never know from this distance what a backward place it is."

92

"You're right," Mr. Booker said.

"Can I sit down?"

"Be my guest."

Anna took a seat on the sofa with her legs crossed and her hands in her lap. She seemed content to be in Mr. Booker's cabin, and she looked around. "Is that a picture of your wife?" she asked, noticing a framed photograph on the wall near the window.

"Yes," Mr. Booker said. "It was taken by a professional photographer on her thirtieth birthday. It's one of my favorites."

"Did you love her?"

"Of course I loved her. That's why I married her."

"But you didn't have any children."

"No, we didn't."

"Didn't you want children?"

"We didn't think we'd have time for them. Our lives were too busy."

"Ogonites love children."

"So I've heard," Mr. Booker said.

"Sit next to me," Anna said.

"I can do that," Mr. Booker said. He took a seat on the sofa, leaving about twelve inches of distance between their hips.

"Why don't you move in a little closer?"

"You want me to sit closer?"

"Yes, so we're next to each other."

Mr. Booker slid over so that their golden robes were touching. "How's this?"

"Much better. Tell me something about your wife, will you? I'd like to know what she was like. I'll bet she was a wonderful woman."

"Yes, she was wonderful."

"Tell me a story about her."

"A story?"

"You know, about something she did or about something that happened to her. You can tell a lot about a person by listening to a story."

Mr. Booker looked at Anna, smiling. It was hard to believe she was nearly a hundred years old. She seemed spry and full of life, and being so close to him, her scent of spearmint was strong. He knew she was an alien, but she seemed divinely human, warm and inviting. He was glad she'd come to his cabin. He'd been feeling a little lonely that evening with nothing to do and no one to talk to, and he appreciated the company. Mr. Booker searched his memories for a story to tell her about Linda, something that would amuse Anna, but he felt put on the spot, and nothing came to mind.

"I can't think of a good story," Mr. Booker said. "The truth is, our lives together were rather uneventful. There aren't a lot of stories to tell."

"What did she do with her time?"

"She spent most of her time working. She worked as a chemist at a pharmaceutical company."

"How about her free time?"

"She did a lot of reading."

"What kinds of books did she read?"

"A little of everything."

"Did she have any favorite authors?"

"She liked Tolstoy a lot. She read *War and Peace* and *Anna Karenina* several times. She also liked Kurt Vonnegut, and she loved James Michener's books. Those are some of the authors that come to mind, but she really enjoyed many others."

"Okay, so I'm going to read *War and Peace*," Anna said.

"Why? Because Linda liked it?"

"Yes, you can learn a lot about people from the books they enjoy. And the title sounds intriguing."

"It's a long book."

"I've got plenty of time," Anna said. "And I want to get to know your wife."

"Why?" Mr. Booker asked.

"If I get to know your wife, then I'll get to know you better. And I want to learn more about you. I want to know everything about you."

Mr. Booker thought that was a strange thing for Anna to say, and he felt embarrassed that Anna was taking such an interest in him. However, as Sid had said, his people were inquisitive. Was it just Anna's nature as an Ogonite, or was it more? Was there more to her interest in him than routine curiosity? Did she have some romantic alien infatuation with him? Wouldn't that be strange? He remembered how she'd held his hand on the way to the basketball game, and now they were sitting close to each other on the couch, talking about Linda. There was something in her eyes, as if she were smitten by Mr. Booker, yet she hardly even knew him.

"Have you read many books by our human authors?" he asked, attempting to talk about something less personal than his wife.

"Yes, I've read a lot. All of us on the ship have read a lot of your human literature."

"Such as?"

"I just finished *Treasure Island*."

"Oh yes, that's a good one."

"Your stories on Earth are so different from the tales that Ogonites write. They're quite interesting and very different."

"How are they different?"

"They pose different conflicts."

"Conflicts?"

"You know, as in man versus nature, man versus technology, or man versus man."

"Yes, of course."

"All good stories have conflict."

"And how are our books different?"

"It's the obsession your writers have with pitting men against other men. This sort of conflict dominates human storytelling."

"And Ogonite literature is different?"

"We seldom write stories about us having problems getting along with each other. This kind of conflict isn't a big concern to Ogonites. We don't fight each other, compete with each other, or constantly butt heads with each other—not the way humans do. It's in our nature to work with each other, to organize ourselves and cooperate to achieve what's best for our civilization. Most of our stories concern the challenges we face with the world and the different ways we work together to bend things in our favor. You just won't find Ogonites struggling against each other, not the way humans constantly are."

"That's hard to believe."

"Actually, humans are hard for us to believe. How your society functions with so many contentious individuals and battles between them is a complete mystery to us. Why do humans have so much difficulty getting along with each other? Why are they constantly fighting between themselves?"

"I don't know."

"I'm sure the council will be asking you about this behavior, if they haven't already. Have they brought it up yet?"

"Not specifically."

"Do you think I'm attractive?" Anna asked, changing the subject.

"Yes, I think you're attractive."

"If you'd met me on Earth, do you think you'd like me? I mean, right off the bat?"

"I'd have to get to know you first."

"Do you know me now?"

"Well, I'm getting to know you."

"And you're getting to like me?"

"You seem like a nice person."

"I've read in some of your literature about a thing you people like to call love at first sight. Some people believe in it, and others say it's a myth. What do you think? Do you believe in love at first sight?"

"I think it's a romantic notion."

"Meaning?"

"I think it's true that people are attracted to others right away. But can you call it love? I don't know if I'd call that sort of immediate attraction love. It seems to me love requires time to develop. It takes months for love to grow and blossom; it doesn't just happen in an instant. Not real love."

"How long did it take for you to fall in love with your wife?"

Mr. Booker laughed. "Now we're on the subject of Linda again."

"How long did it take?"

"It took months. We had to get to know each other. I mean, yes, I was attracted to her right away, but that was just an initial feeling I had. It was months before I was sincerely able to tell her I loved her. Like I said, I had to get to know her."

"So what is it that you learned during those months that made you fall in love?"

Mr. Booker thought for a moment and then said, "I don't recall learning anything specific I can relate to you. I just eventually knew I loved her."

"It just hit you?"

"Yes, I guess you could say that."

"Would you like to kiss me?"

"Kiss you?"

"Yes, on the mouth. Isn't that what you humans like to do?"

"We like to do that."

"Have you thought about kissing me?" Anna asked.

Mr. Booker blushed. If Anna hadn't been so serious with her question, he probably would've laughed—not so much because it was funny but because he was embarrassed. *Kiss her? Now, right here on the couch and out of the blue?* The truth was that Mr. Booker was attracted to the young woman, but he hadn't even thought about kissing her. However, why not? She was nice looking, and she liked him.

The next thing he knew, Anna's face was upon his, and their lips were pressed together in a warm and passionate kiss. It wasn't just a friendly peck. It was a wet and prolonged meeting of mouths, and it gave Mr. Booker goose bumps on his forearms. It lasted for about fifteen seconds. Her mouth tasted like spearmint, as if she'd just brushed her teeth, and her wet tongue rolled against his. It was like no kiss Mr. Booker had ever experienced, for in actuality, he was kissing an alien.

"How's that?" Anna asked when they were done.

"Unexpected," Mr. Booker replied.

"Did you like it?"

"Yes, I did."

"I've been wanting to do that since the first time we met," Anna confessed.

"Have you?"

Anna was smiling, and Mr. Booker smiled back at her. She said, "We have no custom on Og like this act of pressing mouths together. In fact, in all our travels to different planets, we've yet to find another life-form that expresses affection through kissing. Kissing seems to be a uniquely human act. But I enjoyed it. Honestly, I did very much!"

"I'm glad you liked it."

"We'll do it again?" Anna asked.

"Yes, I suppose we can do it again."

"I should go now. You probably want to be alone to read your book."

"My book?"

"*Uncle Tom's Cabin.*"

"You don't have to leave, do you?"

"You'd like me to stay?"

"I think so."

Anna leaned so that her head was on Mr. Booker's shoulder, and she picked up his book from the coffee table and began thumbing through the pages. "Tell me more about this book. Tell me something about slavery and the human condition. We've never had such a thing as slavery on Og. We value our freedom and treasure our independence, not just for ourselves but for all our fellow citizens."

"Why don't I loan this book to you?"

"You want me to read it?"

"Yes, you should read it."

"Are you a slave?" Anna asked.

"Am I a slave?"

"Yes, do you consider yourself to be a slave?"

"No, not at all."

"That's so interesting," Anna said.

"Why is it interesting?"

"Oh, you'll soon see."

"What's that supposed to mean?"

Anna ignored his question. She put the book back on the coffee table, and they were quiet for a moment. Anna then lifted her head from Mr. Booker's shoulder, stood up from the sofa, and walked to his bookshelves, where she ran her finger along the spines of the books he'd collected over the years. "Have you read all these?"

"I've read most of them."

"You know a lot about human history?"

"I think I do."

"That's one of the reasons you were brought aboard our ship. The council wanted someone who had a comprehensive understanding of human history."

"So they told me."

"Can you explain something to me?"

"I will if I can."

"Why is history so unpopular on your planet?"

"Is it?"

"Take your own country, for example. Do you think most Americans have a real interest in history?"

"I suppose some do."

"Of course some do, but I'm talking about the masses. Most people in America could care less about history. I've heard it's said often on your planet that those who don't study history are bound to repeat it, yet those words are often ignored, and history is ignored, and bad decisions are repeated all the time. No one in America seems to care about the past, especially not the masses, and it's the masses who decide who will run your country. By the very structure of your government, the masses pick from the candidates and put leaders into positions of power. We have a very similar system of government on Og, but it's different. Where is the knowledge of history that is so necessary to participating in the democratic process? It seems to me there is an amazing wealth of experience and information that's been recorded over the centuries of human existence, but it's ignored. It's almost as if humans deliberately try to sabotage their ability to make good decisions, to make their lives worse than they need be."

Mr. Booker laughed. "You're right. I'd like to bring you to one of my school classes and have you speak to my students."

"You would?"

"It'd be good for them to hear this from someone other than me, someone other than a boring history teacher."

"Do you think they'd listen to me?"

Mr. Booker sighed. "Now that I think of it, probably not. I don't think they'd listen to anyone, not even you. The kids I teach have their hands full with their more immediate concerns. They're primarily obsessed with how popular they are among the other students, who's going with them to the next school dance, or what kind of clothes they should buy the next time they visit the mall. Or they're worried about what make and model of car they'll be able to talk their parents into financing for them or who they can get to purchase beer for them for an upcoming Friday night. Come to think of it, when they grow up, things don't change much. The minutiae of life overwhelms them and takes up their time. As adults, they're concerned with how much they're making at their job, whether their houses have the right style of hardwood flooring, or whether their flat-screen TVs are as big as their neighbors'. History? No, it's of little importance to them. So you're right; the masses choose our elected leaders from a list of candidates, but most of them have no idea what they're doing. I try to teach kids to know better, so they can grow up into responsible adults, but sometimes I feel as though I'm spinning my wheels. I often feel like I'm getting nowhere, and you ask me why? The truth is that I don't know why humans aren't more interested in history."

"Ogonites view their education about history as supremely important."

"Humans don't."

"And it frustrates you?"

"Of course it frustrates me."

"Do you see this changing?"

"You mean will my feelings change?"

"No, I mean will your people change? Will history ever become important to large numbers of humans?"

"I doubt it will happen in my lifetime, but I suppose there's hope."

"Yes, hope! It's a powerful human concept."

"The concept of hope?"

"Yes, expecting that things may change for the better, when there's no evidence to support any real change is on its way."

"But things can and do get better."

"Do they?"

"I think mankind has made a lot of progress."

"Humans have made technological progress, which all civilizations make. We've seen technological progress on many of the planets we've studied, but that seems to be the easy part. Real progress is a rarity. I'm talking about making improvements to men, such as changing the way they make decisions and changing the way they treat each other and the way they treat outsiders. For thousands of years, human beings have behaved the same. Some people are better than others, and some eras are more civilized, but basically, it's all the same."

At first, Mr. Booker didn't respond. He thought it was weird. Just a little while ago, he'd been sitting with this lovely girl on the sofa and kissing her on the mouth, and now he was getting a speech about the hopelessness of the human condition. He said to her, "I liked it better when we were kissing."

Anna laughed. "Of course you did! And I did too. I shouldn't have gone on like this, belittling your people. I'm sure you'll get plenty of that from the council, so I'm sorry. I didn't come here to lecture you. I came here to make you my friend."

"I just thought of something," Mr. Booker said.

"And what is that?"

"I thought of a story."

"A story?"

"You asked me if I could tell you a story about Linda, and I thought of one."

"Please tell me." Anna stepped to the sofa and took a seat next to Mr. Booker. She held his hand in hers, which made him feel good again.

"It was just a couple years after we were first married," Mr. Booker said. "Both of us were at work. I was at the school, and Linda was at her pharmaceutical company. There was an earthquake that day—not a massive one, but it was strong enough to get everyone's attention. It occurred in the morning, and it gave me an idea. I went home for lunch that day and made a mess of the inside of our house. I adjusted the pictures on the walls so they hung crooked, and I tipped over several knickknacks on our shelves. I even put a couple items on the floor. By the time I was done, it looked like the earthquake had given our home a terrific shaking. It was pretty funny, I thought, and I laughed to myself in my car all the way back to the school. I imagined Linda coming home, seeing the mess I'd made, and thinking it was all the result of the earthquake. I stayed late at school, grading homework assignments, to be sure Linda arrived home before me, and sure enough, she did. When I did finally get home, the front door flew open, and Linda was standing in the doorway, her eyes wide. 'Come in!' she exclaimed. 'You've got to see all this! You need to see what the earthquake did to our house!' All I could do was laugh."

"What did she do when you told her the truth?"

"She was furious. One thing you need to understand about Linda is that she hated to be teased in any way. It wasn't that she didn't have a sense of humor, for she loved to laugh. She just didn't like being the butt of another's idea of a joke. Anyway, when I told her I was responsible for all the mayhem inside our house and that it had nothing to do with the earthquake, she was furious and told me to put everything back where it belonged. She didn't speak to me for the rest of the evening. Despite her anger, I still thought it was funny, and I think it's funny to this day. I smile every time I think about her coming home that evening and seeing the house in such disarray."

"So that's your story?"

"It doesn't end there."

"So what happened?"

"I'd always wanted to own a Mercedes-Benz during those years, but we didn't make enough money to afford a new one. So I found a used one listed for sale in the local paper, and it was for a price we could afford. It was ten years old and had over a hundred thousand miles on it. But I went ahead and bought it, and it was my pride and joy. Jeez, how I loved that car. I washed and waxed it every weekend and took it to a mechanic regularly to keep it in perfect running shape. One thing I didn't like was the fact that I had to park it outside in the driveway every night. Our garage was filled with junk, and I never got around to cleaning it out for the car. One morning, I got ready for work and stepped outside to leave, and the car was gone. Someone had stolen my car! I can't even begin to tell you how upset I was, and I went back into the house to tell Linda the bad news. 'The Mercedes,' I said. 'It's gone! Somebody stole our car!'"

"What does this have to do with the earthquake?" Anna asked.

"Well, all the time I was complaining about the car being gone, Linda was wanting to laugh. She couldn't help herself. 'You're not listening to me,' I said. 'Someone stole our car!' The truth was that she had gotten out of bed early that morning, taken my keys, and moved the car down the street, parking it out of sight. Finally, she did burst out laughing and told me what she'd done. She was getting even with me for the earthquake prank I'd played on her. I hadn't thought she had it in her. She got me good, and while I was a little embarrassed, I was also so proud of her. That was her one and only practical joke in all the years we were married. After setting me straight, she laughed until tears rolled down her cheeks, and I finally had to laugh along with her."

"She sounds like an interesting person."

"I loved her a lot. And I still miss her, even if she was a little on the serious side. I was glad she moved my car that morning. I think her practical joke made me love her even more."

CHAPTER 11

SEMPER FI

O f all the abduction stories I've heard over the course of my writing career, I've never been told about creatures from outer space having much of a sense of humor. They're most often depicted as creepy and curious. They're also described as being arrogant and scheming beings and sometimes even sadistic and ill-intentioned interlopers. However, Mr. Booker's account of aliens was different. His aliens actually liked to laugh. He said there were a number of jokes about us earthlings floating around among the crew members of the ship. When is the last time you heard of an alien telling a joke?

Mr. Booker said Sid told him two of these jokes over breakfast while they were preparing for the third day of questioning. One of the jokes was about a male human who walked into a bar with a loaded gun in his hand. He shouted to the patrons, "Which one of you dirty dogs has been sleeping with my wife? I swear I'm going to shoot you dead!" An old-timer at the bar turned around and said, "You should go home, son. You haven't got enough bullets in that gun."

The second joke Sid told Mr. Booker was about four human beings standing on the edge of a cliff. One of the humans was Hispanic. There was also a Native American, a black man, and a white man. Suddenly, the Hispanic jumped off the cliff, and just before he did so, he shouted, "This is for my people!" Then the Native American also jumped off the cliff, and before he jumped, he shouted, "This is for my people!" Then the black man grabbed the white guy by his collar, dragged him to the edge of the cliff, and threw him over. He shouted, "This is for my people!"

Mr. Booker laughed at the jokes. He wanted to hear more, but Sid said it was time to leave and meet with the council. "It's best we don't show up late," he said, and the two of them left the cafeteria and walked to the council chambers. All the council members were present; some of them were looking up at the ceiling, and the others were staring at their computer monitors. They all looked at Mr. Booker when Rock cleared his throat and called the meeting to order. "Was your breakfast to your liking?" Rock asked.

"It was great," Mr. Booker said.

"That's good to hear. Listen, we'd like to discuss a new topic this morning. We want to talk about one of our most troubling concerns. I'm referring to the human need to take sides and fight. We're hoping you can help us understand this behavior. I'll begin by asking you about the seemingly inexplicable urge human beings have to draw borders on maps and create so many independent countries. Your planet is defined and segregated by these borders. You reside as citizens of different regions, having your own independent governments, currencies, social mores, and languages. It seems so pointless to us. Can you explain the purpose behind so many individual countries?"

"I'm not sure there's an actual purpose."

"Then why do they exist?"

"They're just the result of what's happened to Earth over time—people organizing themselves into geographic entities and calling them countries. It's just the way things have turned out after thousands of years of wars, migrations, and human history."

"But why?"

"Well, how else would things be?"

"Why hasn't your species organized itself into one like-minded group of citizens? Why not just have a single country and government you can call Earth?"

"A single country?"

"Yes, everyone working together. All your citizens would live with and work for each other. They'd be on the same side, speak the same language, pass around the same currency, and follow the same laws. Everyone would be loyal to the whole body. It would be one for all, and all for one."

"Our people would never go for it."

"Ah," Rock said. "It's most unfortunate, but I think you're right."

"For one thing, that kind of cooperation would do away with wars," Ernie said. "Human beings love their wars, and they need countries to justify them."

"I don't think we actually love our wars," Mr. Booker said defensively.

"Then why are there so many of them?"

"I don't know."

"Anyone who's studied human history knows how humans love to take sides and fight against each other," Ernie said. "From the earliest days right up until now, your species has had a special place in its heart for killing and maiming others. Am I wrong about this, Mr. Booker? Your ancestors organized into clans and tribes, crushing each other's skulls with stones and throttling each other with bare hands. These were just the earliest days of combat. They moved forward, inventing spears, blow guns, hatchets, and bows that propelled lethal arrows. And then there were the swords and knives. What better way to inflict a fatal or grossly debilitating injury than to stab and slash with a length of cold, sharpened steel? And then gunpowder arrived on the scene. Oh, what a beautiful thing this gunpowder turned out to be! It gave birth to handguns, rifles, automatic weapons, and cannons of all shapes and sizes. And of course, there are all those wonderful bombs! How humans love to plug their ears with their fingers and set off their deadly explosions! There are bombs dropped in swarms from your aircraft, shrapnel-laden grenades tossed toward enemies, and land mines you bury in the soil, hoping to blow the feet and legs off the boys and men you send to fight. There are torpedoes, missiles, and many other varieties of killing devices your devious minds have created over the years, all inspired by the invention of gunpowder. And let's not forget the atomic bomb. Now you can enter a code, press a single button, and obliterate entire cities. And there's also your chemical and biological warfare. We can't forget all this great weaponry! You promise the world not to use it, because you're humane, but who knows when the time might be right? Why go through the trouble of developing chemical and biological weapons if you don't plan on using them? There's no limit to human ingenuity when it comes to war, and it's become a beloved science and industry on your planet. Killing and maiming are respected and government-funded endeavors for every country on Earth. Human beings love to wage their wars! Your wars are recorded and described in your history books, every sordid and bloody conflict. War is a fact of life on Earth. We're not asking whether this behavior takes place or to what degree. We already know it's a painful reality. We're only asking why it happens. We're asking why humans are so determined to take up arms against their fellow man. What is it about this bizarre behavior that you find so irresistible? What exactly is the point of it all?"

"There are disagreements," Mr. Booker said. "I guess there are bound to be disagreements, and disagreements cause conflicts." He knew this wasn't a good answer as soon as the words left his lips, but he was being put on the spot by the council and didn't want it to appear as though he had no response.

"Seriously?" Rock said. "Disagreements? That's your explanation?"

"Disagreements." Ernie scoffed. "That doesn't cover half of it."

"We have disagreements on our planet," Rock said. "But we don't take up arms to kill and maim each other whenever they arise."

"It's the need they have to take sides and fight," William said. "It's just human nature, isn't it? It's inherent and indefatigable. It's in their DNA, twisted up like a cancer in their double helices and genes. I don't think they can help themselves."

"It isn't just your wars," Rock said to Mr. Booker. "Your need to take sides and fight corrupts all facets of life on your planet. We believe a lot can be said about a civilization by examining its politics, so let's look at your government in America. You view this government as such an exemplary example of tolerance and freedom, yet you're always taking sides and fighting. It's ludicrous, isn't it? You're always busy drawing lines in the sand, forming opposing groups, and coming up with strategies to defeat your enemies. You're always picking sides and sticking with them no matter how preposterous the whole process is. You dig in your heels like you're in some glorious game of tug-of-war, and the deeper you dig in, the more righteous you feel. And the more righteous you feel, the more determined you are to be on the winning side. Before you know what's happening, you're not campaigning for the best possible government; instead, you're just determined to see your side win and the other side lose. Lies are thrown around in place of truths. Both sides start exaggerating, misstating facts, and making all kinds of disparaging insults. Rather than having a thoughtful and intelligent election, you find yourself in the middle of a churlish schoolyard dispute. Doesn't this embarrass you? I'm not even human, and it embarrasses me! Is this what your sons and daughters in the military give their lives for? Ask yourself this: Are you really concerned with creating a better society, or do you just want to be right? Do you just want to win? It seems that aligning yourself with a side and beating the opponent is far more important to Americans than the achievement of success. Yes, I'm talking about real success! Do you consider it to be a success when you've managed to polarize an entire country so that half the population despises the other and simply wants to see it fail?"

"I don't think humans know what real success is," William said. "I don't think they've ever experienced it."

"It's because they're so obsessed with issues," Ernie said.

"Yes, issues!" William agreed.

"Issues are the bane of human politics," Ralph said. "But try telling that to humans. They'll look at you like you're crazy."

The council members stopped talking for a moment and stared at Mr. Booker. Again, he felt as if he were being put on the spot. He said, "What political process doesn't have its issues?" He thought he was making a good point in defense of his fellow men.

"On Og, we never fight over issues," Rock said. "Issues are of no importance."

"Our elections are different from yours," Ernie said. "If an Ogonite candidate takes a stand on an issue, the voters will reject him or her right away. He or she will never get to first base."

"How do you elect leaders if they don't take a stand on issues?" Mr. Booker asked.

"We vote for our leaders based solely on their level of education, experience, and reputation," Lucy explained. So far, she hadn't said much, but she now felt inclined to help Mr. Booker understand. "Our candidates publish their qualifications, and the people decide which of them will be best equipped to do their job. No issues are ever even discussed. None at all. We're not seeking leaders who will take specific actions once they're elected. We're simply seeking out the most capable men and women to run our planet's affairs."

"But how do you know what your leaders will do once they're voted in?" Mr. Booker asked.

"How does anyone ever know?" Lucy said. "How do you know what your own leaders will do?"

"One can't predict the future," Rock said. "No one knows the situations a leader will face until he or she is actually in office, until the time comes for a decision to be made."

"No promises are made, and no promises are broken," Ralph said. "A person's qualifications trump his or her stance on any issue."

"So you're telling me everyone on your planet stands behind your leaders and all their decisions once they're in office?" Mr. Booker asked. "That's a little hard to believe. Don't Ogonites ever disagree with their leaders?"

"Of course we disagree," Ernie said. "But we don't make a big deal out of it. None of our leaders has ever been perfect. An Ogonite accepts imperfections as a fact of life, and imperfections certainly aren't worth fighting over. It would be like fighting over the weather."

"Well said," Rock agreed.

"It's like I tried to say earlier," William said. "I think human infighting is instinctual. Birds fly; fish swim; and given the slightest provocation, humans will take sides and fight."

"It's possible that they could be taught to behave differently," Lucy said.

"Not very likely," William said.

"I'm inclined to agree with William," Ernie said to Lucy.

"Let's step back," Rock said. "I think we're getting ahead of ourselves." It was Rock's responsibility as chairman to keep the inquiry under control. "I think we're getting off track," he said. "We're spending too much time stating our own opinions and not enough time listening to the opinions of our guest. We didn't bring Mr. Booker here to sit and listen to us berate human beings. We brought him here to explain things. We ought to give him a real chance to speak. So, Mr. Booker, you have the floor. Is there anything you'd like to say?"

"About what?"

"About our concerns. Why do you think your species is so contentious?"

"I don't know what to say," Mr. Booker said. "Maybe it sounds simpleminded, but I've always thought this was how all intelligent beings would behave. I mean, isn't this just the way things have to be? Different groups of people will have different opinions, and each side will think it's in the right. Even the best and brightest don't seem to agree on anything. I think disagreements are just a fact of life, and when people disagree, doesn't some discord have to follow? And where there's discord, isn't there bound to be fighting?"

The council was quiet for a moment. They seemed to be considering Mr. Booker's words. Rock broke the silence and said, "Things are indeed different on Og. We simply don't fight like humans, and it's not because we don't have our fair share of disagreements."

"He's just giving excuses," William said.

"Hear, hear," Ralph said.

"A human doesn't need a disagreement to take sides and fight," William said.

"Human sports provide a perfect example," Ernie said.

"Human sports?"

"Yes," William said. "How do you explain them?"

"Explain them how?" Mr. Booker asked.

"Aren't they just another example of your species taking sides and fighting against an enemy for the sake of fighting? Where are the disagreements? They're nowhere to be found, because none are required! In your own country, the most advanced on your planet, what's the favorite sport of your citizens? It's football, isn't it? Do you watch football games?"

"I do at times."

"And you enjoy them?"

"Yes, I do."

"Isn't each game just another war, with one team fighting against the other to win?"

"You could say that."

"Your brave young troops don their helmets and strap on their armor and uniforms. They face off against the opposition, the whole point being to move the ball into the other side's territory and score as many points as possible. It's a very rough game, and it isn't for the weak or timid. Young men are pitted head-to-head against other young men who are equally determined to win. It's just like your military: all troops are trained and well conditioned, all long to win, and all are guided by their coaches and generals. It's the sword and shield, Mr. Booker. Do you know what I mean by this? It's offense versus defense. The defensive players try their best to thwart the advances of the enemy, and the offensive players fight to put points on the scoreboard. There are lots of nasty cuts, bruises, sprains, dislocated joints, fractured bones, concussions, and torn ligaments. The injured are helped off the battlefield to medics who are standing by on the sidelines, or they're carted away to nearby hospitals. There's nothing quite like the organized violence of an American football game, is there? And look at all the spectators! Thousands of fans work themselves up into a nationalistic frenzy, jumping up and down, shouting at the top of their lungs, and rooting for their team to vanquish the despised rival. You can't help yourselves. But it's no surprise to us. There are no disagreements there. There are no differences of opinion lurking behind the sport's violent exhibitions. If fact, everyone involved in the football games agrees! The players agree to fight each other voluntarily. They take sides and fight for the sake of fighting, longing to beat the opposing team and walk off the field as winners."

"Always at odds with each other and always fighting," Ralph said. "How can we trust a species when they revel in such conflict?"

"How indeed?" William said.

"Rah, rah, rah!" Ralph exclaimed.

"Semper fi!" Ernie shouted.

"Just win, baby!" Ralph said, joining in. Everyone on the council was now laughing. Mr. Booker turned to look at Sid, and he was laughing too.

"It is funny, no?" Sid said.

"I guess," Mr. Booker said.

When it came time to break for lunch, Mr. Booker was glad the session was over. Just before he adjourned the meeting, Rock told Mr. Booker that they wouldn't need him for the afternoon. He said Ralph was needed elsewhere on the ship, and all five council members had to be present during any questioning. "We won't need you here until tomorrow morning, so please arrive at eight, and enjoy the rest of your afternoon."

"Okay," Mr. Booker said.

Sid and Mr. Booker left the council chambers and went directly to the cafeteria for lunch. They ordered their food and found an empty table. "I feel I could've said more," Mr. Booker said. "I feel like I dropped the ball."

"They'll give you a chance to say anything you wish," Sid said. "Don't be discouraged. They can sometimes come across as a little opinionated, but they do want to hear what you have to say."

"I get nervous when I feel I'm being attacked."

"They're not attacking you."

"But it feels that way."

"Try not to be so defensive. No one expects you to be perfect. Just be truthful. Just answer their questions to the best of your ability, and don't be afraid of the truth. And if you have something to say, don't be afraid to speak up. The reason you're here is so the council can hear what's on your mind."

"Where did Ralph have to go this afternoon?" Mr. Booker asked. "Why couldn't he be present for the questioning?"

"He's working on his play."

"His play?"

"He wrote a three-act play for the ship's crew. He's also directing it, and performances will start in a few days. They're having a dress rehearsal this afternoon, so he has to be there."

"Ogonites put on plays?"

"Oh yes. And they can be quite amusing."

"What's this play about?"

"It's a comedy."

"I mean, what's the subject matter?"

"It's about life on your Earth."

"A comedy about human beings?"

"Yes, that'd be accurate."

"Can I see it?"

"I'll have to ask Ralph, but I don't see why not. In fact, I think he'd be happy to have you there."

"I'd like to see it."

"I'll see if I can get us seats."

Just then, a visitor appeared at the table: an Ogonite who went by the name of Henry. He looked familiar to Mr. Booker, but at first, he couldn't quite place him. However, when he spoke, he recognized the voice immediately. Henry was one of the cops who'd abducted Mr. Booker from his home—the skinny one with the mustache. He looked different without his police uniform, now being dressed in a golden robe. "Do you mind if I join you?" Henry asked. He was holding his lunch tray and would not sit down until an invitation was confirmed.

"Be our guest," Mr. Booker said.

"Do you remember me?" Henry asked, taking a seat.

"I do," Mr. Booker said.

"No hard feelings, I hope."

"No, I'm fine."

"So how are things going? How are you doing with the council?"

"I'm not so sure."

"He's worried," Sid said.

"Don't let them worry you. It's their job to needle you and ask annoying questions."

"I told him to just be honest."

"Yes, that's good advice," Henry said.

"Ralph has a rehearsal today for his play," Sid said. "So we have the rest of the afternoon off."

"What are you going to do?"

"I'm going to spend some time with my son," Sid said. "I've been so busy lately, and I need to spend more time with him. I thought we might play a little basketball at the fitness center."

"How about you?" Henry asked Mr. Booker.

"Me?" Mr. Booker said. "I suppose I'll do some reading."

"I take it Anna gave you the book?" Sid said.

"She did, and thank you."

"Have you started it?"

"I began last night."

"Which book are you talking about?" Henry asked.

"*Uncle Tom's Cabin*," Mr. Booker said.

"Oh, of course. I think I read it a few years ago. Isn't it about slavery in America?"

"It is."

"Are you a slave?" Henry asked.

"Of course not," Mr. Booker said, giving Henry a curious look. "You know, Anna asked me the same question when she gave me the book."

Sid laughed.

"Is this slavery question some kind of inside joke?" Mr. Booker asked.

114

"You'll learn soon enough," Henry said, and then he changed the subject. "I'm curious, Mr. Booker. What did the council question you about today?"

Mr. Booker looked at Sid as if to ask if it was okay for him to reveal that information. "Go ahead," Sid said. "You can talk about the council meetings to anyone on the ship. We don't keep secrets."

Mr. Booker looked at Henry and said, "They wanted to know why humans spend so much of their time taking sides and fighting each other."

"Seems like a fair question."

"Yes," Mr. Booker agreed.

"Did you have an answer for them?"

"If I did, it wasn't a very good one."

"So what did you say?"

"Now that I think about it, I really gave them no helpful answer at all. In fact, I think they answered the question for me."

Henry turned and said something to Sid, but Mr. Booker wasn't listening. His eyes glazed over, and his mind wandered elsewhere. He was daydreaming, and in his thoughts, he traveled back to a day in his childhood when he was nine years old, walking home from school. It had been raining that day, and the streets and sidewalks were wet. A boy named Artie Duncan rode up on his bicycle and stopped in front of young Mr. Booker. Artie was accompanied by three of his buddies, who were also on bicycles. "Well, if it isn't Booker, the lone bookworm," Artie said. "Look at his gigantic backpack. I'll bet it's full of books! How many books have you jammed into that thing, Booker? It looks like half the school library is riding on your back." The other boys laughed as Artie climbed off his bike and stepped toward Mr. Booker. "Take off your backpack. Let's see what you've got."

"They're just my books," Mr. Booker said. "There's nothing in my backpack you'd be interested in." Mr. Booker said this hoping Artie would leave him alone, but he knew Artie had no intention of going away.

"Hand the backpack over," Artie said. Mr. Booker removed his backpack and handed it over. The boy unzipped it and dumped the books onto the wet sidewalk. Looking down at the pile of books, Artie said, "Do you really think you're smarter than us?"

"No, of course not."

"Then what's with all these books?"

"I like reading them."

"What's this one about?" Artie asked, picking up one of the books and thumbing through the pages. "Who in the heck is Voltaire?" Then, to his friends, he said, "Have any of you ever heard of Voltaire?" Artie's pals all shook their heads while Artie continued to examine the book. "Tell us about him, Booker. What's so great about this guy that you need to be carrying his book around with you?"

"Nothing, I guess."

"Was he a baseball player?"

"No, of course not."

"A football player?"

"No, he wasn't an athlete."

"Was he a US president? Or maybe he was a movie star?"

"No, he was just a great writer."

"A writer?"

"A writer and a philosopher. He lived in France many years ago."

"A Frenchman? I should've known! The French are all faggots, Booker, or didn't you know that? Have you been reading a book written by a fag?"

"I don't think he was a homosexual."

"He had to be, right, boys?" Artie turned to his friends, and they all nodded and laughed. Artie then tossed the book onto the street and picked up another. "Who wrote this one? Plutarch? Who in the heck is he?"

"He was an ancient biographer."

"A biographer?" Artie said. "Probably just another of your fags." His friends all laughed again. They were enjoying Artie's show. "You want to know what I think, Booker?"

"What do you think?"

"I think you're a fag. Only a fag would read books written by other fags."

Mr. Booker did not respond. He stood there staring at Artie. The boy then continued. "I think you're a fag, or else why would you be lugging around a backpack full of books written by queers?"

"I don't know."

"Am I making you mad? I suppose you want to fight me?"

"No, I don't want to fight you."

"I think you do," Artie said. Artie then shoved Mr. Booker backward so that he lost his balance and fell to the sidewalk. "Come on, Booker. Stand up and fight. I'm not afraid of you. Are you afraid of me?" Mr. Booker stood up, and Artie said, "I think this fag is afraid of me!"

Then Mr. Booker did something that shocked even himself: he took a swing at Artie's face. He couldn't believe what he'd done. He'd landed a punch directly on Artie's jaw, and the boy reeled backward from the force of the blow. At first, Artie was surprised, and then he just laughed. "Did you all see that? He sucker punched me! The little freak went and sucker punched me!"

Rather than hitting him back, Artie sprang forward and tackled Mr. Booker so that Artie wound up sitting on his chest. He then held Mr. Booker's arms over his head so he couldn't throw another punch. Mr. Booker struggled to get free, but he couldn't get Artie off of him. Artie had Mr. Booker pinned to the ground, and he told the other boys to grab some mud from a nearby planter. The boys climbed off their bikes and followed his instructions. "Shove it in his faggot mouth!" Artie said, laughing. Mr. Booker struggled again, but Artie was too strong for him. The boys started pressing handfuls of mud into Mr. Booker's mouth. He tried to keep his teeth clenched, but one of the boys pinched his nose so that he had to open his mouth to breathe. The next thing he knew, his mouth was filled with wet soil. The more he tried to struggle, the more dirt they shoved past his lips, until his mouth was completely full. Artie laughed, finally climbing off of Mr. Booker and standing over him, looking down victoriously. Mr. Booker remained on the sidewalk. He sat up, spitting the filth from his mouth. "I hope you enjoy your books," Artie said, and he kicked several of them toward Mr. Booker. Artie and his friends then mounted their bicycles and rode away, leaving Mr. Booker on the sidewalk, spitting dirt.

Mr. Booker truly hated Artie Duncan. After all those years, he still hated him. When they were young, Artie was one of the most popular kids in school. Everyone liked Artie Duncan, even many of the teachers. But why? It never had made any sense to Mr. Booker. Artie was a rotten kid, yet everyone thought highly of him.

"Mr. Booker, are you with us?" Sid asked. Mr. Booker had been sitting in a trance at the cafeteria table, deep in his childhood daydream, recalling the awful encounter with Artie Duncan. Now he was back with Sid and Henry, who were trying to get his attention.

"Sorry," Mr. Booker said. "I guess I was sort of daydreaming."

"Henry asked you a question," Sid said.

"What was your question?" Mr. Booker asked, looking toward Henry.

"What's that you're eating?" Henry asked.

"It's an egg salad sandwich."

"Is it any good?"

"As good as any on Earth," Mr. Booker said. "You want this half? I'm no longer hungry, and I'm not going to finish it."

"Yes, I'll give it a try."

Mr. Booker handed the half sandwich to Henry and then said, "I'm going back to my cabin. I feel like being alone for a while. Will you two excuse me?"

"I'll see you tomorrow morning," Sid said.

"Nice to see you're doing okay," Henry said.

"Thanks," Mr. Booker replied.

Mr. Booker stood up and left. He walked out of the cafeteria and down the hallway to his cabin. He stepped in and closed the front door behind him. He kicked off his shoes and grabbed his copy of *Uncle Tom's Cabin*. He then got comfortable on the sofa and opened the book to read. He'd read about fifteen pages, when there was a knock at the front door. He set the book down to answer it. It was

Anna. She seemed prettier every time he saw her, and he was glad she was there. Just the sight of her made him feel much better. "I heard you had the afternoon off," she said. "Are you by yourself?"

"I am," Mr. Booker said.

"Put your shoes back on. There's something I want to show you."

"Right now?" Mr. Booker asked.

"Yes, right now. Come with me!"

CHAPTER 12

LITTLE LAKE

Anna took Mr. Booker by the hand, and the two of them left his cabin and hurried down the hallway. After passing the cafeteria, they stopped at a large wooden door. Several Ogonites were in the hallway, and Anna told Mr. Booker they would have to wait until the hallway was empty. They pretended to be having a casual conversation several feet from the door.

Mr. Booker remembered the door from his tour. Sid had told him the door led to a restricted area but had never told him what was behind the door. There was a silver touch screen on the wall, and when the hallway was empty, Anna placed the palm of her hand on the screen. The door automatically unlocked with a soft click, and Anna pushed it open and stepped through, pulling Mr. Booker along with her. "I don't think I'm supposed to be in here," Mr. Booker said.

"It's okay," Anna said. "You're with me, and I want to show you something."

"Won't we get in trouble?"

"Only if we're caught."

"What happens if someone sees us?"

"No one will see us. It's right after lunch, and all the farm workers will be taking their naps."

"Naps?"

"You know, something like your earthly siestas. It's very hot in here, just like on our planet, Og, and the workers like to nap this time of day to get a little relief from the heat."

Anna shut the door. The first thing Mr. Booker felt was the extreme change in temperature. It was as if they had stepped into the Sahara Desert, and the heat hit him like a bomb blast. Mr. Booker looked around, but there wasn't much to see. They were in a small corridor that led to a pair of sliding doors, and the corridor's walls and ceiling were decorated with the usual Ogonite wood carvings. A single light fixture hanging from the ceiling provided just enough light to see. He followed Anna down the short corridor to the doors, and she pressed a red button on the wall. The doors slid open. It appeared they were at an elevator, but going where? Anna pulled Mr. Booker into the small elevator cabin, and she pressed another button.

"Where does this go?"

"Up," Anna said.

"Are you sure we won't get caught?"

"I always come here. This time of day, there's never anyone around. We'll have the whole place to ourselves for a couple hours."

The elevator slowly rose to a higher level, and the doors opened after the elevator stopped. Mr. Booker couldn't believe his eyes. They stepped into an interior space the size of several football fields. The ceiling was about forty feet high, crisscrossed with carved woodwork and dotted with large and glaring light fixtures. It was so bright he had to squint and was as hot as a burning furnace. Growing from the ground were varieties of exotic plants and trees organized into orchards and fields of carefully tended crops. The soil was coarse, rocky, and rust colored. Everything was damp, soaked with water from an irrigation system that wound its way around the plants and trees like spaghetti. The place reeked of an unpleasant odor, but Mr. Booker wasn't able to identify the exact smell. It was a little like a city dump, a little like human excrement, and a lot like cooked broccoli. It was pungent, heady, and repulsive. "We're in our ship's plantation," Anna said. "This is where we grow and harvest everything needed to support the crew. The environment here simulates our best agricultural conditions on Og."

"It's so hot," Mr. Booker said.

"Temperatures on Og are much higher than on Earth. This plantation is actually considered moderate for our planet, best for growing trees and crops. Isn't it nice? I love coming up here midday while the farm workers are napping, so I can take everything in. But keep following me. There's something I want to show you."

Anna grasped Mr. Booker's hand and pulled him along a dirt trail that wound through the speckled shade of the trees. "What's that awful smell?" Mr. Booker asked.

"We fertilize with our sewage and garbage. You'll get used to it."

"I'm not so sure I will," Mr. Booker said.

Anna laughed and continued to pull him through the shady orchard. They followed the trail until they came upon a body of water between the trees and the crops. It was a small lake carved into the red soil like a large, inviting swimming pool. The water was crystal clear, and the bright light from the overhead sunlamps glistened on its glassy surface. Fish were visible darting about in the lake, chasing each other and looking for food. "Don't you love it?" Anna said. "We call it Little Lake. It's the only lake on the ship."

"Just how large is this ship?" Mr. Booker asked, suddenly realizing the ship was much larger than he'd imagined.

"It's large," Anna said. "Like a full-sized city in space."

"I had no idea."

"Shall we go swimming?"

"Swimming?"

"You look like you're roasting. The lake will cool you off."

In fact, Mr. Booker was burning up. He was sweating profusely, and the lake water looked inviting. "You want us to swim in this lake?"

"I do it all the time. And there's no one here to stop us. Like I told you, all the workers are taking their naps. Now's the perfect time!" Before Mr. Booker could respond to Anna's proposition, she was removing her golden robe. She tossed the robe aside and then slipped out of her panties and undid her bra. She stepped into the water up to her ankles. "Are you coming?" she asked, standing like a marble goddess under the bright overhead lights, stark naked and smiling, showing off her perfect teeth and lovely body.

"Jeez," Mr. Booker said.

"Come on in!" Anna went in deeper, splashing in the water and then jumping in head first. Mr. Booker watched as she swam and then came up for air. Was he really such a prude? He was terribly embarrassed and had no idea what he should do. Anna laughed and asked, "Are you just going to stand there staring at me?" She was now about chest deep.

"No, I'm coming in," Mr. Booker said, and he took off his robe, dropping the garment onto the rust-colored soil. Then he stepped out of his underwear and tossed the shorts atop the robe. He was completely naked. He hadn't taken his clothes off in front of a girl since he'd been married to Linda. If Linda could only see him now. With one hand covering his groin and the other hand out as if he needed it to keep his balance, he stepped gingerly from the hot soil to the edge of the lake. He stepped into the shallow water of the shore and then jumped in head first where the water was deeper. It was a wonderful sensation. The clear water was the perfect temperature, not too cold and not too warm. He swam out to where Anna stood so that he was also chest deep.

Anna laughed. "Are you embarrassed?"

"Who? Me?"

"You have a funny look on your face, like you're ashamed of your body."

"I guess I am a little."

"You have a fine body."

"Well, so do you."

"There's no one else here to see you. It's just you and me. No need to be shy."

"Okay," Mr. Booker said. Anna swam up to him and, scooping the water with her hands, splashed him several times. Water was now dripping from his face and shoulders, and she giggled. Then she did it again.

"Come on," she said. "Enjoy yourself!" Without any warning,

she jumped to him and hugged him with her warm and slippery arms. "Give me a kiss," she said.

"A kiss?"

"Right here in the water. Give me one big, warm, and wonderful kiss."

"Okay," Mr. Booker said, and before he even knew what he was doing, they were kissing. Her mouth was soft and warm, and her tongue was wet. Her body pressed against his for several seconds, until he stopped the kiss and gently moved her backward with his hands. "That's enough for now," he said.

"You have an erection," Anna said.

"I guess I do."

"I felt it on my tummy. Does it mean you love me?"

"It means I'm aroused."

"Because you love me?" Anna asked.

"A male penis kind of has a mind of its own."

"It has a mind?"

"It's just an expression. It means there's not a lot I can do about it. It doesn't mean I love you. It just means you've aroused me."

"Oh," Anna said. "This is all new to me. Men don't get erections on Og. It isn't necessary for a man to have an erection in order to have sex."

Mr. Booker was twice as embarrassed now, talking about his erection to this girl he'd only known for a few days. "I think we should take things a little slower. I mean, don't get me wrong. This is truly wonderful, being in the lake with you, and I did like kissing you. But I'm a guest on this ship, and I don't want anyone thinking I've taken advantage of you."

"*You* taking advantage of *me*?" Anna said, laughing. She patted Mr. Booker on the cheek. "You're so cute, and you're so funny!"

"Am I?"

"Are you cooled off?"

"Cooled off?"

"Did the water cool you off?"

"Yes, I suppose it did."

"Do you want to get out?"

"Yes, I think so."

"Let's go sit in the shade. We can talk and dry off." Anna waded back to the shore, and Mr. Booker followed her. She took a seat in the shade of the trees. Before sitting beside her, he put on his shorts to conceal the erection that refused to go away. He then sat beside Anna, and she said, "Do you know why I love this place?"

"No," Mr. Booker said.

"I've lived my entire life on this ship, and this is the only spot on the ship where there's soil and plant life."

"And a lake."

"Yes, and a lake. It's the closest I can get to feeling like I'm on my home planet. I've lived my entire life on this spaceship. I was born and raised here, and at times, I feel like I'm in a gigantic cage. I've never even set foot on Og—or any other planet, for that matter—and I often feel I'm missing out. Does that make sense to you? Did you know most of Og is covered with lakes, vegetation, and forests? It's a lot like this indoor plantation. What a wonderful place it must be! On Og, I could choose to be outdoors. I mean, truly outdoors, enveloped in Og's life-sustaining atmosphere, caressed by breezes, refreshed by rains, baked by our sun, and speckled every night with our twinkling stars. What I wouldn't give to go there! All those people back home probably don't appreciate what they have."

"On Earth, we say absence makes the heart grow fonder," Mr. Booker said.

"On Og, we say the greater the distance, the stronger the pull. It's the opposite of gravity. Don't you find that strange?"

"Yes, in a way."

"Tell me about where you live."

"About Earth?"

"About your neighborhood and community. What's it like where you live?"

"I live in a town called Mission Viejo. It's in Southern California."

"Is there a mission there?"

"Not that I know of."

"How many people live in Mission Viejo?"

"I don't know the actual population. But it doesn't really matter. Where I live, it's hard to tell where one city stops and another begins. It's all one big real-estate development."

"Do you live on a street?"

"Yes, I live on a street."

"What's the name of the street?"

"I live on Eagle's Nest Way."

"Are there eagles there?"

"No, I haven't seen any eagles. We have lots of finches, blue jays, and crows. But I've never seen any eagles."

"What does your house look like?"

"It's a beige stucco structure with a red tile roof, just like the rest of the houses in the neighborhood. All the houses are very similar in size and style. My house has a nice front yard and a reasonably sized backyard. There are three bedrooms, two bathrooms, and a family room with a fireplace. I guess there's really nothing special about it, but I like living there. Shopping is convenient, and the weather is nice."

"What are your neighbors like?"

"They're okay."

"That's it?" Anna said, laughing.

"What did you expect me to say?"

"Well, what do they do? Your next-door neighbors, for example. What are they like?"

"On one side are the Cassels, and on the other are the Garcias."

"Tell me about the Cassels."

"Andrew and Vivian Cassel moved into their house about three years after Linda and I moved into ours. They have two children, a boy named Jason and a girl named Courtney. Andrew calls himself a tax adviser, and Vivian is a stay-at-home mom."

"What's a tax adviser?"

"He helps people to avoid paying taxes."

"He helps them to avoid taxes?"

"Yes, within the law, of course."

"I thought taxes were essential to your economy."

"Essential?"

"Don't they support all your schools, roads, bridges, public transportation, health care, social security, and other necessities? How can humans survive without paying their taxes?"

"Well, everyone pays taxes."

"But your neighbor helps them pay less?"

"That's the general idea. The point is to pay the least taxes possible."

"I still don't get it."

"What don't you get?"

"If taxes are necessary to fund all the essentials of your society, what's the point in paying less of them? Do human beings want worse living conditions? Less education? Less health care? Worse roads and highways?"

"No, of course not."

"Then why pay less taxes?"

"It's just the way it is. Only a fool would pay more taxes than he has to. I guess you have to be a human being to see the logic in it."

"I guess so."

"Anyway, Andrew seems to be doing well. He just bought his wife a new Maserati, and both his kids are in private schools."

"Private schools?"

"As opposed to public schools. Private schools are supposed to be better, but they're more expensive."

"So the more money one has, the better education he can acquire for his children?"

"Something like that."

"But you teach in a public school?"

"I do."

"Would you do a better job teaching if you switched to a private school?"

"No, I wouldn't."

"Are history teachers in private schools better at their jobs than you?"

"I doubt it. I'm very good at what I do."

"What's a Maserati?"

"Pardon me?"

"You said Andrew bought his wife a new Maserati."

"It's a car."

"But what's so special about a Maserati?"

"It's an Italian car, and it's more expensive than most other cars. It's a status symbol."

"A status symbol?"

"It tells the rest of the world that you're doing well for yourself financially."

"And the rest of the world needs to know this?"

"It's important to some people, letting others know they're successful."

"At earning money?"

"Yes, at earning money."

"Tell me about the Garcias," Anna said.

"They're in their sixties. I don't think they ever had children. I've never really talked much to either of them except to say hi and comment on the weather, but I've heard things from others. I know Mr. Garcia works at a warehouse as some sort of manager, and Mrs. Garcia works at Target. I think she's a cash register clerk, but I've been to Target several times, and I've never seen her. I know they watch a lot of TV, because when I open our kitchen window for fresh air, I can hear their TV blaring from their family room. It's possible they're losing their hearing; otherwise, why would they have the volume up so high?"

"Why don't you get to know them better?"

"Why should I?"

"Because they're your neighbors."

"I doubt we'd have much in common."

"I like getting to know people."

"I like knowing people too but not necessarily everyone and not just because they happen to live next door to me."

A leaf fell from the tree above and landed on Anna's breast. She brushed it off and said, "We should probably get going." She then stood, bending over to grab her bra and panties. Mr. Booker stood up and put on his golden robe. Once dressed, they walked back through the orchard, staying on the trail, making their way to the elevator.

"I enjoyed this," Mr. Booker said.

"So did I," Anna said. She then planted a kiss on Mr. Booker's cheek. "Maybe we can do this again."

"I'd like that," Mr. Booker said. "Thanks for bringing me up here."

CHAPTER 13

YES, MASTER

It was Mr. Booker's fourth day in front of the council, and he had just enjoyed a terrific breakfast with Sid. The council members all appeared to be in good spirits, talking to each other and laughing. As Mr. Booker and Sid took their seats in the middle of the room, Rock cleared his throat and said, "Good morning, Mr. Booker."

"Good morning to you," Mr. Booker replied.

"Did you get a good night's sleep?"

"I did," Mr. Booker said.

"Did you enjoy your afternoon off yesterday?"

"Yes, it was interesting."

"Fine, fine. Let's get on with this then. Ralph has some questions for you."

"I'll do my best to answer them."

Rock looked over at Ralph, who was leaning back in his chair and stroking his beard with his fingers. "You have the floor," Rock said to Ralph.

Ralph stared at Mr. Booker for a moment and then asked, "Are you a slave, Mr. Booker?"

Mr. Booker chuckled. He was amused by the question—not because it was particularly funny but because he had been asked the same ridiculous question twice already since he had come aboard the ship. The answer seemed obvious. Why did these aliens keep asking him if he was a slave? Surely after so many years of studying Earth and its inhabitants, they would know the answer. "I'm a schoolteacher," he said. "And I'm a free man. No one owns me, and I can do as I please."

"As you please?"

"I mean, more or less."

"Is it more, or is it less?"

"I guess I'd say it's more."

"I see," Ralph said. Again, he stared at Mr. Booker, apparently collecting his thoughts and trying to decide how to phrase his next question.

"Do you think I'm a slave?" Mr. Booker asked.

"My opinion right now isn't important. I want to know what you think. Can I give you a few hypotheticals?"

"Okay," Mr. Booker said.

"Who do you work for?"

"I work for the school district."

"So you have an employer?"

"Yes, of course."

"And they tell you how to do your job?"

"Sometimes."

"But you do work for them?"

"Yes, I do. I have to perform certain tasks. And I have to behave a certain way. There are requirements and expectations."

"Do they own you?"

"Of course not."

"Yet you do have to obey them?" Ralph asked.

"To an extent, yes, that's true."

"Let's say you're teaching an American history class. You have a specific curriculum the school board has asked you to comply with, and you know exactly what you must do in order to satisfy them. But you have a problem with their plan. You don't believe their curriculum will accurately teach your students the true history of their country. You want them to learn about America, but you want them to understand what really happened. And what really did happen in this great country of yours? You choose to put your foot down and take a stand for what you believe in. You opt out of teaching your students about Paul Revere's famous ride, Eli Whitney's cotton gin, or Benjamin Franklin's lightning–ignited kite string. Instead, you focus the entire semester on the brutal annihilation of Native Americans by European immigrants. You teach the history of your country from a Native American's point of view. What happens then, Mr. Booker?"

"I'd probably have a problem."

"You'd have a problem with the school district?"

"No doubt I would."

"And you'd be asked to change your teaching plans?"

"It would be more in the form of a demand."

"And if you refused to go along?"

"I'd probably be fired."

"Fired, yes. You'd lose your job?"

"Most likely," Mr. Booker said.

"And if you applied for a teaching position elsewhere, would the school who fired you recommend you for the new position?"

"Probably not."

"It would be tough to find a new job?"

"It probably would be."

Again, Ralph stroked his beard, seemingly thinking about Mr. Booker's answers. He then said, "Let's look at another hypothetical. Imagine you're no longer a schoolteacher. Let's say you're a bartender."

"A bartender?"

"You work at a local watering hole. You've worked there for several years, and you've begun to notice something about your patrons. Many of them are regulars, and many of these regulars are drinking way too much and too often. They're not doing anything illegal. They call cabs to get rides home, so they aren't endangering anyone on the streets. They're breaking no laws. But they are getting drunk, and they're doing it often. You hear their stories while you're tending bar, and you observe their behavior. You come to the conclusion that these are not happy people. You believe their drinking is interfering with their lives and causing them to be unhappy. You think that if only they would stop, they'd be able to think clearly and move on from their alcoholism. You can see this, Mr. Booker. You know for a fact that by preparing their drinks and taking their money, you're only contributing to their misery. So you decide to put your foot down and become a good friend rather than an enabler. You refuse to serve them any more alcohol, and you tell them to go home to their loved ones. You tell them they need to stop drinking and get their lives in order. My question for you is this: How long do you think it would take before you were fired? Your boss would probably say something like 'Who in the hell do you think you are?' You'd say to your boss that you were just being a loyal friend to your patrons, and what would happen next? Wouldn't you be given your final paycheck and shown the door? Wouldn't you be sent on your way? Am I right about this?"

"Yes, you're probably right."

"Only probably?"

"Yes, you're right, of course."

"And you'd find yourself looking for a new job?"

"I would."

Ralph smiled at Mr. Booker. He thought for a moment and then said, "I have a third and final hypothetical for you."

"Okay," Mr. Booker said.

"This one involves your house. Let's say your house is in need of a new paint job. You ask around and find a friend who recommends a house painter. This friend was very happy with the painter's work and tells you he completed their project for a fair price. You call the painter up and meet with him, and you agree on an amount to pay him for the work. You tell him the color you'd like, and you agree to have him do the work while you're out of town, so his work doesn't interfere with your life. You go out of town, but when you return, you discover the house has been painted a completely different color than the one you selected. You call the painter to find out what happened, and he tells you he started to paint the house using the color you wanted, but it didn't look good. So he picked out a more appropriate color and used it on the house. You don't like the color he used, and you are furious. Who the heck did this guy think he was? What do you do, Mr. Booker? Do you write him a check for the work he did, or do you refuse to pay? I mean, the nerve of this guy, painting your house the wrong color! He thinks he did the right thing, and he insists you pay him for the work. But what do you do?"

"I don't think I'd pay him."

"Because he didn't obey you?"

"He didn't use the color we agreed upon. He had no right to change the color."

"Even though he believed that the color you chose was wrong and that he was doing the right thing in picking a new one? Even though he believed he was acting in your best interest?"

"He had no right."

"Just as you had no right to teach your students your version of American history? Just as you had no right to stop serving cocktails to alcoholics?"

Mr. Booker stared at Ralph for a moment. Then he said, "People in a society can't just go around doing whatever they please."

"So they're not free?"

Ralph stared at Mr. Booker for a moment, stroking his beard and waiting for his answer. "I don't know what to say," Mr. Booker said. Ralph then leaned over toward Rock, and the two of them whispered to each other. As they were whispering, Sid stood up to say something. Rock noticed Sid standing and called upon him to speak.

"I have something to say about all this," Sid said, but Mr. Booker wasn't listening to him. Instead, he found himself daydreaming again about Artie Duncan. In this daydream, he was in high school. Sid continued to speak, but Mr. Booker was oblivious.

Years had passed since Artie had pinned Mr. Booker down and had his friends stuff his mouth with mud. Artie and Mr. Booker were now seniors, and they crossed paths because of a girl named Rose Mathews. Rose was also a senior, and she sat next to Mr. Booker in their world history class. The two were friendly with each other—not outside of class but during class, where they exchanged words every now and again. Rose was a lovely girl, and she was popular. She had a ton of friends and a cheerful personality. She was a cheerleader for the high school football team, and she belonged to several school clubs. Mr. Booker thought she was one of the prettiest girls in school, and he loved it when she spoke to him, even if she was just borrowing a pencil or asking for a piece of paper. However, there was a flaw in the girl. She wasn't stupid, but she had little interest in her schoolwork.

In fact, Rose was failing her world history class, and the teacher had contacted Rose's parents to tell them about her poor performance. He'd told them if she didn't get an A on her final paper, she would likely fail, and if she failed the class, she wouldn't graduate with the rest of her friends. The teacher turned to Mr. Booker. The teacher liked him, and he'd noticed that Mr. Booker seemed to get along with the girl. Mr. Booker had the highest grade of any student in the class, and he was honest and well behaved. He was the kind of student every teacher longed for. After meeting with Rose's parents, the teacher came up with an idea: he would ask Mr. Booker to help Rose with her final paper. Obviously, he didn't want Mr. Booker to do the work for the girl, but he thought he could trust him to assist her. Of course, when the teacher ran this idea past Mr. Booker, he was delighted. Who wouldn't have wanted to spend time with Rose Mathews? It turned out that Rose was also okay with the idea, and the two of them met at Rose's house after school to write a paper that would ensure Rose's passing grade.

Getting a high grade on the paper meant everything to Rose, not because she cared about history but because she wanted to graduate with her friends. She also wanted to go to the senior prom, and her parents had told her if she didn't get an A on the paper, she'd be grounded and kept home.

That was where Artie Duncan came into the story. Artie had asked Rose to the prom, and Rose had said yes to him. Artie was as popular as ever. He was the quarterback and captain of the high school football team. Everyone liked Artie Duncan, the way he led his team to victories, and the way he comported himself. He was especially popular with the girls. Being asked to the prom by Artie was like being asked out by a famous movie star, and he had picked Rose to be his date. That final paper became the most important thing in Rose's young life, so she met with Mr. Booker at her house, determined to do her best. Mr. Booker recalled the first afternoon they met at the Mathews family's dining room table. Mr. Mathews was still at work, and Rose's mom left the two kids alone. Rose was dressed in a maroon turtleneck sweater and a pair of beige slacks. Her blonde hair was tied back in a ponytail, and she had a pencil tucked behind her ear to show she was serious. She was, in Mr. Booker's mind, nothing short of gorgeous.

The teacher had given his students a list of world history topics to choose from for their final papers. Rose was seated with her pencil behind her ear, and Mr. Booker had the list in his hand. "So which subject do you want to write about?" he asked.

"Pericles," Rose said.

"Why Pericles?"

"I like the sound of his name."

"Do you know anything about him?"

"He was a Roman god, wasn't he?"

"He wasn't a Roman," Mr. Booker said. "He was an Athenian."

"An Athenian?"

"He was Greek, not Roman. And he wasn't a god. He was a mortal man."

"What exactly does *mortal* mean?"

"That he would die just like everyone else."

"Is there any other kind of man?"

"I suppose not. I guess all men are mortal."

"Then we can just say he was a man. Although, come to think of it, I like using the word *mortal*. It would be good to call him a mortal man. It'll make me sound more intelligent. It'll show the teacher that I know what the word means."

"That's fine," Mr. Booker said.

"So what was so great about him?"

"He inspired his people."

"Inspired them?"

"He lived during the greatest period of time in Greek history. Because of his influence, historians call that period the Age of Pericles. They also call it the Golden Age of Athens."

"What was so great about it?"

"That's exactly what you're going to find out."

"Can't you just tell me?"

"I'm supposed to help you with this, not do the actual work."

"Oh," Rose said. She sounded a little disappointed. A couple strands of hair had fallen across her face, and she blew them away.

"I'm going to write down several topics for you to research, and we'll see what you come up with. Then we can sit down and write your paper. First is the Acropolis. I want you to find out what it is and tell me why it was so important to the Athenians."

"The Acropowhat?"

"The Acropolis," Mr. Booker said. He then spelled the word out, and Rose removed the pencil from behind her ear and wrote the word on a sheet of paper.

Mr. Booker then gave Rose several other items to research, spelling them out for her. When he was done, she had a list of six topics. "This is going to be a lot of work," she said.

"It should only take you a couple nights."

"When the teacher said you'd help, I had the idea you were going to do this research with me."

"There wouldn't be much point to any of this if I did all the work with you. You're supposed to be learning how to do this on your own."

"Why would I want that?"

"Don't you plan to go to college?"

"I'm not so sure."

Sounding like a counselor or teacher, Mr. Booker asked Rose, "What will you do when you graduate from high school?"

"I was thinking of becoming a dental hygienist. You don't need to write papers about Romans to clean people's teeth, do you?"

"I suppose not."

A week before Rose's paper was due and two weeks before the night of the prom, Artie Duncan approached Mr. Booker at school during their lunch break. Mr. Booker was eating his sandwich alone, minding his own business. Artie stood in front of him with his arms folded over his muscular chest, wearing his letterman's jacket. His hair was perfectly combed, and his brow was furrowed because he was about to say something important. "So, Booker," he said, "how's the paper coming?"

"It's coming," Mr. Booker said.

"Is she going to get an A?"

"She should."

"You know, if she doesn't get an A, I won't be able to take her to the prom."

"I'm aware of that."

"If I'd known she was this stupid, I would've asked someone else."

"She's not really stupid."

"So you're sticking up for her? Look, you little fag, don't tell me you've got a crush on her."

"No, I just don't think she's stupid."

"We'll see, won't we?"

"Yes, we'll see."

"An A, Booker. She has to get an A."

"I'm aware of that."

Was Artie threatening him? It certainly felt like a threat. Artie smiled at Mr. Booker but not in a friendly way. He then walked away, having delivered his message, and Mr. Booker went on to finish his sandwich.

The next day, Mr. Booker overheard a couple of Artie's friends talking. They were talking about Artie's plans for prom night, and they were joking about how Artie planned to get Rose drunk. Rose was still a virgin, they said, but Artie would change that before the night was over.

Mr. Booker was appalled.

He thought long and hard about what to do. He could see to

it that Rose got a bad grade on the paper, and that would be easy enough. But if he did that, everyone would be disappointed. Rose and her parents would be upset, the teacher would be let down, and who knew what Artie would do to him?

As it turned out, Mr. Booker did his job. He did not sabotage the project, and when the paper was turned in, Rose received an A. Her graduation from high school was ensured, and so was her prom night with Artie. It made Mr. Booker sick to think about it.

Sure enough, the day after the prom, Mr. Booker heard Artie bragging about how he'd had sex with Rose after the prom. He even had the nerve to approach Mr. Booker to convey his appreciation. "You're a good man, Booker," he said. "I still say you're a fag. But the truth is, I couldn't have done it without you!"

The boy was such a rat. Why couldn't anyone else see that? Poor sweet Rose. Had she really succumbed to Artie, or was he making the whole thing up?

Mr. Booker suddenly snapped out of his daydream and found himself looking back at Sid, who was still talking to the council.

When Sid finished speaking, he sat down. Rock looked at Mr. Booker and asked, "Do you have anything to add?"

He hadn't heard a word of what Sid had said, so he shook his head.

"Sid has made his points," Ralph said. "But isn't that precisely what slavery is?"

"We wish to be neither your masters nor your slaves," Rock said to Mr. Booker. Mr. Booker didn't say anything, because he didn't know what they were talking about.

"It's who they are," William said. "They spend nearly all their time and energy bossing each other around and telling one another what to do."

"It's hard to imagine," Ralph said.

"You'll do as I say," Ernie said firmly to Ralph, as though talking to a servant.

"Yes, master!" Ralph replied.

"Ho, ho!" Ernie bellowed, and the rest of the council laughed along with him.

"Let's break for lunch," William said. He had removed his glasses, and he rubbed his eyes as he talked.

"Yes, I'm starving," Ralph said.

"I hear the chef has decided to serve us his oofla today."

"Seriously?" Ralph said.

"What's oofla?" Mr. Booker asked.

"You should give it a try," Rock said. "You'll be in for a real treat."

"A real treat," Ralph agreed.

Chapter 14

Hot Needles

When we came to this point in his story, Mr. Booker wanted to stop. He was hoping I'd do a favor for him. His recollections of Artie Duncan had stirred his curiosity, and he asked me to use my investigative skills to find out what had happened to the boy. Mr. Booker hadn't seen Artie since high school, and he had no idea where he lived or what he'd been doing for the past twenty years. I told him he could easily do the research on his own, but he wanted me to handle it. I think he knew I'd do it for him. After all, what choice did I have? I didn't want to risk Mr. Booker taking his story elsewhere, so I agreed to look for Artie. "I'll do this for you," I said. "I'm not sure what I'll find out, but I'll do my best. I'll let you know what I come up with. But you have to promise to continue telling me your story once I'm done. I've invested a lot of time in your project, and I want to see it all the way through."

"You have my word," Mr. Booker said. "I just need to know what happened to Artie."

We stopped having our meetings for a couple weeks so I could go to work on Mr. Booker's request. Mr. Booker and Artie were raised in the suburbs of Santa Ana, about thirty miles north of Mr. Booker's current home. Researching Artie was easier than I'd thought it would be, for he'd never moved out of the Santa Ana neighborhood. He married a local girl, and during the early years of their marriage, they lived in a rental house just a few miles from where the boys grew up. After high school, Artie went to college. He was accepted to USC, and his grandparents paid the costly tuition. He didn't receive an athletic scholarship, but he was put on the college football team. He was a fourth-string quarterback. Unfortunately for Artie, he didn't play a single game, so despite all his football success in high school, his career as a college athlete was a bust. He majored in business administration and almost graduated with a degree. He dropped out in the middle of his junior year, and that was when he got married. He got a job at a local insurance agency, working as an assistant, where he coordinated claims, helped write policies, and did a lot of paperwork. The work was drudgery, but he stuck with it.

As the years passed, he and his wife had three healthy children, all of them daughters. When Artie turned thirty-two, he purchased a home in Tustin and opened up his own insurance agency. He had business cards and stationery with his name printed on them, a small office in Tustin, and a small but growing list of clients. He wasn't getting rich, but he was doing well enough to keep the bills paid and finance a boob job for his wife. Two years later, she left him for another man, taking her boobs and the three girls with her. Artie continued to sell insurance, living alone in the Tustin house.

A single man approaching middle age, Artie was unrecognizable from his high school years. He was no longer the handsome and self-confident young man of his youth. He was prematurely bald, and he'd gained a great deal of weight. His body was shapeless and flabby, and his clothes never quite fit; they looked as if they'd come from someone else's closet. I learned Artie started drinking heavily after his wife and daughters left him, although the drinking might have started before then. In fact, it'd be a good guess to say his drinking was a problem during the years he was married. When I talked to his ex-wife, she told me Artie had always been a drinker but not a happy one. She didn't get into any specifics, but I suspected his drinking was one of the reasons she left him.

Artie got his first DUI when he was thirty-seven. The judge required Artie to go to AA meetings, and shortly after he started attending the meetings, Artie joined a local church. He went to the church every Sunday for several months but soon lost interest and stopped showing up. He cut back on his drinking for a while, but he never actually quit. Three years ago, he began seeing a psychiatrist for chronic depression. He might have been depressed earlier, but that was the first time he sought professional help. His psychiatrist prescribed a number of antidepressants, and Artie has been taking the medications ever since. I was unable to find out whether the pills helped him. He never did marry again, but he began seeing a woman he met in AA. The woman's name was Beatrice Gibson. She was a frumpy, overweight artist who lived in Laguna Beach, and she wore lots of lipstick and oversized Hawaiian muumuus. She too drank despite her involvement in AA. She lived off a trust fund her father had set up years ago. To keep busy, she painted portraits of people's cats and dogs from photographs they gave to her. I saw some of the paintings, and they weren't good, but people love their pets, so there was a market for her work.

Most of the information I got about Artie was told to me by his father, Jaspar Duncan. Artie's mom had passed away years ago, and Jaspar was living alone in the same house where they'd raised their son. "Artie was such an odd boy," Jaspar told me. "Neither his mom nor I could figure him out. He was always so popular and athletic but also very insecure. And he had a mean streak in him. I never was able to figure the kid out." Jaspar last saw Artie several years ago, when Artie came to visit for his father's birthday. They weren't estranged, but there wasn't a strong father–son bond. Artie seldom saw his father, and when he did, their conversations were brief and superficial. Jaspar told me, "When his mom passed away six years ago, the boy didn't even bother to come to her funeral. At first, I was angry, and then I just felt sorry for him."

So that's the brief version of the report on Artie Duncan I handed over to Mr. Booker. There's more I could tell you, but Artie is only a small part of this story, and there's no need to spend a lot of time on such a minor character. Mr. Booker read my report slowly and carefully but didn't show the slightest emotion while reading. When he was done, he finally smiled and said, "It warms my heart. All these years, I was worried that the son of a bitch had a good life."

"Can we now continue?" I asked.

"We can," Mr. Booker said. "Where were we?"

"You were describing your fourth day with the council. You just broke for lunch."

"Yes, the oofla!"

"The what?"

"It's what we had for lunch that day. All four of us ordered the oofla." He said he was sitting with Sid and a young couple who'd joined them. By *young*, I mean they looked as if they were in their early thirties, but of course, they could easily have been in their hundreds. The male's name was Jared, and the female's name was Agatha. Sid told Mr. Booker they were members of the ship's large research crew, and they'd come to that end of the ship hoping to meet Mr. Booker in person.

Mr. Booker told me the oofla was a delicious dish of several different Ogonite ingredients molded into a cylindrical mass about the size of a Campbell's soup can. It sat upright in the middle of his plate, and he carved at it with his fork, starting at the top and working his way down. The outside of the oofla was stiff and flakey, like a pie crust. The crust held the soft interior together. The inside of the cylinder was a moist variety of salted vegetables and spicy protein cubes, something like the inside of a chicken pot pie, except richer and more flavorful.

"How do you like it?" Sid asked.

"It's actually very good," Mr. Booker said.

"It's one of my favorites," Jared said.

"Same here," Agatha agreed.

Everyone continued to eat, and Sid said, "Jared and Agatha are planning to get married."

"Is that so?" Mr. Booker said.

"Very soon," Jared said.

"We want to have children," Agatha said.

"When is your wedding?" Mr. Booker asked.

"About eighteen years from now."

"Eighteen years?"

"Right around the corner," Sid said.

"We can't wait."

"Of course not."

"Jared is hoping our first child will be a son. Of course, he'll be happy whether it's a girl or a boy."

"Did you have any children?" Jared asked Mr. Booker.

"No," Mr. Booker said.

"Don't most humans have children?" Agatha asked.

"Yes, but my wife and I didn't feel we'd have the proper time for them."

"But you had sex?"

"Of course we did, but Linda took birth control pills."

"That's funny," Agatha said, laughing. Jared also laughed.

"Why is that funny?" Mr. Booker asked.

"Having sex but not wanting children."

Sid began to chuckle as well.

"What does human sexual intercourse feel like?" Agatha asked. "Is it as pleasant as they say?"

"Pleasant?" Mr. Booker said.

"It's a pleasurable experience, isn't it?"

"You could say that."

"Can you describe it?"

"You don't know what sex is like?"

"It's much different for Ogonites," Sid explained.

"How is it different?" Mr. Booker asked.

"Ogonite sexual intercourse is extraordinarily painful," Jared said. "We only put up with it so we can have children."

"It's painful?"

"It's difficult to describe. It's like having your private parts poked and skewered by a dozen hot needles."

"Doesn't sound like much fun," Mr. Booker said.

"But you feel pleasure?"

"Yes, we like sex. In fact, I think you could say that we like it a little too much."

"What does it feel like?"

"It's hard to describe."

"I read that for many humans, it's like scratching an awesome itch," Agatha said. "It's like you have this nagging and insatiable itch, and you're able to scratch it just right. Is that an accurate description?"

"Sort of."

"Do you look at pornography, Mr. Booker?" Agatha asked. "Do you masturbate?"

"That's kind of a personal question."

Sid laughed. He then put his hand on Agatha's forearm and said to her, "Humans love having sex as much as they love eating, but they don't like to talk about it. It embarrasses them."

"Does it embarrass you?" Agatha asked Mr. Booker.

"Sort of," Mr. Booker said.

"I didn't mean to embarrass you."

"Are you a Christian?" Jared asked, suddenly changing the subject.

"I was raised a Christian. My parents made me go to church and Sunday school."

"Do you know your Bible?"

"I do," Mr. Booker said.

"Do you believe in Adam and Eve?"

"Perhaps as a parable."

"As a parable?"

"I don't believe the story literally. I mean, I don't think there was an actual Adam and Eve whom God made from the soil, but I understand the point of the story."

Jared and Agatha looked at each other. Mr. Booker then stuffed a forkful of oofla past his lips. He chewed and swallowed and then smiled at Sid. "Your people certainly do like asking questions."

"I told you we were inquisitive creatures."

"Does it bother you?" Jared asked.

"Does what bother me?"

146

"All of our questions."

"Not at all," Mr. Booker said. "It's refreshing to come across beings who are so eager to learn."

"We mean no harm by it," Agatha said.

"Honestly, I wish my high school students on Earth showed half your curiosity."

"So it doesn't bother you?"

"He's not bothered," Sid said.

Jared took a bite of his oofla. He then said, "We have our own ancient legend similar to your story about Adam and Eve. It's similar yet also very different. According to our Ogonite legend, there was a place like your Garden of Eden with its tree of knowledge. But instead of a tree, it was a thorny bush, and instead of apples, the bush was laden with red berries. And it was our God himself, not a conniving serpent, who encouraged our first male and female to eat the berries from the bush and open their minds to the remarkable possibilities of knowledge. You see, we see knowledge as something to be grateful for, not something to regret. Knowledge has never been viewed in a bad light on our planet. According to legend, it was ignorance that caused sin. And there's another thing that makes our folklore different. Our God never told us to be fruitful and multiply. Instead, his command was to propagate prudently, to raise each and every one of our children with great care. Be fruitful and multiply? It sounds like you're talking about rabbits."

"This is why our sex is so painful," Agatha said. "We don't copulate for the fun of it. It's something we endure in order to have children. The goal isn't to seek constant physical gratification. The goal is to promote a society that graces the hills and valleys of our planet in moderate numbers so that we can care for our children and properly tend to our God-given surroundings."

"But Ogonites do believe in God?" Mr. Booker asked.

"All of us believe in God," Jared said.

"Do you go to churches?" Mr. Booker asked.

"We have no churches."

"Do you go to church, Mr. Booker?" Agatha asked.

"No," Mr. Booker said. "I haven't been inside a church for many years. Churches are places of worship, and I don't think God cares whether he's worshipped or not. I think he cares about how we behave, and if people really want God to think highly of them, they ought to just behave themselves. Dressing up and sitting through sermons every Sunday proves nothing. Anyone can sit on his or her butt and listen."

Everyone at the table thought about what Mr. Booker had said as he stuffed another forkful of his lunch into his mouth. He chewed and swallowed his oofla, and Sid suddenly blurted out, "I got us tickets for Ralph's play!"

"Did you?" Mr. Booker said.

"It opens tomorrow. We'll be there for the opening night."

"We're going next week," Jared said.

"Ralph's productions are always worth seeing," Agatha added. "He's a genius, isn't he?"

"That's what they say," Sid said.

"I'm looking forward to it," Mr. Booker said.

"Are you about done with your lunch?" Sid asked.

"I suppose."

"Did you like it?"

"Yes, it was great."

"We should probably get going. We don't want to keep the council waiting."

"No, of course not," Mr. Booker said.

"We have a saying on Og," Jared said. "We say, 'God looks unfavorably upon the procrastinator.'"

"We have a similar saying on Earth," Mr. Booker said. "We say, 'There's no time like the present.'"

"I like that one," Sid said.

"So do I," Jared agreed.

Sid and Mr. Booker stood up from the table, and Agatha and Jared said goodbye to them. The two men made their way out of the cafeteria and toward the council chambers, Sid with his wooden staff and Mr. Booker with his belly full of oofla. "I feel a lot better now that I've eaten lunch," Mr. Booker said.

"That's good to hear," Sid said.

CHAPTER 15

ORDER IN THE COURT!

R ock called the afternoon session to order as soon as Sid and Mr. Booker took their seats. Ralph was stroking his beard again, and William was rubbing his glasses on the lapel of his golden robe. William polished his glasses so often that Mr. Booker figured it was more a nervous habit than a need to clean the lenses.

Rock leaned forward and asked, "Mr. Booker, have you ever been to court?"

"To court?"

"Yes, civil or criminal court."

"Well, besides a few short stints for jury duty, I've been to court three times."

"Can you describe your experiences? Were you being sued, or were you suing someone else? Were you being prosecuted for a crime? Let's hear about your first time before a judge."

"The first time was years ago," Mr. Booker said. "I was fifteen years old. I did something stupid. I guess I just wanted to fit in with the other kids and earn their respect. There was a small convenience store across the street from our high school, and the owner of the store was a man named Leon. I don't know his last name, but he was a very nice fellow who went out of his way to get along with us. Even though he was old enough to be a parent, all the kids seemed to like him. Every day when school let out, his little convenience store would fill with students crowding the aisles and lining up at the cash register to buy snacks and drinks. It was always kind of a madhouse, and looking back, I honestly don't know how Leon tolerated all of us. I mean, sure, he was making some money, but teenagers can be a real nuisance.

"One day after school, when the store was filled with its usual throng of students, I decided to do something—something I'd immediately regret, it turned out. The cash register was located on a counter in the middle of the store, and Leon was there, ringing up sales. Behind Leon was a tall cabinet filled with packs of cigarettes, and while Leon was busy at the register, I snuck behind him and nabbed a box of Marlboros, holding them up for the others to see. Why a pack of Marlboros? I have no idea. I didn't even smoke, but it seemed like a cool thing to do, to steal the cigarettes behind Leon's back. Noticing the kids were now all looking at me, Leon turned around to see what was going on. Just as he turned, I was stuffing the stolen pack of cigarettes into my jacket pocket. 'You!' he said. 'Stay right there!' When he was done ringing up his sale, he stepped toward me and grabbed my arm. Then, with his free hand, he removed the stolen cigarettes from my pocket and held them about an inch from my nose. 'You're going to learn a lesson,' he said loudly so all the other kids could hear. He had an assistant named Chuck, a young man who was in his early thirties, and Chuck was wiping down the counters over by the coffee machine. He told Chuck to take over at the cash register, and Chuck did as he was told. Leon then dragged me into the store's back office. There was a phone in the office, and Leon used it to call the police.

"Within minutes, a patrol car rolled into the parking lot, and an officer came into the store. Chuck led the cop to the back room where I was waiting with Leon, and Leon instructed the cop to arrest me. He told the cop he'd caught me trying to steal cigarettes and wanted to press charges. 'Why don't we just call his parents?' the officer said, offering a less extreme course of action, but Leon insisted that the cop handcuff me and take me away. 'I know this arrest may seem extreme,' Leon said to the officer, 'but I need to show these kids there's a price to be paid for shoplifting. If I let this boy go, the other kids won't have any respect for me. I need to set an example. Take this kid away, and lock him up!'"

"So were you arrested?" Rock asked.

"I was," Mr. Booker said. "The cop took me down to the station, where I was fingerprinted, photographed, and placed in a holding cell. A detective at the station asked me if I'd tried to steal the cigarettes, and I confessed to the crime. Yes, I'd been a thief, but I wasn't going to be a liar. My mom then had to pick me up and take me home. I was to appear in court several weeks later, and since I was under eighteen, a parent had to come with me. My dad agreed to join me, and we appeared before a judge. It took the better part of a day, sitting in the courtroom and waiting for my name to be called, and when our time finally came, it was late in the afternoon. The judge was nothing like I expected. He was a younger man, well groomed and energetic. I'd expected some scruffy old codger with whiskey on his breath and a gavel in his hand, like in the movies, like in an old black-and-white western. But this judge had a very youthful face, almost like a choir boy. He had sparkling blue eyes and a head of neatly styled blond hair. He read the charge against me methodically, as if it were the first case ever brought before him. Then he looked at me and asked, 'Do you deny stealing the cigarettes?' I said no, I didn't deny it, and he then said to my dad, 'We can't condone this kind of behavior. Have you talked with your boy? Do you think he'll do this again?' Dad said I'd been punished for my bad behavior. And that was true. He'd grounded me for two weeks, and he'd taken me to see Leon so I could formally apologize. It was awful, having to stand before Leon and say I was sorry. I felt like an idiot for having done such a stupid thing. The judge said, 'I'm giving you twenty hours of community service. The clerk will give you some paperwork to sign.' And that was it. My dad and I signed the papers, and the next thing I knew, we were in Dad's car, driving home."

"Did you do the community service?"

"Of course I did."

"What did you have to do?"

"I picked up litter at a public park for several weeks after school.

You'd be amazed at how many people just toss their trash on the ground rather than putting it in the waste cans. There were waste cans located in the park, but no one bothered to use them."

"So how would you describe your experience in court, facing a judge?"

"It was not what I expected."

"What'd you expect?"

"I'm not sure. I guess I thought the judge was going to rake me over the coals. I thought he was going to lecture me for an hour about shoplifting and why it was wrong for me to steal. I thought I was going to get an earful; instead, I got a quick and expedient punishment. He gave me twenty hours of community service, and that was it. It was so easy, like a transaction at Leon's convenience store—a bag of potato chips for a dollar sixty-nine. In my case, it was a pack of cigarettes for twenty hours of picking up trash."

"Did you know stealing was wrong before you grabbed the cigarettes?"

"Of course I did."

"But you took them anyway."

"Yes, that's true."

"This is what we don't understand," Rock said.

"What don't you get?"

"I don't understand why humans are constantly doing things they know are wrong. This happens all the time on Earth. Your courtrooms are full of people who get caught doing things they know they shouldn't do."

"I suppose that's true."

"How can we trust a species so prone to doing what it knows is wrong?" William asked.

"Trust is the issue," Ernie said.

"We want to be able to trust you," Rock said. "We really do."

"But how can we?" Ernie asked.

"Yes, Mr. Booker," Lucy said. "How can we?"

Mr. Booker looked at the council, wondering what to say. "I don't have a good answer for you."

"We think you do have an answer," William said. "We just think you don't want to admit it."

"And what would that answer be?"

"Simple," William said. "It's that humans can't be trusted."

"They know the difference between right and wrong," Ernie said. "Yet so often, they intentionally choose to do the wrong thing."

"Yes, more often than not," William said.

"It is troubling," Lucy said.

"Let's move along," Rock said to the council. Then, to Mr. Booker, he said, "Tell us about the second time you went to court. You said you went to court three times, and we'd like to hear about your second experience."

"The second time involved a traffic ticket I got seven years ago."

"A traffic ticket? You were breaking a law again?"

"I was cited for rolling through a stop sign rather than coming to a complete stop. It was five in the morning, and there wasn't a car or pedestrian in sight. So yes, I rolled through the stop sign, just like anyone else would have. What was the point of stopping, when there were no oncoming cars or pedestrians? I argued with the officer when he gave me the ticket, but I got nowhere with him. I told him what I'd done was safe and acceptable, but he was a by-the-book sort of fellow, a real Dudley Do-Right. He said, 'The law is the law,' and he handed me the citation. I went before a judge and argued my case, thinking I could convince him I hadn't been driving recklessly and didn't deserve to be cited."

"And what did the judge say?"

"He didn't agree with me. He backed the officer and said I had to pay the fine. He asked me only one question—whether or not I'd rolled through the stop sign. When I said yes, he said, 'Well, that's all I need to know.'"

"But you were driving safely?"

"Yes, of course. I'm a very careful driver. If there had been any cars or pedestrians around, I would've come to a complete stop."

"What would have happened if you'd refused to pay the fine?" Rock asked.

"They would've thrown me in jail."

"In jail?"

"It's illegal to ignore traffic fines."

"Ah, illegal," Ernie said, smiling.

"The law is the law!" Ralph said. He was being firm with Mr. Booker, mocking a judge. He banged his fist on the table, and when he started to laugh, William and Ernie joined in.

"Order in the court!" William said.

"Objection overruled!" Ernie said. The three men were all still laughing.

"Okay, okay," Rock said. He turned his attention back to Mr. Booker. "Tell us about your third time in court," he said. "Why a third time?"

"I was being sued."

"Sued by whom?"

"By a tree trimmer. He did some work at my house, and I refused to pay him. He sued me because he wanted to be paid for the work he'd done."

"So you were in civil court?"

"Yes, civil court."

"Why didn't you pay the man?"

"Because he did a lousy job. I hired him to trim all the trees in my backyard, but he butchered them. You should've seen what his workers did to my poor trees. His name was Angus Gonzales. He'd left a business card at my front door a couple weeks earlier, advertising his services. I called the number on the card, not knowing a thing about him, and he came out to the house to give me a price for the work. The price was reasonable, and I asked when he could start. I know I should've asked for some references. I should've checked the guy out. But he seemed like such a competent and personable fellow, and he had a very professional-looking business card. I asked if I needed to sign anything, and he said it was such a small job that no written contract was necessary. 'We do these kinds of jobs all the time,' he said. 'We can do a job like this with our eyes closed.' Well, in fact, when his crew was done, it looked like they *had* done it with their eyes closed. Jeez, what a mess it was! My backyard looked like it'd been ravaged by a tornado. It was the worst tree-trimming job I'd ever seen, and when Angus came by the next day for his check, I told him I'd pay him when hell froze over."

"So he sued you?" Rock asked.

"Oh yes," Mr. Booker said. "When I refused to pay, Angus's demeanor completely changed. He was no longer the personable man I'd met earlier on. Now he was very rude to me. And after we exchanged a lot of angry words, Angus ended our meeting by saying he'd see me in court. And sure enough, just a week or so later, I was served with papers saying that I had to appear. I couldn't believe this crook actually had the nerve to sue me when he'd done such a bad job! I took pictures of my backyard and had a landscape architect friend of mine check out what'd been done. He wrote me a letter giving me his opinion on Angus's poor workmanship. I planned to give the letter to the judge as evidence. When the time came for me to appear in court, I was ready to argue my side of the case, and I was confident I would win."

"So you convinced the judge?"

"Not exactly," Mr. Booker said.

"What happened?"

"The judge said obviously, Angus had done work on my trees, and he should be paid for his time. Angus told the judge the trees had simply been trimmed the same as he would have trimmed anyone else's trees; he trimmed trees all the time; and if I hadn't wanted them looking like they'd been trimmed, I should've just left them alone."

"What about the letter from your landscape architect friend about the quality of work?"

"The judge wouldn't even look at it. He said he would've questioned my friend as a witness had he come to court in person, but he wouldn't accept a letter from him. The letter was worthless."

"So you lost the case?"

"Sort of. The judge split Angus's invoice down the middle and told me to pay half. I guess it was a compromise. I don't think either of us was happy with the outcome."

"Do you still think Angus did a lousy job?"

"Of course I do."

"Do you think he did a lousy job deliberately?"

"No, probably not."

"Probably not?"

"No, I'm sure he thought he did a perfectly acceptable job."

"So he had good intentions?"

"Yes, he probably did."

"That's interesting," Rock said.

"It's typical," William said. "Your courtrooms are overflowing with this sort of nonsense."

"Don't you have the same problem on Og?"

"Never," William said.

"He doesn't know," Rock said.

"Apparently not," William said.

"What don't I know?" Mr. Booker asked.

"We have no courts on Og."

"None at all?"

"No laws, no police, no jails, and no judicial system. And best of all, we have no attorneys."

"That's hard to believe. How do you prevent people from misbehaving?"

"How would you define *misbehaving*?" Rock asked. "As in breaking laws? We have no laws to break. It is not an Ogonite's nature to do wrong. There's no point to it. Doing wrong serves no purpose, and it only causes harm to others. Why would we want to cause harm to others?"

"You don't have any bad people?"

"We have a few."

"How do you deal with them?"

"They're usually ostracized. Sometimes they're just killed."

"Killed?"

"It's perfectly acceptable to kill a misfit. Usually, they're just banished and sent off to live on their own, but sometimes they're killed. And anyone is allowed to kill them."

"And who determines if they're to die?"

"Whoever does the killing."

"And what's to keep people from killing for the wrong reasons?"

"Ogonites don't kill for the wrong reasons. I already told you we don't have any desire to do wrong. It serves no constructive purpose."

Mr. Booker stared at Rock for a moment. This all seemed unbelievable. He said, "You place an awful lot of faith in your people."

"We place no more faith in our people than you place in your laws. We'd rather place faith in people than in written laws."

"How can a society function without laws?"

"We trust ourselves," Ralph said.

"Yes, that says it all," Rock said.

"Yes," William said.

"Don't you people ever disagree on what is right and what is wrong?"

"We disagree all the time," Rock said.

"If you have no laws or courts, how do you settle your differences?"

"We settle them between ourselves, like adults. Since when do adults need a third party to come to the rescue and settle every dispute?"

"But what if the two sides can't agree?"

"What does it matter?" Rock said. "Life goes on, Mr. Booker. Life moves on whether the parties settle their dispute or not. This is something humans don't seem to understand. An unresolved dispute doesn't stop the world from turning."

"Don't you have issues that *have* to be resolved?"

"Such as?"

"I don't know. How about abortion?"

"All our children are wanted."

"How about wars?"

"We don't wage wars. There's no need for them."

"Heck," Mr. Booker said. "How about taxes?"

"We have no taxes."

"I have a question for you," Ernie said to Mr. Booker, leaning forward.

"Yes?" Mr. Booker said.

"Why are human beings so afraid of themselves? Why don't they have more faith in each other?"

"I'm not sure I understand."

"Why is it necessary to write down every little rule, law, and regulation you can imagine and force yourselves to follow them? Why do you need police departments? And why do you need all your courtrooms? If you know how you should be living, why can't you trust yourselves to live that way?"

"It's a good question," William said.

"I don't have an answer," Mr. Booker said.

"We avoid the law trap," Ernie said.

"That we do," William said.

"The law trap?" Mr. Booker said.

"All civilizations that write laws become victims of what we call the law trap. You're hardly alone. We see it happen all the time."

"I have no idea what you mean."

Lucy spoke up. "My good friends on the council are referring to a social phenomenon we discovered several hundred years ago. We call it the law trap. We made the observation that societies that write laws for their citizens become victims of those very laws. It's a trap, if you will. You think you're creating order, when in fact, you're encouraging the opposite. We've seen that the more a society tries to define morality through laws, the more immoral its behavior becomes."

"I don't get it."

"Think for a moment. Isn't it true that your people on Earth assume if they're following the laws, they're behaving morally?"

"Yes, I suppose so."

"Intuition is ignored," William said.

"But the law is revered," Lucy said.

"You know in your hearts what is right and what's wrong," Ernie said. "But it's the laws you pay attention to. It's the laws you respect."

"I'll give you a simple example," Lucy said. "When that police officer gave you the ticket for rolling through a stop sign, he was following the letter of the law, wasn't he?"

"Yes," Mr. Booker said.

"His decision to write you a ticket had nothing to do with what was right or what was wrong. You simply broke the letter of the law."

"Yes, I did."

"And laws are not morals," William said.

"Laws are just laws," Lucy said. "The fact is that you really did nothing wrong. The police officer who gave you the ticket was wrong, not you. He shouldn't have harassed you for driving in a safe manner. Surely he knew you weren't posing any threat to anyone. He may have somehow convinced himself that he was acting morally, but he was wronging you."

"It's the law trap," Ernie said.

"It can be dangerous," Lucy said.

"Very dangerous," Ernie agreed.

"And it concerns us."

"Why?" Mr. Booker asked.

"It means humans can't be trusted to behave morally," William said. "They can only be counted on to follow their written laws. Because of these laws, their morality has atrophied."

"I'll give you an example," Ernie said. "Do you remember the Iraq War?"

"Of course I do."

"Let me ask a question about President Bush. What would've happened if, around the same time as this war, he had suspected his wife of cheating on him with another man? Let's say he had no proof, but he was sure of her infidelity. What if he hired a hit man to do away with Laura? I know it sounds crazy, but follow along. You'll see this premise isn't at all far-fetched. What do you think would've happened if Laura was murdered by the hit man, and the truth came out in the press? Let's say the police caught Laura's killer, and he told them everything about his relationship with George. Would the president still be loved and respected, or would he be despised for what he did?"

"He'd be despised, obviously. You can't go around murdering your wife."

"He would've broken the law, and humans don't like it when you break their laws. They cry for justice! Bush would've been prosecuted, and a judge would've locked him up, maybe even putting him on death row. His charmed life would have been over."

"To be sure," Mr. Booker said.

"But that's not what he did."

"No, of course not."

"But what did he do?"

"To Laura?"

"No, to the people of Iraq. He suspected Saddam Hussein of developing weapons of mass destruction just as he might have suspected Laura of being unfaithful. He mobilized an all-out war against Iraq, and under his leadership, the United States searched high and low for the weapons. And guess what. They didn't find a thing! The entire war was over nothing at all. Do you know how many humans died in the war?"

"Not exactly."

"Nearly a quarter of a million."

"Okay."

"It was a catastrophe measured not just by loss of life, senseless injury, and a phenomenal destruction of property but also by the hundreds of thousands orphans the war left in its wake. Orphans, Mr. Booker! Innocent and parentless children by the thousands. I don't think most Americans realize the extent to which their country ravaged the people of Iraq. And what about George Bush? Yes, he would've been hated and prosecuted for killing Laura, a single person, but for his part in the bloody Iraq War, he was given a pass. And why was this? How did he get away with such blatant murder and mayhem? I'll tell you exactly why. It was because he followed the letter of the law. His actions were all legal and proper. You may laugh and think Ogonites are completely crazy for having no laws, but we think you're foolish for having them. Only in a country that abides by laws with such blind fervor would such a monumentally immoral act be allowed to occur. It's the law trap, Mr. Booker, and it worries us. Human beings cause us concern."

"Grave concern," William said. He took his glasses off again to wipe them on his lapel. Ralph stroked his beard for the umpteenth time, and Lucy stared at Mr. Booker and sighed. She'd been hoping for some encouraging words from him, but he just sat there without saying a word. He was speechless.

CHAPTER 16

FIRE WITH FIRE

Mr. Booker and Sid were eating dinner in the cafeteria following the afternoon session with the council. Mr. Booker said, "I feel like I'm climbing up a sand dune. Every time I take one step forward, I feel like I'm slipping two steps back. It's so frustrating. It's like I'm getting nowhere."

Sid reached across the table for a salt shaker and said, "I've got a good one for you."

"A good what?"

"A good joke."

"Let's hear it," Mr. Booker said. "I could use a good joke. I need something to make me laugh."

Sid sprinkled some salt on his dinner and proceeded to tell the joke to Mr. Booker. "I heard this one yesterday," Sid said. "There's a human being named Joshua Smith. He goes to a cardiologist, complaining of chronic chest pains. The human doctor performs all sorts of tests and examinations and then meets with Josh in his private office. 'There's no sense beating around the bush,' he says. 'You need a heart transplant, and you need it right away.' Josh asks the doctor if there are any hearts available on such short notice. 'There are three hearts you can choose from,' the doctor says. 'But they vary in price.' Joshua asks what the difference is, and the doctor describes the hearts to him. 'The first heart is from an eighteen-year-old kid who was a nonsmoker and swimmer. He was in excellent shape, but he hit his head on the edge of a swimming pool and died. His heart is available for a hundred thousand dollars, and this is the lowest-priced heart I have available. There's a second heart we can get that comes from a twenty-four-year-old marathon runner. He too was in great condition and never smoked or drank a day in his life. He was hit by a bus while running a race, and he died instantly. His heart is going for a hundred and fifty thousand. Then, of course, there's the third heart, and this one costs more than the first two. It's from a fifty-one-year-old heavy drinker, cigar smoker, and steak lover. His heart is priced at a little over five hundred thousand.' Josh is surprised by the price of the third heart, and he asks the doctor why it's so expensive. 'It's from a lawyer,' the doctor explains. 'It costs more because it's never been used.'"

Both Sid and Mr. Booker laughed. "That is pretty funny," Mr. Booker said.

"I have more," Sid said, and he proceeded to tell Mr. Booker more jokes while they ate. The jokes cheered Mr. Booker up, and by the time they were done eating dinner, Mr. Booker felt a lot better than he had when they'd first sat down.

When they'd finished their meals, the two men stood up and left the cafeteria. Sid put his hand on Mr. Booker's shoulder and told him not to worry. "You're doing fine, my boy. Don't let the council get you down. It's their job to be a little cynical."

When Mr. Booker returned to his cabin, he plopped down on the sofa and picked up his copy of *Uncle Tom's Cabin*. He struggled through several pages but found it difficult to get into the story. He didn't feel much like reading, so he set the book down.

Mr. Booker told me sometimes he could read books with great ease, yet other times he found it impossible. This was one of those impossible times, so he leaned back, propping a throw pillow behind his head. He looked up at the ceiling and thought about his recent sessions with the council. The more he thought about them, the more uneasy he felt. "Think about something else," he said out loud to himself. He tried to let his mind relax and go to a more pleasant place, but for some reason, Drew Mathews popped into his thoughts.

Drew had been a student in Mr. Booker's world history class the previous fall. Mr. Booker had taught all kinds of kids over the years, but Drew stood out.

The kid had some serious behavioral issues and was the kind of student every teacher dreaded having to teach. He was disruptive, galling, and, at times, outright belligerent, and he had a reputation for stirring up all kinds of trouble. He had no desire to be in school and was only there because the law required it. Mr. Booker had learned a lot about Drew prior to the day he showed up for his class. He'd heard other teachers gossiping and complaining about him during breaks between classes in the teachers' lounge. It was just one dreadful story after another.

Mr. Booker didn't fear the boy. He was intrigued by him, and he told me about his experience with him. He said there was nothing outrageous about his appearance. He was unlike kids who tried to get attention through crazy hairstyles and provocative clothing. He looked like any other kid at school. He was about the same height and build as most boys his age, and his blond hair was cut conservatively short. He was not extraordinarily handsome, nor was he ugly. He had a forgettable and generic face, the sort of face that could be easily lost in a crowd. If you were to judge Drew solely by his appearance, nothing would grab your attention or cause you any alarm. But he was Drew Mathews. Mr. Booker told me, "Everybody in the school knew about Drew, teachers and students alike. Most teachers feared him, not because he was dangerous but because he was so annoying and unpredictable. He wasn't a violent boy, nor was he a bully. He just did a lot of weird and mischievous things. You could often find him smoking in the boys' room or sitting in the principal's office, being reprimanded for his behavior."

Mr. Booker believed in his skills as a teacher. He considered himself one of the school's best instructors. He prided himself on being able to inspire even the most difficult students, so he saw Drew as a challenge, not a thorn in his side. When the other teachers asked how Drew was doing in his class, he'd always say the same thing: as long as Drew showed up and sat at his desk, Mr. Booker would treat him fairly and no differently than any other student. He'd say, "All children deserve a break and a decent education. That's what public school is all about. That's why we're all here." He'd also say, "No one ever said teaching would be easy." He liked to say these things to the other teachers, and he felt strongly about them. No matter how much grief Drew tried to cause, he wasn't going to give up on him. Drew was a boy, not an adult. He was only sixteen years old, still legally a child, and didn't all children deserve a chance to learn and grow into well-adjusted and productive adults? If anyone could provide such a chance, it was Mr. Booker. No, he would not give up on the boy.

It didn't take long for Drew to test Mr. Booker's resolve. During one of Mr. Booker's first lectures, while he was explaining the six basic characteristics of a civilization, he asked the class to come up with their own examples. The six characteristics were cities, government, religion, social structure, writing, and art. The categories came directly from the class textbook, and Mr. Booker stood in front of the class and wrote them on the whiteboard. Drew immediately raised his hand, not just casually but up high in order to get Mr. Booker's attention. He was determined to be called upon. He was using his other hand to hold up his arm, as if the raised arm were heavy and needed support. "Mr. Booker, sir?" he said. Mr. Booker was surprised at Drew's desire to start things off.

Had he inspired the boy already? What would Drew have to say? Which category would he pick, and what kind of example would he give? Mr. Booker called on Drew and asked, "Do you have an example for us?"

"No," Drew said. "Not really."

"But you raised your hand."

"I need to ask you something."

"What is it?"

"Can I be excused?"

"Excused?"

"I need to crap," he said. The kids in the class laughed.

"You mean now?"

"I really have to go."

"But we just started. Couldn't you have gone between classes?"

"I can't help it. It just suddenly came on." Drew wriggled in his seat and added, "Seriously, dude, I've got a turtle head poking out."

"A turtle head?"

"It's nearly touching cloth!"

Mr. Booker stared at the boy for a moment and then, realizing there was no point in denying him, said, "Fine. You can go."

"I'll need a pass."

"Yes, I guess you will," Mr. Booker said. He went to his desk, wrote Drew a hall pass, and handed it to him. Drew then left the room, and Mr. Booker began where he'd left off with the rest of the class.

Just a few minutes later, the class was interrupted by the loud bleating of the school fire alarm. Someone swung open the door to the room, and everyone looked. It was the school janitor, Mr. Higgins, and his eyes and mouth were open wide, as if he'd just seen a ghost. "There's a fire!" he exclaimed. "You've got to evacuate! Everyone needs to leave right now!" The kids stood up from their desks and hurried toward the door. Some of them seemed frightened, while others were laughing and enjoying the drill, pleased that class was being interrupted. Mr. Booker made his way to the doorway, and as he passed through it, sure enough, he saw that the hallway was filled with smoke.

"Don't panic," Mr. Booker said to his students. They spilled into the hall and made their way to the exit doors. For a short while, the hallway was a madhouse, but in no time, the entire school had been evacuated, and the teachers and students were all standing outside in the fresh air and sunlight. The kids were talking about the fire, describing what they thought they'd seen while inside the burning building. Several fire engines showed up at the scene, and firemen wearing all their gear ran into the building, searching for the fire. It didn't take long for them to find what they were looking for. In fact, there was no fire at all. Instead, the firemen found the charred rolled-up newspaper and tinfoil remnants of a homemade smoke bomb. It was behind a waste can near the boys' restroom. The entire evacuation had been the result of a prank. When Mr. Booker found out about the smoke bomb, he immediately thought of Drew Mathews.

Had it been Drew? Mr. Booker had given the boy a hall pass and let him loose without any supervision. It was just the sort of thing Drew would do, wasn't it?

The firemen opened the windows in the hallways and classrooms, and they turned on fans to blow out all the smoke. It took a couple hours for the rooms to clear. Mr. Booker looked for Drew outside, but he was nowhere to be found.

The next day, Drew showed up in class as though nothing had happened. Mr. Booker asked Drew to see him after school. He wanted to talk about the smoke bomb and ask Drew if he was responsible for setting it off. He didn't want to get the boy in trouble, and he didn't want to send him to the principal. He just wanted to know the truth, and he wanted to talk to the boy privately. He wanted to see if he could get through to him and help him understand why what he'd done was wrong. As it turned out, the principal spoke over the intercom system that morning and asked the students to provide any information they had about the incident. It was promised that their names would be kept confidential, and that afternoon, three kids from Mr. Booker's class came forth and informed the principal that Drew had been excused to use the restroom just several minutes before the smoke bomb was set off. Mr. Booker was subsequently called in to meet with the principal to confirm whether or not that information was true, and he had to be honest and say yes. The principal asked Mr. Booker why he hadn't come forward, and Mr. Booker told him, "We have no proof that Drew did this, and I didn't want the boy to be accused of something he didn't do."

"We all know he probably did it," the principal said. "What the hell, Booker?"

"What the hell what?"

"What the hell were you thinking? We're talking about Drew Mathews. We know the kind of kid he is. Why would you try to protect him?"

"Someone has to," Mr. Booker said. He knew he shouldn't have said that. It was a dumb thing to say, and the principal looked at him as if he were crazy.

"You know, what he did was a crime."

"I know."

"This is a serious matter. One that should be handled by the police."

"I was planning on talking to Drew after school."

"Christ, Booker," the principal said. "What were you thinking? The kid's a bad seed. After all the years you've been teaching, I'd think you'd have learned to spot a bad seed when you see one."

Mr. Booker told me, "Just between you and me, I never did discover any evidence that proved Drew set off the smoke bomb, but if I had, I probably would've kept it to myself. I didn't want to see Drew get kicked out of school, and that's exactly what would've happened. He would've been expelled, and then what chance would the boy have had to get his life together?"

Weeks passed following the smoke bomb incident, and with the exception of a few minor classroom disruptions, Drew was behaving himself. There were no major incidents until the altruism project. The altruism project was one of Mr. Booker's favorite class assignments. Each semester, he had his students carry out the project in each of his classes. He'd have the kids come up with a favorite charity and a money-raising idea, and then he'd have them use their time outside of class to earn donations. That particular class decided to wash cars during a weekend, and they wanted to give the money they earned to the Make-A-Wish Foundation, a charity that made wishes come true for children with terminal illnesses. Mr. Booker thought it was a great cause, and he helped the kids organize their plans by calling a property manager and securing a portion of a shopping center parking lot on a busy Mission Viejo street corner. Over a Saturday and Sunday, the kids worked their tails off washing cars, and they brought in nearly five hundred dollars.

The money was all cash, and Mr. Booker kept it in the locked drawer in his desk at school. He was going to have a representative of the foundation come to the class, where the kids would present him with the money they'd earned. However, two days before the presentation, something awful happened: the window to his classroom was broken at night, and someone made his or her way through the opening, pried open his desk drawer, and took all the money. Mr. Booker found the broken window and jimmied drawer the next morning. He had a terrible feeling in the pit of his stomach. He knew right away who probably had done it, despite his desire to feel otherwise. Surely, it had to have been Drew. Everyone in the class, including Drew, knew where he kept the car wash earnings, but only Drew was the kind of kid who'd actually have the nerve to steal it. To say Mr. Booker was disappointed was an understatement. He tried to decide what to do. Would he confront Drew with his suspicions and ask him outright if he'd broken into the desk? No, that was the wrong way to go about things. Instead, he told the class what had happened. "I'm not going to point fingers at anyone," he told them. "I have no idea who did this. I simply want whoever was responsible to see me after school and return the money. I'm not going to make a big deal out of it. I only want to talk to you. And I do want the money returned."

Well, days went by, and no one fessed up. The more he thought about it, the more convinced Mr. Booker was that Drew was responsible. Finally, Mr. Booker had Drew stay after school so he could talk to him. He was careful how he worded his question to Drew. He said, "Drew, you're a pretty bright kid, and you seem to have a finger on the pulse of what's going on at this school. Do you have any idea who stole the car wash money? I need your help."

"You think I did it," Drew snapped.

"No, that's not what I'm saying. I just think you know a lot of things."

"You think I did it," Drew said again.

"I didn't say that."

"But it's what you think. It's what everyone thinks, isn't it? You're just like everyone else at this stupid school. When something bad happens, you automatically suspect Drew Mathews. I may as well have done it. You think I did it, so I may as well have done it. And now I wish I had done it. I could use a few hundred dollars."

Was that an admission of guilt? Who knew? Or maybe he was right to be angry. Maybe he hadn't stolen the money. Maybe it was wrong to assume the worst of him.

Mr. Booker never did come out and accuse Drew of setting off the smoke bomb or stealing the car wash money. He wanted the boy to feel someone had faith in him despite his reputation. He said to me, "I don't believe there's such a thing as a bad seed. I think some kids are just a little misguided, for whatever reasons. It's no cause to write them off. And having some faith in them might just be the very thing that helps them. After all, who of us is perfect? Haven't we all done things we're not proud of?"

When the world history class was over, Mr. Booker no longer had Drew in any of his classes. He felt as though he'd made some headway with the boy and was a little disappointed he was no longer Drew's teacher. Given more time, he might have been able to help the kid more. As for Drew, things would take a serious turn for the worse. Drew quickly became the talk of the school the next semester. He found himself taking chemistry with Mr. Bishop, a teacher known to have little patience for unruly or disrespectful students. Drew deliberately belched loudly in the middle of one of Mr. Bishop's lectures, and Mr. Bishop told Drew to see him after school. According to Drew, the two of them met after school, and Mr. Bishop scolded him. However, according to Mr. Bishop, things got ugly. He wound up being pummeled by Drew in a fit of adolescent rage. There were no witnesses, but everyone believed Mr. Bishop. The story had the whole school talking. It was true that Mr. Bishop's eye was swollen shut, and his lip was split. He had obviously taken a beating from someone. He maintained the boy had assaulted him, and the principal immediately called the police. Drew was arrested and charged with the crime. He was expelled from school, and Mr. Bishop no longer had Drew in his class.

Were Mr. Bishop's wounds self-inflicted? Mr. Booker told me he thought they were. He'd never known Drew to be violent, and he found it hard to believe he'd actually beat up one of his teachers. Drew was incorrigible and annoying, but he was not a violent boy. Mr. Booker heard Mr. Bishop talking to one of the other teachers several weeks later in the teachers' lounge. He said, "Sometimes you just have to fight fire with fire." The other teacher smiled and nodded. The problem of Drew Mathews had been solved.

Mr. Booker said to me, "You're probably wondering what any of this has to do with the Ogonites."

"Yes," I said.

"We were their problem child," he said. "Don't you see? They were keeping us after class, and what was I supposed to do? So far, I'd answered all their questions, and I'd listened to their complaints. When the sessions with the council first started, I thought we might have a chance. But the proceedings may just have been a deceptive formality, and for all I knew, they'd already made up their minds. Who really knew? I certainly didn't know. As I lay on my couch in my cabin, I realized I had no way of knowing what they were really thinking. I didn't have a clue if my answers meant anything to them at all. For all I knew, they were just covering their tracks so that they could wipe us out and say, 'Well, folks, we gave them a chance!'"

"Wipe us out?" I asked.

"That's what I was thinking. That's where my mind was going. We were about to be expelled from school."

CHAPTER 17

A TEAM EFFORT

The next morning, it was a few minutes before eight when Sid and Mr. Booker walked from the cafeteria toward the council chambers. It had been Mr. Booker's suggestion that they both have buttermilk pancakes for breakfast. Sid seemed to like the pancakes, and Mr. Booker said they were as good as any on Earth. As Mr. Booker entered the council chambers with Sid, he could still taste maple syrup, molten butter, and pancakes in his mouth, a sensation that ordinarily would've invigorated him. However, that morning, his eyes felt heavy, and his stomach was distended. Perhaps he'd eaten too much. Or maybe his lethargy was due to the fact that he'd had so much difficulty falling sleeping the previous night. He wished he could've slept another couple hours. He wanted to feel alert for that morning's session, but the truth was, he was not in the mood for being grilled by the council.

He and Sid took their seats in the middle of the room, and Rock called the meeting to order. The council members looked at Mr. Booker as if there were something wrong with him. "Are you okay?" Rock asked.

"I'm fine," Mr. Booker said.

"You look tired."

"I am tired."

"Trouble sleeping last night?"

"A little," Mr. Booker said.

"Did you forget to comb your hair this morning?"

"Did I?" Mr. Booker asked, and he turned to look at Sid, who just smiled and nodded. "Why didn't you tell me?" he whispered to Sid.

"Go on," Sid said. "It doesn't matter."

"Are you able to continue?" Rock asked, and Mr. Booker turned to look at him.

"Yes, I'll be fine."

"We need you to be coherent and attentive."

"Don't worry about me."

"Very well. I'm going to turn the questioning over to Lucy. She'd like to get things started."

"Can I ask a question first?" Mr. Booker said.

"Of course," Rock said.

"Do my answers to your questions really matter? Do you really care what I have to say?"

"Of course we do. Why would you even ask that? We're listening to everything you tell us."

"Sometimes I feel these council sessions are just an empty formality, like you're trying to make me feel as though what I say matters, when you already know what you're going to do."

"No, Mr. Booker. I can promise you no decisions regarding your planet have been made by any of us. If our minds were made up, we'd go ahead and take action without wasting your time. But our minds are not made up, and we're listening to everything you say. Your answers to our questions are important."

"Okay," Mr. Booker said.

"Does that make you feel any better?"

"I'm not sure."

"Just be honest," Rock said. "Your honesty means a great deal to us."

"Okay."

"Can we now proceed?"

"Yes, I guess."

"Like I said, Lucy has some questions for you."

"I do," Lucy said. Mr. Booker looked at her, and she smiled. Hopefully she would go easy on him. He wasn't in the mood for being ridiculed.

"Good morning," Lucy said.

"Good morning," Mr. Booker replied.

"First, I have a very simple question for you. It requires only a yes-or-no answer. Mr. Booker, do you own any guns?"

"I don't," Mr. Booker said.

"None at all?"

"No, none at all," Mr. Booker said.

"Isn't that unusual?" Lucy asked.

"Unusual?"

"Don't most Americans own at least one gun?"

"Not necessarily."

"Do you know how many guns are in your country?" Lucy asked. She was looking at her monitor when she asked this.

"I have no idea."

Lucy read from the screen. "There are approximately three hundred sixty million guns in the United States. That's about forty million more guns than there are people. Does that figure surprise you?"

"Actually, yes, it does."

"Is there a reason behind this?"

"A reason?"

"We're looking for a reason. There must be some logical reason why Americans find it necessary to own so many guns. Why are human beings so obsessed with having the ability to kill one another? That's what a gun is for, isn't it? Isn't the purpose of a gun to kill another living thing?"

"Yes, it is."

"Do you all plan to kill each other?"

"No, of course not."

Lucy stared at Mr. Booker for a moment and then asked, "Are you familiar with a man named George Zimmerman?"

"The name rings a bell."

"He shot and killed a seventeen-year-old high school student named Trayvon Martin some years ago. It was a sensational story at the time, in the newspapers and on TV. Do you recall the incident?"

"Yes, I do remember it."

"Tell me what you think about it. What do you have to say about a country that condones a grown man getting into a physical scuffle with a seventeen-year-old boy and then shooting him dead with a gun? Doesn't it seem odd to you that Mr. Zimmerman was found not guilty?"

"It was a complicated situation."

"What was so complicated about it?"

"Zimmerman felt threatened. He said he feared for his life."

"Feared for his life?"

"That's how the court saw it—that he was defending himself."

"Defending himself from an unarmed seventeen-year-old boy? You don't think there's something terribly wrong with this?" Lucy asked, raising her voice a little. "Don't you think there's something wrong with a society that says it's okay for a man to murder an unarmed child? Trayvon was just a kid, wasn't he? He could've been one of your students, Mr. Booker. And he wasn't doing anything wrong or anything suspicious. He had every right to be where he was. He was walking from a nearby convenience store on his way back to his father's fiancée's home, where he was an invited guest. What was so threatening about that?"

"I don't know."

"When Zimmerman called the police, he told them, 'These assholes—they always get away.' He just assumed Trayvon was a criminal. Isn't there something seriously wrong with this?"

"Yes, I guess so."

"Then he killed him."

"He did do that."

"Shot him dead with his handgun."

"Yes, he shot him dead."

"I'll tell you something about this story that you probably don't know. Do you know what happened to the handgun that was used to kill Trayvon?"

"No, I don't."

"The police gave it back to Zimmerman."

"They did?" Mr. Booker said.

"Yes, they did, and do you know what he recently did with the gun?"

"No, I don't."

"He put it up for auction."

"For auction?"

"It was advertised as the weapon used to kill Trayvon Martin. People from all over submitted bids, hoping to get their hands on it. Zimmerman finally found a gun collector willing to pay a quarter of a million dollars. Doesn't this upset you? Don't you find it kind of sick? When people found out about this auction, they were outraged, and Zimmerman told them he was giving the proceeds to charity. It sounds to me like he made that up. Do you believe he planned to give the money to a charity?"

"I don't know."

"And don't you find it bizarre that someone would pay so much money for the gun? Why did the buyer want it?"

"I don't know."

"Can you explain it?"

"I don't think I can."

Lucy didn't roll her eyes or show any other signs of being disappointed with Mr. Booker's answer, but she looked to her left, toward the other council members. It was her way of turning the inquiry over to them, and Ernie spoke first. He said, "Seldom, in all our travels, have we come across civilizations so head over heels in love with their weapons."

"It's a love affair," Ralph said.

"If it weren't so alarming, it'd be amusing," Ernie said. "But we find it very disturbing. Humans are as obsessed with injuring and killing each other as they are with having sex."

"Is that really true?" Mr. Booker asked.

"It's a wonder," Ralph said.

"A real wonder," William agreed.

"What's a wonder?" Mr. Booker asked.

"It's a wonder, with all these weapons floating around, humans have managed to survive at all."

"Are you a science-fiction fan?" Ralph asked, looking at Mr. Booker.

"I can take it or leave it," Mr. Booker said.

"But you've read a few of these science-fiction books? And surely you've seen a few movies?"

"Yes, a few."

"We've noticed something revealing in these stories," Ralph said. "It's something troubling but also clear and inescapable."

"Clear as the nose on your face," Ernie said.

"I don't know what you're talking about," Mr. Booker said.

"The most common theme of your science-fiction stories is war, Mr. Booker," Ralph said. "War, war, and more war. You can't seem to get enough of it. You imagine your species at war either with itself or with machines or evil and marauding aliens. But no one ever seems to get along in your stories. The overriding mind-set is always one side pitted against the other, shooting at each other and blowing each other up."

"The *Star Wars* movies," Ernie said. "They seem to be the most popular of them all. The movie's title says it all, doesn't it?"

"War, dammit!" Ralph said, and he slammed his fist down on the table. Everyone laughed.

"Man the cannons!" Ernie said.

"Bombs away!" William said.

"They can't help themselves," William said. "It's in their DNA."

"It's how you see your future," Ralph said. "You're always shooting at each other with ray guns, deadly lasers, and photon torpedoes or taking swings at each other with your lightsabers."

"Is that how you see your future?" Ernie asked. "Is that the sort of world that comes up when you look into your crystal ball?"

"I guess I've never really thought about it," Mr. Booker said. "But now that you mention it, it does seem kind of weird."

"I have another question for you," Ernie said. "Do you know how much your country will spend on its military this year?"

"No, I actually don't."

Ernie looked at his computer monitor and read the statistic. "It will be over six hundred billion dollars. More than half your country's discretionary spending will go into your weaponry and into maintaining and building up your military forces."

"Yes, it's a dangerous world," Mr. Booker said.

"Only because human beings make it dangerous," Ernie said.

"Would you have us become a weaker nation? Would you have us fall to our enemies?"

"Your human enemies," Rock said.

"Yes, our human enemies."

"Don't you hear yourself?"

"I don't think he gets it," Ralph said.

"I don't think any of them get it," William said.

"Get what?" Mr. Booker asked.

"Our concern isn't with America," Rock said. "And it isn't with Russia, China, or Iran. Our concern is with the whole lot of you. Our concern is with human beings."

"It's the big picture," Ralph said.

"The human picture," William added. "Your entire civilization."

Mr. Booker looked at Lucy, who had been quiet during all of this. He was hoping she'd join in and say something encouraging. But instead, she shook her head and said, "I have to agree with the rest of the council, Mr. Booker. Unless you have some sort of explanation, we'll continue to have serious concerns with the behavior of your species. Are we wrong about humans? Now's the time to tell us how we're wrong."

Mr. Booker thought about this for a moment. He said, "No, you aren't wrong. It's like you say. I'm ashamed to admit it, but it's all true."

"I have another question for you," Lucy said.

"Go ahead," Mr. Booker said.

"It's a very simple one. And maybe it will help to make our concerns clearer."

"Okay," Mr. Booker said.

"We know George Zimmerman pulled the trigger of his gun, but who do you think actually killed Trayvon Martin?"

"I don't understand the question."

"Did Zimmerman kill the boy?"

"He did. That's never been disputed."

"With his gun?"

"Yes, obviously, with his gun."

"And where did the gun come from?" Lucy asked.

"A gun store, I suppose."

"So someone sold him the gun?"

"Yes," Mr. Booker said.

"This person sold the gun in order to make a business profit?"

"I would assume so."

"Isn't the purpose of a handgun to shoot people?"

"Yes, that's fair to say."

"So doesn't the gun store owner share some of the blame for Trayvon's death, having sold a deadly weapon to a man he barely knew? The gun shop owner was fully aware of the purpose of a handgun. It's not all his fault that Zimmerman killed the boy, but certainly he should be held partially accountable."

"I can agree with that."

"And where did the gun shop owner get the gun?"

"I don't know," Mr. Booker said. "From a broker? Or maybe directly from the manufacturer?"

"Let's say he got it from the manufacturer. How did the gun get from the manufacturer to the gun store owner? I mean, what was the means of transport?"

"A delivery truck?"

"So a driver was hired to operate the truck and deliver the gun? No doubt the driver knew what he was delivering since he unloaded the merchandise at the gun store, and certainly, just like the shop proprietor, he knew the purpose of a gun. Everyone knows what guns are for. Isn't all of this a fair assumption?"

"Yes, I think so."

"So doesn't the driver bear some blame? He could've refused to deliver the gun. He knew he was delivering a lethal weapon to be sold to the general public, but he made the delivery and was paid for his efforts."

"True enough."

"So we've established that both the gun store owner and the truck driver share some responsibility. Now, what about the government agency that allowed Zimmerman to carry a concealed firearm? He was licensed to carry a gun, no? Didn't anyone bother to check the guy out and ask why he needed to be walking around with a loaded handgun? Isn't the agency responsible for seeing to it that only the appropriate people are allowed to arm themselves? I mean, honestly, Mr. Booker, do they just hand out permits to anyone who walks through their doors?"

"I don't know."

"Someone in the government bears responsibility for this. Some person didn't do his job. Why did Zimmerman need to carry a gun? I can't think of a good reason for it. Can you? He wasn't a cop. He wasn't trained by any expert on the proper use of lethal force."

"No, he wasn't."

"Yet he was given a license."

"That's true."

"Maybe the person in charge of his application didn't ask the right questions. But shouldn't this person have known what questions to ask? I'm not saying the person effectively pulled the trigger or that he told Zimmerman it was okay to shoot a defenseless kid, but he does have culpability. Otherwise, what's the purpose of him even having his job?"

"All good points."

"So think about this. Now we have the person at the government agency, the gun shop owner, and also the man who made the delivery to the gun shop. That's three people who had a hand in setting up the shooting. But it doesn't end there. What about the company that manufactured the gun? They didn't tell Zimmerman to pull the trigger, but certainly they bear some blame. They make deadly weapons, as many as they possibly can, and deliberately distribute them to the public. They know full well what the purpose of a handgun is, which is to shoot people. So how much blame should we assign to them?"

"I don't know."

"How much blame to their executives, their employees, and their subcontractors? They're all in on it, aren't they? They're all a part of this scheme to sell lethal weapons to the public for a profit. Think of all the people involved. There are the engineers who design the guns and draw up plans describing every detail of their manufacture and assembly. There are people who procure the raw materials required, and clerks sign for the deliveries. Workers then forge and anneal the steel into the needed parts, and machinists work on the frames, cylinders, and other components. Then there are other workers who assemble all the parts and carry out the product's quality control. And don't forget the pencil pushers, the employees who manage all the paperwork. There's the accounting staff, the professionals who keep the financial books up to date and write all the checks. There are secretaries, janitors, and security guards. I'm sure I'm missing someone. The point is that manufacturing a simple gun requires a whole slew of people, and all of them know exactly what they're doing and what their company is producing. They're helping to put as many guns as they possibly can into the hands of your citizens. Are you getting the picture?"

"I think so," Mr. Booker said.

"And this is only the beginning."

"It is?"

"There are many more to blame. There are all the characters who were vandalizing and stealing from residents at the townhouse project that Zimmerman was patrolling. Someone needed to take charge and stop them, and Zimmerman was only trying to help. Shouldn't we be pointing a finger at those people? What gave them the right? They're the ones who created the perilous environment in the first place. Without them and all their illegal shenanigans, there would've been no shooting. Nothing would ever have happened."

"I see what you mean."

"And I'm still not done."

"No?" Mr. Booker said.

"There's the media," Lucy said. "They contributed as much to this killing as anyone."

"The media?"

"Yes, I blame the media. Don't you suppose George Zimmerman watched television?"

"I suppose he did."

"Don't all human beings watch TV?"

"Most do."

"Have you ever watched the six o'clock news? You must be aware of the stories these networks push on their viewing public. Watching this nonsense, you'd think every citizen ought to be armed. They make the world out to be a perpetually threatening place filled with crime and dangerous miscreants. It's a matter of self-preservation. You need to protect yourselves, right? You have a right and obligation to keep yourselves safe and protect your loved ones. Who can blame Zimmerman for carrying a gun? Watching the news, you'd think trouble was lurking around every corner. It's a paranoia constantly induced by your media. It's hard for us to believe there aren't more shootings than there are."

"I see what you mean."

"And of course, there's also Hollywood."

"Hollywood?"

"The film industry, Mr. Booker. All your crazy movies and TV shows. It's all of them combined! Do you watch any of these?"

"Not too often."

"Problems between humans aren't solved with reason or intelligence. Problems are solved with guns. Yes, all those deadly guns! What would Hollywood ever do without them? From James Arness as Matt Dillon to Clint Eastwood as Dirty Harry to Bradley

Cooper acting out the deadly accomplishments of Chris Kyle, they're all the same. If you were to exclude guns from movies and TV shows, you'd literally shut the industry down. You'd bring the writers to their knees, and the actors and directors wouldn't know what to do with themselves. It's pathetic, isn't it? And think of the influence this all has on the citizens of your country. Your species has been brainwashed! Everyone thinks he or she needs to own a gun to protect him-or herself from the other guy who has one. One gun begets another, and around and around you go, until everyone is armed and ready to pull the trigger."

"So you blame Hollywood?"

"I say everyone is to blame. I blame your actors, film editors, directors, writers, costume designers, poster artists, musicians, carpenters, and electricians. They're all responsible, the whole lot of them. They all play their roles. No one can plead ignorance, for everyone knows precisely what they're doing. The purpose of a gun is no secret. It is a weapon devised to kill. From the laborer who sweeps the movie set floor to the most powerful producer, they all know precisely what they're doing, promoting the public's use of guns. And don't forget the audience! They don't just watch it; they demand it. They can't wait for the next gun-worshipping movie release or television episode. Without this audience, Hollywood would be nothing."

Lucy stopped talking, and Mr. Booker stared at her, wondering if she was done. Apparently she was, for she was now just staring back at him. "You've indicted a lot of people," he said.

"The killing of Trayvon Martin was not an individual act. It was a team effort."

"Yes, a team effort," Ernie said.

"It was your civilization that killed Trayvon Martin. George Zimmerman pulled the trigger with his finger, but your society set the whole thing up."

"Can you see now why we're so concerned about your species?" Ernie asked.

"I guess so," Mr. Booker said.

"How can we trust any of you?" Rock asked. "How can we trust people who have such little regard for life and such a love of killing? It's a little crazy, the way humans adore their weapons."

"A lot crazy," Ralph said.

"Too many weapons," William said.

"We're under no moral obligation to endanger ourselves by condoning your irrational obsessions," Lucy said. "It's not a risk we should be expected to take."

Mr. Booker thought for a moment and then said, "I guess I understand. I wish I could argue with you, but I think I get it."

"So what should we do with you?"

"I don't know."

"Given the opportunity, do you think you can talk your fellow human beings into disarming themselves?"

"No, it would never happen."

"We don't think so either."

CHAPTER 18

THE BIG FOUR

The morning session with the council adjourned right before lunch. Rock told everyone there'd be no afternoon session since it was the opening night of Ralph's play. Ralph was needed in the ship's auditorium to help get things ready for the event. Sid and Mr. Booker left the council chambers together and walked toward the cafeteria to grab their lunch. After eating, Mr. Booker was on his way to his cabin, when Anna caught up to him. She approached him from behind and tapped him on the shoulder. When he turned around and saw it was her, his spirits were lifted, and he laughed. "Anna!" he exclaimed.

"I heard there's no council session this afternoon," she said. "Sid told me."

"He told you right," Mr. Booker said.

"Will you come with me?"

"Where are you going?"

"There's a couple of people I'd like you to meet."

"Can I go to my cabin first? I want to comb my hair. I forgot to comb it this morning."

"No one cares if your hair is combed," Anna said, laughing.

"But I care," Mr. Booker said.

"Fine. Let's go to your cabin. But then you'll come with me, right?"

"I'll come," Mr. Booker said. "Who do you want me to meet?"

"You'll see," Anna said.

Mr. Booker and Anna arrived at his cabin, and Mr. Booker went to his bathroom to take care of his messy hair. "I can't believe you sat through an entire council session looking like you just crawled out of bed," he said to his image in the mirror. When Mr. Booker was done making himself presentable, he and Anna left the cabin, and Anna held Mr. Booker's hand. She walked briskly, pulling him along. "Are we in some sort of hurry?" he asked.

"No, not at all."

"Then why are we walking so fast?"

"Because it's fun. Don't you like to walk fast? It's invigorating."

"If you say so," Mr. Booker said.

They passed the council chambers and cafeteria and then the fitness center. When they came to the door at the end of the hallway, Anna pressed her hand on the silver screen beside the door. The door unlatched, and Anna pushed it open. She then pulled Mr. Booker with her into the hall beyond the door. "Am I supposed to be in here?" Mr. Booker asked.

"Where you are is where you're supposed to be," Anna said, sounding as if she were reciting a proverb.

"Where I'm what?"

"Never mind. I was just joking around. You'll be fine here as long as you're with me. You can think of me as a chaperone."

Anna led Mr. Booker to an elevator. The doors opened, and they stepped inside. Anna pressed the appropriate button, and they quickly dropped down seven floors. When the elevator came to a stop, the doors opened, and the two stepped into a new hallway. "It's right down here," Anna said. "They're going to be so surprised."

Anna held Mr. Booker's hand again, and she pulled him along. Finally, they reached a large wooden door that was slightly ajar. Anna pushed the door open and pulled Mr. Booker into a large office. She suddenly proclaimed, "Here he is!" There were two people in the room, a man and a woman, working at their desks in front of their computer monitors. They both turned their heads. The man stood up from his chair. "Well, I'll be a monkey's uncle," he said. He reached out to shake Mr. Booker's hand, and Mr. Booker obliged.

"I want you to meet my mom and dad," Anna said to Mr. Booker.

"My name is Jacob," her dad said. "This is Anna's mother, June."

"It's nice to meet both of you," Mr. Booker said.

"The pleasure is ours," June said.

"Wow," Jacob said, looking up and down at Mr. Booker. "A live earthling! As I live and breathe!"

"He looks just like his pictures," June said.

"Mom and Dad are tuperloos," Anna said.

"Tuperloos?"

"It's an Ogonite profession," Anna explained. "I don't know that there's a human word for it. They're very important people on the ship. Tuperloos are sociologists who've been specifically educated and trained to identify myths in the cultures we study. We've found that most of the cultures we observe have a variety of myths, and Mom and Dad sort through them and present their findings to the council. Their work uncovering all these myths helps the council make better decisions."

"We cut through the bullshit," Jacob said.

Bullshit? Mr. Booker laughed. The word sounded funny coming from an alien. "I think I get the picture," he said.

June stood up from her chair and reached out to shake Mr. Booker's hand. She was shorter than Jacob by several inches. There was no telling how old they actually were, but they looked as if they were in their fifties. Of course, both of them were wearing golden robes just like everyone else aboard the ship. Jacob had a friendly yet slightly daunting countenance. His face was dominated by his Roman nose and black-framed glasses, the lenses of which were thick and made his eyes appear small and especially piercing. His hair was thin and ragged, yet his glistening teeth were perfect. Jacob had an unbending air about him, as if he were the sort of man who would tell others, "The buck stops here." He looked like a man who didn't suffer fools gladly and who lived in the here and now.

Mr. Booker looked at Anna's mom. Unlike her husband, she had a gentle and more disarming appearance. She was a mom, obviously, and she looked compassionate and motherly. Like Anna, she wore a little too much rouge on her cheeks. She also wore bright red lipstick, and her red lips made her perfect teeth look especially white. Her hair was soft and red, piled atop her head in a complicated hairdo with every strand in place. Mr. Booker figured she must have spent an hour each morning just working on her hair. Clearly, her appearance was important to her, and given his own compulsion to keep his hair combed, Mr. Booker could relate to her.

What a pair they were. June was the empathetic and feminine matron, and Jacob was the no-nonsense spouse, June's rough-and-ready counterpart. "Sit down, both of you," Jacob said. Anna and Mr. Booker obeyed and took their seats in a couple of carved wooden chairs. "Anna has told us a lot about you, Mr. Booker."

"Has she?"

"She likes you," June said. "She says she likes you a lot." This made Mr. Booker blush.

"Well, I guess I like her too."

"We heard you went skinny dipping," Jacob said.

"At Little Lake," June added.

Mr. Booker didn't know what to say. "I think you're embarrassing him," Anna said.

"It's nothing to be ashamed of," Jacob said.

"No," June said. "Nothing to be ashamed of."

"So you're a teacher?" Jacob said.

"Yes, a high school teacher," Mr. Booker said.

"A teacher of history," June said.

"Yes," Mr. Booker said. "I teach history to human teenagers."

"Such a noble calling," Jacob said.

"Yes," June said. "A noble calling."

"Tell me about what you do," Mr. Booker said.

"As Anna said, we're tuperloos. We cut through the bullshit. I can tell you something interesting about most life-forms in the universe. Civilizations in the universe are riddled with bullshit. Life is a blessed miracle to be sure, but the shit is deep. We see it all the time, more often than not. Bullshit, Mr. Booker. It's as far as any telescope can see."

"As far as any telescope can see," June said.

"Faith in so many falsehoods and myths," Jacob said. "Are you following me?"

"I think so. I'm guessing you're referring primarily to religions?"

"No, no, not religions. All cultures establish religions early on, but in time, their inaccurate stories and silly explanations of the world fall by the wayside. As knowledge progresses, men see religion for what it is: a childhood attempt to make sense of the world. No, I'm not talking about that kind of bullshit. Cultures eventually grow up, Mr. Booker. They learn Earth was not made in a week. They learn there are good reasons to kill, despite the Sixth Commandment. They learn no one is really paying any attention to their prayers. No, we don't worry about religions at all. What concerns us is a more cunning form of mythology."

"More cunning," June said.

"Such as?" Mr. Booker asked.

"Ah, he wants an example," Jacob said to June. "Where should I begin?"

"Tell him about the Big Four," Anna said.

"The Big Four?" Mr. Booker asked.

"In our report to the council, we identified the four biggest myths of modern humanity. There are many others, but we believed these four to be the most critical and prevalent. I suppose you'd like to hear them?"

"I would," Mr. Booker said.

"Very well. The first is the invisible hand. Are you aware of this myth?"

"I think so," Mr. Booker said. "If I'm right, Adam Smith coined the term many years ago. I think he was an economist."

"You're correct," Jacob said. "Do you understand how the myth works?"

"It's a theory that in a free-market economy, people's pursuit of their own selfish interests results in endeavors that benefit their fellow man."

"Well put, Mr. Booker."

"Yes," June said. "Very well put."

"But it is bullshit, isn't it?" Jacob said.

"Is it?"

"How can a deliberate pursuit of self-interest possibly be better than an economy in which people try to help one another? Really, there's no comparison. Ah, the mysterious invisible hand! It sounds so intriguing and alluring, as myths are inclined to sound. But what does the hand really do? It causes employers to pay the lowest possible compensation to its workers, and it motivates its workers to contribute as little as possible for the highest possible wage. It encourages producing the lowest-quality products for the highest possible prices. It feeds on greed. It instigates backstabbing, pilfering, and swindling. Men and women are encouraged to hoard everything they can get their greedy hands on, giving little back. The rich get richer, and those who are not adept at playing this selfish game find themselves with lousy living conditions, poor-quality health care, and far less effective educational resources for their children. Honestly, Mr. Booker, I could go on describing the ill effects of this invisible hand for hours! Yet the world buys into it like a throng of wide-eyed fools believing a salesman's pitch for the latest and greatest snake oil remedy. They think to themselves, *Someday I'll be rich. All I need is to buy a winning ticket for next month's state lottery, to find oil bubbling up in my backyard, or to have one lucky pull on a progressive slot machine.*"

"One lucky pull," June said.

"But the reality falls short of the promise, doesn't it? In fact, the truth is that your world is an ugly and selfish place for all citizens. The rich and stingy live lonesome and unfulfilling lives, the middle class wallow in their competitive mediocrity, and the poor try to assuage their sorrows with pipe dreams and vicarious fantasies. These are the consequences of your hallowed invisible hand, the fruits of your mythology."

"I think you're making it sound a little worse than it actually is."

"You only think that way because you don't know any better."

"Maybe," Mr. Booker said.

"A year on Og would change your mind."

Mr. Booker thought about this. A year on Og was an intriguing prospect. He then said, "Give me another."

"Another what?"

"Another of your Big Four."

"Okay, I'll give number two. This one is true for all humans, especially Americans. It's the idea that all men are created equal. It's absurd, and nothing could be further from the truth. Yet modern human beings believe in this as if it were carved into a stone tablet by God himself. In fact, if you don't believe in this myth, you're seen as a heretic. And in America, you're called unpatriotic."

"Unpatriotic," June said.

"Do you really think all men are created equal?" Jacob asked Mr. Booker.

"I believe in the idea," Mr. Booker said. "It means all men are born as human beings and should be treated equally under the law."

"Typically human," Jacob said.

"Am I?" Mr. Booker asked.

"Under the law?" Jacob said, and he laughed.

"Under the law," June said. She too was laughing, and even Anna was smiling.

"Why is that so funny?"

"Why is it that you all strive for equality, when in fact, you're all so different? Is a leader a follower? Is a slothful man a go-getter or an entrepreneur? Is a concert pianist the same as an architect or engineer? What does an artist have in common with a brain surgeon? Are lawyers the same as volunteers at a soup kitchen? Some people have a talent for writing novels, and others have a talent for selling shoes at a shoe store. Would you have a fireman go to the same school as a policeman, the same school as an economist, or the same school as a nurse? Differences, Mr. Booker. They're everything and everywhere! Differences are what make the world go around. Rather than trying to treat everyone the same, you should be celebrating the fact that they're all so unalike."

"But I think we do. We celebrate by rewarding those who are hardworking and successful. Each lot in life is rewarded according to its value."

"These are mostly financial rewards," Jacob said. "You hand out the wrong kinds of prizes. A man should be rewarded for his contribution with his own sense of self-fulfillment. Money should have nothing to do with his motivation. A high school history teacher should make the same as the CEO of a multinational corporation. A shoe salesman should be cashing the same-sized paycheck as a doctor. This is something human beings don't understand. Money is the last thing people should be thinking about. They should be concerned with how well they're doing their jobs and how much they're contributing to the welfare of others. They should all be individuals, all empowered to succeed free from greed. The measuring stick for their success should be how much they've been able to help others and not how much money they've managed to deposit into their checking accounts."

"Aren't you describing a utopia?"

"Not at all," Jacob said. "It's simply a healthier way to organize a society. We've been living this way on Og for centuries."

"For centuries," June said.

Anna's parents were quiet for a moment, and Mr. Booker thought about what they'd been saying. He then adjusted his weight in the wooden chair and asked, "So what is number three?"

"Ah," Jacob said. He smiled at Mr. Booker. "Number three is the human notion that money is the root of all evil."

"That's it?"

"It's a myth, Mr. Booker."

"But you just got done telling me how misguided and awful money is."

"I did no such thing. I only pointed out that money is an ineffective reward. Money is very important. In fact, money is critical. It's as necessary to intelligent living as the air we breathe, the food we eat, and the cool and refreshing water we drink. It is absolutely not evil, Mr. Booker."

"Not evil," June said.

"Now you're confusing me."

"Money, if properly shared, makes it possible for economies to function, allotting the goods and services everyone needs in order to enjoy his or her life. So why do humans think that money is the root of evil? It's not the money, Mr. Booker. It's the people who handle it. It's the human desire to accumulate and spend as much money as possible. It's the desire to have more of it than your neighbor, more than your associates at work—more than anyone! It's the need to have power over others. The evil that humans attribute to money isn't in the money itself. It's in their own selfish hearts and souls. On Og, we all love money, because we have enough of it. No one has any more than the other, and no one desires to get more than his or her fair share. There's enough to go around for everyone, and our citizens are free to pursue their ambitions and dreams without having to worry about whether they can pay their bills, drive more expensive cars than their neighbors, or bribe public officials. The truth is that money is the root of good. It's the stuff that makes all things possible. It's the power that lights up cities and the medicine that cures diseases. It's the roads we travel and the food we put on our tables."

"The food on our tables," June said.

"You look confused," Jacob said to Mr. Booker. "Do you get what I'm trying to say? Am I forcing a round peg into a square hole?"

"Maybe," Mr. Booker said.

"Tell him number four," Anna said.

"Do you want me to continue?" Jacob asked.

"Yes, please," Mr. Booker said.

"Number four is my favorite," Anna said.

"Do you believe in justice?" Jacob asked Mr. Booker.

"Doesn't everyone?"

"Justice for all, right? Like your children say in the Pledge of Allegiance."

"Yes," Mr. Booker said. "Something like that. I suppose you have a problem with justice?"

"Do you know who has been the most influential man on your planet? I mean, of all time? According to your own experts, the man is Jesus Christ."

"I guess I can agree with that."

"Historians and sociologists all say he's the most influential man in all human history."

"All human history," June said.

"Millions of people still look up to him and worship the ground he walked on, yet none of them take his words to heart. The truth is that he isn't influential at all. Humans write about him, paint pictures of him, chisel statues of him, and talk about him until they're blue in the face, but he may as well have never said a word to anyone. This justice thing, Mr. Booker. It flies in the face of his best advice."

"Which is?"

"To turn the other cheek."

"To turn the other cheek," June repeated.

"Justice is the exact opposite of this. What exactly is justice? Isn't it just a well-organized and powerful institution devised to slap people back? That's its sole purpose: getting even over perceived wrongdoings. When someone crosses the line with you, you don't turn your cheek to him. No, forget what Jesus said. You sue the son of a bitch or call the police to throw the bum in jail. Call it assault, breach of contract, theft, larceny, fraud, murder, or patent infringement; you file the appropriate papers and seek revenge. A justice system affords men an opportunity to hit back at their aggressors with the full force of the law."

"I can see that," Mr. Booker said.

"You know, humans have always had a choice. They had the opportunity to follow the advice of Jesus, the most beloved man in history. Or they had the option to do the opposite. I'm sorry to say they chose the latter. People believe in justice like they believe the Earth is round. Everyone seeks justice when they're wronged, and no one questions it. Amen, Mr. Booker. In God we trust, but in Jesus we defy."

"I guess I understand what you're saying, but without some system of justice, wouldn't societies just fall to pieces? There'd be nothing holding us together."

"No, you're wrong. The need for justice is a myth, and it's a myth of the highest order. There is no need for justice, Mr. Booker. But there is a need for better people. There's a need for people to love and respect each other. There's a need for people to live and behave virtuously. Slapping someone in the face when you feel you've been wronged doesn't solve anything. It only perpetuates a fight that should never have started in the first place. Jesus had it right, Mr. Booker."

"So you do believe in religion?"

"I never said that."

"But you believe we should listen to Jesus."

"In this case, yes. Let's just say there's no reason to throw the baby out with the bathwater."

Mr. Booker laughed. "No, I suppose you're right," he said.

Everyone sat quietly for a moment, staring at each other and thinking about what had just been said. Then Anna spoke up, changing the subject. She said to Mr. Booker, "Sid told me that the two of you are going to Ralph's play tonight."

"I asked if I could go, and Ralph said yes," Mr. Booker said. "Sid picked up the tickets from him yesterday."

"The three of us are going next week," Jacob said.

"It should be a good performance," June said.

"Ralph's plays are always worth seeing."

"Sid told me this one's a comedy," Mr. Booker said.

"That's great," Jacob said. "There's nothing more uplifting than sitting for a couple hours in an auditorium full of laughing Ogonites."

"Nothing more uplifting," June said. Jacob and June looked at each other. For a moment, they just stared, and then they broke out laughing.

CHAPTER 19

GEORGE'S BIRTHDAY

M r. Booker was impressed. Elaborate and imaginative Ogonite wood carvings crawled over every square inch of the soaring auditorium ceiling and walls. Large chandeliers were suspended every thirty or so feet and shone like captured suns. Every seat in the house was filled, and the people were all talking and laughing. There seemed to be a lot of good cheer and anticipation in the air. Mr. Booker had never seen so many Ogonites in one place, and the scent of spearmint was powerful; it was like being in a Wrigley's chewing gum factory. And what a sight it was! Hundreds of golden robes glistened under the chandeliers, and a sea of mock hairstyles and faces filled the room. Everyone was waiting for the play to begin at eight, and the lights dimmed just before the hour. It was the one thing Mr. Booker could rely upon—his alien friends' punctuality. Sid turned, placed his hand on Mr. Booker's forearm, and said, "I hope you have a sense of humor."

"I think I do," Mr. Booker said.

"Good, good. Just don't forget to laugh. Remember, this is a comedy."

"Yes," Mr. Booker said. "I'll remember."

The name of Ralph's production was *George's Birthday,* but Mr. Booker had no idea what the play was about. He knew only that the main character was a human being named George, and the story had something to do with his fortieth birthday. Obviously,

George lived somewhere on planet Earth, but Mr. Booker wasn't sure where—probably somewhere in the United States and maybe even in California. It would be interesting to see what sort of story Ralph had cooked up and what sort of dialogue he'd written for his characters.

There was one thing Mr. Booker did know: Ogonites liked to laugh. Did they ever like to laugh! Mr. Booker also knew that Ogonites found humans especially amusing. Would the play seem funny to Mr. Booker, or would one have to be an Ogonite to appreciate it? It was all crazy, wasn't it? There he was on an alien spacecraft, orbiting Earth, about to watch a comedy written by a man who wasn't really a man, the parts acted out by actors who weren't even human. Who back on Earth would believe any of this?

Suddenly, the chandeliers went dark, and for a few seconds, the room was pitch black. Then the stage curtain was drawn open, and light flooded the set. It was a bright and cheery kitchen with cabinets, modern appliances, and a breakfast table and chairs. At the right side of the stage, a woman appeared. Her voluptuous body was barely covered by a scant two-piece swimsuit. The woman carried a cardboard sign from one end of the stage to the other. The sign said, "Act One." As she strutted across the stage, the audience laughed, and the men all whistled. Sid nudged Mr. Booker's arm with his elbow. "Funny, no?" he said. "It's just like a boxing match."

"Yes," Mr. Booker said. "I can see that."

When the woman was done, the play began. A female actress came out from the side of the stage, stepping into the kitchen. She was dressed in an athletic outfit and wore a white terrycloth headband. She appeared to be in her late thirties and had an attractive middle-class face. Her skin glistened with perspiration, probably water that had been sprayed on her backstage. It made her appear as if she'd just been exercising. She proceeded to remove food from the refrigerator and several pans from the cupboards. She then pretended to prepare a meal, and as she did, her young son stepped into the room and plopped his backpack on the floor beside the breakfast table. "Good morning, Elroy!" she said.

"Morning, Jane," Elroy said.

"It's Mom to you," she said. "You should know by now that it's inappropriate for little human boys to call their mothers by their first names."

The audience laughed at this. Apparently, there was something funny about it.

"Fine, *Mom*. What's for breakfast?"

"Fatty strips of dead pig flesh and some scrambled chicken ovum and albumen."

"I can't wait!"

Again, there was laughter. Already the audience was enjoying Ralph's show. If they kept this up, they'd be laughing all night.

"Hang on, and I'll pour you a big glass of pasteurized white liquid secretion from the mammary gland of a large farm animal."

"You mean a cow?" Elroy asked.

"Yes, of course. A cow. A big, hairy, runny-nosed, cud-chewing cow!"

"Yum," Elroy said.

Jane held the egg carton up to the light to examine it. "It says here that they're farm fresh."

"What's that mean?" Elroy asked.

"Farm fresh? Why, they're the best eggs money can buy. It means your breakfast will have come from a farm where the workers stuff chickens into feces-encrusted cages that are so cramped they can't even spread their wings. They lay eggs at a painful rate just for you and me. It's sort of like a chicken hell on Earth. But don't worry your little head; chickens are just dumb and ignorant farm animals. If God didn't intend for us to eat their eggs, he wouldn't have made them so stupid. I'll have your breakfast ready in a jiffy."

Now the daughter entered the kitchen from the side of the stage. Her name was Judy, and she too was ready to eat breakfast. She was dressed in jeans and a red halter top. She was wearing pink sneakers sewn up with bright red shoelaces, and her backpack was the same shade of pink as her sneakers. She plopped her backpack down beside Elroy's and took a seat at the breakfast table. Judy was a junior in high school, just a few years older than Elroy. "What's for breakfast?" she asked.

"Scrambled chicken ovum and albumen," Elroy said. "Farm fresh!"

"And fatty strips of dead pig," Jane said. "Nice and crispy, the way Rosie does it."

"Yum!" Judy said.

"The best foods always come from killing and abusing animals," Jane said knowingly.

Jane really made the audience laugh when she delivered this line, and Mr. Booker laughed along with them. He didn't want them to think he wasn't getting any of the jokes.

"I'm starving," Elroy said.

"Remember, kids," Jane said, "today's your father's birthday, so mum's the word! Don't say anything to him about it; I want him to think we forgot. And remember that we're having a surprise party for him tonight when he gets home from work. Yes, I really do want him to be surprised."

"Got it," Elroy said.

"Can I have a friend come to the party?" Judy asked.

"Which friend?"

"I don't know yet."

"I suppose there's no harm—as long as it isn't a boy. You know how funny Daddy gets about your boyfriends and about your youthful predilection to having sexual intercourse with them."

"Oh, he's such a stick in the mud."

"But he's our stick in the mud," Jane said. She smiled at her kids and then turned to the stove top. She stirred the scrambled eggs with a wooden spoon. "Speaking of sexual intercourse, Judy, did you take your pill this morning?"

"I always take it right after I brush my teeth. That's how I remember to take it."

"The last thing we need in this house is a little baby to care for. I mean, I'm sure Rosie could help, but it's really the last thing we need."

"Where is Rosie this morning?" Elroy asked. "And why are you cooking breakfast?"

"Rosie's coming in late today so she can stay tonight and help with the party."

"Who's picking me up today after baseball practice?" Elroy asked.

"It won't be me," Jane said. "I'm going to be busy with Rosie, preparing for the party. There's a lot to do. Judy can get you."

"Do I have to pick him up again?" Judy asked.

"It won't kill you."

"Okay, but I'm not giving a ride to any of his creepy baseball friends," Judy said. "Who was that little pervert you brought along last time I picked you up? You let him sit in the front seat, and he stared at my boobs all the way to his house."

"That was Tommy," Elroy said, laughing.

"Your friends are weirdos."

"I don't know why you thought Tommy was staring at your chest," Elroy said. "There isn't anything there to look at."

"Freak!" Judy exclaimed.

"That's enough from the both of you."

"Good morning, everyone!" George exclaimed. He had just entered the kitchen from the side of the stage, and the audience applauded his arrival. He was humming "Happy Birthday" and was dressed for work in slacks, a white shirt, and a tie. He was carrying his coat when he entered, and he draped it over one of the chairs. "Where's the paper?" he asked.

"It's still in the driveway," Jane said.

"Where's Astro?"

"He's is the backyard. I let him out first thing this morning so he could urinate and relieve his bowels all over our vegetation."

There was more laughter. George went offstage to retrieve his morning paper, and while he was gone, Jane said to the kids, "Remember, we're to say nothing about his birthday."

"Got it," Elroy said.

"Yes, we've got it," Judy said.

When George returned, Jane turned to look at him. He was

shaking his head and clearly was irritated. He said, "I thought you were going to ask Carlos to adjust the sprinklers so they didn't hit my paper."

"I asked him to, but I don't think he understood what I was talking about."

"Why can't we get a gardener who speaks English?"

"You're the one who hired him."

George looked at Jane and said, "Oh yeah, I guess you're right."

George took a seat at the breakfast table and unfolded his wet newspaper. He then looked around and noticed things were different. "Where's Rosie this morning?" he asked.

"She called in sick," Jane said. "I'll be making your breakfast."

"What are we having?"

"Scrambled chicken ovum and albumen," Elroy said. "Farm fresh!"

"And fatty strips of dead pig," Judy added. "Nice and crispy, like Rosie does it."

"Ah, all my favorites," George said, rubbing his hands together, and then he exclaimed, "Thank God for all our dumb farm animals! Where would we be without them?"

"Hear, hear," Elroy said.

Opening the wet newspaper and looking over the first page of the sports section, George asked, "How's that curveball coming, Elroy?"

"I've been working on it."

"It says here that Blaine Smith signed a new contract pitching for the Yankees. They're paying him ten million a year for six years."

"How old is he?" Jane asked.

"He's only twenty-three."

"I heard he's dating Cynthia Pike," Judy said.

"Who's she?" Elroy asked.

"She's a famous movie actress. You should keep up on current events."

"She does those perfume commercials," Jane said. "She has her own perfume."

"Keep working on that curveball," George said to Elroy. "You never know."

"No," Jane said. "You never know."

"Say," George said, pointing to the date at the top of his newspaper. "Any of you know what day today is?"

"Thursday?" Elroy asked.

"I mean besides that."

"It's just another Thursday," Jane said. "And we won't have Rosie to straighten up the house. Nothing to get excited about."

"I suppose not," George said. He then looked at the audience, and the curtain closed.

That was the end of act one, and everyone cheered and applauded. The lights dimmed, and it took a few minutes for the stagehands to rearrange the set behind the closed curtain. When they were ready, the woman in the swimsuit walked across the stage again, holding a new cardboard sign that said, "Act Two." Again, there was laughter, and the men in the audience whistled. When the woman was done, the curtain was pulled open, revealing an office. There was a drawing table with a lamp, and to its right was a cabinet with a coffee maker sitting atop it. George was working at the drawing table and drinking a cup of coffee. He turned around and looked at the audience, saying, "Can it really be? Did my own family forget about my fortieth birthday? None of them even mentioned it. No one said, 'Happy birthday, George.' No one said, 'Wow, I can't believe you're forty!'"

When George was done talking to the audience, a big bowling ball of a man rolled onto the stage, and the audience applauded his arrival. Sid turned and whispered to Mr. Booker, "He's one of the ship's favorite character actors."

"I see," Mr. Booker said.

"You'll like him."

"I'm sure I will."

The actor was playing George's boss, the owner of the company where George worked. He was the tough-as-nails and inimitable Cosmo Spacely. He said, "Good morning, George."

"Good morning, Cosmo," George said.

"That's Mr. Spacely to you."

"Of course, Mr. Spacely."

The audience laughed. George laughed along with everyone else. He didn't laugh as hard as they did, but he did chuckle.

"How's the Azula-Bar account coming?"

"It's coming," George said.

"The client wants to launch the campaign in June."

"I think we'll be ready."

"Do you have a film crew picked out?"

"Everything is set up. We bought their plane tickets to Peru last week. Once they land, it'll take them about two days to get into the rain forest. They'll spend three or four days shooting the footage. Once they return home, we can see what they've got and put the ad together. We won't know exactly what the ad will look like until we see what we have to work with."

"By Jingo, I'm expecting big things from you, George. I want to see what these natives look like. Do they really live to be over a hundred?"

"That's what they claim, and that's the story we're sticking with."

"Most of them probably can't even count to a hundred," Mr. Spacely said, laughing.

"Does it really matter?"

"No, as long as we're not lying."

"We won't lie. No, we won't have to lie at all. I'm picturing something like this: We start with a shot of an elderly native who's as fit as a fiddle. He's stringing a bow or mending the roof of his hut. The narrator says something like 'Here were are, deep in the Peruvian rain forest of Azula. Like so many other local residents, this astonishing man claims to be over a hundred years old! And look at how active he still is. So what's the secret behind this man's good health and longevity? Is it in the local air? Is it in the water? We think it's in the cocoa beans. Yes, the cocoa beans!'"

"Marvelous!" Mr. Spacely exclaimed.

"Yes, it works, doesn't it? The narrator will go on to explain how Azula-Bars are manufactured exclusively from chocolate made from Azula cocoa beans. Then we work in the slogan 'Azula-Bars are good for life.' These are just my initial thoughts. We'll have to get a writer to create the actual script, and we'll have to use an editor to work out the visuals. But I think it'll be a winner. They'll be selling Azula-Bars like hotcakes, like there's no tomorrow. I mean, who doesn't want to live a long and healthy life? And all you have to do is plunk down a couple bucks for a chocolate bar!"

"I love it," Mr. Spacely said, patting George on the back. "And I like what you're saying about the old man *claiming* to be over a hundred. We don't want to get caught in a lie."

"No lie is necessary. Humans believe what they want to believe, and a claim is as good as a fact."

"Yes, yes," Mr. Spacely said.

George smiled and winked at Mr. Spacely, and the man winked back at him. Then they both turned their heads and winked at the audience, and everyone in the auditorium burst out laughing.

"By Jingo, you're my kind of man, George. I do like the way you think!"

The two men went on to discuss several of their other advertising campaigns, each a little more ridiculous than the last. When they were done talking about all the campaigns, George asked, "Do you happen to know what today is?"

"I believe it's Thursday, isn't it?"

"Yes, I suppose it is," George said.

"Something I should know about it?"

"No, it's nothing," George said. Then he looked at the audience with a disillusioned look on his face. Once again, they laughed. Poor forgotten George!

That scene marked the end of act two, and the lights dimmed while the curtain closed. The stagehands worked behind the curtain to install the new set. Meanwhile, the woman in the swimsuit strutted across the stage for a third time with a cardboard sign that said, "Act Three."

When the curtain opened, the stage was set up to look like the inside of a restaurant. In the middle was a round table with two chairs. Coming from the left side of the stage, George and another man followed a young hostess to the table. The man was George's best friend from work, Jeff. The hostess handed them their menus and then walked off the stage. "Do you know what today is?" George asked.

"Thursday?"

"I mean besides that."

"Is there something I should know about it?"

"No, not really," George said. Then, to the audience, George said, "Heck, he doesn't know either, and he's my best friend." Everyone laughed.

"What are you going to get for lunch?" Jeff asked, putting his glasses on so he could read the menu. "I could really go for a French dip sandwich. Or maybe I'll just get a Reuben. I had a Reuben yesterday, and it really hit the spot. They don't skimp on the meat here. They know how to make a sandwich."

"A Reuben sounds good."

"Did you see Sarah Michaels today?"

"No, why? What about her?"

"You have to see what she's wearing. I mean, talk about a low-cut dress! I mean low, George! I could almost see her little areolas trying to come up for air. Jeez, I'm such a sucker for low-cut dresses and areolas. They give me such a wicked erection. What do you think she'd say if I asked her out? She's fifteen years younger than me. Do you think she'd say yes?"

"She might."

"And how about Dina Marshall?"

"What about her?"

"Did you see what she was wearing the day before yesterday?"

"No, I guess I didn't."

"She was wearing a plaid skirt. Can you believe it? Wearing a plaid skirt to work!"

"What's so special about a plaid skirt?"

"She looked like one of those girls going to a parochial school.

I've always been a sucker for girls who go to parochial schools. There's something mysterious and nasty about them, George. They give me an erection every time I think of them."

"Well, since we're on the subject of women at work, what about Sally Andrews?" George said.

"What about her?" Jeff asked.

"Have you noticed her pouty lips? Don't those lips drive you crazy?"

"You like pouty lips?"

"I'm a sucker for them," George said. "They give me an erection for sure. Every time I pass Sally in the hall, I see those lips, and I have to get to my chair pronto and take a seat. Sometimes it takes minutes before I can stand up again."

Jeff laughed. "Do you want to know what I'm really a sucker for?"

"What?" George said.

"Braids," Jeff said.

"You mean hair braids?"

"Instant erection, my friend. And I'm talking about the kind of erection that won't go away. I once dated a girl named Julie Anne Whipple, and she always braided her hair, sometimes in a single braid and sometimes in a pair. But it drove me crazy. I had to stop dating her. I couldn't walk anywhere with her."

The audience was laughing hard, and Mr. Booker was laughing too. Then George asked, "How about Marsha? What about her?"

"My ex-wife?"

"Yes," George said.

"Once upon a time, maybe. Yes, once upon a time, I'd get an erection just thinking about her. That was all it would take. But five years of marriage cured me of that. All it took to throw water on that fire was for me to get to know her better. It's hard to get an erection when your love mate is constantly telling you what to do—always telling you to change the lightbulbs, take out the trash, walk the dog, fix the door, wash the car, clean the dirty windows, and mow the lawn. Jeez, it was hell on Earth, George. Now if I need to get rid of an erection, I just think of her. Yes, that's all it takes. I just picture her face, and down the old boy goes. So what about your wife, Jane?"

"What about her?"

"Erection—yes or no?"

"It depends."

"On what?" Jeff asked.

"On what sort of mood we're in."

Just then, the waitress appeared at the table to take the men's lunch orders. Her name was Rhonda. Mr. Booker knew her name was Rhonda because the first thing she said was "Good day, gentlemen. My name is Rhonda. Are you both ready to order?"

"I'll have a Reuben sandwich," Jeff said.

"Same here," George said.

"Anything to drink?" Rhonda asked.

"I'll have an iced tea," Jeff said.

"A Coke for me," George said.

"Is that it?" Rhonda asked.

"Yes," Jeff said. "That should do it."

"I'll be right back with those drinks," Rhonda said, and she walked away and off the stage. George and Jeff watched her as she walked.

"Nice girl," George said.

"Erection?" Jeff asked.

"Not for me," George said.

"Not for me either."

"I'm looking forward to my sandwich."

"I think you're going to like it," Jeff said. "Their waitresses might not be much to look at, but they know how to make a sandwich."

The two men were quiet for a moment. Then George smiled and said, "Braids? Really?"

"Yes," Jeff said. "Braids."

The audience had been laughing the whole way through this conversation, and Mr. Booker turned to look at Sid. Sid had been laughing so hard that he'd been crying, and his cheeks were wet with tears. He reached to wipe the tears away, saying to Mr. Booker, "Oh God, was that ever funny!"

"Yes, it was," Mr. Booker said.

"I haven't laughed this hard for years," Sid said. "Humans are too much."

"Too much," Mr. Booker agreed.

The curtain was now closed. After a couple minutes, the woman in the swimsuit walked across the stage again, and then the fourth act started. This time, the stage was set up to look like a doctor's examination room. George was sitting in his boxer shorts, waiting for the doctor to arrive. In the room was a cabinet with a countertop, and on top of the counter sat a big electronic cash register. The doctor arrived from the left side of the stage and said hello to George. He was a tall, good-looking man wearing a white lab coat with a stethoscope hanging from his neck. "So we're here for our annual physical, are we?" the doctor said cheerfully.

"Yes," George said.

"I see today's your birthday," the doctor said, looking at George's file.

"I come in on my birthdays so I won't forget. When my birthday comes around, it reminds me that it's time to get my annual physical."

"Last time you were here, your blood pressure was a little high," the doctor said, still looking at George's file.

"You said it was a little high but not high enough for me to need medication."

"Ah, so I did," the doctor said. "Let's see what we have now. Hold out your arm, and roll up your sleeve. I should tell you that a blood-pressure check is going to cost you two hundred dollars." The doctor punched the amount into his cash register.

"Two hundred dollars?" George said. "That's just to check my blood pressure?"

"It's the going rate. Everything is figured in to the price. It doesn't all go straight to my pocket. The price includes all my overhead. I've got to pay my receptionist every week, and my rent is due once a month. Then there's my electric bill, phone charges, and cable

Internet costs. And there's also my insurance. Do you have any idea how much my insurance costs? Listen, do you want me to check your blood pressure or not? I've got other patients I could be seeing."

"Go ahead and check it," George said. "It just seemed a little expensive." The doctor stepped up to George, attached the device to his upper arm, and pumped it full of air.

"Ah, not too bad," the doctor said, reading the numbers. "You're still looking pretty good. It's a tad high but still in the ballpark. You've got nothing to worry about. Now let's check your lungs. Do you want me to warm up my stethoscope, or are you okay with it being a little cold? Some patients like it warm. Warming it up costs an extra hundred dollars."

"I'll go with cold," George said.

"Cold it is. So that'll be three hundred dollars." The doctor punched the amount into his cash register and then placed the cold stethoscope against George's naked back. "Big breath in," he said. He listened carefully and then said, "Now you can let it out." He had George do this several times. "Your lungs seem to be okay to me," he said. "Do you smoke?"

"No," George said. "I don't smoke."

"We'll pass on the x-ray then. I think you're in good shape."

"That's good to know."

"Lungs are important."

"Yes," George said.

"Now I need to look down your throat. That'll be two hundred for my labor and another fifty for the tongue depressor."

"Fifty dollars for a tongue depressor?"

"That's what they cost. I buy the best on the market. These things don't come cheap, you know. I buy them in quantity, but they still don't come cheap. You wouldn't want me poking any old dirty stick into your mouth, would you?"

"I suppose not."

The doctor punched the charge into the cash register and then told George to open wide. He looked down George's throat and told him to say, "Ah," several times. "Fine, fine," the doctor said. "You're looking healthy here too."

"I guess that's good," George said.

"Now for the ears. I need to look into your ears. We can do this one of two ways. I can look into one ear for three hundred dollars, or I can look into them both for five hundred. You get a hundred-dollar discount for doing both ears in one sitting. It's a pretty good deal. Or you can just have me look into one ear, and we'll just take the chance that one ear is the same as the other. It's up to you."

"I'll go with one ear," George said.

"One ear it shall be," the doctor said. He punched the price into his cash register and then grabbed the ear scope. He peered into George's left ear and said, "Good, good. You're still looking good. I don't see anything wrong with your ear at all."

"That's reassuring," George said. The audience was loving this entire routine. They were laughing loudly, some of them starting to cough because they were laughing so hard.

"Now comes the worst part of the exam," he said. "You're not going to like this, but I have to stick my finger up your butt."

"You did this last time."

"Yes, I'm sure I did. This procedure will cost you a thousand dollars."

"A thousand dollars?"

"It's what I charge."

"But a thousand dollars for a few seconds of work?"

"It's not the time, George."

"Then what is it?"

"Ask yourself how you'd like to stick your finger up the butt of another man. I can tell by the look on your face that you wouldn't like it, not at all. So what would you charge? Do you honestly think I went through years of medical school and internship hoping I'd be sticking my finger up butts day in and day out? It's combat pay, my friend. If you want me to stick my finger in you, I'm going to charge a thousand dollars. It isn't a rip-off. It's what any other self-respecting doctor would charge. Unless, of course, you go to someone less reputable. But ask yourself if you really want someone with a questionable reputation sticking his finger up your butt."

"Probably not," George said. The audience was now roaring, and the actor playing the doctor had to suppress his own laughter when he looked at George's face. George said, "Aw, what the hell? I guess if you have to do it, you have to do it. Go ahead and ring it up!"

"A thousand dollars," the doctor said as he punched the amount into his cash register. He then put on a latex glove, jellied up his finger, and told Mr. Booker to drop his shorts and bend over.

When they were done with the physical exam, the doctor pressed a big red button on his cash register. It spit out a long receipt that listed all the items George had purchased, and the list included a grand total. "Ah," the doctor said, looking the receipt over and smiling. "Your choices saved you some money. They certainly did. Earlier this morning, I did an exam on a woman that cost her twice this amount. She went for the whole nine yards, no expense spared. You got off easy, George." The doctor handed over the strip of paper and told George to take it to the receptionist. "She'll take your payment for the services," he said. "Did you happen to bring cash?"

"Not this much," George said. He was looking over the receipt.

"That's too bad," the doctor said. "We give a five percent discount for all payments made in cash."

"I'll keep that in mind for next year."

"If it's any consolation to you, it's good you came in when you did."

"Why is that?"

"We're raising our rates starting next week. I bought a new Porsche, and my monthly country club fees are going up. And my wife wants to go to Europe this summer. Cost of living, you know. Everyone and his brother thinks health care is a rip off, but it isn't exactly cheap living the life of a doctor."

"Of course not," George said.

"I guess I'll see you next year."

The doctor walked off the stage, and George stepped toward the audience. He grimaced and then stuck out his tongue as if he were going crazy. Everyone, including Mr. Booker, broke out laughing, and the curtain closed while he was still making the face.

"Too much, I tell you," Sid said, laughing.

"Too much," Mr. Booker agreed.

"Your doctors ought to be drawn and quartered. That cash register gag? What a great idea!"

"Yes," Mr. Booker said.

It was time for the final act of the play. The set was made to look like George and Jane's living room. George wasn't home yet, but his friends and family had arrived for the surprise party. Among the guests were Jeff and Mr. Spacely from work and a couple other business associates. Some neighbors and other friends were there, and so were Elroy, Judy, and one of Judy's girlfriends. They were all in the living room, talking to each other and waiting for Jane to give them the word. Jane was at the front window, looking out for George. Finally, she hollered, "Okay, he's here! Everyone down!"

They all stooped and hid behind the sofa, and George entered from the left side of the stage. "Jane?" he said. "Elroy? Judy? Is anyone home?"

Suddenly, everyone jumped up and yelled, "Surprise! Happy birthday, George!" Jane then ran up to George and gave him a hug.

The look on George's face was priceless. "I thought you'd all forgotten about me," he said, grinning from ear to ear.

"How could we forget your fortieth birthday, dear?" Jane said. "It's a milestone!"

"We really had you wondering," Jeff said.

Mr. Spacely laughed. "He didn't have a clue!"

"No, I didn't," George said.

"How does it feel to be forty?" Elroy asked.

"If you'd asked me this morning, I would've said not so great. But now I'll tell you it feels terrific."

"Wait right here," Jane said.

"We have something for you," Judy said.

Jane left the room and promptly returned with a large birthday cake. There were four candles in it, one for each decade of George's life. Jane set the cake on the living room coffee table. Then everyone sang "Happy Birthday," and George's eyes welled with tears. Jane put her hands on George's shoulders and guided him to sit down on the sofa in front of the cake. "Blow out the candles, George."

"Don't forget to make a wish," Elroy said.

"Yes," Judy said. "Don't forget a wish."

George stared at the cake for a moment, silently making his wish. Then he leaned over and blew out the candles in a single breath.

"Hurray!" Mr. Spacely exclaimed, and everyone else in the room cheered.

"May all your wishes come true," Jane said.

"I don't know what to say," George said.

"Let's have a speech!" Jeff said.

"Yes, speech!" Elroy said.

"Speech, speech, speech," the guests all chanted in unison. George just sat there staring at his cake. Then, looking up at his friends and family, he spoke.

"What can I say?" he said. "I can't begin to tell you all how happy I am right now. You've all made my day. You really have. And it's been an interesting day, to say the least. It's been one of those days I'll remember for as long as I live. You know, I have everything a human being could ask for. I mean, I really have everything. Forty years ago, I was brought into this world with nothing but my own ten fingers and ten toes. My loving parents raised me to the best of their ability, and I grew up. I studied hard and graduated from high school and then from college. I got my first job. It wasn't a great job, but it paid the bills. Then I married Jane, and we had our two children, my lovely daughter, Judy, and my wonderful son, Elroy. And now here I am after forty years of living on planet Earth, a man who is so enthusiastically grateful for all he's received. I now have a terrific and well-paying job working for a thoughtful and supportive boss. My love for my wife is stronger than ever, and I couldn't be any prouder of my two children. And I have many good friends, like Jeff. I thank God for my good friends. I learned today that I also have my good health. According to my doctor, I'm as fit as a twenty-year-old athlete. My ears, throat, lungs, and heart are in perfect shape. And to top everything off, I'm not impotent. Yes, the old boy has some life in him yet. Wow, I have so much to be grateful for that I just feel speechless." Again, George's eyes welled with tears, and Jane moved closer and held his hand, squeezing it tightly.

"I think I'm going to cry," Jane said.

"We love you, Daddy," Judy said.

"Yeah, Pop," Elroy said. "We all love you."

"By Jingo, this is what life's all about," Mr. Spacely said firmly. "Loyal friends, a loving family, a good job, great health, and the ability to get an erection."

"Hear, hear," Jeff said.

"Today is such a great day," George said. "What more could a human being ask for? What else is there to life? Now, let's carve up the cake and fill our glasses to the brim with some pasteurized white liquid secretion from the mammary gland of a large farm animal. It's time to eat, drink, and celebrate!"

With that, the curtain closed, and the play was over. Everyone in the audience stood up and clapped, and several people shouted, "Bravo!"

Sid and Mr. Booker were standing, and Sid looked at Mr. Booker and asked, "Well, what did you think?"

"It was great," Mr. Booker said.

"Are you just saying that to be polite?"

"No, I really liked it."

"That's good to hear," Sid said. "I love Ralph's productions. He's one of a kind."

"Yes," Mr. Booker said. "I guess I can't argue with that."

CHAPTER 20

THE FINAL SESSION

The next morning, Mr. Booker found himself deep in another of his dreams. Like in his other recent dreams, he was seated at a crackling campfire. He was discussing a final plan of attack with his two most trusted comrades, and every aspect of the offensive was discussed in dreamlike detail. They talked about points of attack, the timing involved, and the weapons to be used. It was decided they would advance in the early morning darkness, catching the Ogonites groggy and unprepared. It was cold, and the warmth of the campfire flames felt good. Mr. Booker placed his hands close to the fire, rubbing them together, thawing out his freezing fingers. Then he said to Lucius and Titus, "Tomorrow morning will be critical. Will our men be ready?"

"Our men are always ready," Titus said.

"The Ogonites are going to be a formidable opponent," Mr. Booker said.

"They'll be no match for us," Titus said. "We are both disciplined and brutal."

"By the end of this week, they'll all be under Roman rule for sure," Lucius said. "They'll be begging for our tolerance and mercy."

"They asked for this," Mr. Booker said.

"They did," Titus agreed.

"They should've left well enough alone," Lucius said. "They had no right to threaten us."

"They're such a queer breed," Mr. Booker said. "Their council preaches peace and harmony, yet at the same time, their troops are poised to kill. Their mistake was in making their intentions toward us known. They were fools to think we'd just roll over and let them have their way. Clearly, they've left us no choice."

"It's either us or them," Lucius said.

"Us or them," Mr. Booker repeated. "Us or them, us or them. The alarm is ringing again."

"The alarm?" Lucius asked.

"Yes, the alarm," Mr. Booker said. "I need to get up and turn it off."

"Are you okay?" Titus asked.

"I'm fine. No, maybe I'm not. I don't know for sure what I am."

"We need you to lead us."

"We're depending on you, sir."

"I need to see the council again," Mr. Booker said. "I have to be there at eight."

"But they've already told you," Lucius said.

"Told me what?"

"That they're not our friends and that they never were."

"I agree with Lucius," Titus said.

"You two actually agree on something?"

"We do!"

"I must be dreaming!"

"The council and all its irrelevant words have just been a stall tactic," Lucius said.

"A stall tactic," Titus agreed.

"Yes, the council!" Mr. Booker said. "I must meet with them again. They're expecting me."

"Don't be a fool, Caesar!"

"Caesar?"

"Don't be a fool!"

"What the heck?" Mr. Booker said, and he opened his eyes. The dream was over. His body ached all over, and he was sweating profusely. He was dressed in nothing but his shorts, and he'd kicked off his covers while sleeping. The alarm clock on the nightstand was ringing. He reached over and turned it off and then climbed out of bed. He went to the bathroom and looked at his face in the mirror. "Ah, Mr. Booker," he said. "So it is just you."

What a laugh that dream had been! As if Caesar would've stood a chance against a foe like the Ogonites. What had he been thinking? It had seemed so real while he was sleeping, and now it was just ridiculous.

After showering and getting dressed, Mr. Booker met Sid at the cafeteria. They ordered breakfast and sat down at a table. "I had the strangest dream this morning," Mr. Booker said.

"About what?" Sid asked.

"I was Julius Caesar."

Sid laughed. "That's a good one."

"We were about to go to war."

"You are such a human. If you're not waging war, you're dreaming about it."

"Do you really think it's that simple?"

"I do," Sid said. "How's your ovum and albumen?"

"Pardon me?"

"Your eggs, Mr. Booker. How are your eggs?"

"They're good," Mr. Booker said. "Just like the real thing."

"Are you ready?" Sid asked.

"Ready for what?"

"To return to Earth."

"Am I going back?"

"Of course you're going back. You're being returned to your house in Mission Viejo tomorrow. Today is your sixth day here. Your time with us is about up, Mr. Booker. Your vacation to England was only scheduled for seven days, and your doppelganger will be returning from Europe. Today is your last full day aboard the *Peacekeeper 102*."

"I guess I'm ready to go."

"But not homesick?"

"Strangely, no."

"Tell me how you're feeling."

"The truth?"

"Of course the truth. I wouldn't have it any other way."

"I feel like a patient in a mental hospital who's been allowed to live in the outside world for a week, only to be told he has to return to the confines of the hospital. I got a brief taste of what it's like to live like a free man in the outside world. I got a taste of what it's like to live with people who aren't crazy. But now I'm being told that I have to return to the asylum. Every morning, I wake up in my cabin and look at Earth through my front window. It's such a beautiful planet, isn't it? From a distance, it seems so colorful, peaceful, and full of life, floating like an island in space. It's an oasis among the stars, a shining jewel in space. But when you're actually on its surface, it is all quite different. It's a vicious and corrupt place teeming with conniving, self-centered human beings. Seven billion of them crawling, scheming, killing, and taking from one another. Am I really ready to return? I don't know, Sid. I honestly don't know what to tell you. I don't know where I belong."

"Men like you are needed," Sid said.

"Needed for what?"

"Isn't it obvious?"

Just then, Sid and Mr. Booker were interrupted by Anna, who seemed to have appeared from nowhere. She sat down at their table with a tray of food and a cup of coffee. "It's your last day," she said to Mr. Booker.

"So I've just been told," Mr. Booker said.

"I'm going to miss you," she said.

"We're all going to miss him," Sid said. "He's been one of our best guests."

"You're probably looking forward to going home."

"A little," Mr. Booker said.

"We should get to the council," Sid said, looking at his wristwatch. "It's almost eight."

"I'll come see you tonight," Anna said. "I'd like to spend some time with you before you go."

"That'd be nice," Mr. Booker said.

"Let's have at it," Sid said, and he stood up to leave. Mr. Booker also stood, and they left Anna sitting by herself.

They went straight to the council chambers, and Sid opened the big wooden door. It creaked loudly, something Mr. Booker hadn't noticed before. They stepped inside the room and took their usual seats. They didn't have to wait long. Rock called the meeting to order at precisely eight o'clock, and he started things off by asking Mr. Booker about Ralph's play. "We understand you were there last night," he said.

"I was," Mr. Booker said.

"Well, what did you think?"

"It was a good play," Mr. Booker said. "Not like anything I've ever seen on Earth but interesting and entertaining."

"You laughed?" Ralph asked.

"Yes, I laughed."

"Good, good. I was worried you'd be offended."

"No, I wasn't offended," Mr. Booker said. "I thought it was very amusing."

"I'm glad you have a sense of humor."

Everyone in the chambers was quiet for a moment. Then Rock said, "I guess we should get moving along. We'd like to wrap things up today, but rather than ask you more questions, we'd like to give you a chance to talk. Do you have any questions for us? Is there anything you'd like to say to us?"

"What do you plan to do?" Mr. Booker asked.

"With human beings?" Rock asked.

"Yes, with my fellow men. With Earth. With the whole ball of wax."

"Right now, we honestly have no idea," Rock said. "We don't take these decisions lightly, and there are a lot of different considerations. Our decision-making process could take anywhere from a few months to several years."

"But you must have some idea."

"We can tell you this," Ernie said. "The decision we make will be in accordance with our High Rule."

"Your High Rule?"

"It's the one rule that all Ogonites live their lives by," Ernie said. "You have a million and one laws, but we have just one High Rule."

"And what is the High Rule?"

"Roughly translated to English, it is 'Live and let live.'"

"We say the same thing on Earth."

"You say it, but you don't live by it," Rock said.

"They say a lot of things," William said.

"It's important that you don't get us wrong," Rock said. "We're very fond of human beings. We like you despite your obvious flaws. Most Ogonites find Earth fascinating, and we've grown to appreciate and admire your many cultures and civilizations. Despite all its shortcomings, Earth is an astonishing planet. How humans are able to thrive and advance in such a deleterious environment truly intrigues us, and how you're also able to see certain truths is encouraging. Your art, music, and literature are true treasures of the universe. So I would answer your question by saying no, we don't want to see an end to human life, but we must honor the High Rule. It's live and let live, Mr. Booker. That's the maxim we follow. That's the rule that has guided us for thousands of years. And living is important to us, as it is for any life-form. To stay alive and remain a prospering species is our primary objective. To let live, well, we can only afford this as long as the life-forms we are allowing to live do not pose a threat to us. Our lives must come first. In a perfect world, we would let all species in the universe live, but we do not live in a perfect world. Alas, what we want and what we must settle for can be very different things."

"Right now, human beings pose no threat to us," Lucy said. "But the ball is rolling. You're going to discover something about science and technology that we learned many years ago. Technology doesn't just advance. It explodes! It wasn't that long ago that humans were riding horses and lighting their homes with candles and kerosene lamps. Now look at you! You've already landed on your moon. They're already taking reservations for trips to Mars. It won't be long before the human species is on our doorstep, and we have to decide what kind of danger this is for us. We plan to live in peace. It's live and let live, yes. But we live first and then let live only if it doesn't destroy our way of life. We know you're a bright man, Mr. Booker. Can you see how important this is? It isn't a question of whether humans are worthy to live; it's a question as to whether allowing your species to continue on threatens us and our way of life."

Mr. Booker thought about that and then said, "I have a question for you."

"Please ask," Rock said.

"How many species have you destroyed in your travels? What sort of chance do we have?"

"I'll be honest with you. Since our ship first left Og, we've destroyed six different species. This doesn't mean humans are soon to be extinct. The life-forms we destroyed were far more obvious threats. In fact, you've benefitted from their destruction. Believe me when I say that the last thing you would've wanted was for these aliens to visit your planet. And in time, they would've come knocking."

"Humans are a unique lot," Ernie said.

"Indeed, very unique," Lucy said. "Different in many ways from the life-forms we've terminated."

"How are we different?" Mr. Booker asked.

"Never have we encountered a species that can be so good and bad at the same time," Lucy said. "It's a true marvel."

"A marvel," Ralph said.

"Even William would have to admit there is much to admire in your species."

"I can admit that," William said. "I'm reluctant, but I do admit it."

"Here is what we really don't understand," Rock said. "How can you have such a good grasp of what's right and wrong yet also behave so badly?"

"It's very confusing," Lucy said.

"Humans like to call it hypocrisy," Ralph said. "But with humans, it's not just a foible. With humans, it's a way of life."

"Why is this?" Rock asked.

"I don't know," Mr. Booker said.

"But can you see our dilemma?" Ralph asked.

"I can," Mr. Booker said.

"You've been honest with us. Now we've been honest with you."

"I guess I appreciate it."

"You guess?"

"I would've preferred to hear you say that humans simply weren't in your crosshairs."

"Yes, of course. We can understand that."

"Can I ask you another question?" Mr. Booker asked.

"Certainly," Rock said.

"I've been told Ogonites believe in God."

"We do," Lucy said.

"All of us do," Ralph said.

"What would your God think of you destroying his creations?" Mr. Booker asked. "Wouldn't your God object to this?"

"Our God is quite different from yours," Rock said. "Our God isn't a creator."

"Not a creator?"

"The universe creates itself. It always has and always will. It has no morals, and it knows no love. It swirls, boils, freezes, and explodes. It shines, orbits, pulls itself apart, and bonds together. It has no dreams, desires, or longings, and while it is often beautiful to behold, beauty is a stranger to it. It can be frightening and horrifying, but it knows nothing of fear or horror. This is the palette from which life is painted. It is not painted by the hand of God but by sheer natural laws and happenstance. Life comes in all shapes and sizes, and like the rest of the universe, it knows nothing. There are gentle living creatures that wouldn't harm a flea, and there are vicious beasts who thrive on the thrill of having blood and flesh in their teeth. There is everything in between. And then there is God, Mr. Booker. God is what separates the pointless from the thoughtful. God is rational, and God is love. God is a way of living but not a living thing. God does not meddle in the lives of the living. God doesn't throw lightning bolts from the heavens, shake the ground, or overflow rivers. God is what happens when matter becomes moral, when gravity has feelings, when electrons seek to do what is right. God is a miracle, Mr. Booker. Yes, God is both miraculous and inexplicable.

"Ogonites do not drop to their knees to worship God. There is no point in doing this, because God has no eyes. And Ogonites do not pray, because they know God has no ears. We know God exists because we see evidence of God every day of our lives. We see God when two parents love and care for a child, when a doctor gives of himself to cure an ailing patient, when a teacher passes wisdom down to a youngster, and when a man reaches out to console a friend who is grieving or suffering. There is no law or mathematical formula for it. It simply is—as small as a pinhead and as large as an entire galaxy. But the point is that God does exist, and this is what an Ogonite means when he tells you he believes in God."

"Amen," Mr. Booker said. The council looked at him curiously, unsure whether he was confirming his own faith or being facetious.

"Did we answer your question?" Rock asked.

"Oh yes," Mr. Booker said.

"Fine, fine," Rock said.

"Can I ask you more?"

"You have the floor, Mr. Booker. Ask us anything you like."

Mr. Booker did indeed have more questions, mostly about the particulars of life on Og. The council members answered to the best of their ability, describing in great detail the planet and its people. The session went on for nine hours. They talked right through lunch and up until dinnertime. Things became clear to Mr. Booker. For the first time since he'd been abducted, he began to see what it meant to be an Ogonite and what it meant to be a crew member of this ship. While he'd once had a suspicious fear and distrust of this advanced species, he now felt a powerful sense of admiration and even a little envy. Despite the fact that the destruction of his species was still on the table, he had a feeling the Ogonites would do the right thing. God would lead them in the right direction, toward the proper action, for if anyone was in touch with God, it was the Ogonites.

After the session was adjourned, Sid and Mr. Booker went to the cafeteria for dinner. For a while, they didn't say a word to each other. They took their food and drink to an empty table, and before they started eating, Sid broke the silence. "We're not perfect," he said.

"Pardon me?" Mr. Booker said.

"Despite how it may seem, we're not perfect. We make mistakes like any other life-form."

"Meaning?"

"Just saying," Sid said. "Don't be surprised by the council's decision, whatever it turns out to be. It's as humans like to say: there are no guarantees in life. You can't be sure of anything, except that you'll die. Death is for certain, no matter how or when it happens to come around."

"And?" Mr. Booker said.

"I'm just trying to manage your expectations."

"I don't expect anything. But being human, I hope for the best."

"That's a good attitude," Sid said. He smiled at Mr. Booker, and Mr. Booker felt they understood each other. Sid then picked up a fork and began to eat, and Mr. Booker did the same.

Chapter 21

Sparky

Mr. Booker stopped talking to me about the Ogonites and told me he wanted to tell a story about something that had taken place a week after he returned to Earth. When I asked him why we were jumping ahead to a new topic, he just said it was important. He said the relevance of the story would be obvious, and he promised to get back to telling me about the Ogonites as soon as he was done. Of course I agreed to his plan. After all, who was I to argue about it? It was his story, not mine. If he felt it was important to leap ahead a week, I had to assume there was a good reason for doing so. If you like dogs, you might want to skip this chapter. Things do not end well for a little dog named Sparky.

I've already told you about the Garcias. They were Mr. Booker's next-door neighbors, a childless couple in their sixties. Mr. Garcia was a blue-collar Hispanic who worked as a manager at a warehouse, and Mrs. Garcia was a chubby little Caucasian woman who worked a cash register at the local Target. Mr. Booker didn't know much else about the Garcias, and although he was always politely friendly with them and they with him, they'd never been close. After Mr. Booker returned to Earth, he came to know the Garcias better. He came to know them by way of a dog named Sparky, a little yapping mixed-breed mop of an animal with dirty gray-and-white fur and a pair of rheumy dark brown eyes.

The dog was new. That is to say, he was new to the Garcia

household. Sparky once belonged to Mrs. Garcia's sister, but the sister died of cancer, and she willed the animal to the Garcias. The couple had never owned a dog, but they took it in. This happened while Mr. Booker was with the Ogonites. Mr. Booker said to me, "Imagine my surprise when I returned home and heard this noisy mutt barking in the Garcias' backyard. And I don't mean to say it barked once in a while. The dog barked morning, noon, and night, and the sound was shrill and annoying—so shrill that it penetrated walls and windows. I could hear it in every room of my house."

After a week of putting up with the dog's intolerable barking, Mr. Booker decided he had to speak to the Garcias and see if there was something they could do to stop the dog from barking. They'd always seemed like nice people, and surely they would do something to rectify the situation. Surely they would have to recognize that the dog's barking was unacceptable. So one Saturday morning, Mr. Booker walked to their front door. He rang the doorbell and waited for someone to answer. Mrs. Garcia opened the door. She was wearing an apron and apparently had been working in the kitchen. "Mr. Booker!" she exclaimed. She seemed to be in a good mood. "What brings you to our door? Won't you please come in? I'm right in the middle of baking cookies. Come along and follow me. I was about to remove another batch from the oven when you rang the doorbell."

"Okay," Mr. Booker said. He followed Mrs. Garcia, and she led him through the front room to the kitchen. Mrs. Garcia put on a mitt and then opened the oven door. She reached in, pulled out a baking sheet covered with hot chocolate chip cookies, and set the sheet down on the counter. "How do they look to you?" she asked.

"They look good," Mr. Booker said.

"Do they look done?"

"They do," Mr. Booker said.

"I love baking cookies on Saturday mornings. It makes the house smell so good."

"Yes, it has a good smell."

"Mr. Garcia loves my chocolate chip cookies."

"Is he home?" Mr. Booker asked.

"No, he's at work this morning. They're very busy at the warehouse this time of year."

Mr. Booker decided to get to the point of his visit. He said, "I couldn't help but notice you took in a dog while I was gone."

"You mean Sparky?"

"Yes, Sparky, if that's his name. When did you and Mr. Garcia decide to get a dog? I didn't realize you two were dog lovers."

"We inherited Sparky from my sister. She just died of cancer. She left Sparky to me in her will."

"Sorry to hear about your sister," Mr. Booker said.

"Thanks, but we knew her time was coming. It wasn't a surprise, so we were all prepared for it. By the time she finally passed away, it was more a relief than it was a shock. And she was able to say goodbye to each of us. That's the good thing about knowing you're about to die—being able to say your goodbyes."

"I can understand that."

"Sparky was her companion. How she loved that little animal. He saw her through thick and thin."

"I'm sure he did."

"So what did you want to know about him?"

"Well, I didn't actually want to know anything about him," Mr. Booker said. "I wanted to see if you could get him to stop barking."

"Stop barking?"

"I'm sure he means a lot to you, but his barking is kind of annoying. I can hear him in all the rooms of my house. He barks all day long, and he barks at night while I'm trying to sleep."

"Oh dear. I'm so sorry. He does like to bark, doesn't he?"

"Do you think you can get him to stop? Or maybe you could keep him indoors?"

"You don't like dogs?"

"I like dogs. I just don't like hearing them bark at all hours of the day and night."

"I see," Mrs. Garcia said.

"Do you think you can help me?"

"Here," Mrs. Garcia said. "Try one of my cookies, and tell me what you think." Mrs. Garcia handed him a warm cookie from the baking sheet. "It's my mother's recipe. I got it from her recipe book."

Mr. Booker took a small bite. "It's good," he said, and it was good. But that wasn't why he'd come to visit. "About the dog," he said. "Do you think you can keep him quiet?"

"I can try, dear," Mrs. Garcia said.

"I'd really appreciate it."

"Here. Take a few of these home with you," she said, and she put several cookies on a paper plate, covering them with a paper napkin. "I wouldn't want you to go home empty-handed."

"Thanks," Mr. Booker said.

That was Mr. Booker's first attempt to quiet the barking dog, but the situation didn't improve. Following his visit, there was a brief period of peace and quiet that lasted about an hour, and then the dog started up again. "Jesus," Mr. Booker said to himself. "This is going to drive me out of my mind!" Rather than going right back to the Garcias' house, Mr. Booker decided to leave his own house and run some errands. He thought that maybe by the time he returned, Mrs. Garcia would've figured out some way to quiet the dog. However, when he arrived back home, Sparky was still barking. In fact, the animal barked all that afternoon and into the evening. It barked all night, and Mr. Booker was only able to sleep for a few fitful hours.

Mrs. Garcia had seemed like such a nice person, so why was she letting the dog carry on like that? Hadn't he made himself clear? The barking had to stop. Something had to be done.

The next day was Sunday, and Mr. Booker went to the Garcias' front door again. He rang their bell, and this time, Mr. Garcia answered. He was not a tall man. He was dressed in a jacket and tie, ready to leave for church. He had kind brown eyes and jet-black hair. "Ah, Mr. Booker," he said. "I heard you came by yesterday."

"I did," Mr. Booker said.

"About Sparky?" Mr. Garcia said.

"Yes, about Sparky."

"Who is it, dear?" Mrs. Garcia asked.

"It's Mr. Booker again," he said.

Mrs. Garcia appeared in the doorway beside her husband. She too was ready for church. She was wearing a nice dress and hat. "I suppose you want more cookies," she said, smiling.

"They were very good," Mr. Booker said. "But I'm here again about your dog."

"What's the problem with him now?" Mr. Garcia asked.

"It's his barking," Mr. Booker said. "Isn't there any way you can get him to stop?"

"What do you want us to do?"

"I don't know," Mr. Booker said. "There must be some way to keep him quiet."

"We think he's just getting used to his new home. He isn't used to the surroundings."

"And he misses my sister," Mrs. Garcia said.

"Give him a few more days, and I'm sure he'll be as quiet as a mouse."

"A few days?"

"He's probably just nervous," Mrs. Garcia said. "I think it's just a case of the nerves."

"Can you keep him in your house?" Mr. Booker asked. "It would help if you kept him indoors."

"We tried that," Mr. Garcia said. "He just barks in our house."

Mr. Booker stared at the Garcias for a moment. They were friendly enough, but he seemed to be getting nowhere. "Give him a few more days," Mr. Garcia said. "I'm sure he'll calm down in a few days. He just needs to get used to us."

In the days that followed, the situation didn't get any better. In fact, things were getting worse. The dog barked even more consistently, and the barking became even more intense. Sometimes it sounded as if someone were torturing the poor beast. On and on the barking continued. Mr. Booker had never heard anything like it. He decided to pay the Garcias another visit to see if he could convince them to actually do something about the problem. This time, he went over on a Thursday evening. He saw Mr. Garcia's car parked in their driveway, so he knew he'd be home. He wanted it that way. He wanted to have a man-to-man talk with Mr. Garcia to let him know something had to be done. Mr. Booker was at his wit's end. He'd been deprived of sleep, and his waking hours were unbearable.

Mr. Booker rang the doorbell, and Mrs. Garcia answered. "Is your husband home?" Mr. Booker asked. "I'd like to talk to him again."

"Of course," Mrs. Garcia said. "I'll get him for you." She disappeared from the doorway, and then Mr. Garcia appeared, this time wearing shorts and a T-shirt. He seemed to be in a good mood.

"What is it?" Mr. Garcia asked.

"It's about Sparky," Mr. Booker said.

"What about him?"

"He's still barking."

Mr. Garcia sighed and then said, "I don't know what you want me to do. We've tried everything. We bought him a couple toys. We put his favorite blanket on the patio to make him feel at home. We just can't get the little guy to shut up."

"There must be something," Mr. Booker said.

"He's my wife's sister's dog. I can hardly get rid of him after all that has happened."

"You don't have to get rid of him," Mr. Booker said. "You just have to keep him quiet. Can't you keep him inside your house?"

"I told you before: he's too noisy."

"But at least I won't have to hear him."

"Can't you just keep your doors and windows closed?" Mr. Garcia asked.

"It doesn't do any good."

"I use earplugs," Mr. Garcia confessed.

"Earplugs?"

"To go to sleep. I bought a pair of earplugs, and now I sleep like a baby."

Like a baby? The nerve of this guy, telling me to wear earplugs in my own house just so I can fall asleep! Mr. Booker didn't reveal his true feelings, but he was now becoming angry. In fact, he felt like kicking Mr. Garcia in his shin.

"That's about all I can suggest," Mr. Garcia said. "I don't know what else you expect me to do. He just seems to be a barker. Some dogs are quiet, and some are barkers."

Mr. Booker stared at the man. He then turned to walk back to his house, and Mr. Garcia said, "Sorry I couldn't be of more help."

Mr. Booker went back into his house without responding to Mr. Garcia. It was better that he keep his cool and say nothing. But the barking continued.

Mr. Booker told me that he didn't dislike dogs. In fact, he liked them a lot. When Linda was alive, they had a dog of their own, an energetic little Boston terrier by the name of Sir Lancelot. They called him Lance for short. Mr. Booker adored the dog. Since they didn't have any children, Lance served as a kind of surrogate son. Linda and Mr. Booker doted over Lance, buying him all sorts of chew toys, playing with him during their free time, taking him on long walks, and letting him sleep at the foot of their bed at night. Lance lived to be sixteen. Mr. Booker had to put Lance to sleep when he finally reached an age where he was having difficulty controlling his bowels and walking. His body was giving out on him, and his eyes were the eyes of an animal who knew it was time to leave. It was sad, knowing that the life of his beloved dog was coming to an end. He took Lance to the vet, and thirty minutes later, Lance was no longer alive. Both Linda and Mr. Booker cried for hours. It was like losing a child.

So Mr. Booker understood the love people have for their pets. He knew the love firsthand, and he was fully aware of the feelings Mrs. Garcia probably had for her awful dog, Sparky. But the dog was interfering with Mr. Booker's life, and something had to be done to quiet the little dog once and for all.

At three in the morning on a Tuesday night, Mr. Booker finally decided to take action. Sparky had started barking again, and the sound had awakened Mr. Booker. He climbed out of bed and put on a pair of sweatpants and a T-shirt. He then put on a pair of socks and sneakers. He paced back and forth across his bedroom for fifteen minutes, contemplating the details. "It's either him or me," he said to himself while pacing. Finally, he stepped out of the bedroom and walked to the patio door. He slid open the door and stepped outside into the cool night air. There was a full moon, and its light shone on everything, including the wood fence that separated his backyard from the Garcias'. There was nothing between Sparky and Mr. Booker other than the wooden fence.

Mr. Booker grabbed one of the patio chairs and brought it to the fence. He then stood on the chair and looked into the Garcias' backyard. There he was, the mangy little mop of an animal. He was standing on the lawn, barking at nothing. The dog just stood there, foolishly barking for the sake of barking. Mr. Booker proceeded to grab the top of the fence, pulling himself up and swinging over one leg and then the other. He jumped and landed in the Garcias' flower bed. He was trying to keep quiet to be sure he didn't wake anyone. Of course, with the dog yapping so loudly, who would have noticed his footsteps?

He made it to the Garcias' back lawn and immediately got down on his knees. The grass was damp, and his knees were now wet. "Here, Sparky," he whispered. "Come here, boy." The dog continued to bark, at first ignoring him. He needed to gain the dog's trust, and he continued. "Come on, boy," he whispered. "Here we go. Be a good boy, and come to Mr. Booker."

The dog suddenly responded. He stopped barking for a moment and wagged his tail. He seemed pleased that someone was paying attention to him. At first, Sparky remained where he stood, wagging his tail and panting. Then he let out a whimper and lowered his head. He slowly approached Mr. Booker. "That's a good boy," Mr. Booker whispered. "Be a good boy. Come to Mr. Booker."

When the dog was a foot or so away, Mr. Booker reached out and petted the little scoundrel. He patted Sparky on the head and then scratched his back with his fingers. Sparky liked this, and his tail wagged nonstop. He barked a couple more times, as though trying to talk to Mr. Booker and express his gratitude.

Then, in one quick motion, Mr. Booker grabbed Sparky by his neck with both his hands. He rolled the dog over onto his back and then, pressing his thumbs deep under the dog's chin, did what he'd come to do. He began to strangle the little beast with all his might. Sparky immediately put up a fight, so Mr. Booker squeezed even harder. Sparky opened his mouth, coughing and gasping for air, but it was a futile and pathetic gesture. He squirmed and kicked his legs, trying to break free from Mr. Booker's strong hands, but Mr. Booker held his ground, squeezing the dog's neck even harder. It had to be one of the worst things Mr. Booker had ever done. The dog's tongue was now hanging out, and his eyes were bulging. Finally, after a minute or so, the dog began to succumb. Sparky's eyes looked sadly at Mr. Booker, as if to say, "Why have you done this to me?" But Mr. Booker didn't let up; he choked the poor dog until he forced out a final bowel movement, until his little body went as limp as a wet rag. "No more barking for you, little fella," Mr. Booker said. Finally, he released the dog and stood up, looking down at the dead animal.

Mr. Booker was shaking, and his forehead and armpits were wet with perspiration. He was out of breath, as if he'd just gotten done running around the block. There was a large terra-cotta pot alongside the fence, and Mr. Booker stood on its edge to get himself up and over the fence. Just before jumping into his own yard, he looked back at the dog on the Garcias' lawn. Sparky was on his side in the moonlight, motionless and dead. The barking had finally ceased, and the nightmare was over.

Mr. Booker tried to go back to bed that night, but he couldn't fall asleep. When he shut his eyes, all he could see was Sparky wagging his tail and approaching him, trusting him. It was about five in the morning when Mr. Booker began to cry. He wasn't ordinarily a crier, but he found himself sobbing uncontrollably. "That fucking little dog!" he exclaimed, and he punched his pillow with his fist over and over. Finally, at about six, worn out from crying and punching his pillow, he was able to fall asleep. He didn't wake up until noon the next day. The first thing he said to himself was, "I'm not a bad person. It was either me or him. I was given no choice."

A couple days later, Mr. Booker was in his front yard, trimming the hedge that led to his front door. He looked to his left and saw Mr. Garcia stepping out of his house to go to work. Mr. Garcia noticed him and waved. Then he walked toward Mr. Booker, wanting to tell him something. "Sparky died," he said.

"I'm sorry to hear that," Mr. Booker said. "What happened?"

"We think he had a heart attack. We found him on the lawn, dead as a doornail."

"Poor dog," Mr. Booker said.

"Mrs. Garcia was devastated. First her sister and then her sister's dog. It was a bit much."

"I can imagine."

"Just between you and me, I'm glad the little fella is gone. All that barking, you know."

"He was a barker," Mr. Booker said.

Mr. Garcia smiled, as if remembering the dog fondly. Then he said, "The hedge is looking good."

"Thanks," Mr. Booker said. "It just needed a little trimming."

The two men stared at each other for a moment. "Well, I guess I'll see you around," Mr. Garcia said. Mr. Booker nodded and smiled.

It was nice having things back to normal. Mr. Booker went to work on his hedge, and Mr. Garcia climbed into his car and started the engine.

Did Mr. Booker feel guilty? Did he feel any remorse at all? It was truly an awful thing to do, but it was as Rock had said during the last council session: "In a perfect world, we can let all species in the universe live, but we do not live in a perfect world. Alas, what we want and what we must settle for can be very different things."

Yes, it was just as Rock had said. Mr. Booker said so long to Sparky and hello to some peace and quiet.

CHAPTER 22

A TIME TO LAUGH

"I guess this will be my last dinner in the cafeteria," Mr. Booker said.

"Are you going to miss our food?" Sid asked.

"I think I will."

"And our prompt service?"

"Yes, the service has been good."

"Eating is so important, isn't it? To eat! We call it the seventy-five-year verb."

"The what?" Mr. Booker asked.

"It's like this," Sid said. "Given that the average Ogonite lives to be over six hundred years old, and given that he spends approximately three hours a day preparing and consuming food, he spends over seventy-five years of his life in the act of eating. Think of it! Over seventy-five years making food and stuffing it into his mouth! That's a significant chunk of time by any measure, and it's not time to be squandered. 'Make the best of it,' we like to say. 'Enjoy every second.'"

"I guess that makes sense," Mr. Booker said.

"Of course it does," Sid said. "If it didn't make sense, why would I bother to tell you about it?"

"I don't know."

"Mind if we join you?" a voice said from behind Mr. Booker, and he turned to see Rock and the other four council members.

They were holding their dinner trays, hoping to sit with Sid and Mr. Booker.

"Yes, please sit with us," Mr. Booker said.

"Pull up a table and chairs," Sid said. Rock set his tray down and moved an adjacent table closer. They all pulled up chairs and took their seats.

"Are we all hungry?" Rock asked the group.

"I'm famished," Lucy said.

"I could eat a horse," Ernie said.

"I was just telling Mr. Booker about the seventy-five-year verb," Sid said.

"Yes, of course," Rock said.

"It works out to about ten years for humans," William said, looking upward and doing the math in his head.

"Ten years," Mr. Booker said. "Imagine that."

"Not to be squandered," Sid said.

A new voice asked, "Do you have any room here for us?" Mr. Booker turned to see Anna's father, Jacob. He was with his wife, June. They too were holding dinner trays, hoping to join the group.

"Please join us," Mr. Booker said.

"Pull up another table," Sid said.

"We'll be one big, happy family," Rock said.

"One happy family," June repeated.

Jacob pulled up a table and a couple chairs, and he and June took their seats. "I take it the council session went well today?" Jacob asked.

"It did," Rock said.

"Today was the last day," Lucy said.

"So we heard," Jacob said.

"Mr. Booker has probably had enough of us to last a lifetime," Rock said.

"It wasn't so bad," Mr. Booker said.

"You did a fine job," Ernie said.

Two more men approached the group, and one of them asked, "Do we need an invitation to join this party, or can we just sit down?" Again, Mr. Booker turned his head. This time, it was Henry, the guy with the mustache who had pretended to be a cop at his house. He was there with his partner, Chuck.

"Please join us," Sid said. "Pull up another table and chairs."

"Where is Anna?" Mr. Booker asked Jacob. "She should be here too."

"She had an emergency in Sector Four," Jacob said. "She'll be eating dinner late."

"She said she'd come see you later," June said. "She said she'd come to your cabin right after she finished dinner."

"She's developed quite a liking for you, Mr. Booker," Jacob said.

"Quite a liking," June said.

"We're just friends," Mr. Booker said. "It's really nothing more than that."

Ralph suddenly stood up. "Let's toast our fine earthling friend!" He held up his glass, and everyone else did the same. They then clinked the glasses together and looked toward Mr. Booker.

"He's been one of a kind," Rock said.

"Yes," Ernie said. "One of a kind."

"We're going to miss you," Lucy said.

"You are?" Mr. Booker replied.

"He was nothing at all like D'Orfo," Rock said to the group.

"Or Ignaratiz," Lucy said.

"Or Blacher," Ernie said.

"Who are you talking about?" Mr. Booker asked, not recognizing the names.

"Those are some of our other guests," Sid explained. "The ones who drove us crazy."

"D'Orfo was the worst," Rock said.

"The absolute worst," Lucy agreed.

"He was from the planet Towd," Sid told Mr. Booker. "He gave us a lot of trouble. Our computer said he was one of the best ones, but if he was a good one, I can't imagine what the rest of his kind were like."

"Awful people," Ralph said.

"Just begging to be destroyed," William said.

"Did you destroy them?" Mr. Booker asked.

"Oh yes," Rock said. "Not a trace of them remains. They're completely extinct. And good riddance, I say. The universe is a much better place without them."

"They were a cancer," William said.

"What was so bad about them?" Mr. Booker asked.

"I don't even know where to begin," Rock said, rolling his eyes. "Does anyone here want to describe the Towdians for Mr. Booker?"

"Murder, rape, and theft," Ernie said. "They thrived on mayhem and immorality. They were a godless and hateful civilization. As smart as whips but a despicable species with no redeeming qualities."

"The stories about them we could tell you," Ralph said. "They'd curl your hair."

"Stories that would make your stomach turn," Lucy said. "Their behavior would even offend Earth's worst criminals and psychopaths."

"Ah, the Towdians," Rock said. There was a strange look on his face as he recalled them.

"Now they won't be bothering anyone," William said. "Not ever."

"Thank God for that," Rock said.

Everyone stopped talking for a moment. The group was eating and lost in thought. Then Jacob broke the silence by asking Mr. Booker, "What do you plan on doing once you're home?"

Mr. Booker swallowed a mouthful of food. "I'll be teaching summer school."

"History classes?"

"Yes, world history."

"Do your students like spending their summers at school, studying and doing classwork?"

"Some of them do. But others, not so much. I have two kinds of students during the summer session. I get all the kids who flunked their history class during the regular semesters. They have to repeat the class to keep up with the rest of the students. I also get kids who simply like to go to school. These are the kids who want to spend their summers learning about world history. It's a weird mixture of kids."

"You'd enjoy teaching Ogonites," Lucy said. "They all like to learn."

"We should've had him sit in on a few classes here on the ship," Rock said.

"That would've been a great idea," Lucy said.

"There wasn't enough time," Sid said. "We were pressed as it was."

"True enough," Rock said.

"What do you think of the other teachers at your school?" Ralph asked. He had dribbled some soup on his beard while eating, and he cleaned it off with a napkin while he spoke. "Are the other teachers as honest and thoughtful as you?"

"I think most of them are."

"Do you think they're good people?"

"For the most part, yes. I would say they're good people."

"Do you know Miss Applecart?" Lucy asked.

"Yes, of course."

"What do you think of her?"

"She's a nice person," Mr. Booker said.

"Anything else about her?" Lucy asked.

"She has an odd last name."

Everyone laughed, but Mr. Booker had no idea what was so funny. "Did you know one of our Ogonite operatives spoke to Miss Applecart?" Ernie asked. "I mean, before you were abducted."

"I didn't know," Mr. Booker said.

"We spoke with most of the teachers at your school. But we found Miss Applecart to be most interesting."

There was laughter, and Mr. Booker now felt a little embarrassed at not knowing what the Ogonites were laughing at.

"Did you know she likes you?" Lucy asked.

"I like her too," Mr. Booker said.

"I mean, she really likes you," Lucy said. "She likes you a lot."

"And she's about your age," Ernie said.

"And she's nice looking," Rock said. "Well, at least as far as humans go."

"Yes," Mr. Booker agreed. "She's a good-looking woman, and she is about my age."

"Why haven't you pursued a relationship with her?" Lucy asked. "Why haven't you ever asked her out to lunch, to dinner, or to a movie? You like her, don't you?"

"Yes, of course. I just told you I liked her."

"Well?" Lucy asked.

"I don't know," Mr. Booker said. "Ever since Linda passed away, I just haven't been motivated to date other women. It would be weird. It would be like I was cheating on her."

"She's no longer alive," Rock said. "It would hardly be cheating."

"Don't you think Linda would want you to be happy?" Lucy asked.

"Yes, she probably would."

"Are you happy, Mr. Booker?"

"I don't know. I mean, I think I am, but I guess I don't honestly know."

"I'm going to give you some advice," Rock said. "It's about love, Mr. Booker. Love is critical. A life without love is like a planet without a sun. Life without love is a cold and dark place. It's true, isn't it? You're alone, Mr. Booker. You have your students, but they aren't the same thing as having a loving mate. You have your history books to read, but do they really complete you? I think I can speak for everyone here when I say it's time for you to open your eyes. Love is right on your doorstep, and all you have to do is let it into your home. Linda wouldn't be upset. She would want to see you happy. She would want you to be loved. I'm sure she would agree with me when I tell you to move on and end your loneliness. Applecart, Mr. Booker. Remember that name."

"Hear, hear," Ralph said.

"Love conquers all!" Ernie exclaimed, slapping the table with the palm of his hand.

"Love means never having to say you're sorry!" Jacob said.

"Better to have loved and lost than never to have loved at all!" Henry said.

"Love is a many-splendored thing," June said.

"All you need is love!" Lucy said.

"Love, love, love!" Ernie sang.

Everyone was now laughing, and Mr. Booker could feel his face turning warm.

"We've embarrassed him," Lucy said.

"Someone had to tell him," Ernie said.

"Yes," Rock agreed. "We're doing him a favor. Now it's up to him."

"Humans have a saying on Earth," Ralph said. "They say, 'When one door shuts, another door opens.' Have you heard this saying?"

"Yes," Mr. Booker said. "I've heard it."

"We have a similar saying on Og," Ralph said. "We say that all endings are beginnings. It's the same idea, only using different words. Do these sayings tell you anything?"

"I suppose they do."

"When I was a boy," Ernie said. "My father died from a rare and fatal Ogonite disease. He died when I was only forty-two. It was an awful time in my life. I loved my father dearly, and we had always been very close. He was a great father and a wonderful teacher. But best of all, he loved me with all his heart. I think my father would've done anything for me, and I would've done anything for him. When he was first diagnosed with his illness, all of us were devastated. My mom took it especially hard. Mom and Dad had been so close, and they'd thought they'd be together for the rest of their lives. It took four years for my father to die following the day he was diagnosed, and during those four years, we tried to pack in a lifetime of experiences. We traveled all over Og and saw all the cities and sights. We went to plays together, and we went to restaurants afterward. We went to athletic events, art exhibits, and music concerts. We were always doing things as a family. When it finally came time for Dad to say goodbye, he made us promise to do something. On his deathbed, he made us promise to go on living. He said, 'I ask only one thing of you: that you promise to live your lives so that the last day of my life is the first day of yours.' Then he said, 'All endings are beginnings.' That was the first time I'd heard that saying, and it stuck with me into adulthood. I still believe in it, Mr. Booker. We all should believe in it. Endings are indeed beginnings. Each and every one of them."

"Did you keep your promise?"

"It wasn't easy," Ernie said.

"But you did?"

Ernie smiled. "Five years later, my mom met another man. This man was nothing like my father. At first, I was furious that Mom was trying to replace my dad with a new partner. I didn't want this ape to be my stepfather. I wanted nothing to do with the poor guy. But Mom reminded me of my father's last words and the promise we'd all made. 'Endings are beginnings,' she said to me, repeating my father's words. And it is true, isn't it? It's like you say on Earth: when one door closes, another door opens. I hunkered down and learned to accept my mom's new lover as my stepfather, and I grew to love him as much as he loved me. Today we're best friends. He's not my father, and he never will be, but that doesn't mean I love him any less. That doesn't mean he doesn't have an important place in my life. He's been a wonderful teacher and a supportive friend. What I'm trying to tell you is that when a loved one dies, life keeps moving forward for the survivors, as it should. There's nothing perverse about it, and there's nothing to be ashamed of. There's no reason for you to feel guilty. Your new life may not be the same as your old life, but it doesn't have to be any less rewarding. You need to understand this. Take this advice as a gift from us to you."

"Yes, a gift," Rock said.

"All wrapped up with a ribbon around it," Lucy said.

"With a cherry on top," Ralph said. Everyone laughed at this, including Mr. Booker.

The Ogonites stared at Mr. Booker for a moment, and then Rock said, "Consider this advice the next time you talk to Miss Applecart."

"Miss Applecart?" Mr. Booker said. "Jeez, so we're talking about her again?"

"Yes, about her."

"Just what I needed," Mr. Booker said, chuckling. "A roomful of men and women from outer space telling me how to manage my love life."

Ralph said, "Don't sell us short. Good advice can often come from the most unlikely sources."

"It happens all the time," Rock said.

"All the time," June said.

"I suppose that could be true," Mr. Booker said, mulling their words over.

"Would you like some more advice?" Rock asked.

"About what?" Mr. Booker asked.

"About what you do when you return home."

"What's there to do?"

"You could tell others about your experience."

"Yes, I could do that."

"But we strongly advise against it," Ernie said.

"Do you think anyone on Earth will believe your story?" Ralph asked. "Who'll believe you other than a lot of gullible kooks and crackpots?"

"The people you respect will all say it's bullshit," Jacob said. Apparently, he couldn't resist interjecting his favorite noun.

"They'll call you crazy," Ernie said.

"And there's a good chance you lose your job," Lucy said. "No parents are going to want a lunatic teaching their children history. It would be a problem for you. If you lost your job, how would you pay your bills? And what other kind of job are you qualified for?"

"We've seen it happen," Rock said.

"Tell him about Queep," Henry said.

"Who's Queep?" Mr. Booker asked.

"Like you, we brought him aboard our ship," Rock said. "We'd never met a nicer and more intelligent man. We extracted Queep from the planet Nara, and he spent two full weeks with us. The

Naranites were wonderful people, and we had no need to destroy them. Their civilization was far more advanced than Earth's, so you'd think they would've been more open to the idea of aliens orbiting their planet. But they weren't. When we returned Queep to his province, the first thing he did was tell everyone about where he'd been. He told them about our spaceship, our planet, our council, and all the questions we asked. The Naranites take their mental health very seriously, and upon hearing Queep's ramblings, the authorities immediately had him committed to a mental hospital to treat his delusions. He lost his job and then his family. He refused to recant his story, and when we left ten years later, he was still a patient, still locked up."

"Still locked up," June said.

"And for what purpose?" Rock asked. "What was the point of it all?"

"To be honest?" Mr. Booker said.

"Ah, to be honest. But there's a time to be honest and a time to prevaricate."

"There's a time to weep," Ralph said.

"A time to laugh," Ernie said.

"A time to mourn," William said.

"And a time to dance," Lucy said. Everyone broke out laughing except for Mr. Booker.

"I thought Ogonites didn't lie," he said.

"Did someone here tell you that?"

"I thought they did."

"Listen," Rock said. "The truth is a wonderful thing. And we believe everyone should be true to themselves. But to always be truthful to others is a different story. A much different story. We asked you to be truthful to us during our council sessions because it was necessary. Without your honest answers, we wouldn't have been able to make a sound decision. But ask yourself this, Mr. Booker. If you were introduced to a woman at a party, and you felt she was especially ugly, would you blurt out, 'Nice to meet you. You sure are an ugly woman'? Or if you were talking to one of your students who wasn't very bright, would you say, 'You can study all you want, but odds are you're barely going to pass my class'? Or if you'd just experienced a serious bout of depression, would you tell your classroom, 'Nice to be here, but just a few days ago, I was trying to decide between jumping off a bridge and slitting open my wrists'? No, Mr. Booker, we don't always need to tell the truth. Sometimes the truth is pointlessly harmful, and sometimes it's unnecessarily discouraging. And sometimes it's just personal and no one's business. In the case of your visit to our spaceship, the truth is just going to be more than the average human can handle. You'll have nothing to gain by telling them and everything to lose."

"I guess that makes sense," Mr. Booker said.

"A month or so ago, before we abducted you, if someone had told you he'd been aboard an alien spaceship for a week, would you have believed him?"

"Probably not."

"Of course not. And if you go tell others now that you spent a week aboard such a spaceship, went skinny dipping with an alien girl named Anna, and ate dinner every night in an alien cafeteria, do you think they'd believe you?"

"No, they wouldn't."

"That is the truth, Mr. Booker. The truth is that the truth will get you nowhere."

"Nowhere," June said.

"So mum's the word," Ralph said.

Mr. Booker thought about that for a moment. Of course, the Ogonites were right. Then he changed the subject and asked, "Will there be a warning?"

"A warning?"

"If you decide to destroy us, will we have any warning? Will there be an explanation?"

"No," Rock said. "There'll be no warning."

"It'll happen very quickly," Ernie said.

"Our weapons are very effective," William said. "It'll be over in a matter of minutes."

"You people criticize humans for all their weapons. But what of your own weapons?"

"There's a difference between how we use our weapons and how humans use theirs," Rock said. "Our sole aim is to survive and keep the peace. For humans, weapons provide a means to attack."

"We don't just attack. We also use our weapons to defend ourselves and survive."

"You use them to survive the aggression of other humans."

"There are always aggressors," Ralph said. "That's the problem."

Mr. Booker didn't know how to respond. They'd been over this before, and they were right. There were always aggressors.

"Don't worry," Rock said. "We'll consider everything and make the right decision."

"Our God will guide us," Ernie said.

"And God is love," Lucy said. "We are guided by love and peace."

"Okay," Mr. Booker said.

"You know," Henry said, jumping to a new subject, "This hamburger isn't half bad." Everyone at the tables looked at him. He was eating a juicy hamburger and had taken several big bites from it. "It's not bad at all," he said. "In fact, it's very good!"

"I tried one several years ago," Ralph said.

"Did you like it?"

"It was different."

"Have you tried the enchiladas?" Rock asked.

"Aren't they Mexican food?" Lucy said.

"Yes, yes, Mexican food."

"Do you like to eat Mexican food?" Rock asked Mr. Booker.

"I do," he said. "Linda and I used to eat it all the time. There was a little Mexican restaurant in Santa Ana we used to frequent."

"It's funny how much Mexican food Americans eat while simultaneously trying to keep Mexican people out of their country. What is it with you Americans? Do you like Mexicans or not?"

"It's complicated," Mr. Booker said.

"Complicated?" Ralph said.

"Excuses, excuses," William said. "Whenever a human being can't justify his actions, he calls the situation complicated."

"Amen," Ralph said.

"Enough of this blather!" Rock suddenly exclaimed. He threw his arms up in the air. "It's time for us to laugh! It's time to dance! This is the last night any of us will see our guest. First thing tomorrow morning, he'll be on his way home to his house in California, and we'll never see him again. So why are we talking about Mexicans? Why are we talking about dead loved ones, weapons, and the end of the world? Someone needs to come forward and tell us a good joke. We should see our friend off with a laugh to remember us by."

"I know a good joke," Henry said.

"Which one?" Rock asked.

"Have you heard about the Ogonite who walks into a bar?"

"I haven't," Rock said.

"Neither have I," Ernie said.

"Have you heard it?" Ralph asked Mr. Booker.

"No, of course not," Mr. Booker said.

"Then let's hear it," Ralph said to Henry.

"Yes, tell it," Rock said.

Everyone stared at Henry, waiting for his joke. He plopped his half-eaten hamburger onto his plate and wiped his lips with the back of his hand. He leaned forward and said, "An Ogonite walks into a tavern and takes a seat at the bar so he can order a drink. The bartender asks him what he wants, and the Ogonite orders a Scotch and water. The bartender says, 'You're not from around here, are you?' The Ogonite says no, he's an alien from another galaxy. The bartender makes the drink and pushes it in front of the Ogonite. The Ogonite then asks how much he owes for the drink. Figuring the alien hasn't got a clue what a drink on Earth should cost, the bartender says to the Ogonite, 'That'll be two hundred dollars.' The Ogonite reaches into his back pocket and pulls out his wallet. He removes two hundred dollars from the wallet and slides it toward the bartender. The bartender grabs the money and smiles ear to ear. He then goes to work cleaning the bar with a rag, and the Ogonite enjoys his drink. Finally, after a couple of minutes, the bartender says, 'You know, we don't get many aliens in this place.' The Ogonite laughs and says, 'At these prices, it doesn't surprise me.'"

Rock laughed. "That was good."

"Ho, ho!" Ernie bellowed.

"Bravo!" Ralph exclaimed.

Everyone laughed, including Mr. Booker. He said, "I'm really going to miss you guys. However this all works out, I'm going to miss all of you."

CHAPTER 23

PLAYING HOUSE

Mr. Booker was alone in his cabin. The cafeteria dinner with his Ogonite friends had concluded two hours ago, and he was reading *Uncle Tom's Cabin*, waiting for Anna to show up.

Was this amazing adventure really almost over? It was an adventure, wasn't it? He hadn't climbed a mountain, blazed a trail through a jungle, or climbed to the top of a mountain, but it was a great adventure. How many people on Earth could say they'd been aboard an alien spacecraft, not just in their imaginations but for real? He'd seen real creatures from outer space, real golden robes, and real Ogonite woodwork. He'd eaten real cocopees with kambert sauce, ooflas, and sides of salted arponots. He'd watched real aliens try to play basketball.

It was an adventure he would never forget, and now it was coming to an end. He was looking forward to being home in his stucco and red-tile-roofed house on his sleepy tree-lined street, on his beloved planet Earth, whirling around its axis every twenty-four hours. There would be real days and nights. He would be able to get a real hamburger for dinner, with a real side order of fries. He was looking forward to the fresh air, wispy clouds, and gentle breezes of summer. How he missed all the sounds of home. There would be the ruckus of children playing in the neighborhood, the chirping of birds from the trees, the drone of airplanes passing overhead, and the noisy whir of power lawn mowers being pushed across front yards on Saturday afternoons. He had been gone only a week, but it felt as if he'd been away from home for years—and he would be returning tomorrow.

There was a knock on the front door, and he jumped off the couch to answer it, hoping it was Anna. Instead, it was a kid who looked about fifteen or sixteen with a glass of water in one hand and a couple pills in the other. "Sid asked me to bring these to you," he said. "They're for your trip tomorrow."

"What do they do?" Mr. Booker asked, letting the kid place the pills in the palm of his hand.

"They're to help with relocation sickness. You need to take them now."

"Okay," Mr. Booker said.

"Sometimes they work, and sometimes they don't. Sid thought you may as well give them a try. He said you were pretty sick when we first brought you here."

Mr. Booker popped the pills into his mouth and washed them down with the glass of water. "Thanks," he said, handing the glass back to the kid.

"Can I ask you a question?" the kid asked.

"Sure," Mr. Booker said.

"I'm just curious."

"Go ahead."

"Is it true humans don't like the way they smell?"

Mr. Booker laughed. It seemed like such an odd question. "Who told you humans don't like the way they smell?"

"My father told me," the kid said. "He said human beings will do about anything possible to avoid smelling human."

"Why did he say that?"

"Dad says perfumes, colognes, deodorants, breath mints, and mouthwashes are a multibillion-dollar industry on Earth. Is that really true?"

"I suppose it is."

"So is there a reason?"

"Maybe it's because we don't smell so good," Mr. Booker said, laughing.

"Can I smell you?" the kid asked.

"I suppose there's no harm," Mr. Booker said. The kid leaned forward and sniffed at him. He sniffed at his face and then at his chest.

"You don't smell so bad to me," he said.

"What do I smell like?"

"I guess you smell like a human."

"Is that good or bad?"

"It isn't anything. It's just the way you smell. But you're the only human I've smelled. Maybe if I had a chance to smell other humans, I'd see what all the fuss was about."

"Maybe," Mr. Booker said.

"I finally made it!" a voice said. It was Anna. She was now behind the kid, tapping him on the shoulder and motioning for him to step aside. "Jeez, what an afternoon I had," she said. "I never thought I'd get here."

"Who's this?" the kid asked.

"This is my friend Anna," Mr. Booker said.

"And who are you?" Anna asked.

"Sid sent him over here with some medication," Mr. Booker explained. "It's supposed to keep me from getting sick when they send me home tomorrow."

"Sometimes it works, and sometimes it doesn't," the kid said.

"He's all mine now," Anna said to the kid.

"He's yours?"

"Off with you!" she said. "Shouldn't you be at home with your parents? Shouldn't you be doing homework?"

"He wanted to smell me," Mr. Booker said.

"Smell you?"

"I just wanted to see what all the fuss was about," the kid said.

"Take a hike," Anna said to the boy.

The kid looked a little dejected.

"Thanks for the pills," Mr. Booker said, trying to be nice.

"You're welcome," the kid said. Anna was now in the cabin, and the kid turned to leave.

When Mr. Booker shut the door, Anna plopped down on the sofa and kicked off her shoes. "Ogonite curiosity can be so annoying," she said.

"I didn't mind," Mr. Booker said. "Besides, he was just a kid."

"I heard you had a big dinner this evening," Anna said.

"I did," Mr. Booker said.

"I'm sorry I wasn't there."

"Your dad said you were busy."

"One of the farm workers got his hand caught in a reaper. It was a mess. It took three of us to take care of him."

"Is he going to be all right?"

"He'll be fine in a few days. Dad told me your dinner went well. He said you all had a good time."

"It was nice," Mr. Booker said. "But it did leave me wondering."

"Wondering?"

"About what the council plans to do. One minute they're raking me over the coals with all their questions, and the next minute we're all telling jokes and laughing. I honestly can't make heads or tails of it."

"Don't worry about it," Anna said.

"I have to worry, don't I?"

"Listen, Earth could be hit by a giant meteor before they even make up their minds. Worrying won't get you anywhere."

"They seemed encouraging tonight."

"Maybe that's a good sign."

"I'd like to think it is."

"Or maybe they're just trying not to alarm you. Who really knows what they're thinking? At this point, I don't think even they know what they're going to do. Let's talk about something else."

"Like what?"

"Tell me what you plan to do when you get home."

"What I plan to do?"

"The first thing you'll do when you're home."

"Well, I'll check my voice mail for messages. Everyone knew I was leaving for England, so I'm not expecting any messages. But you never know. I'll also go through all my mail. I had my neighbor bring it in while I was gone. And I suppose I'll have to unpack my suitcase, the one my doppelganger took with him overseas. And I'll have to wash all my clothes. It's kind of gross to think a stranger has been wearing my clothes, so I'll probably wash them twice. And I'll probably check the yard to be sure nothing died. I was only gone a week, so the yard should be fine. But I'll check it anyway, just to be sure. I'll also probably start up my car, just to be sure the battery didn't go dead. Sometimes when you don't drive your car for a while, the battery dies. I guess that's about it. I'll sit down on the couch and turn on the TV news to see if I missed anything important."

"I think it's sad."

"What's sad?"

"You have no one to return to. No one will be waiting for you. You have no one to call to tell that you've returned home."

"I'm used to living alone."

"But it's sad."

"Let's change the subject."

"So it does bother you."

"It does a little."

"Have you ever been on death's doorstep?" Anna asked, now seeming to change the subject.

"Death's doorstep?"

"I mean, have you ever been about to die? Have you ever been so close to the end of your life you could taste it, smell it, and feel the Grim Reaper breathing down the back of your neck? Have you ever been sure your life was about over and that there was nothing you could do about it?"

"No, I guess I never have."

"I have," Anna said.

"What happened?" Mr. Booker asked.

"Ah, what happened to me? That is the sixty-four-thousand-dollar question."

"I don't understand."

"I am not the same person today as I was before it happened. That's what happened to me."

"I still don't understand."

Mr. Booker stepped over to the couch and sat down next to Anna. She leaned against him and told her story. "When I was younger, I was afraid," she said.

"Afraid of what?"

"Of everything, I guess. I don't know how else to describe it. People frightened me. Situations frightened me. Life frightened me, so I kept to myself. I never went out on a limb for anyone or anything. I felt there was too much at stake—getting humiliated, being betrayed, having others laugh at me. My father grew concerned, and he had me read several self-help books about building up self-confidence and dealing with fears, but I didn't find them helpful. He then had me go to the ship psychologist, and I spent months with him, working on my problem. But no matter what the psychologist said, and no matter what I tried to do, I remained a frightened little girl. Then everything in my life turned around when I was fifty-six."

"What happened?" Mr. Booker asked.

"Something awful."

"Something awful?"

"I'm going to tell you about it because you need to know. I'm going to tell you every horrible detail of the event so you can understand."

"Okay," Mr. Booker said.

"When I was fifty-six, we were studying a civilization who occupied a planet called Towd."

"I've heard of it."

"You have?"

"They were talking about Towd at dinner this evening. Rock said they were destroyed."

"They were," Anna said. "But before we destroyed them, we brought one of their citizens aboard the ship, much the same as we abducted you. The council wanted to question him. The creature's name was D'Orfo."

"I've heard of him too."

"Did they tell you what he did to me?"

"No," Mr. Booker said.

"When we first put him in his cabin, he was completely out of control. He was running into walls and beating his head against his front door. We were worried he was going to crack his skull, and we had to stop him. We sent four people into his cabin to take care of him, three of them being guards and the fourth being me. The guards were supposed to restrain him, and I was supposed to administer a mild tranquilizer to calm him down and stop his self-destructive behavior. I had just started my career as a medic, and that was my first assignment. D'Orfo was a typical Towdian—about eight feet tall, very muscular, completely hairless, and covered with scales. Something like a cross between a lizard and a large human being. Anyway, the guards wrestled D'Orfo to the floor, and they had him pinned down and ready for the tranquilizer. I opened my medic bag and got what I needed, when suddenly, D'Orfo was able to throw the guards off him. We had made sure there were no weapons available to him, but there was a large vase in the room. D'Orfo grabbed the vase and smashed it against the wall. He then grabbed one of the large ceramic shards, and using it like a knife, he proceeded to fight with the three guards, cutting their throats one by one. When D'Orfo was done, the guards were writhing on the floor, holding their severed throats and dying. In the meantime, I had been off to the side of the room with my back against a wall. D'Orfo looked at me, growling and grimacing. I was frozen in place, too scared to run. I was petrified! D'Orfo came after me and held me from behind with his strong arm around my neck and with the knife–like ceramic shard pressed to the jugular vein of my neck."

"Jesus," Mr. Booker said.

"He then told me to hold still and keep quiet, or he would kill me. He was holding me as a hostage. His hot reptilian breath was panting against the top of my head, and the scales on his arms were scratching my throat. It was the worst experience of my life, having this out-of-control eight-foot-tall beast holding me from behind, threatening to kill me. I swear he smelled like he'd just swum in a lake of raw sewage, and the angrier he got, the worse he smelled. And he drooled when he spoke, and the shoulders of my robe were growing wet with his saliva. I felt like vomiting, but I didn't dare do anything that might make him angrier. I just kept quiet and let him have his way with me. And that included being raped.

"Towdian men rape their women when they feel stressed. It's how they release their anxiety. He tore off my robe, pushed me up against a wall, and went after me with a vengeance until globs of his yellow semen were running down my legs. It was the worst feeling ever! When I started to cry, he slapped my face. I regained my composure, and he then told me to open the front door of his cabin. I did what he said, since he was still holding the ceramic shard at my neck. The two of us went out into the hall. Others saw us, and they ran to get help. I remained in D'Orfo's clutches for two or three hours until Sid showed up and was finally able to convince him we meant no harm. He let me go, and I ran into Sid's arms. D'Orfo was then escorted back to his cabin, and I was taken to the nearest medic station. I was crying like a baby. Never in my life had I come so close to losing my life. Sid met with me later, and instead of commiserating with me, he patted my cheek and said, 'You've been given a wonderful gift, Anna, all wrapped up with a ribbon around it.' It took a few weeks for me to get what Sid meant, but once I got it, I saw the purpose in the whole awful event. My fears were gone, and I was ready to start living."

"I don't get it," Mr. Booker said.

"I should've died that afternoon. D'Orfo should've slit my throat."

"But he didn't."

"Precisely. And why didn't he? There are purposes to all the things that happen in life. I'm not talking about anything magical or mysterious. I'm not talking about the guiding hand of a supernatural god. I'm talking about something very real. Purposes just are, and the purpose to the awful experience I had that afternoon was now as plain to me as the nose on my face. Isn't that what you humans like to say—as plain as the nose on your face? There was no question about it. I owed it to myself to live each day to its fullest. I was grateful for the opportunity to go on living, and I would no longer take life for granted. I would no longer let my fears consume me, and I would treasure every second of life given to me, serving and loving others, exploring the universe, and jumping in the water without always testing the temperature first with my toes. I would box up my shyness and reticence and put them in storage along with the rest of my childhood toys and immaturities. I would be a woman, Mr. Booker. I would no longer be a frightened little girl, keeping to herself, fearful of life. I had survived the worst of the worst, and I knew I could and would be able to survive anything. I don't hate D'Orfo for what he did to me. He threatened my life and raped me, but I'm grateful for it. I'm glad he came into my life when he did. I needed him like I need the food I eat, like I need the air I breathe, and like I need my own blood."

Mr. Booker was quiet for a moment. He thought about what Anna had said. He and Anna then continued to talk late into the night. They remained on the sofa, Anna nestled at his side with her head on his chest and her hand on his forearm. Mr. Booker loved hearing Anna talk. She told him more about Og and how she longed to visit her planet and about all the sights and cities she would see. Likewise, Mr. Booker told Anna about Earth, the places he and Linda had visited in their travels, and the people who lived there, including their customs, history, and different forms of government. Finally, Anna looked up at Mr. Booker and said, "I can't imagine anyone I would rather be with right now than you."

"I feel the same," Mr. Booker said.

"I wish tonight could last forever."

"Yes, forever." Mr. Booker was exhausted, and when he said this, his head fell backward as he began to doze off.

"Here. Why don't you lie down?" Anna said.

"Yes," Mr. Booker said, now half asleep. "I can lie down." She tipped him over, and he stretched out on the couch. Anna put a throw pillow under his head, and she snuggled up beside him, resting her head on his chest. She could hear his heartbeat, counting away the time they had left together aboard the ship, and then the two of them fell sound asleep.

When Mr. Booker woke up the next morning, he was alone on the couch. Anna was in the kitchen, preparing breakfast, and Mr. Booker sat up to look at her. "Were you here all night?" he asked.

"I was here."

"We fell asleep on the couch?"

"We did," Anna said.

"I must've been exhausted."

"You were," Anna said. "I hope you like pancakes."

"I love pancakes."

"I found the mix in your cabinet. I put the butter and syrup on the table."

"That sounds great."

"What do you want to drink?"

"Is there any milk left?"

"There's enough," Anna said. "Get your lazy bones off the couch, and take a seat at the table. I'm almost ready for you."

Mr. Booker stood up and stepped to the table. He sat while Anna brought his breakfast to him. "It's like we're playing house," he said.

"Playing house?"

"It's what kids on Earth do when they pretend to be adults, when they pretend to be their parents."

"Here are your hotcakes," Anna said, and she plopped several pancakes onto Mr. Booker's plate. He reached for the butter and then the syrup. Anna proceeded to clean the pan, bowl, measuring cup, and spoon she'd been using, and she put them all in the dishwasher.

"These are great," Mr. Booker said.

He was halfway done with the pancakes, when Anna said to him sweetly, "Goodbye, Mr. Booker."

He was about to turn around and look at her, when he felt something cold touch the back of his neck. "No, not yet," he said, but it was too late. In an instant, everything went black.

CHAPTER 24

A MAN'S HOME

Another crazy dream began. This time, Mr. Booker was Jesse James, on the run from the law. He was seated at a crackling campfire, talking to his brother and warming his hands. It was an especially cold night in the backwoods of Mississippi, and the fire felt good. They were on their way to Louisiana. Only Frank and Mr. Booker were at the fire; the rest of the gang were sleeping. "I think there may still be a chance for us to redeem ourselves," Mr. Booker said. "No doubt they're watching us."

"Who's watching us?" Frank asked.

"The Ogonites," Mr. Booker said.

"Who the fuck are the Ogonites?"

"They're from the planet Og."

"Oh, of course they are," Frank said, rolling his eyes.

"You don't believe me? Haven't I told you about them before? Of course I did! I remember telling you all about them."

"I don't remember anything about it," Frank said.

"I told you their spaceship was orbiting Earth and that they'd been up there watching us for the past twenty years."

Frank looked at Mr. Booker, squinting one eye. "What are you, fucking crazy?" he asked.

"Didn't I tell you?"

"I think I would've remembered a dipshit story like that."

"We need to change our ways," Mr. Booker said.

"Change what ways?"

Mr. Booker stared at his brother. The yellow light from the campfire danced on Frank's skeptical and unshaven face. Was it true? Had he never talked to him about this before? "They're going to destroy us," he said. "We need to care for one another. We need to disband the gang and earn honest livings."

"Now I know you're fucking crazy," Frank said. "Or maybe you just think our luck is about to run out."

"After the jobs in Washington and Fayette, I wouldn't be surprised. They're all going to be searching for us, and everyone's going to want to see us hang for sure. But that's not what I'm talking about."

Frank laughed. "I think you're just scared. You're losing your nerve."

"Hell yes, I'm scared. What we've been doing is wrong. We've got it all wrong, Frank. There is another way."

"Now you sound like a preacher."

Just then, Mr. Booker noticed a dog barking. In fact, it had been barking during their entire conversation. "Where'd the dog come from?" Mr. Booker asked.

"It doesn't seem to have a home," Frank said.

"You mean it just came up to our campsite?"

"Appears so."

"Can't you shut the thing up?"

"I've tried," Frank said.

"What do you mean you've tried?"

"Watch," Frank said. Mr. Booker could see the dog about twenty feet away. He couldn't tell the breed, but it was a persistent barker. Frank pulled his gun from his holster, took aim, and shot the animal in the head. The dog's head jerked sideways, and it fell over onto its side. "Keep watching," Frank said. Miraculously, the dog stood up as though nothing had happened, and it began barking again. "It won't die," Frank said. "I've shot the fucker four times, and it just keeps getting up."

"Jesus," Mr. Booker said.

"Shoot it yourself," Frank said. "See if you can do any better."

"I'm not going to shoot a dog," Mr. Booker said.

"Have it your way."

One of the other men then appeared at the campfire. "How's a man supposed to sleep with all this barking?" he asked.

"How *is* a man supposed to sleep?" Mr. Booker asked.

"Are you asleep, or are you awake?" Frank asked.

"Which is it?" Mr. Booker said. "Am I asleep? What am I doing here?"

"And where the hell did this dog come from?" Frank asked.

"I think it's hungry."

"I don't feel so good," Mr. Booker said.

"What's wrong with you now?" Frank asked.

"I feel like I'm going to puke."

"Well, go somewhere else to do it."

"Go to the bathroom."

"Yes, the bathroom," Frank said.

The bathroom? What were the two men talking about? Why would there be a bathroom in the woods? Suddenly, Mr. Booker woke up, and the campfire was gone, as were Frank and the other man. He found himself in his bed, dressed in nothing but a pair of shorts. His head was spinning something awful, and the urge to throw up was overpowering. He leaped out of bed and ran to the bathroom, where he fell to his knees and vomited into the toilet bowl. Over and over he puked, until there seemed to be nothing left in his stomach. When he was finally done, he wiped his mouth and blew his nose into a wad of toilet paper. He flushed the toilet and stepped to his front room to confirm what he suspected. He looked out the window, and it was all there: green trees, bushes, a front lawn, and several cars parked against the curb. He saw the stucco and red-tile-roofed houses across the street. He no longer had a view of the distant Earth. The sky was blue, and the stars were gone. He was home. The Ogonites had returned him to his house. He went into the kitchen and checked the clock on the wall; it was three o'clock, and this time, he knew it was in the afternoon, because it was light outside, and the sun was beaming in through the kitchen window. Then his head started spinning again, and he went back to the bathroom.

When he was done vomiting for the second time, he heard the barking again. How could he help but hear? It seemed to be coming from the Garcias' backyard, which he thought was strange. Since when did the couple have a dog? The barking was loud and annoying, but Mr. Booker tried to ignore it for the time being. He was just happy to be home and back on planet Earth.

The pills the kid had given him the night before hadn't done much of anything. He was just as sick this time as he'd been when the Ogonites had first abducted him. It took about an hour for the nausea to run its course, and then Mr. Booker felt better. Now he was ravenously hungry. He checked the refrigerator, but there wasn't anything to eat. It wasn't stuffed with food, as the refrigerator in his cabin had been. It was his refrigerator. He decided to go to the grocery store to pick up something to eat. He walked back to his bedroom and found that all the clothes he had packed for the trip had been washed and neatly put away. His wallet was on top of the dresser with his keys. He got dressed, put his wallet in his back pocket, and went to the garage to start up his car. "You don't appreciate what you have until it's taken away," he said to himself, backing the car out of the garage and reaching for the dashboard. He turned on the radio, and music blared. He sang along to the songs all the way to the grocery store. After parking his car, he stepped into the store and was astonished. It was as if it was the first time he'd ever been there. There were so many things to choose from—so many brightly lit aisles packed with boxes, cans, and jars of goods. They were real goods, not chemicals and plant bulk. This was the real McCoy!

"First things first," Mr. Booker said to himself, and he wheeled his shopping cart to the meat section. There he picked out the bloodiest and thickest steak he could find. Then he went to the dairy section, where he grabbed some butter, sour cream, and milk. Then he went to the produce department, where he grabbed a large russet potato, a huge brown chunk of starch about the size of two fists. He wheeled his shopping cart to the checkout lane, where he waited behind a couple of shoppers. When his turn came, the cashier smiled at him. "I see you're a steak-and-potatoes man," she said.

"I am today," Mr. Booker said.

"This is a big steak."

"It probably isn't big enough."

"I like men who have an appetite."

Mr. Booker laughed. "Well, I certainly have an appetite today."

The cashier rang up the food and told Mr. Booker the total. He swiped his credit card, grabbed his bag, and made his way back to his car.

When Mr. Booker arrived home, he put the groceries on the kitchen counter and lit the backyard barbecue. He then popped the potato in the microwave. While he was waiting for the grill to heat up and the potato to cook, he checked his voice mail messages on the kitchen phone. There was only one message, and it was from Graham Perth. "Call me when you get back from your trip," he said. "I finally did it! I'm in the ring, old man. I've put on the gloves, and I'm ready to fight. I'm giving notice as soon as Hawthorne is back in his office. Give me a call, and I'll tell you all about it."

Graham was one of Mr. Booker's fellow teachers at the high school, and he was probably the closest thing Mr. Booker had to a best friend. Hawthorne was Abe Hawthorne, the school principal. To understand Graham's message, you need to know about the Supernova Seminar. Two years ago, Graham purchased two tickets to a motivational seminar, one seat for himself and a second seat for his wife. The Supernova Seminar featured speakers from all over the country, men and women who'd achieved success and were enthusiastic about sharing the secrets of their success with anyone willing to pay the high price of admission to the seminar. On one of the nights, Graham's wife had to work late and was unable to join him, so Graham asked Mr. Booker if he wanted to come along. Mr. Booker said yes, and the two men went to the seminar. There were several speakers that night, one of them being Rusty McGee.

Rusty was a famous heavyweight boxer. Mr. Booker sat and listened as Rusty told the audience about how he'd come up in the world from being a bagger at a grocery store to being a champion prizefighter and best-selling author. Rusty's autobiography, *Jump in the Ring*, sold millions of copies. They called it an autobiography, but he didn't actually write the book. I know for a fact that a ghostwriter by the name of Charlie Watkins did all the writing. Rusty simply told Charlie the stories, and Charlie did the heavy lifting. Nevertheless, Rusty became well known not just as a boxer but also as an author, and following the success of his book, he was in big demand as a public speaker.

People loved listening to Rusty talk with his gravelly voice and colorful language. I don't know this for sure, but I suspect Charlie or someone else was paid to help Rusty write his speeches. I checked out a couple of his speeches on the Internet. It's hard for me to believe that someone who spent his entire youth getting punched in the head day after day, month after month, would have the kind of brainpower required to put together the cogent thoughts evidenced in the speeches Rusty was delivering. If Rusty had been writing his own speeches, he probably would've sounded like a five-year-old.

Anyway, while the barbecue was heating up and the potato was still cooking, Mr. Booker called Graham back, and Graham told him about his plans. These plans had nothing to do with teaching high school. Graham said his days as a high school teacher were over. He'd passed his state exam and was now a licensed real-estate salesman. Further, he'd talked his way into being hired by one of the county's most exclusive residential real-estate firms, and he was going to tender his resignation to the school as soon as Abe Hawthorne was back in his office. "I'm jumping into the ring, just like Rusty McGee."

"You're quitting for good?" Mr. Booker asked.

"I'm done with it," Graham said.

"Are you sure you know what you're doing?"

"I've never been surer of anything in my life."

"What about your students?"

"They'll do fine without me."

"But you were a good teacher. Good teachers are hard to come by."

"High school teachers are a dime a dozen."

"I think the same could be said of real-estate agents," Mr. Booker said.

"Yes, there are plenty of them. I'll grant you that. But in real estate, you get paid for your ingenuity and hard work. In real estate, you can make something of your life. A schoolteacher shows up for work, struggles to teach his students, gets his payroll check, and then goes home. No matter how good or bad a job he does, he gets paid the same inadequate allowance. In real estate, the sky's the limit, old man."

"Teaching is noble," Mr. Booker said.

Graham laughed. "Who do you think you're fooling?"

"No one," Mr. Booker said.

"High school teachers aren't noble. They're glorified babysitters. No one in their right mind wants to look after teenagers all day, so they send them to school and let teachers do the dirty work. Do you think they're sent to school to learn? What exactly do they learn, Booker? A lot of facts, equations, theories, and other useless bits of information, ninety-nine percent of which they'll forget before they get interviewed for their first jobs. It's a joke, Booker! It's a joke no one laughs at, because to laugh would be to admit the absurdity of it. Do you want to know what really matters? Do you want to know what your students will obsess over when they grow up, when they become adults? They won't be thinking about the Magna Carta, Gutenberg's printing press, or Watson and Crick's amazing discovery. They'll be thinking about how many square feet their houses are, what part of town they live in, what brand of hardwood floors they have in their front rooms, and whether their kitchen appliances are as good as their neighbors'. I respect you, Booker. And I like you as a friend, but you really need to wake up and smell the coffee. Real estate is the heart and soul of America. High school is its babysitter. High school is just a way to keep unruly teenagers under control while their parents work, connive, scheme, and sweat to get the nicest house on the street. Home sweet home. Home is where the heart is. A man's home is his castle. Need I say any more?"

"I have to go," Mr. Booker said.

"Are you disappointed in me?" Graham asked.

"No, I just need to make my dinner. I haven't eaten anything all day."

"So how was England?"

"It was fine," Mr. Booker said.

"Did you get a dog?"

"No, why?" Mr. Booker said.

"I can hear a dog barking in the background."

"It's the neighbors'."

"That would drive me crazy. You should probably say something to them. If I were you, I'd say something. Well, anyway, it's good to have you back, Booker."

"Thanks," Mr. Booker said. The two men said goodbye, and Mr. Booker took his steak to the barbecue. He dropped it onto the grill, and the meat sizzled. He then went back into the kitchen to remove the potato from the microwave. He was about to cut it open, when the doorbell rang, and he went to answer it. When he opened the door, he found Vivian Cassel holding a large paper bag. "Mail delivery," she said. She was her usual cheerful self. The Cassels had said they would collect Mr. Booker's mail from his mailbox while he was gone, and now Vivian was turning it over to him. The bag was about half full.

"Thanks," Mr. Booker said, taking the bag and smiling.

"You get an awful lot of junk mail," Vivian said. "So do we."

"I guess we all do."

"There's a letter in there from the IRS."

"There is?"

"You should probably open it first. Do you owe them money?"

"I don't think so."

"You don't want to mess with the IRS," Vivian said. "Andrew can help if you owe them money."

"I'll keep that in mind."

"There's also a letter from the school district. What do you suppose it says?"

"I don't know," Mr. Booker said.

"Do you suppose they're laying you off?"

"No, I'm sure it isn't that."

"Andrew had a friend who was an elementary school teacher in another district. That's how they laid him off. There was no warning at all. They just sent him a letter in the mail, and the next thing he knew, he was looking for a job."

"That's tough," Mr. Booker said, shaking his head.

"It's a dog-eat-dog world."

"It can be," Mr. Booker said.

"There's also a letter in there from your accountant. At least I assume he's your accountant. The return address says the letter is from an accountancy firm in Anaheim. Maybe it has something to do with the IRS letter. Maybe they made a mistake filing your taxes."

"Maybe," Mr. Booker said.

"You can't depend on anyone these days."

"No," Mr. Booker said. He was agreeing with Vivian not because he agreed with her but because he hoped that if he agreed, she would go away.

"I had our son bring in the mail."

"Should I pay Jason something?" Mr. Booker asked.

"No, no, it was the neighborly thing to do."

"Here," Mr. Booker said, and he removed his wallet from his pocket. "Let me pay him something."

"It really isn't necessary."

"Here's a twenty. Tell him I said thanks."

"Okay, if you insist."

"I do," Mr. Booker said.

"I'm sure he'll appreciate it," Vivian said.

"I'd love to talk more, but I've got to go," Mr. Booker said. "I have a steak cooking on the barbecue, and I don't want it to burn."

"Oh my," Vivian said, smiling. "Go take care of your steak. We can talk later."

Mr. Booker smiled at Vivian, and she smiled back sweetly. He then closed the front door and carried the bag of mail into the kitchen. He stepped outside to turn over the steak. When he returned to the kitchen, he dumped the mail onto the counter.

He found the letter from the IRS and opened it. It was a notice stating he owed eight dollars. *Leave it to the IRS to send a bill for eight dollars.* The letter from the school district was his schedule for the summer session, and the letter from his accountant was an invoice for the preparation of his taxes. So far so good with the mail. Mr. Booker went outside to retrieve his steak. It had been grilled to perfection, and Mr. Booker could feel his mouth watering.

He decided he would eat in the family room, and he set a placemat and some silverware down for himself on the coffee table. He put the steak and baked potato on a plate and poured a tall glass of milk. He brought his dinner and milk to the coffee table and turned on the TV so he could watch it while he ate. Then he surfed through the stations until he reached the evening news. People were lying to each other. People were swindling one another. People were shooting guns and setting off bombs. Movie stars were checking into celebrity rehabs. A five-year-old boy had been hit in the head by a stray bullet from a drive-by shooting, and an elderly pedestrian had been hit by a drunk driver. It was the usual assortment of nonsense, no different from a week ago; nothing had changed since the last time he'd watched the news.

Mr. Booker sighed and then laughed. He was thinking of Ralph's play. He thought, *Who exactly am I?* Why, he could easily have been George's next-door neighbor. He could've been Judy's teacher at school. He continued to chew on what Ralph would have described as his grilled chunk of dead animal flesh, washing it down with mouthfuls of white mammary gland secretion. He'd only been home for a few hours, and already he was a character in a play, right in the thick of it.

CHAPTER 25

SUMMER SCHOOL

It was as if he'd never been abducted. He was back in the familiar arms of his normal routine, proceeding with the usual chores and activities. Mr. Booker kept himself busy by doing some gardening in his front yard, replacing many of the flowering plants, mowing and edging the lawn, and trimming the hedge that grew alongside the walk to his front door. He took time to read several books he'd been meaning to start for the past year or so, and he got things ready for summer school, putting together his teaching plan and organizing the classwork. He also opened up his checkbook and paid all his bills, which included sending his eight-dollar payment to the IRS and the amount he owed to his tax accountant. Then there was Sparky. Sadly or happily, depending on how one looked at it, the dog was no longer a nuisance. Mr. Booker wasn't a callous man, but if you were to ask him how he felt about strangling the little beast, he would've said, "It was either him or me."

When summer school finally started, Mr. Booker's first class was at nine. He arrived in the room at eight thirty and wrote an outline of the day's lesson on the large whiteboard at the head of the class. As he wrote, he found himself daydreaming. He imagined what might happen if he did things a little differently. What would happen, for example, if he taught his world history class the way it ought to be taught? What would happen if he were to take his students back in time millions of years, traveling back much further than the school textbook and class curriculum dared to go? He could teach his kids some real world history. He could prove that Graham was wrong. He would be more than a glorified babysitter. He could be a real teacher.

"It would be funny, wouldn't it?" he said to himself. He chuckled as he thought of what he might actually do. He pictured himself standing before the class and introducing himself. "Good morning to all of you," he would say. "For those of you who don't know me, my name is Mr. Booker, and you're in for a treat." After taking roll, Mr. Booker would begin his lecture, speaking about early human beings—not as the descendants of Adam and Eve but as the descendants of a six-million-year-old African species of earthling known as *Ardipithecus.* He'd write out the word on the whiteboard and instruct the kids to write it in their notebooks. "It will be on your exams," he'd say. "And I'll expect all of you to know what it means and spell it correctly."

Sure, the Bible had it all wrong. Sure, the parents wouldn't mind. Sure, Mr. Hawthorne wouldn't object to him teaching the kids a little evolution. "Sure, sure, sure," Mr. Booker said. Then he laughed out loud at the absurdity of his daydream.

"What's so funny?" a girlish voice asked. But it wasn't a girl. Mr. Booker knew who it was.

He looked to his left. It was young Gary Lindstrom with his trademark wire-rimmed eyeglasses, high-pitched voice, and backpack full of books. Of course Gary would be the first student to arrive. He was dressed in a plaid button-down shirt and pressed khaki slacks. His short brown hair was neatly combed, and he was looking at Mr. Booker, wondering why he was laughing.

Everyone in the school knew about Gary. He had a reputation for being one of the smartest kids, if not the smartest, and he also had a reputation among the teachers for being polite and well behaved. Mr. Booker liked the kid. Gary had been in his US history class the previous semester, and Mr. Booker had found him to be a serious student and a nice young man. Gary reminded Mr. Booker of himself when he was in high school, always carting around a load of books in his backpack, never hanging out with the cool or ne'er-do-well kids, and always being respectful to adults. Unfortunately, Gary often got picked on by bullies, who reminded Mr. Booker of his own nemesis, Artie Duncan, the rotten kid who sat on Mr. Booker's chest while his friends stuffed dirt into his mouth. "Can I help you, Gary?" Mr. Booker asked.

"Is this the world history class?"

"It is," Mr. Booker said.

"Good, good. I always like to confirm that I'm in the right room before I pick my seat. Sometimes they switch rooms on us. Last semester, I sat for thirty minutes in an algebra class before I figured out it wasn't the trig class I'd signed up for. Don't ask me why, but they'd switched the rooms without telling me. When I finally went to the right classroom, everyone had already picked their seats. I had to sit in the fourth row back. But I like sitting in front. I always sit in front."

"You're in the right class."

"Good, good. Do you mind if I sit here?" Gary was pointing to the center front-row desk.

Mr. Booker nodded. "You can sit wherever you wish, Gary."

There were stories about Gary Lindstrom. One of the stories was that Gary was gay. Supposedly, Mr. Brooks, one of the PE teachers, had found Gary and Andy Pendergrass in one of the gym's toilet stalls. Andy was gay by his own admission, but Gary was not. The kids in the school said that Mr. Brooks had caught Andy performing oral sex on Gary in between classes. They also said that because Gary was so well liked by the teachers, neither boy had been punished. I heard about this story from another teacher. The teachers all knew that the story was an outright lie, but none of them did anything to stop the lie from spreading, including Mr. Booker. It wasn't the kind of gossip a teacher could do anything about. What was he supposed to do? Ask Mr. Hawthorne to get on the school intercom and tell everyone that there had been no blow job? The kids would've had a field day with it. It would've made things worse than they already were.

Another Gary Lindstrom story that made the rounds at school

had to do with Gary's grandmother and her dolls. Gary's parents had died in a car accident when Gary was eight, and he was being brought up by his grandmother. He lived with his grandmother in her house, with her collection of dolls. She had hundreds of them on display throughout the house, even on the shelves in Gary's bedroom and on the pillows of Gary's bed. She was obsessed with her dolls, almost as obsessed as she was with raising her grandson. The story about the dolls had been started by a boy named Billy Hellman. Billy was one of the few kids from school who'd gone inside Gary's house. Gary and Billy were paired in Miss Jaspar's English class to complete a book report together. The boys met at Gary's house to work on the report the night before it was due. They completed their work, and then Billy went home. Then Billy couldn't resist. He told his buddies at school about the dolls, especially the dolls in Gary's bedroom, especially the dolls on Gary's bed. He said Gary slept with the dolls at night. So now, according to the rumors, Gary not only had had sex with a boy in a toilet stall but also slept with dolls. The news traveled fast, and all the kids at school were talking about how Gary slept with his grandmother's dolls. The poor kid. Mr. Booker was sure that was also a lie, but there was nothing he could do. It was his experience that the more one tried to argue with a rumor, the more traction it got. That was the unfortunate truth.

"I read the book," Gary said.

"Which book?" Mr. Booker asked.

"The textbook."

"You read it already?"

"I like to be prepared for my classes."

"Of course you do."

"Are we going to start with Mesopotamia?"

"We are," Mr. Booker said.

"Will we get to write reports in your class?"

"There will be a couple papers."

"I like writing papers. It's a lot more fun than just studying for tests."

"Yes," Mr. Booker said. "Reports can be fun. I liked writing reports when I was your age."

Two girls suddenly stepped into the classroom, and they were both giggling. Mr. Booker knew them from the previous semester. They had both flunked and were now making the class up in summer school. One girl was Amber Halstead, and the other was Cindy Beechum. "Here we are again," Amber said. "Gluttons for punishment."

"Hello, girls," Mr. Booker said.

"What's he doing here?" Amber asked, referring to Gary, who was now seated at his desk and removing his textbook from his backpack.

"He's taking this class."

"Don't tell me he flunked too."

"Of course not," Mr. Booker said.

"This is my first time," Gary said.

"Who said you could talk to me?" Cindy said. Gary smiled, not knowing what else to do. The girls giggled and then took their seats at the back of the room.

"The doll boy," Amber said.

There was more giggling.

Gary's face turned red. He knew about the doll rumor, but what could he do?

Then four more kids stepped into the room. Then five more after that. They were all talking and selecting their seats, plopping their backpacks on their desks. More kids entered, and the next thing Mr. Booker knew, the classroom was nearly full. It was almost time for the bell to ring, and Mr. Booker stood before the kids.

Dammit, Mr. Booker thought. He was looking at the last kid to enter, a boy named Biff Perkins. Biff had also flunked Mr. Booker's class last semester, but no one had warned him that Biff would be in his summer class. He knew it wasn't healthy or proper for an adult to dislike a child, especially if the adult was a teacher, but Mr. Booker couldn't help it. He couldn't stand this kid. Biff stood for everything Mr. Booker despised. He was the younger generation's version of

Artie Duncan. He was a new and improved Artie Duncan—Artie Duncan 2.0, the sequel, volume two.

"Well, who have we here?" Biff said, stopping at Gary Lindstrom's desk. "It must be the boy genius. Are you a genius, Gary?"

"No," Gary said.

"You know, I think it's the glasses that make you so fucking smart," Biff said. "Is that why you wear the glasses?"

"I'm farsighted."

"No, I think your glasses have magical powers," Biff said. "Let me try them on. Let's see if they'll work for me." Gary looked over at Mr. Booker, hoping he would stop Biff from picking on him, but before Mr. Booker could say or do anything, Biff snatched the glasses from Gary's face. He put them on his own face and then blinked his eyes. Looking at the rest of the class while imitating Gary's high-pitched voice and raising his index finger as if to make an important point, he said, "The square of the hypotenuse equals the sum of pi minus the divisors." At first, the room was quiet. Then everyone burst out laughing, even the smart kids.

"That makes no sense," Gary said.

"You make no sense," Biff said. "You and your stupid dolls."

"That's enough," Mr. Booker said. "Find a desk, and sit down, Biff."

There was a smirk on his face, but he decided to obey Mr. Booker. He handed Gary his glasses, and Gary put them back on his face. Biff took a seat, and just as his butt hit the chair, the school bell rang. Class had officially started, and Mr. Booker cleared his throat and asked the kids to be quiet.

"Okay," Mr. Booker said. "For those of you who don't know me, my name is Mr. Booker. You're in my summer world history class. If you belong somewhere else, now's the time to say something. Does anyone here belong somewhere else?" No one raised a hand, so he continued. "I need to begin by taking roll. When you hear your name, say, 'Here,' or 'Present,' so I can mark your name and tell the attendance office you showed up." Mr. Booker proceeded to go through his list of names, and as was often the case with a first day of class, everyone was present.

From the back of the room, one of the boys suddenly shouted, "She never said that!"

"She did!" another boy said back.

"Take it back, or I'll break your fucking arm!"

"You and who else?"

"Me and me, you little faggot."

"Who's the faggot?"

Then all hell broke loose. The two boys leaped out of their seats and started swinging their fists. It had all happened so fast. "Whoa!" Mr. Booker said, but neither boy heard him, or if they had heard him, they didn't care what he had to say. They continued to throw punches at each other, and Mr. Booker ran toward them. "Stop it!" he shouted, but they fought on furiously. Then one of the boys flew backward and cracked his head on the rear wall. He crumpled to the floor and began groaning. Rather than letting the fight stop there, the other boy jumped on top of him, pounding on his face. "Stop, stop!" Mr. Booker shouted. He was now right on top of them, and he grabbed the boy who was doing the punching by the collar of his shirt, pulling him off the other boy. "When I say stop, I mean stop!" he said. The boys were both bruised, bloody, and out of breath, and Mr. Booker had a hold of both of them by their shirt collars. "Both of you, come with me," he said, and he pulled up on them so that they were standing.

"Where are we going?" one of the boys asked, wiping his bloody nose with the back of his hand.

"We're going to the principal's office."

"Both of us?" the boys asked. "But he started it!"

"You can tell that to Mr. Hawthorne, not to me."

"But he won't believe me."

"Of course he won't believe you," the other kid said. "You're a fucking liar! A liar and a moron."

"You're the liar!"

"Enough," Mr. Booker said. He then dragged the boys out of the classroom. He took them down the main hall to the administration offices. Mr. Hawthorne's door was closed, which meant he was meeting with someone, but his secretary was seated at her desk. "We're here to see Mr. Hawthorne," he said to her.

"He's busy right now."

"How long will he be?"

"He should be done soon. He's just meeting with Mr. Higgins."

"We'll wait," Mr. Booker said. Mr. Booker and the boys sat on the wooden bench across from Mr. Hawthorne's door. Mr. Booker sat in the middle, with the boys sitting on either side of him. He didn't dare let them sit next to each other, and he didn't dare leave them alone.

Mr. Booker could hear Mr. Hawthorne speaking loudly to Mr. Higgins. He couldn't hear Higgins responding, but he could certainly hear Mr. Hawthorne. He was angry, and his voice was raised. He told Higgins, "Listen, I don't want to hear any more excuses. You are the janitor at this school, and goddammit, you're going to do your job. I've had it up to here with all this chewing gum. It's an epidemic, Higgins. The stuff is everywhere. It's stuck under desks, on walls, and on the floors. I even saw a piece of it stuck to one of the water fountains. Do you have any idea how disgusting that is? And have you ever tried to clean gum off the bottoms of your shoes? That's what I was doing this morning. Cleaning up chewing gum! Haven't we had this talk before? How many times do I have to bring up the same old problem? Chewing gum, goddammit! It's a filthy curse. But I'll be damned if I'm going to sit on my hands and put up with it. I didn't get to be principal of this school by sitting on my hands!"

You wouldn't think a rant about chewing gum could last long, but Mr. Booker sat and waited with his boys for at least five minutes. Mr. Hawthorne went on and on while Higgins sat in his office and listened. When Mr. Hawthorne was finally done, the beleaguered janitor opened the door and stepped out of the principal's office. "Hi," Mr. Booker said, trying to be friendly.

"Oh, hi, Booker," Mr. Higgins replied. He looked as if his dog had just died or as if he'd just been evicted from his home. He walked away, looking down at his feet.

Mr. Hawthorne's secretary then stood up and walked to Mr. Hawthorne's doorway. "Mr. Booker is here to see you," she said.

"What does he want?"

"Looks like he broke up a fight."

"A fight?"

"He has the boys with him," she said.

"Tell him I have to make a phone call first. Shut the door. I'll just be a couple of minutes."

The secretary closed the door and looked at Mr. Booker. "I heard," Mr. Booker said.

Fifteen minutes later, the door swung open, and Mr. Hawthorne was standing in the doorway. "Well, come on in," Mr. Hawthorne said. Clearly he was not in a good mood. The chewing gum issue still had him upside down.

"In we go," Mr. Booker said to the boys.

"Do we have to?" one of the boys asked.

"We do," Mr. Booker said.

When he brought the boys into Mr. Hawthorne's office, Mr. Booker explained what had happened. "Well, for crying out loud," Mr. Hawthorne said.

"Can I go back to class?" Mr. Booker asked.

"Of course."

"I'm leaving these young men with you."

"Close the door behind you," Mr. Hawthorne said. "This could get ugly."

When Mr. Booker returned to class, the students were talking, mostly about the fight. However, they settled down once Mr. Booker cleared his throat and took his place in front of the whiteboard. "As I was saying, this is a world history class. Is there anyone who doesn't belong here?"

No one said anything.

"Does anyone have any questions before I begin?"

A boy in the third row raised his hand, and Mr. Booker called on him. The kid asked, "Will you be giving us any extra credit? Some teachers give us extra credit in case we don't do well on a test, or in case we get a bad grade on a paper."

"Do you plan on getting bad grades?"

"No, I'm not planning on it," the boy said.

"Then why would you need extra credit?"

"I don't know. I guess just in case."

"Yeah," another kid said. "Just in case."

"How many of you want extra-credit assignments?" he asked the class, and nearly everyone raised his or her hand. "Fine," he said. "I'll come up with something. But the extra-credit work won't be easy. It'll be challenging and time consuming. My suggestion is for you to do your best on your exams and papers in the first place."

Another kid raised his hand, and Mr. Booker called on him. "Will you be marking us down for showing up late to class?"

Mr. Booker sighed. "Do you plan on showing up late to class?"

"I don't plan on it," the kid said. "But it might happen."

"We might not be able to help it," said another kid. "Sometimes things happen."

"No, I won't mark your grade down," Mr. Booker said. "But if you make a habit out of being late, I'll probably give you detention."

"How much detention?"

"As much as I think you deserve."

"How about bathroom breaks?" a boy asked.

"Bathroom breaks?"

"What if we have to go to the bathroom?"

"There's plenty of time to use the restroom before you come to class," Mr. Booker said.

"But what if we didn't need to go before class, and then when we got in class, we suddenly had to go?"

"Then I guess you could go."

"Would you mark down our grade?"

"Of course not."

"Even if we had to go more than once?"

"Why would you have to go more than once?"

"I don't know," the kid said. "I'm just saying what if." Some of the kids laughed.

"Listen, just try to go before class," Mr. Booker said.

A girl now raised her hand, and Mr. Booker called on her. She said, "Last semester, Mr. Prescott wouldn't let any of us go to the restroom during his math class. Do you know Mr. Prescott? Do you know who Tami Roberts is? Tami raised her hand and told him she really had to go, but he made her stay in her seat. He said she should've used the restroom before coming to class. Then she peed herself. She peed, and her jeans got all dark and wet, and it was dripping off the seat. It was all over the floor."

"I wouldn't let that happen."

"Do you like Mr. Prescott?"

"Actually, I don't know him that well."

"I think he's mean."

"No one likes him," another girl said.

"Listen, you won't think I'm mean. I'm on your side. I just want you kids to learn."

"Whatever happened to Tami?" a boy asked. "I haven't seen her around."

"I heard she transferred to a different school," the girl said. "She was too embarrassed to come back to school."

"Who can blame her?" the boy said.

"Shit, she should've just walked out of the class," Biff said. "It's not like Mr. Prescott would've been able to stop her. What an idiot. Sitting there and pissing herself!"

"Are there any more questions?" Mr. Booker asked, ignoring Biff's commentary. "I'd like to get the class started."

No one said anything.

Then he heard it. One of the students was whimpering and sniffling. It sounded like a girl. The sound was coming from somewhere near the back of the room. "Is someone in here crying?" he asked.

"Just ignore her," a girl said.

"Ignore who?"

"It's just Betsy. She's upset about her father." The girl who was talking was sitting behind Betsy, and she was rubbing Betsy's back with one hand, trying to make her feel better. "She'll be all right."

"Are you all right, Betsy?" Mr. Booker asked. He had stepped sideways and could now see the girl plainly. Her eyes were bloodshot, and her cheeks were wet with tears. When she saw that Mr. Booker had spotted her, she suddenly began to sob loudly, and she dropped her face into her hands. The girl behind her continued to rub Betsy's back, but it wasn't making her feel any better.

The girl behind Betsy said, "Her dad didn't come home last night. He's an alcoholic. Sometimes he's gone for days."

"Is this true, Betsy?" Mr. Booker asked.

Betsy lifted her head and nodded. Then she dropped her face back into her hands, sobbing again.

"Jesus," Biff said. "Tell the girl to get a grip."

"Be quiet, Biff," Mr. Booker said. He walked to Betsy's desk and held her hand. "Come with me, Betsy," he said.

"Where are you taking her?" the girl behind her asked. "She's not in trouble, is she?"

"Of course not. We're going to see Mrs. Crumb." Mrs. Crumb was the school counselor, and Mr. Booker figured she would know how to best handle a situation like this. Mr. Booker kept holding Betsy's hand, and he led her to the door. "I'll be back in just a minute," he told the class. Then he walked with Betsy to the guidance offices, opened the door, and stepped inside. Mrs. Crumb's secretary was at her desk, shuffling through some papers, and Mr. Booker said, "We'd like to see Mrs. Crumb."

"She's not here," the secretary said.

"Where is she?"

"She's in her car."

"In her car?"

"She's smoking a cigarette. She's not allowed to smoke on campus, so she drives off campus and smokes in her car."

"Do you think she'll be back soon?"

"As long as it takes for her to smoke a cigarette," the secretary said.

"Then we'll wait for her."

"Be my guest," the secretary said. Mr. Booker and Betsy sat down to wait. Betsy's crying had subsided, but she was still sniffling. "Do you have any tissues?" Mr. Booker asked the secretary.

"I do," she said. She lifted her purse onto her desktop and pulled out several tissues. "Here you go, dear," she said, and Betsy took the tissues. Betsy wiped her eyes and blew her nose.

"Rough morning?" the secretary asked.

Betsy nodded.

"Can I leave her here with you?" Mr. Booker asked. "I need to get back to my class."

"No, no," Betsy said, and she started crying again. "I need you to stay with me."

"But Mrs. Crumb will be here soon."

"Stay until she gets here," Betsy pleaded. "I need you to stay."

"How much longer do you think she'll be?" Mr. Booker asked the secretary.

"Just a few minutes."

"Okay, I guess I'll wait," Mr. Booker said. He held Betsy's hand again, since that seemed to calm her down.

"Thanks so much," Betsy said. She had stopped crying, and she leaned her head against Mr. Booker's shoulder. He hardly knew the girl, yet for some reason, she'd grown attached to him.

Mr. Booker waited and waited with the poor girl leaning against him. It took more than fifteen minutes for Mrs. Crumb to finally show up. As she passed them, Mr. Booker said, "I've got someone here who needs to see you."

"Oh?" Mrs. Crumb said.

"Can we talk in your office?"

"Of course we can," Mrs. Crumb said. They stepped into Mrs. Crumb's office, and Mr. Booker told Betsy to take a seat while he remained standing.

"She has problems at home," he said.

"My daddy's gone," Betsy said.

"He might be an alcoholic," Mr. Booker said. "That's the story I'm getting. Apparently, he didn't come home last night. That's all I know. Betsy is very distraught. She was crying in class, so I brought her to see you. I thought you could help her."

"Poor dear," Mrs. Crumb said.

"You're in good hands," Mr. Booker said to Betsy. "But I've got to go now. Mrs. Crumb is here to help you. I need to get back to my class."

"I'll take good care of her," Mrs. Crumb said.

"I know you will," Mr. Booker said. He patted Betsy on the top of her head and said, "Everything's going to be all right." Betsy looked up at him as he left and shut the door behind him.

When he arrived back at his class, his students were talking and laughing. Surprisingly, everything seemed to be okay, and the room was still in one piece. He told the kids to be quiet and listen, and then he looked at his watch to see how much time was left.

"Mr. Booker?" one of the girls said. She was raising her hand, and he called on her. "Can I go to the restroom?"

"Class is almost over," he said. "Can't you wait until the bell rings?"

"I've got to go right now."

"Very well," he said. He opened the desk drawer and removed a pad of paper and a pen. He wrote the girl a hall pass and handed it to her.

"Me too," another girl said.

"You too?"

"I need to go bad. If she can go, I ought to be able to go. I really need to go."

"Fine," Mr. Booker said, and he wrote out another hall pass. The girl left, and just as Mr. Booker was about to speak, the boy sitting next to Gary Lindstrom raised his hand. "Yes, what is it?" Mr. Booker asked.

"Sorry," the kid said. "But all this talk about going to the bathroom made me realize that I have to go. I mean, I have to go real bad."

Mr. Booker looked at his watch again. "Listen, the period is over in eight minutes." He was now speaking to the entire class. "We won't be able to get anything done in eight minutes. So you all can go."

"You mean right now?" the boy next to Gary asked.

"Class is dismissed."

Everyone in the room cheered, and it was amazing. You would've thought there was a raging fire in the room as quickly as all the kids evacuated. In no time at all, the students were all gone, except for Gary Lindstrom. He was having some difficulty stuffing his large textbook into his full backpack. He looked at Mr. Booker and asked, "Are we going to learn anything tomorrow?"

"That's the plan," Mr. Booker said.

CHAPTER 26

KATIE

"What would you have done?" Mr. Booker asked me. "I was sitting on the story of the century. Perhaps it was the greatest story of all time. To keep this story to myself was unconscionable, yet to tell it to others would be like committing social suicide. Rock was right. Who would believe a word of it? On the other hand, many people would benefit from it. Everyone had to hear about this. Yes, I decided the story had to be told! Then I realized how it could be done without jeopardizing my reputation or putting my job on the line. I would have the story published anonymously, using a false identity. I'd be a teacher at a nonexistent school, and I'd say I lived in a different town. None of my personal information would be revealed to the readers. What mattered was my story about the Ogonites, not who I was, who my friends were, or where I came from. Anonymity was the perfect way to go about this.

"This revelation came to me during the third week of summer school, while I was driving home. I decided that I needed to find a respectable author who would write and publish my story in this manner. And I needed to find this person soon, before time took its toll on my memories and I forgot all the extraordinary details of my trip. When I got home that night, I immediately started searching the Internet. I was up until five in the morning, drinking coffee and going from site to site. When I was done, I had twenty-three names and e-mail addresses of writers I thought might be interested. The next day, I sent e-mails to each of them, telling them I was sitting on an amazing story, the likes of which they'd surely never seen. I told them it was a once-in-a-lifetime opportunity. I told them I'd be the goose that laid their golden egg. I said if they were interested, they had to contact me as soon as possible for more information. I heard back from eight of them, and those eight asked me to describe the story I was raving about. But then came the hard part, which was convincing them I wasn't some crackpot wearing a tinfoil hat who'd escaped from a mental hospital. They had to be assured I wasn't just some nut wasting their time with an insane fantasy or using them in a deliberate ploy to get my fifteen minutes of fame. I had to be credible." Mr. Booker stopped talking and took a deep breath.

"So how did you come across my name?" I asked. "That has never been clear to me. I wasn't one of those eight writers."

"I'm getting to that," Mr. Booker said. He took another deep breath. "I e-mailed a synopsis of my story to the eight writers, and I waited for them to reply. I quickly got responses from all of them, but none were interested. One just said, 'You've got to be kidding,' and another said he'd meet with me as soon as he got back from his vacation to Mars, ha-ha. Two of the writers suggested that I see a psychiatrist and offered advice on how to find one. Three were outright angry, chastising me for wasting their time with such a blatant attempt to get attention."

"And me?"

"You were in the eighth response."

"But the eighth response wasn't from me."

"No, as you already pointed out, you weren't even on my original list."

"I still don't understand."

"The eighth response I received was from a writer in Florida named Tucker Wilson. He was a kind and thoughtful man, which I've learned is unusual in the book-publishing business. He wasn't sarcastic, patronizing, or angry. He didn't act like he had no time for me, and he didn't make me feel like a kook. He replied and told me very politely that my story wasn't the sort of subject he wrote about.

But he said if I was serious about seeing my experiences published, I ought to contact someone who specialized in alien abductions. He said he'd read several of your books out of curiosity, and he said you seemed like a sincere and intelligent man. Coincidentally, you and he had the same publisher, and he called the publisher to get your contact information. He gave me your name and number. He said not to bother mentioning his name if I called you, as you wouldn't know who he was. He said he only knew of you. But he did think you were my best bet. The same day he wrote back to me, I called you on the phone."

So there you have it. That was how Mr. Booker found me. He called me that day. I wasn't home when he called, but he left me a long voice mail summarizing his remarkable story. I called him back later that night, and we agreed to meet in person. I told him I wasn't making any promises, but I said his story had potential. It took only one face-to-face meeting with Mr. Booker to convince me that his tale was worth writing about. You know, he said something to me that struck a chord. It was a simple statement, but it conveyed a notion that had been on my mind for years. He said, "There's something wrong with the world we live in." That was it. That's all he had to say to pique my interest, for I believed he was right—there was something wrong with the world we lived in. The story about being abducted was interesting, but I think that statement closed the deal for me.

We decided to meet at his home in the evenings, and our meetings went on for about two months. During the meetings, he told me everything that had happened to him while he was aboard the Ogonite spaceship. I wrote everything down and discovered the man had a truly remarkable mind. He was able to recall every facet of the abduction—every conversation, every mood, and every little nuance with the most astonishing attention to detail. I don't think he left out anything. By the time September rolled around, when his summer classes were over, I sat down in my office to write the book. It was the only active project I had, and I was able to concentrate on it without any distractions.

By December, I'd completed the first draft of the book, and I printed out a copy for Mr. Booker to read. He read through the manuscript twice and then called me on the phone. He had a few minor changes to make, but for the most part, he was delighted with what I'd done. "When can we get it published?" he asked. I could tell he was excited.

"First, I need to have my publisher look it over," I said. "He has to think the story is compelling and that the book will be marketable."

"How long will that take?"

"A few weeks," I said.

"And then?"

"If my publisher is optimistic about it, he'll have the manuscript edited."

"And how long will that take?"

"Probably two to three months."

"So the book will be published in about four months?"

"If everything goes smoothly. It'll be four, maybe five months. We're probably going to have a live book sometime in April or May."

"Exciting, isn't it?"

"It is," I said, and I meant it.

Then, in a more serious voice, Mr. Booker asked, "Are you sure there's no way anyone will be able to tie me to the book?"

"You're not mentioned anywhere. Even my publisher doesn't know your real name."

"This is important."

"I know it is," I said. "Don't worry about it. You're virtually invisible."

"When do we start?"

"I'm going to give my publisher the manuscript tomorrow."

So the ball was rolling. I gave the manuscript to my publisher, and it took him three weeks to read. When he was done, he called and said he loved the story. "It's so different," he said. "I love these Ogonites. They're not like all your other crazy aliens. Seriously, I don't know how you come up with this stuff, but I think you're onto something here."

The book went straight to editing. Meanwhile, Mr. Booker did something that surprised me. He did it in the month of January, right after the school's holiday break. He did it on a Monday. He had spent the entire weekend mustering up the courage he would need. He drove to school just as he did any other day of the week, but on that Monday, he would dive in head first. He knew when and where he would do this. It would be in Miss Applecart's classroom at precisely five after twelve. Her students would all have been dismissed for lunch, and she would be in her room, tidying up for the next class. She would be alone, just as she always was that time of day. He knew she would be by herself. Had he been stalking her? In a way, he had. He knew her habits, and he knew the best time to catch her alone.

Mr. Booker told me he'd had a long talk with his wife about his intention. "It wasn't a real talk," he told me. "I mean, it was, and it wasn't. I do talk to Linda sometimes, and I pretend she's alive. I pretend she can hear me. I ask her for advice, and I often tell her how much I miss her. But I finally brought up the subject I've never discussed with her: my loneliness. Well, we have discussed it before, but never in terms of me dating someone of the opposite sex. I just never felt it was appropriate for me to bring the subject up. When we said our wedding vows to each other, they meant a lot to me. I realize we were to remain faithful only until death did us part, but somehow, I always interpreted that to mean until both our deaths did us in. I tried to imagine how I would feel if I was the one who'd died and she was the one who'd gone on living. How would I feel about her chasing after a new man, kissing him, and making love to him? Heck, just the idea of it was so repulsive to me that I couldn't imagine doing that to her. When we got married, we promised to be loyal to each other forever. We'd be forever faithful. Our love would be undying. We'd always be husband and wife. Isn't that what love is supposed to be? Anyway, that is how I saw it."

"I can understand that," I said. "But do you really think she'd expect you to be alone for the rest of your life?"

"That's exactly what I asked her, almost in those very words. And she spoke to me. I don't mean out loud, but in a voice I could hear. It made me realize how much I missed the sound of her voice. God, I really did miss her, but she told me it was time to move on. 'Go ahead and ask her out,' she said. 'She likes you. Who knows? She might even come to love you. Take her out to dinner, or take her to a movie. Or take her to a play, baseball game, or concert. I don't need you to prove your love to me, and I certainly don't want you to live the rest of your life being lonely and unhappy. I think she'll bring joy to your life. It will probably prove to be one of the best things you ever did for yourself.'"

Anyway, on that Monday at the high school, while our book was being edited and while everyone else in the world was going about the business of his or her life, Mr. Booker opened Miss Applecart's classroom door. She was sorting some papers on her desk, and she looked up at Mr. Booker, a little surprised. "Hi, Mr. Booker," she said. "Can I help you with something?"

"Maybe," Mr. Booker said.

"Yes?" she said.

"I wanted to ask you something."

"Okay, what is it?"

"I wanted to know if you'd have dinner with me."

"Dinner?"

"You know, like at a restaurant."

"As in a date?"

"Yes, I guess. A date."

"After all these years, now you want to have dinner with me?" she asked, smiling.

"I do," Mr. Booker said.

Miss Applecart smiled again. "Well, I'd love to have dinner with you."

"You would?"

"Where do you plan on taking me?"

"I haven't picked out a place. I thought I'd leave that up to you."

"Up to me? Very well then. I'll pick a nice place out. When are we going out on this date?"

"How about tonight?"

289

"You don't waste any time," she said, laughing.

"Is tonight too soon?"

"No, no, tonight is fine."

"I'll pick you up at your house at seven. But I'll need your address. I don't know where you live."

"Seven is good," Miss Applecart said, and she grabbed a piece of paper from her desk and wrote down her address. She handed the paper to Mr. Booker.

"All right, Miss Applecart," Mr. Booker said. "It's a date. I'll see you at seven."

"It's Katie," she said.

"Katie?"

"That's my first name. Call me Katie. My friends all call me Katie."

Are you wondering how I came to know the details of this private conversation? Mr. Booker told me about it, word for word. In fact, he told me a lot about Katie Applecart. We met at a restaurant near the beach a month or so after he first asked her out to dinner, and Mr. Booker wanted to fill me in on Katie. It wasn't really any of my business, but I think because he'd grown so accustomed to telling me about his life, he felt he should tell me about her too. Or maybe he now thought of us as close friends. During all our dealings, I'd tried to keep our relationship businesslike, but I suppose it's easy to feel you're friends with people when you tell them your secrets. And his story was a secret, wasn't it? I was the only person who knew anything about the abduction. The man trusted me. Trust requires closeness, so maybe we were close friends. Maybe I had made friends with him without having intended it.

Anyway, he went on about Katie, telling me what a wonderful woman she was. "You should see her," he said. "Next time we meet, I'll bring a picture of her."

"Do you have any pictures on your phone?"

"I do! What was I even thinking? Of course I have pictures on my phone. I'll find one for you."

As Mr. Booker fiddled with his phone, looking for a shot of

Katie, I looked over my menu, trying to decide what I'd have for lunch.

"Here!" Mr. Booker said. "Here's a good one. I took this when we went to LA last weekend."

I looked at the photo, and indeed, she was an attractive woman. I mean, she wasn't drop-dead gorgeous, but I could see why Mr. Booker thought she was so pretty. She had wavy blonde hair, big blue eyes, and a nose that was a little too big but not huge. It was big but not big enough to warrant a nose job. In fact, her nose gave her face some personality. She was smiling in the picture, and she had a nice mouth: full lips and two rows of healthy white teeth. If I was to use a single word to describe her, it would be *wholesome*. Whereas Linda was handsome, this woman was definitely wholesome. She was a schoolteacher, and she looked like a schoolteacher, the sort of person you would want your children to learn from and look up to. "She's very pretty," I said.

Mr. Booker looked at the picture himself. "She is, isn't she?"

"What are you getting for lunch?"

"I'm getting a hamburger," Mr. Booker said. He didn't even look at the menu. "They have the best hamburgers here."

"You come here often?"

"It's one of my favorite restaurants."

"I'll get the hamburger too."

"You won't be sorry."

A waiter stepped up to the table and introduced himself. He took our orders. We each asked for the hamburger. Mr. Booker asked for a Diet Coke, and I asked for a cup of coffee.

"This is where Katie and I came on our first date," Mr. Booker said.

"Katie picked this place?"

"She did. She has good taste."

"Yes," I agreed.

We then sat there staring at each other a little awkwardly. Mr. Booker finally said, "The strangest thing happened to me earlier this week. It happened in class while I was speaking to my students. I was lecturing them on the Peloponnesian War, when I suddenly had this overpowering urge to take the class outside. It was a beautiful, warm day. The sun was shining, and the sky was bursting with big white cumulus clouds, the kind of clouds little kids like to look at while letting their imaginations run amok. 'I see a dinosaur! I see an enchanted castle! I see a giraffe eating the leaves from a tree!' What did you see when you looked at clouds? Do you even remember? Anyway, it occurred to me it was the perfect day to take the class outside into the fresh air. We could all sit on the lawn, in the shade of the oak trees. Jeffrey Hauser was in my class that day. You don't know Jeffrey, but he's a wonderful guitar player and singer. He carries his guitar with him everywhere he goes, and he had it with him that day. I was being beckoned, lured, and cajoled, so you know what I did? I stopped my lecture, and I told the class we were going outside. 'Let's go,' I said. 'Let's all go outside.'

"They all grabbed their backpacks, and Jeffrey grabbed his guitar. We marched right out of the classroom and down the hall to the exit doors. We then walked to the lawn, and I had everyone sit down in the shade of the oak trees. Then I asked Jeffrey to play us a song. 'I don't care what you play,' I said. 'Play anything you wish.' Jeffrey removed his guitar from its case, and he played it and sang a song I'd never heard before. The kids recognized it, and many of them sang along. It was such a great moment! It was a spiritual and joyous moment, and you know what? I wouldn't have traded that moment for all the world history lectures in the world. I was truly happy, and all my students were having a good time. The sky above was endless and blue. The grass, oak trees, and clouds all glistened as if they were made of glass, and Jeffrey's music fell around us like a sparkling, refreshing rain shower. I was hoping the school bell would never ring. That's what I was hoping for."

Mr. Booker stopped talking, and he had a faraway look on his face. He was still remembering that afternoon. He was on the school lawn with his students, appreciating and enjoying life. Our waiter brought our beverages to the table, and that was when it dawned on me. Right there, at that moment, I understood what was going on. Mr. Booker was no longer Mr. Booker the history teacher. He was in love. He was head over heels in love. Puffy white cumulus clouds, shady oak trees, music, and sunshine—it all added up.

CHAPTER 27

THE BOOK

"You've got to be kidding," I said. I said it as angrily as I could. I was talking to Jerry North, but before I tell you what we were talking about, I need to introduce you to Jerry.

Jerry liked to say he was the man who discovered me. He was employed by Waterman and McKnight, my publisher, and for years, he'd handled my books and talked his superiors into printing and marketing them. Physically, he was not an imposing figure. About five foot six inches tall and weighing about two hundred pounds, he looked like someone who spent his life reading books. He was nearly bald, wore glasses, and had a physique like that of the Pillsbury Doughboy. But he knew his business, and his business was selling books. He had an uncanny sense for determining what would go over with the public and what manuscripts weren't worth bothering with. I wouldn't say the two of us were close friends, but we were friendly. I had always gotten along well with Jerry, and we seldom had rifts over my work. My books always earned a decent little profit for his company, and while I wouldn't say Jerry's superiors were exactly proud to have someone who wrote about alien abductions and UFOs on their author list, they tolerated me because I added to their bottom line. Without Jerry, it's unlikely I would've ever become so popular with my readers.

But now I felt betrayed—and that's putting it lightly. I had just received a sample copy of my book in the mail, and I immediately called Jerry to complain. It was the middle of May, almost a full year since Mr. Booker had been abducted. I had put my heart and soul into this project, trying to be truthful and accurate, trying to tell Mr. Booker's remarkable story just as he'd told it to me, and now Jerry was making a six-hundred-page mockery of the thing. First, there was the title. It's true I'd always left the titles up to Jerry. In fact, his responsibility for titles was in my contract. I would write the manuscripts, but Jerry would be responsible for the titles, covers, and marketing. I can't argue with the fact that he had a real knack for coming up with titles that simultaneously conveyed the contents of my books and captured the attention of potential readers, ensuring that my public would want to part with their hard-earned money to buy another one of my books. But holding the sample book in my hands, I suddenly realized I shouldn't have left the title up to Jerry, not this time. It was a big mistake. He'd titled the book *Council of Death*. I mean, what the hell? I thought he'd read the manuscript, so what was he even thinking? "It's all wrong," I said. "You couldn't have come up with a more inappropriate title. It's misleading and wrong."

"It's a perfect title," Jerry said, remaining calm despite my anger.

"It sounds like a science-fiction novel."

"It is a science-fiction novel," Jerry said. "And that's how we're marketing it."

"You're what? And who is Jack Sterling? It says the book was written by someone named Jack Sterling."

"That's your new pen name."

"A pen name? Who came up with that idea?"

"I did," Jerry said.

"Why would I need a pen name?"

"Because you're now writing science-fiction novels. It's a new genre for you, so a pen name is needed. We don't want to confuse your readers."

"I never said this book was a work of science fiction."

"Then who is Mr. Booker?"

"He's Mr. Booker."

"I mean who is he? Where does he come from, and where does he live? Where does he actually teach?"

"I can't tell you that."

"Because he doesn't exist."

"But he does exist."

"Sure he does. And he was transported to an invisible spaceship orbiting Earth. And he watched aliens play basketball. And he went skinny dipping with one of their young females. Oh, wait a minute. By young, I mean she looked thirty but was a hundred years old!"

"Listen, it's no crazier than the other stories I've brought you."

"But you had real sources for those—real living, breathing human beings who were telling you about their experiences. Granted, they were probably all crazy, but they stood behind their stories. But Mr. Booker doesn't exist. We have no picture of him. We have no bio on him, and you can't claim a work of nonfiction from a fictional character. So be real about this. *Council of Death* is a work of fiction."

I thought about that and then said, "Even if I were to agree with you, the cover art is all wrong."

"What's wrong with it?"

"A pile of human skulls?"

"It's the end of humanity."

"That's not what happens in the story."

"It's implied, isn't it?"

"It's considered, but it never happens. It's left up in the air. The council makes no decision. There's an optimistic angle to the story, which you completely ignore with this pile-of-skulls idea."

Jerry was quiet for a moment. Then he said, "*Council of Death*. That's what's going to sell your book. A pile of skulls, the doomsday plague, the end of mankind, and the apocalypse."

I shouldn't have done it, but I hung up on Jerry. I slammed down the phone receiver, and I looked at the book again. Through no fault of my own, now I was a science-fiction writer named Jack Sterling. My breakout book was titled *Council of Death*, and it featured a pile of human skulls on its cover. I was reporting on one of the most amazing stories of all time, and Jerry had stuck a big red nose on it and dressed it up like a clown. "Step right up, ladies and gentlemen, and read about Mr. Booker and the Ogonites! Buy your kids some cotton candy, and see what happens next!"

I got drunk that night. I don't ordinarily drink, and there was no booze in my house, so I drove to the local liquor store and bought a big bottle of Crown Royal to celebrate. Of course, I'm using the world *celebrate* sarcastically. I drank and stared at the book, thinking of how I was going to explain all this to Mr. Booker. About halfway into the bottle, I turned on the TV. I watched an old black-and-white movie. It was perfect. I sat sipping my whiskey and watching *The Thing from Another World*, a Howard Hawks production from 1951. It was a story about an alien spacecraft that crashed into Earth, into the arctic ice. Some scientists and some military men tried to blast the ship out of the ice, and in the process, they destroyed it. But lo and behold, they found the alien pilot who'd been tossed from the craft during the wreck. Apparently, aliens were smart enough to build a spaceship that traveled light-years through space but not smart enough to invent any seat belts. The alien was in the ice, and the men dug it out in a big block of the ice. They took the block to their arctic outpost, and while they were trying to decide what to do with it, one of the men standing guard over the frozen alien carelessly left an electric blanket on the block of ice. The ice melted, and the alien came to life, terrorizing the outpost. This alien was a seven-foot-tall groaning, grunting, arm-swinging beast played by James Arness, of all people. Matt Dillon the alien! He had one thing in mind: drinking the blood of earthlings. The really weird thing was, they soon discovered this alien was not a mammal, reptile, or giant insect or arachnid. It was a vegetable! It was a seven-foot-tall hunk of broccoli with powerful arms and legs, whose sole purpose in life was to murder humans and drink their blood. *Jesus, who came up with this stuff? People like Jerry North? Sure, he probably saw this movie on TV as a kid and loved every minute of it*, I thought. "Fucking Jerry North," I said, raising my glass of whiskey to the TV, toasting it.

I fell asleep on my couch and missed the end of the movie, but I assume they figured out a way to kill the alien. The next day, I was hungover. I knew I'd have to call Mr. Booker, but I didn't want to talk to him with a hangover, so I waited until evening. When I called his house, a woman answered the phone. I assumed it was Katie, but I acted as if I didn't know who she was. I had no idea whether he'd told Katie anything about us, about the book, or even about the abduction. "Is Mr. Booker home?" I asked.

"Who's calling?" she asked.

"My name is Jack Sterling."

"Just a minute," she said, and I could hear her talking to Mr. Booker, telling him who was on the phone.

I heard Mr. Booker say, "I don't know anyone named Jack Sterling. I wonder what he wants." Then he came to the phone and said, "Hello. Can I help you?"

"It's me," I said.

"Oh yes," Mr. Booker said. He recognized my voice immediately. "What can I do for you?"

"We've got to meet," I said.

"I'm busy tonight."

"How about tomorrow?"

"Sure, we can meet for lunch."

"That would be fine," I said. "Does Katie know anything about us? Does she know anything about your abduction?"

"No," he said.

"Sorry to call you at home."

"It's okay."

Mr. Booker gave me the name of a restaurant and told me to be there at twelve. I could tell by the way he was talking to me that he was trying to think of a story to tell Katie to explain the phone call. "See you for lunch," I said.

"See you," he said, and he hung up the phone.

The next day, I went to the restaurant, and I arrived before Mr. Booker. I waited in the lobby, and he finally showed up about thirty minutes late. We had the hostess seat us at a table in the rear, so we could have some privacy. I had brought the book with me to show him. I was sure he was going to be angry. In fact, I thought he'd be livid. I put the book on the table and pushed it toward his place setting. "Here it is," I said.

At first, he said nothing. He picked the book up and looked it over, revealing no opinion one way or the other. Then he set the book down and looked at me. *"Council of Death?"* he asked.

"It wasn't my idea," I said.

"And who is Jack Sterling?"

"He's me. Jack Sterling is my new pen name. My publisher wants to call me Jack Sterling."

"I see," Mr. Booker said.

"The manuscript is the same as you approved. They didn't make any changes to it. They only changed my name. And they came up with the cover and the title."

"A pile of skulls?" he asked, looking over the cover art.

"My editor thought it would sell more books. It's being marketed as a science-fiction novel."

"Science fiction?"

"Since we're not using your real name."

"I see," Mr. Booker said.

"Are you disappointed?" I asked. I was sure he'd say yes. If fact, I was sure he'd be very disappointed. I wouldn't have been surprised if he threw the book at me and left the restaurant. But he just laughed and set the book down on the table.

"It doesn't matter," he said.

"No?" I said.

"You know," he said, "Katie wanted to know who you were and why I was having lunch with you."

"I figured that."

"Do you know what I told her? I said you were from a community college. I said I'd called the college looking for a job as a history professor. Of course, I made this all up. I've never looked for another job in all the years I've been teaching. But you should've seen the look on her face. I know she wanted me to stay at the high school, so the two of us could be together. I explained I'd called you before I met her, and now, obviously, I didn't want to leave the high school.

So that's why the two of us are now having lunch. As far as Katie is concerned, we're meeting so I can tell you that I'm no longer interested in teaching at the college. I'm telling you I changed my mind, and I've decided to remain at the high school. Katie knows nothing about us, and I intend to keep it that way. I'm happy with the way things are."

"That's good to hear."

"We're going to get married soon."

"Married?"

"Not right away, but soon. We're going to be husband and wife, the two of us. And we're going to have a baby. We're going to have a child of our own."

"And what about the Ogonite threat?"

"I guess they'll do what they do."

"I have to ask you a question," I said.

"Yes?" Mr. Booker said.

"It was all true, wasn't it? Everything you told me? You weren't pulling my leg, were you?"

"Pulling your leg?" Mr. Booker laughed. "No, it was true—all of it. I wasn't pulling your leg. But do you remember Anna's story about being raped and held hostage? She said, 'There are purposes to all the things that happen in life.' That sentence stuck with me, word for word. And there *are* purposes. The purpose behind my abduction wasn't for me to tell my story to the world and change the behavior of seven billion people. The book you wrote about my experiences will be just a drop in a very large, empty bucket, if even that. No, I'm not angry about the book. The book is fine. *Council of Death*, a pile of human skulls, and a new pen name? Who cares? What difference does it make? The purpose behind my abduction was love! I took Rock's advice and asked Katie to go out with me. It was good advice, and no one but Rock had ever suggested it. No, my experience with the Ogonites wasn't about the end of the world. It was about one insignificant pair of lonely adults meeting each other, getting to know each other, and eventually getting married and having a child. That was the purpose of the abduction."

"And what about everything else?" I asked. "What about all the subjects you discussed with the council? All the points they made? Everything they had to say about human beings? They had a lot to say."

"And they were right."

"And?"

"That's all I can say—they were right. Human beings are violent, selfish, and confused. But what are we going to do about it? Do you really think a science-fiction writer and a high school history teacher are going to change the world?"

"But I thought that's why we wrote the book."

"We did what we set out to do. People will read your book. Some will take it seriously, and others will call it nonsense. I read your manuscript, and I think you did a terrific job. You have nothing to be ashamed of, and neither do I. Will the Ogonites destroy us, or will they let us live? That's ostensibly the primary question my abduction raises, isn't it? Or is it really? Isn't there a more appropriate question? What will we do with our lives in the meantime? We're all going to die eventually—if not by a thumbs-down decision by the Ogonite council, then by getting cancer, being hit by lightning, getting crushed in a fatal car accident, or simply succumbing to old age. It makes no sense to worry about something that is inevitable. It makes more sense to worry about what we're doing right now. It's all about now. And as for me? I now plan on marrying Katie, and we plan on having a child. We plan on living together and enjoying our lives for as long as we can, until we die."

"So the book was a waste of time?"

"Not at all," Mr. Booker said. "No effort to make the world a better place is a waste of time." He smiled and then picked up his menu. "The hamburgers here aren't very good. I've tried them twice, and I didn't like them much. I don't know what you feel like eating, but the French dips here are excellent. That's what I'm going to order. And I'm going to get a side of their onion rings. The onion rings here are good too."

CHAPTER 28

A LITTLE NIGHT MUSIC

E nough about Mr. Booker. Let me shift gears and tell you a few more things about myself. I've told you I'm an author, and I make my living writing about alien abductions and UFOs, but that's about all you know. I haven't even told you my name. My full name is Thomas Benny Gilchrist III—Thomas because that was my father's name and Benny because my parents were both big Benny Goodman fans. I prefer that people call me Tommy, since that's the name I've been going by since I was a kid. I was born under the sunny skies of Los Angeles in the summer of 1955, and I was raised in the foothills of Altadena, just a short drive from Los Angeles. I'm now sixty-two years old, and I've lived in Southern California my entire life.

My marriage has been a good one, and I've been with the same woman for more than forty years. My wife's name is Rachael, and she's three years younger and two inches shorter than I am. We have one twenty-six-year-old son who's been in and out of colleges and low-paying jobs for the past eight years, trying to find himself. He's had a few girlfriends but still hasn't found the love of his life. I've written twenty-one books, and he hasn't read a single one of them. Come to think of it, neither has Rachael.

Rachael and I now live in Huntington Beach, an hour's drive south of my birthplace. I do my writing at home, and Rachael works as a loan officer for a local bank. We make decent money, but we're by no means rich. Our house is a little three-bedroom tract affair in a neighborhood of similar houses. We've lived in the same place for about twenty-five years and have no intention of moving anytime soon. We like the house, and I like my den. It's quiet, cool, and private, just right for me to do my writing. I started writing about alien abductions and UFOs when I was forty-six. Prior to that, I was the manager of a local grocery store. I wrote my first book while I was working at the grocery store. I wrote during the night and worked at the store during the day. The story I wrote was about one of our stock boys and his incredible claim that he'd been abducted by aliens. I heard him talking about it to another worker at the store in the lunchroom. Okay, so I was eavesdropping, but his story was intriguing, and I wanted to learn more. He seemed sincere, and except for his bizarre story, he was normal in every other respect. I'd always wanted to be a writer, and alien stuff had always interested me, so I asked him if I could write a book about his experiences. I think he was surprised at my offer, and he jumped at the opportunity. We immediately went to work on the project. It took me a year and a half to write that first book. I'm a lot faster at it now. I can write a book in a few months.

Long story short, I sent my first manuscript to several different publishers, and Jerry North wrote me back, offering to print and market the book. I was overjoyed! I signed a contract with his company, and the next thing I knew, the book was published. It sold quite a few copies, thanks to Jerry and his marketing skills. I told Rachael that I thought I was onto something with this writing thing, and she encouraged me to continue. She said, "Who would ever have guessed we had a writer in our family?"

Well, who would've thought? A ton of fan mail came in because of my first book, mostly from people with their own abduction and UFO stories, people hoping I would write about them too. Well, by "a ton," I really mean about twenty or thirty letters. But it seemed like an awful lot. I continued to write using the stories I was receiving, and one book led to another. The next thing I knew, I became something of an expert on the topic. Not only did people continue to buy my books, but they were also now asking me to speak at gatherings and review their own books. It's funny to think this all started with a stock boy talking in a lunchroom. I have no idea what happened to the kid. He took a payment from Jerry when he signed over his rights to the story. He quit his job at the store when they cut him his check, and I never heard from him again.

Anyway, here I am some sixteen years later, telling you about Mr. Booker. You've been patient with me, and I appreciate that. Not everyone likes to listen to these kinds of stories. A lot of people would just laugh or brush me off. As for *Council of Death*, it's doing well. Jerry made sure everyone knew that Jack Sterling was actually me, so all my regular fans are buying the book. I've also acquired a lot of new fans, people who like science fiction. Jerry started a rumor that the story of Mr. Booker was true, which helped sales a lot. I'm not getting rich off this book, but it looks as if I'll be getting some hefty royalties, more than the royalties I've received from any of my other books. Jerry thinks I ought to stop writing "true" stories and stick to science fiction. I told him I'd think about it. To be honest, it doesn't sound like such a bad idea.

I bought plane tickets yesterday. I bought three tickets to Cairo: two for Rachael and me and one for our son. I still have to arrange for the ground transportation and a hotel room, but I'll do that soon. I can't wait to go! All my life, I've wanted to see the pyramids near Cairo, not just in picture books but for honest-to-God real. I've heard the photographs don't do them justice. I want to stand in the desert with the sand at my feet, the scalding sun overhead, and a faithful camel at my side, looking in awe, taking it all in.

Ah, the pyramids! One of the Seven Wonders of the World! It took two million blocks of stone, each weighing two and a half tons, just to build the Pyramid of Khufu. You know, there are still people today who believe the pyramids could never have been built without the help of aliens. Does that make you laugh? When I first heard the theory about aliens helping the Egyptians build the pyramids, I was in high school. You can call me young and naive, and I probably was, but the theory seemed entirely plausible to me. I asked myself how ancient human beings could possibly have carved two million blocks of stone from the ground and carried them into place, building what are still touted as the largest man-made buildings on Earth. It seemed impossible. They had to have had some assistance. It wasn't until I was in my forties, after doing a little more research, that I came to accept the fact that aliens had had nothing to do with it. It was a human endeavor. It showed just how amazing humans could be if they set their minds to a task. Humans, I now believed, were the most remarkable creatures on the planet. I can't believe it's taken me more than sixty years to finally fly to Cairo, but it was important that I visit.

Who built the pyramids? Who was responsible for the actual work? Today it's no longer popular to say that the pyramids were built by slaves. Now the experts want us to believe the workers were treated well, fed well, clothed, and buried honorably. But seriously, who do these experts think they're kidding? Cutting out and hauling two-and-a-half-ton blocks of stone day after day in the blistering desert heat, those men toiled for masters. For how many years did they do this, and under what awful conditions? I think Herodotus had it right the first time. Saying the laborers who built the pyramids weren't actually slaves is like saying blacks weren't slaves in America because they were given three square meals a day, clothes on their backs, and decent burials in Christian graveyards. Sure, I can just picture the ancient Egyptian workers—Sneezy, Grumpy, Dopey, and Merkha—cutting stone and yanking on ropes, whistling while they worked. Fat chance of that.

The pyramids are the penultimate example of something magnificent coming directly from man's worst and most callous inclinations. The good and the bad. The bad and the good. Do you see what I mean by this? Bad things happen all the time, but so do good ones. When one thinks of humanity, it's easy to see the worst. It's easy to be cynical. But I prefer to see all the pyramids in our lives, reaching into the clouds, standing magnificently—like Michelangelo's *Pietà*, Neil Armstrong's footprints on the moon, or a Mozart performance outdoors on a warm summer evening. Or maybe a Monty Python movie shown late at night on TV. Or a toddler trying to eat his first ice cream cone on a hot August day at a county fair or a youngster sitting on his grandfather's knee and listening politely and attentively to same old stories, pretending he's hearing them for the first time. Good and wonderful things take place in our world every day, and they don't happen by accident. They happen because we're human beings.

If I had the opportunity to speak before the council, this is what I'd tell them: we're not nearly as bad as we appear. Despite all our written laws, avarice, self-centeredness, weaponry, borders, slavery, and taste for each other's blood, we're really a pretty decent lot of people. If you've listened to Mozart, you know what I'm talking about. My dad used to recite a little saying to me when I was feeling cynical. He'd sit me down and say, "Don't complain because a rose has thorns. Instead, smile because thorns have roses." Tonight I'm going to stand in my backyard and look up at the sky, and I'm going to recite this saying out loud. I'm going to do this every night, as if I'm saying a bedtime prayer. Maybe if I say it often enough, the Ogonites will hear me, and then maybe they'll reach the right decision.

Sid? Rock? Lucy? William? Can you hear me? I'm talking to you!

Printed in the United States
By Bookmasters